THE FLORILEGIUM OF MADNESS

ALSO BY D. J. BUTLER

THE FLORILEGIUM OF MADNESS

D. J. BUTLER

Edited by

CALLIE BUTLER AND JOE MONSON

HEMELEIN PUBLICATIONS

The Florilegium of Madness

Cover artist: Rob van Hal / Shutterstock

Cover and interior layout and design: Joe Monson

Managing Editor: Joe Monson

Publisher: Heather B. Monson

Published by Hemelein Publications, LLC.

http://hemelein.com/

First Edition. First Hemelein printing, July 2021

10 9 8 7 6 5 4 3 2 1

ISBN:
978-1-64278-008-6 (trade paperback)
978-1-64278-009-3 (ebook)
978-1-64278-011-6 (audiobook)

Library of Congress Control Number: 2021940699

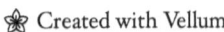 Created with Vellum

For Nathan Shumate,
who invited me early and often.

TABLE OF CONTENTS

LEGACY OF THE CORRIDOR

Way back in 1994, M. Shayne Bell put together *Washed by a Wave of Wind,* an anthology of short works by authors from "The Corridor", an area that covers Utah, most of Idaho, parts of Wyoming and Nevada, and stretches into Arizona and parts of northern Mexico. Sometimes, the area around Cardston, Alberta, Canada, is included, too. For those unfamiliar with this area, it was settled by Mormon pioneers, members of the Church of Jesus Christ of Latter-day Saints.

Bell's anthology highlighted science fiction and fantasy works by authors from the area, as The Corridor contained an unusually high number of successful authors, for the population in the area, both genre and non-genre, both members and non-members of the predominant religion. That legacy continues today with an impressive list of authors such as Jennifer Adams, D. J. Butler, Orson Scott Card, Michaelbrent Collings, Ally Condie, Larry Correia, Kristyn Crow, James Dashner, Brian Lee Durfee, Sarah M. Eden, Richard Paul Evans, David Farland, Jessica Day George, Shannon Hale, Mettie Ivie Harrison, Tracy and Laura Hickman, Charlie N. Holmberg, Christopher Husberg, Matthew J. Kirby, Brian McClellan, Stephenie Meyer, L. E. Modesitt, Jr., Brandon Mull, Jennifer A. Nielson, James A. Owen, Brandon Sanderson, J. Scott Savage, Jess Smart Smiley, Eric James

Stone, Howard Tayler, Dan Wells, Robison Wells, Brad R. Torgersen, David J. West, Carol Lynch Williams, and Dan Willis. This list only barely scratches the surface.

Hemelein Publications is starting a publication series that will highlight authors from The Corridor, both well-known and lesser-known. You can learn more about the series at:

http://hemelein.com/go/legacy-of-the-corridor/

ON THE TOPIC OF HATS AND MUSTACHES

I first met Dave around ten years ago at *Life, the Universe, & Everything*, the annual science fiction and fantasy academic symposium held in Provo, Utah. Since then, we've attended various conventions together, worked booths together, participated in panels together, had long discussions on many different topics, shared meals together, and even won Kovel Awards in the same year multiple times. That's just a long way of saying that we hardly know each other.

Despite that, Dave was talking about trying to get together a collection of some of his short works (he has a lot more than are found here), and I suggested that Hemelein could put one out for him. He looked at me for a few moments, then asked, "Who are you, again?" while slowly backing away. Yet here we are, and you have this amazing collection of dark fantasy and cosmic horror in your hands (and hopefully are reading this introduction).

Dave is a man of many talents, and he shares them freely. He loves running tabletop and roleplaying games (and he's great at it, too!). He has a growing collection of painted minis. He looks great in a good hat, and his mustache is a thing of legend. He's written a bunch of really good books and shorter works. He's written and performed folk music (some of it set in his *Witchy Eye* world). His scratch-made brownies can give you diabetes from across the room, and the flavors are constantly changing (all good changes, mind you).

He (before all this COVID stuff, and hopefully again now that things seem to be getting back to normal) regularly opens his house to all comers for book release parties (for other authors), musical and poetry performances, and presentations on a very wide variety of topics. He's always trying to help out other authors, no matter where they are in their careers. I've seen him do things for which he doesn't want attention, but which would make your heart melt with joy. He is a kind person, which is becoming increasingly rare these days.

The stories here are really good. There is a lot of variety in them, and I hope you enjoy them. I had a lot of fun working with Dave and Callie to get everything pulled together, and I hope we get to put out additional collections like this in the future.

Joe Monson
MANAGING EDITOR
HEMELEIN PUBLICATIONS

EDITOR'S NOTE

Wow! I am happy to be here today accepting the Kovel Award for Youngest Professional Editor. I can't say I'm surprised. It was about time. I have indeed met all the requirements as specified by the Kovel jurors: I rode here on a sixty-year-old tortoise, I am wearing twelve shirts, and I haven't clipped my toenails for six weeks in preparation.

We all know one of the most celebrated winners of previous Kovel Awards, David Butler. But his time is over now. Which is why I took on the challenge of helping this poor soul with his collection, for an exorbitant fee.

But in all seriousness, I really enjoyed editing these stories for my dad. One day, we were talking about the possibility of *The Cunning Man* (one of his novels) becoming a film. I was really excited because—on the cover of the book—Hiram is extremely hot, and I would get to meet a handsome actor. My dad then told me that he would cast a homely-looking fellow, much to my disappointment. All of the stories in this collection are tied together through their adventurous nature, especially the Hiram Woolley stories, which were my favorite to edit.

The stories in this collection are very remarkable. Whether the adventure was set in outer space or in some ancient civilization, I was always entertained. So—especially if you like a one-hundred page story about horny astronauts or stories about a woman with seven living boobs—you will definitely like this book.

There is a range of genres here, which kept things interesting for me. We had a very interesting working dynamic, the two of us. He would write a story in an afternoon, and it would take me three weeks to edit it. I got to seek out my father's mistakes and fix them, which was highly satisfying. Ironically, my dad edited this document for me.

But honestly, this was one of the best working experiences of my life. If you want a kind boss who cuts you an enormous amount of slack, work for my dad.

I love you, Dad, thanks for giving me the chance to edit for you. And you're welcome for turning your so-so writing into perfection.

Callie Butler
January 16, 2021

THE SEVEN NIPPLES OF MOLLY KITCHEN

This is the untrue origin story of a true cartographical curiosity. In the State of Utah, there are numerous geographical features named "Mollie's Nipple" (as of this writing, according to Wikipedia, at least seven peaks, one butte, and a well).

The nearest to my home is a peak at the south end of Utah Valley, so travelers watching their Google Maps or other navigation app as they round the mountain from Payson to Santaquin may be surprised to see the name drifting past them on the software. The various nipples were named by a man named John Kitchen, in the early days of Utah's Mormon settlement, and one presumes Mollie was his wife or paramour.

As I have it in the story, though, the records of the time are imperfect, so Mollie herself has left more trace on Utah's maps than on its written history.

"There are seven, scattered all over the state", Hiram Woolley said. His voice echoed in the mineshaft.

Looking over his shoulder, he saw the last light of the day splash pink over his Model A, sitting on the shoulder of the mountain. Below, the lights of Payson would be winking into life, though Hiram couldn't see them. Payson was a small enough town that many of those lights came from kerosene lanterns, though the beet processing plant and the city buildings were all electric.

Then the shaft turned, and his car disappeared from view as well.

No breeze brushed Hiram's face; this was a mine with only one way out.

"Seven nipples?" Rose Callaghan asked.

"Seven mountain peaks named for her nipples. There's also a butte, but that strikes me as a stretch. There's a well, too. Some say eleven features in total, but on the maps I trust, I count seven."

"You gotta pick your maps real careful, in this life."

"Yes", Hiram agreed. "And be willing to switch maps when you find you've been following a bad one."

"This Molly Kitchen must have been a strange woman."

"Hmm."

Hiram followed Rose down into the mine, listening intently for footfalls other than hers and his. She was large, though he would have said she was bulky rather than fat, and her step was light. The sound of sand and pebbles grinding under the soles of his Harvesters was gigantic by contrast. The denim of his overalls, crusted with dust from the road and from the farm, scraped together as he walked with a noise like the sound of a woodsaw.

The shaft's supports were rough-hewn logs rather than regular timbers, the work of a solitary miner or a small crew. The tunnel walls were irregular and its ceiling low, which suggested the same thing. Given the valley's history, it had most likely been one man, solitary and half-crazed, during the silver boom.

They passed one side tunnel after another, and he reached into the bib pocket of his overalls at each, scattering a small handful of the pocket's contents in every opening.

"Who was she, then?" Rose asked.

"There's not much about her in the record", Hiram said. "She's not alone in that; records were a bit sketchy around here, seventy years ago."

"You went up to Salt Lake and poked around in their cupboards, did you? They were the only ones writing anything down, back then. The Shoshone just remembered things, or told them to each other in songs."

"I have a friend at B.Y. High", Hiram said. "He's a librarian, and I find there's little he can't ferret out for me, in the way of facts on the record."

"And facts *off* the record?"

"John Kitchen shows up clearly enough. Frontiersman type, like your John D. Lees and your Orrin Porter Rockwells. Led an early expedition, back before the Shoshones and the Utes had cleared out of the valleys and left them to the white settlers. And everywhere he went, he named a mountain peak after Molly."

"After her nipple."

"I guess he found that her most memorable feature."

"Ain't that just like a man?"

Hiram heard rustling at his feet. Shining the light of his electric torch deliberately ahead of him to keep his hands in obscurity, he threw grains down into the shadow. With a hiss and a scuffling sound, something unseen retreated, and then fell silent.

Callaghan stopped. Had she heard?

"I reckon that might be it", Hiram admitted. "Men can be pretty predictable, especially that way. Though there's another possibility, too."

He kept walking. After a moment's hesitation, Rose joined him. In the darkness of the mine, her bulk appeared to shift and twist underneath her calico dress.

"The missing children", Hiram said. "What do you make of them?"

"Well, you know how it is", Rose answered slowly. "Anytime anything happens that folk can't explain, it must have been a witch. And if it was a witch, then all the widows have to keep their heads down."

"Oh, it wasn't a witch", Hiram agreed.

"I suppose you've known your share of witches?" Rose asked slyly.

"As many as the next fellow", Hiram admitted.

"More, I heard."

Hiram felt a shiver in his spine. "What did you hear, then?"

Rose Callaghan purred with satisfaction. "You were sent down from Salt Lake, but you ain't exactly a Salt Lake man, are you?"

"I'm from Lehi", Hiram said. "I farm beets."

Rose clucked her tongue. "That ain't what I mean. I mean, you ain't the regular Sunday School type."

Sweat dripped into his eyes, and Hiram badly wanted to lift his fedora and mop the sweat with a handkerchief. "I guess you better speak clearly, Mrs. Callaghan." Instead, he reached into the hip pocket of his overalls and put his hand on the cold butt of his pistol. The hairs on the back of his neck stood up. Where were the rest of the creatures?

Were they behind him, about to pounce?

Rose didn't stop walking. "Your grandma was a witch. Payson ain't so far away from Lehi that there ain't a few around here who'd heard of her, in her day. Especially once the beet plant got built, and Payson started taking all of Lehi's beets."

"She was a cunning woman." Hiram blinked, sweat stinging his eyes. "She knew herbs, and some German prayers, and she could read the almanac."

"And I heard tell you're a cunning man, yourself."

Who had she been talking to? Had R.J. made some well-intentioned, off-hand remark? She had a tendency to mock Hiram, to gain credibility herself. Hiram grunted without commitment. "I'm willing to try whatever does the job."

"Stone-peeping? Rod-work? A heavenly letter?"

"Whatever gets the task done", Hiram repeated. "And doesn't compromise my soul."

It was Rose's turn to grunt, a contented sound that might have come from a sow.

"We're almost there."

"What were you doing so far down the mine, that you found the body?" Hiram asked. He knew the answer would be a lie, of course.

"Lost one of my dogs", she said. "Followed it down here, and the poor creature came across the dead child."

They walked a few steps in silence.

"If it ain't a witch", Rose said, "what do you think killed those children? You don't agree with the fellow from the *Star-Courier*, the one who thinks it was an accident."

"No accident drains the body entirely of blood like that."

"A vampire, then?"

Hiram forced himself to chuckle. "Have you *read* Stoker's novel? Do you imagine there might be a Transylvanian nobleman wandering around in Utah Valley, looking for sanatorium patients to enslave?"

Rose laughed lightly. "Then what? An illness? That would be a horrible abomination of an illness to drain so much blood out of a child."

"It would be an abomination", Hiram agreed. "I think something drank the blood from those children. But not a vampire. A monster. Something horrible, something without a name."

"You ain't much of a wizard, if you can't name your foe."

"I didn't say I was a wizard." Hiram *had* a name to give his foe, but Hiram wasn't quite ready to share it. "I'm just a cunning man. More of a beet farmer than anything else, and I delivery groceries to people who have lost their jobs. I dig out collapsed ditches, settle fights over irrigation times, things like that."

"You help the poor."

"I *try* to help them."

"Widows and orphans. Pure religion and undefiled."

"You've read your Bible."

"Ain't everyone? And you try to solve the mysterious deaths of children in a small farming town."

"The way I see it", Hiram said, "those children were poor in life, but they're even poorer now. They have no one to hear their story, no one who would even believe how they died. If nothing else, I can do them this last service. Even if I never really figure out what killed them. Even if I can't stop the monster from killing again. I can do them the service of believing, and of trying to help."

"Sad." Rose Callaghan didn't sound the slightest bit sad.

"We almost there?"

"Almost. Bear with this fat old woman a little longer, Salt Lake City man."

"Another possibility", Hiram said, "is that John Kitchen was trying to give a warning."

"What kind of warning does a man give by naming mountains after his wife's breasts?"

"Some say it wasn't his wife", Hiram said. "No record, as such. Some remember it was his betrothed. But Molly Kitchen left no birth certificate and no death certificate. No record of baptism or marriage, nothing."

"Maybe they never married."

"Maybe not", Hiram allowed.

"Maybe they were just poor. Records are especially bad where poor folk are concerned."

"True", Hiram said. "Or maybe she ate him."

Rose laughed, a sharp edge that shaded into a cackle. "That's a dark joke, cunning man."

"I see it like this", Hiram said. "This very mountain was the first. It was where John started, and somehow he got the right to put a name on the map for it. Then as he traveled, he left a string of 'Molly's Nipples' behind him. Seven of them all told, just counting the mountains, but it started here. He was warning us about something, and we missed it. We missed it for seventy years and more."

Rose Callaghan snorted. "Warning us his bride was deformed? Maybe that's why he ran off and joined Brigham's expedition."

"Maybe he was trying to get away", Hiram agreed. "His end in the record is a bit mysterious, too, but folks around here agree he came back, and he died here. Of sickness, some say, or accident. Some say the death was a surprise, and a bit mysterious."

"Folks will repeat all kinds of nonsense."

"Seventy years isn't all that long. There's old folks in the valley who were alive then. Even old folks who were adults when John Kitchen came back from his journey."

"And you think Molly Kitchen killed him?"

"No." He meant it. She was toying with him now, trying to draw out what he'd learned. Perhaps she wanted to find out who else knew, and whether she should strike at his young son Michael, in the boarding house back in town, or against the Roosevelt administration agent, R.J. Lazarus, who thought Hiram was insane but helped him anyway, because she was also on the side of the poor.

He could try to take her now.

Only he hadn't accounted for them all. If she wanted to draw him deeper into the mine, there might be more of the beasts.

"No", he said again, "I don't think Molly Kitchen killed her husband. And I don't think she killed any of the other people who have died in these hills since, missing without trace or found drained of blood."

"Then what do you think it was?"

"Monsters", Hiram said. "Things beyond human ken. Things that have no name. Things about which nothing is written in any of our books."

"That sounds terrifying." Molly's voice was cold and remote.

And lonely.

Hiram felt a pang in his heart and swallowed it. What had her life been like, all these years with such a dark secret? All these years, with no one to tell it to?

And had she told John Kitchen, before he died?

Did she mourn his death still, the death of her last companion?

He heard a slithering in the darkness. He almost missed it, distracted by his strangled feelings of compassion for Molly Kitchen, but he was alert enough to shine the light on ahead and throw a handful of crystals into the crack from whence the slithering sound emanated.

"We're here", Rose Callaghan said.

The tunnel had ended in a sudden wall, no chamber as such, but just a termination of the mine shaft.

"There's no body, Molly", Hiram said.

If she noticed his use of her name, she showed no sign. "There will be."

Hiram shone the light on the calico that sheathed Molly Kitchen's torso and shuffled his feet as if uneasy. The silver beam hid the action of his other hand, scattering crystals on the dirt, and his Red Wings masked the sound.

"What's it like?" he asked.

"I don't kill them", she said.

"I guessed that. I believe you, and I don't mean what's it like to kill. I mean, what's it like to be alone? With . . . *them?*"

"They don't talk", she said, after a brief pause. "And who would I tell about them? Who would believe it, other than you? Who could bear the knowledge?"

Hiram's shoulders felt heavy. He nodded.

"Do you want to see them?" she offered.

He didn't. He felt ill. He wanted to flood the entire shaft with gasoline and drop a match.

He nodded.

She undid the buttons down the front of her dress. Responding to the touch of her fingers, the fabric moved as if it were itself a living thing.

Or as if there were other creatures moving beneath it.

She opened her dress.

"I count two", Hiram said. They clung to her body, jaws clamped fiercely onto her flesh, long and red, like serpents with a single powerful pair of legs, just behind their skulls. If they had skin, Hiram couldn't see it—they seemed to be composed entirely of blood, not clotted blood, but red, living blood, holding itself together in this shape by some sorcery so foul, Hiram could scarcely imagine it.

And he could not countenance its survival.

"You destroyed two", Molly said. She wasn't, after all, a fat woman. Her face was swollen and puffy, but in this light it looked like the swelling of rot and corruption. Her body was skeletal. "With fire."

"It wasn't just me", Hiram said, and then regretted it. It had been R.J. Lazarus who had sloshed gasoline on the two feeding monsters and then ignited them. Despite what she had seen, the federal agent insisted she had killed a couple of large reptiles. Gila monsters, perhaps, or some desert lizard that had not yet been added to the catalog.

"But you didn't bring your gas-can down here, did you, Salt Lake City man?"

"No." Hiram felt a deep sense of sorry and pity. He must not let it stay his hand. "Were they actual nipples, once?"

Molly Kitchen nodded. "I was born with them. Mere nubs of flesh, no use to me any more than yours serve you. I never had a natural child. Just these queer body-memories of an ancient time and a more ancient pact."

"What pact?" Hiram asked.

"My family." Molly didn't volunteer any more.

"What family is that?" Hiram pressed. Were these same monsters killing elsewhere, clinging to the grotesque form of some cousin of Molly's? And where would that be? Hiram had no idea where Molly came from, or who her kin were.

Molly said nothing.

Hiram tried another approach. "And you renewed that pact?"

"They came to me", Molly said. "It was before I knew John. And I had two of them before he and I were engaged to be married, and seven by the time of our wedding night. I tried to keep them from him. I . . . I thought I had."

"Until he published his warning to the whole world."

"I had to kill him. *They* had to kill him. My only other choice was to flee into the wilderness, and live the life of a monster. Can you understand that, cunning man?"

Hiram sighed. "You . . . nurse them."

"It isn't milk."

"It's blood", Hiram said.

The two monsters on Molly's body unlatched their mouths from their hostess and glared at Hiram, gripping Molly's thigh and her upper arm. Hiram saw nothing that any longer resembled a human nipple, but seven oozing bloody sores. Two of them rested on Molly's chest where an ordinary woman's nipples would have been.

He stepped back, scattered more of the crystals on the ground.

They only had forelegs, but was it possible that the monsters could jump? Or worse, fly?

"They're made of blood." He hoped fervently he was right.

"Are they?" Molly furrowed her thinning eyebrows and glared at Hiram.

"We'll find out", he said.

The creatures leaped from Molly's body toward Hiram. They landed on the dry dirt, where Hiram had scattered two handfuls of rock salt.

The monsters shrieked in pain. Their forward momentum died, and they flopped on the salt and sand like caught fish on the bank of a lake.

"No!" Molly's face curled into a fist as she wailed.

Was she dangerous? Hiram had to worry about her later. He shot a hand into his other hip pocket and grabbed the large glass bottle of Vi-Jon Hospital Brand Solution of Hydrogen Peroxide. Fumbling, he lost the cap.

Molly leaped at him over her foul offspring—

He sloshed peroxide on both the monsters, spilling too much in his efforts but hitting both of them—

They erupted into bubbles and pink fizz, spattering blood in all directions. Tiny bloody jaws opened and tiny claws clenched and unclenched as they sank into the pink foam and disappeared.

Molly crashed into Hiram.

He fell down under the surprising force of her charge. She was much heavier than she looked, as if her bones were plated with lead. He dropped the Vi-Jon solution and lost sight of it. He kicked the flashlight spinning away into darkness, and the bottom of the tunnel became a funhouse nightmare of flashing light, shrieking, spittle, and nails clawing into his forearm.

"Don't!" he bellowed.

She didn't slow down, and then the same weight that had knocked him prone grabbed Hiram around the throat and squeezed. She bore down on top of him, howling and reeking of blood. In the darkness, he couldn't see her face.

But he found the pistol in his pocket.

"You murdered my children, cunning man!"

He jerked the weapon out and managed to thumb back the

hammer. He only ever used the pistol when he had to, which was rare, but he cocked it with only one hand, then squeezed the trigger.

Click.

Of course, the hammer had been on an empty chamber for safety.

"Molly!" he shouted, one last time.

Molly Kitchen sank her teeth into his neck.

He cocked and squeezed again, and this time was rewarded with a kick and a bang, and the infernal stink of gunpowder.

Molly slumped onto him, still.

Hiram's ears were ringing. He stood and found the light. Checking, he found the bloody puddles that were all that remained of Molly Kitchen's two monster-children. He clapped a hand to his neck and it came away red as well, but not so much so that he had to worry about bleeding to death on the spot.

He checked Molly. Her body sagged like a waterskin with a bullet-hole in it, blood pouring out into the sand. He stared as the last of the gore exited, leaving behind a slack husk with facial features, rucked about a distorted skeleton. Dead, she appeared to have no muscles or viscera. Skin, bones, and blood, that was all that had remained of Molly Kitchen.

Had she been a bright young child once? Had she been quiet and watchful, like Michael?

He could still see the seven nipples, like seven wounds.

"I'm sorry."

Hiram tried not to think of what he was feeling. He found the peroxide bottle on its side, with some solution still in it. Slowly, he trudged back up the mineshaft. At each side passage or hollow where he'd heard movement and responded by throwing down salt, he found another of the blood-beasts, trembling in pain on the bed of white crystal.

He poured down a little Vi-Jon on each monster, bursting each in turn. He patiently watched them dissolve into nothing under the firm light of his electric torch, to be certain nothing survived.

At the mouth of the mine, a cool breeze blew over his Model A. He brought the gas can down into the shaft, along with a box of kitchen matches and a long-handled shovel.

How must it have felt to be Molly Kitchen? Separated by her grue-some nature, by the realization in her body of what she had called the "ancient pact", and severed from her husband by the same. A lonely woman would talk to herself. Eventually, she would talk to the monsters clinging to her flesh, and decide they were her children.

When had Molly Kitchen become a monster herself?

He dug a shallow trench in the ground at the bottom of the shaft and laid Molly in it. Staring down at the distorted sack of skin, he tried to think of words to say. At the end, all he could do was repeat: "I'm sorry."

He doused her with gasoline, then burned her, then covered the ashes with dirt.

He burned the bloodstains that had once been her monstrous chil-dren, for good measure.

Then he stood in the night breeze, leaning against the Model A, and staring down at the lights of Payson.

He would tell Michael nothing, of course. They would drive together back to Lehi in the morning, and they would talk only of the irrigation ditch they'd dug out together. This was knowledge of the sort one kept from the young.

The sky was pale blue over the eastern mountains before he finally started the car to drive back.

THE GUNS OF PERDITION

William Morris is an editor, anthologist, short story writer, and novelist. When he published an invitation to submit alternate history stories about Mormons, I knew I had to throw my hat into the ring. This story of necromantic guns made from the bodies of Joseph and Hyrum Smith and auctioned by the ghost of Joseph Smith through Jonathan Browning, the Nauvoo gunsmith and father of John Moses Browning, as a way to sort out Joseph's possible successors—a business Joseph seems to have left unfinished in life, or at least unfinished enough that multiple men thought they had a good claim—struck me as perfect.

It is a tale of alternate history (these guns were not made, and this auction did not happen) about possible alternate histories (how else might the succession have gone?). Also, I love the gloomy, almost-gothic, almost-steampunk feel. Also, I felt that the story allowed me to actually, you know, say something.

My favorite notice of this story came from a reviewer who read the entire anthology and whose comment on this tale was that it followed actual history, and therefore was "the least interesting" of the lot.

"Couldn't you have held this auction some other time?" asks the man with the bushiest beard and the most elaborate dress; his waistcoat is crimson, and thickly embroidered with squares, compasses, trumpets, and eight-pointed stars. "It's freezing, and I have things to do on Beaver Island."

Always impatient.

I nod. "Forgive me, brother—"

"Call me Jesse." The man in the elegant waistcoat eyes the other two men quickly, and especially the younger of the two, the youngest man in the room. The uncertain light from the room's kerosene lantern darkens the caverns around his eyes with the result that his face looks like a skull.

"Yes, Jesse. Forgive me, but the timing was not my choosing."

"No? Whose was it, then?"

Mine, you knobwit.

I ignore the question. Opening the Imseti-jar, I remove the three cards therefrom and lay them on the cherry-wood desk. I confuse the cards with my fingers after the fashion of a St. Louis street-corner charlatan stealing his daily bread with a game of Find the Lady. The gestures are pure theater.

It is January of the year of our Lord eighteen hundred fifty-six. We are in Nauvoo House, an unfinished hotel a stone's throw from the Mississippi River that might someday, with the right attention, be grand. I have taken two rooms here, just for the night. Nauvoo House is a place that will be noticed by history, as it is owned and operated by Mr. Bidamon and his wife, once wife of the man they called the Prophet in this, his city: Joseph Smith, Jr.

Dead these twelve years.

We are all eternal beings, Brother John.

I nod, but the other men in the room don't know why.

The Bidamons do not know my purpose here. They have rented me a room as they have rented rooms to many strangers, though I am not a stranger. I was once a friend, at least to Emma. Having sold my land and bundled my wife and children into the adjacent room to this one, I do not know where I will be going next. I only know for certain that this is my last night in Nauvoo.

The three men in the room watch me shuffle the cards. They have each written on one of the cards an offer for what I am selling tonight.

We.

They have each written an offer for what we are selling tonight. Brother Jesse, as he wishes to be called, has come from his throne on Beaver Island. He is the wealthiest of the three, and the most suspicious; he looks through slitted lids and he leans with one shoulder against the wall. His presence here, rather than the presence of a messenger, suggests... I don't know what. That he wants to see our offering for himself? That he trusts no subordinate to do his work faithfully in this grave matter?

Oh, your wit.

Brother Isaac Haight is, like Brother Jesse, a man in his early forties. He has come from Deseret, and having arrived only this afternoon, he still has the dust on his trousers to show for it. Brother Haight bounces on the balls of his feet, perpetually rubbing the knuckles of one hand with the fingers of the other. What makes him so anxious? Does he desire so greatly the success of his President, Brother Young? Is he ambitious for his own account? Does he pray for the downfall of an enemy?

The third man is twenty years younger than the others. Like all of us, he wears a thick, dark beard, but his is the only facial hair in the room not streaked with silver. He is the Bidamons' son Joseph, or rather the son of Emma and the Prophet. He stands stiff as a hat rack.

I take all three cards into my hands and peruse them together.

"The highest bid in this first round", I announce, "is one thousand dollars."

Joseph exhales sharply around his teeth. The other two men eye each other.

"What do you mean, this round?" Haight asks.

"There will be two more rounds of bidding", I say. "After the next round, I will again announce only the highest bid. After round three, we will select and announce the winning bid."

"Three rounds. I think we can all agree three is a significant number." Jesse's eyes focus in the distance. I believe he means to create the effect of him looking through the red-wallpapered walls of the room into eternity.

Or maybe he's cross-eyed. It would surprise you how many people will take a cross-eyed man for a prophet.

"What do you mean, *winning bid?*" Haight presses.

"I mean the bid of the winner of the auction."

"Do you mean the *highest* bid again?" Haight rubs his jaw with all ten fingers, as if by doing so he can elongate his chin.

Well noted.

I nod in recognition of the point. "Not necessarily."

Young Joseph has been gazing at me coolly, but now his brow furrows. "That's not really the interesting question, though, is it?"

Have I let something slip? "Oh?"

"Who do you mean by *we?*" Joseph asks. "Surely you don't mean that the four of us together will select the winner. That could only result in deadlock. You imply that you have a confederate."

"Have you considered the bar as a profession?" I counter the question with a question. "Your father had considerable practical experience with the law. If he'd had the training, who knows what his legal career might have looked like?"

You gain nothing by this flattery, John.

Joseph's brow unfurls. "Mr. Bidamon runs a boarding house."

Jesse cuts back in. "A thousand dollars is a heap of money. And the logic of an auction suggests the winner will probably pay even more than that. Don't you think you'd better show us the... the goods?"

"The pistols", Haight adds.

Do it.

"The Guns of Perdition", I announce. Opening the left-hand drawer of the desk, I remove the box that holds the guns; I set the box on the table and open it.

"You're a gunsmith, Brother Browning." Haight grins at me, but it isn't a friendly grin. "Stay away from the theatrics."

I nod and try to keep my smile humble. "Allow a craftsman a little pleasure in his work, Brother Haight."

Jesse takes a step forward and leans to look into the box. Resting inside he sees what I see: two very ordinary pistols, plain but for ivory in their grips and astrological signs engraved in careful arrangement upon their recoil shields. The signs and their arrangement were taught to me, and I cannot interpret them, though I know that one gun bears signs tied to Joseph and the other bears signs that mark it as Hyrum's. There is also a small jar of grease. Jesse sniffs and steps back. "Look like pistols."

"I don't understand", Joseph says. "One thousand dollars is a lot of money for two pistols."

Brace him.

"I will explain." I gesture at the divan behind Joseph. "But first, please, would you sit? I have some strange happenings to report. You, of all four of us, ought to hear them sitting down."

Joseph shakes his head. "I will stand."

Haight takes a flask from inside his coat and holds it to the young man. "If you're going to keep your feet, take a slug of this, at least."

Joseph waves Haight off as well. Haight shrugs, takes a long sip from his own flask, and then returns it to his pocket. "I'm ready, anyway." Haight wipes his mouth with the back of his hand.

I hesitate.

Go ahead.

"Several days before your father's death", I begin, talking directly to Joseph, "he gave me an unusual blessing. In this blessing, he warned me of his own impending murder. He tasked me with certain solemn errands, he directed me to carry out... strange operations. He promised me that he would guide me in those operations, and that the Lord would protect me from the consequences."

"Consequences?" Joseph frowned.

"Criminal", I say. "And other. You know your father and uncle were buried here for a time? Under this building, I mean."

Joseph nods.

I try to continue, but my words catch in my throat.

Go on.

Joseph is staring at me.

"I dug them up. Their bodies."

I am looking at the red and gold carpet now, so I do not see their faces. I do, however, hear their shocked intake of air. I give them a moment to let the simple statement sink in before proceeding to elaborate. While I wait, I try not to remember the sound of my shovel biting into the packed earth floor of the basement that night, or the groaning of coffin lids.

Or the rasping and sucking noises that followed.

I manage not to shudder.

"You need not imagine the usual gothic appurtenances", I say after a moment. "There were no ravens, or hunchbacks, or phantasms. As directed, I dug up both men, then I... took something from each of them. Then I returned the bodies to their graves."

Jesse steps away from the wall, smile widening. "These pistols, you mean? These are pistols possessed by the Prophet and the Patriarch? That's hardly what you implied in your—"

"No." I say it forcefully, and the word shuts Jesse's mouth. "I took things from their very bodies. Blood, and fat, and bone."

Young Joseph staggers back as if I have struck him in the mouth. "The whisky", he says in a loud whisper. "Quickly."

Haight supplies the requested article. Then, with aqua vitae in his belly to fortify him, the Prophet's son decides to sit on the divan after all. He buries his face in his hands.

I let him sit unmolested. The other men stare at him and me in alternation.

"Go on", Joseph says after a minute. He is still hiding his face.

I gesture at the guns. "As directed, I have made these guns. They are inscribed with astrological symbols communicated to me by your father. They are handled with his very bone and the bone of his brother Hyrum. They are greased—anointed, if you will—and have always and only been greased by the Martyrs' very fat and blood."

"Perdition!" Haight hisses; his voice sounds triumphant.

"Sorcery!" Jesse growls; he approves.

Joseph looks up, but says nothing.

I bow my head. "I have only done as instructed."

Jesse steps forward, beaming. "And you have done well, Brother Browning. I am prepared to bid again."

I set three more cards on the front of the desk, beside the pen and bottle of ink. "The highest bid in round one was one thousand dollars." I stand the Imseti-jar with its painted human face beside the cards, and then I withdraw to the window.

I hear the scratching of the pen behind me as the men step forward, one at a time. Each will write his bid on a card, and on the reverse of that same card a glyph of his own design. Each will drop his card into the Imseti-jar and retire.

Nauvoo is lit by lanterns and fires as the evening deepens. It was lit by more and greater lights, once, but it is a city recovering from a grievous wound.

I shall miss it.

You miss it already. This is no longer Nauvoo the Beautiful.

True.

I turn on my heel. "Finished?"

The three men nod. Joseph's is a distracted bob of the chin from the divan, where he sits staring at his feet. Jesse tips his head fiercely, staring through the walls again. Haight nods three times and cracks the knuckles of both hands.

I again examine the three cards. "The highest bid this round is five thousand dollars."

Again Joseph exhales sharply. Isaac Haight whistles. Jesse snaps his fingers.

"Do we really need a third round?" Jesse asks. "Can Brigham's impoverished eaters of crickets really match my bid?"

Haight glares at him. "You think that possessing these pistols will make you King."

Jesse's eyes flash. "No! I think the Lord has made me King. And I think the King should wear the pistols of the King before him. As the Nephites handed down the sword of Laban and the brass plates, so shall the Kings of Beaver Island hand down to their successors the Guns of Salvation, embodying in them the implacable witness of the brothers Joseph and Hyrum Smith, cut down as to this world, and exalted as to the next!"

"I know you now", Joseph says. "You're James Strang. Folks around here say queer things about you and your people."

"Ha!" Haight guffaws.

Joseph shakes his head. "They say strange things about the followers of Brigham Young, too. All of you. Despotic rule. Multiple women."

It is hard to see him like this. Say something.

"They said strange things about your father, too", I proffer. "Some of them were even true."

Joseph springs from the divan. For a moment I fear he will attack me, but he recoils away into a corner. "No!"

He could take the guns. He could know the truth. He could be the Prophet.

I cannot tell whether those are alternatives, or the results of a single course of action. I cannot ask, without making a fool of myself.

"I know your father", I say.

"Yes?" Joseph steps forward. The placement of his feet resembles the fighting stance of a pugilist. "And my mother?"

"Emma. Yes."

"And did you ever hear my father introduce any other woman, any woman other than my mother, as his wife?"

I hesitate. "Well, I also know—"

Joseph raises his voice. "Did my *father* ever introduce another woman as his *wife?*"

I try again. "It wasn't ever that simple."

Joseph lunges forward half a step. "This is a yes or no question, Brother Browning. This is what the Lord teaches us, is it not? Yea, yea, or nay, nay, with no tricks. I will give you one more chance to answer the question, and then I will walk out the door. Did my father ever introduce any woman other than my mother as his wife, in your presence?"

Let it go.

My shoulders slump. "He did not."

Joseph collapses on the divan. He is trembling.

"It is sad to see the seed of the Prophet fallen so low." Haight shakes his head. Joseph ignores him.

"Show respect." Strang stands straighter, somehow taller. "He was your King."

Cross-eyed men.

"No", I say, "the Lord was and is the King."

Strang hisses through his teeth, but doesn't challenge me.

"There will be a third round", I continue. "But first you must understand why Brother Joseph calls these the Guns of Perdition. They are not mere symbols. Anointed with the blood of the Martyrs, like the Title of Liberty, like the sword of Laban, like the portable Throne of God itself, these guns will bring victory to their wielder in this world."

Strang steps forward. "I am ready."

"There will, of course, be a cost."

I place three final blank cards on the desk, but before I can withdraw to permit the last round of bidding, Joseph rises from his seat. "Wait."

Good.

"Yes?" I ask.

He chooses his words carefully. He really *should* be a lawyer. "You say you received direction from my father in this matter."

"I did."

"You speak of him in the present tense. As if he speaks to you now."

Excellent!

"That is correct."

"It is correct that you speak in this fashion, or it is correct that he speaks to you now?"

I laugh softly. "Now I am caught in the cross-examination. What shall I tell him, Brother Joseph?"

Tell him the truth.

I steady myself with a deep breath. "Your father has never left my presence since the day he gave me that blessing. I see him always at the corner of my vision. I hear his voice. I ask him questions, and he answers. I am acting in this matter, in every detail, at his direction."

As I speak, Joseph shrinks. When I finish, he springs up like a shot anvil. "Madman!"

"I am not mad." I think I am telling the truth, but looking at the Guns of Perdition I cannot be certain.

"You are a necromancer and a resurrection man", Joseph snarls. He is right, I suppose, though I never intended to be either. "And you hear voices in your head."

"Nephi heard voices", I point out. "I'm not mad."

"Then prove it."

At my words, and at Joseph's accusation, the other men have stepped back from the Imseti-jar and the bidding cards. The expressions on their faces now suggest that they would also like to see evidence of my sanity.

"Well, Brother Joseph?" I ask.

I am *stepped forward* in that moment. I choose my words carefully in this matter, because what happens to me is beyond my prior experience. My legs spring forward, perfectly balanced and agile, but not at my choosing. Then my hand is thrust forward to grip young Joseph by the forehead. Joseph wavers, but I hold him upright by a strength beyond my own. My mouth is opened.

"*Joseph Smith my son*", my mouth utters, "*in the name of the Lord I command you to doubt.*"

"The Prophet's face", Haight murmurs.

"His voice!" Strang gasps.

"*In the name of the Lord I pronounce these blessings upon you, my son. You shall live a long and happy life. You shall be a great leader of your flock. And you shall not suffer from the curses of your father. In the name of the Lord Adonai the Everlasting, amen.*"

At that, I step back and lower my arm.

"Amen", pronounce all three men.

Joseph collapses into my arms.

It seems after that there is no more to say. When Joseph has regained his feet I return to the curtain for a last look at Nauvoo. She was Beautiful once. I am still uncertain what wrecked that beauty.

When I have heard three cards deposited in the Imseti-jar, I replace its human-head lid, shake it gently, and then remove the cards. I sit at the desk and spread the cards before me. I do not shuffle them this time.

"Well, Brother Joseph?" I ask.

You know which it has to be.

I nod and raise the winning card to examine its reverse. "Whose emblem is the beehive?"

"Well, obviously", Haight begins, but then Strang punches the other man in the face.

What occurs next happens quick as snakebites. Haight crashes against the desk, Strang pulls a knife from his pants, and as Strang lunges forward to stab at the man from Deseret, Haight's hand falls on the Guns of Perdition. He snatches one up, aims at the King of Beaver Island, and pulls the trigger.

The explosion in the room is loud.

Strang falls to the ground and drops his knife. Haight drops the pistol to the desk and steps away, shaking. Joseph presses himself against the wall.

"I had not loaded those pistols", I say. It is the truth.

The look on Haight's face suggests he believes me.

The look on Joseph's face suggests he now thinks us all mad.

Strang stands slowly, examining himself. When he looks up, his eyes are the baffled eyes of a bull that has been mortally shot in the temple and has not yet realized it. "And yet I am unhurt."

Again, I am seized. *"James Strang, King of Beaver Island, in the name of the Lord I pronounce a doom upon you. Within the year you shall die, in your absence your Kingdom shall wither, your name shall be forgotten upon the face of the earth, and you shall have no seed after you!"*

Strang's face is shocked. "But I didn't hurt him! And I didn't mean to!"

"I pronounce this doom upon you, James, not for your violence, but for your blasphemy. For your trivial treatment of sacred things will the Lord Adonai the Everlasting strike you dead, amen!"

Strang says, "amen." He is the only one.

He throws back his head to emit an inhuman noise, something like the howl of a wolf, and then he crashes through the door and is gone.

There is a long silence.

Isaac Haight steps forward to shake my hand. He steps carefully, so as not to be too close to the Guns of Perdition. I hand him his winning bid, with the beehive scratched onto the reverse, and on the obverse the words *A PLACE AMONG THE SAINTS IN DESERET.*

"Brother Joseph will hold you to this promise", I tell him.

"I hope he does", Haight says. "When will you join us?"

"My family and I will depart for Salt Lake City tomorrow."

"What did the King of Beaver Island promise you?"

I pick up the second card. On its reverse is sketched a simple image of a crown, and on the obverse are the words *A PRINCE FOREVER AFTER THE ORDER OF MELCHIZEDEK.*

Haight nods. He carefully replaces the fired pistol with its mate. He closes the box and takes it to the door.

"I must remind you", I call to him. "Joseph tells me the Guns promise success in this world only. And there will be a price to pay."

"What price?" he asks from the doorway.

"I don't know." I shrug. "In general, the greater the victory, the steeper the price."

Isaac Haight nods one last time, and then he is gone.

Joseph is sitting silently on the divan. I pick up the third card, his card, marked on the back side simply with his initials *J.S.*, and I sit beside him.

"You bid nothing", I say. "In each round, you offered nothing."

He is slow to answer me. "My father was indeed a king", he says finally. "His kingdom was not of this world."

Very good.

"So the question for you, Brother Smith, is this: of what world will your kingdom be?"

Joseph stands slowly, nodding and straightening his coat. "Yes", he says. "That is the question."

He leaves, and I am alone.

Completely alone; for the first time in twelve years, I do not see another man standing in the room with me.

"And now, Brother Joseph?" I ask.

Silence.

"What next?"

A WILD WOMAN HATH COME AMONG US

This story is set in the world of Aaron Michael Ritchey's Juniper Wars, in which North America has been hit by a couple of simultaneous catastrophes: a loss of electrical power in the Rocky Mountain region, and also a plague that means that male children mostly die in utero, resulting in a population that skews female, 10:1. With this background, Aaron asked if I'd be willing to write a story, speculating about what Utah might look like.

EXPLANATORY NOTE TO FILE: THE FOLLOWING TRANSCRIPT IS PART OF THE RECORD OF THE POSTHUMOUS DISCIPLINARY ACTION OF A MEMBER OF THE CHURCH OF JESUS CHRIST OF LATTER-DAY SAINTS. IT IS INCLUDED FOR ITS VALUE AS BACKGROUND BECAUSE OF THE INFORMATION IT CONTAINS ABOUT NOTORIOUS OUTLAW TAMAR JOHNSON.

BRACKETED ENDNOTES FOLLOW THE TEXT OF THE EXCERPT.

WITNESS TRANSCRIPT
WITNESS: LUCY SORENSON
IN THE MATTER OF THE MEMBERSHIP OF CLAYNE
EBBERS (DECEASED)[1]
HIGH COUNCIL[2]
OAK HILLS SECOND STAKE[3]
PROVO, UTAH

Begin Transcript:
WITNESS: I never trusted that new girl, not from the start.

YOUNG: Please stay focused, Sister Sorenson. We're interested in your memory of the events surrounding the death of Brother Ebbers.

WITNESS: Well, that's no secret. Brother Ebbers shot himself. It was right in front of all of us.

YOUNG: Thank you for confirming that. We had heard that from Sister Oaks, of course, and a few of the other young women. We're hoping to find out a little more. The question, you see, is whether Brother Ebbers should lose his standing in the church due to the nature of his death.

WITNESS: You mean should he be excommunicated because he killed himself?

OLDHAM: Since we're being recorded, I want to say again that I fail to see the necessity of this proceeding. Surely God in His infinite wisdom can decide what to do about Brother Ebbers now.

PACKET: That sounds like Godbeite[4] talk to me.

OLDHAM: The twentieth century is over, and I don't hold on to any dreams of it coming back. I'm happy where I am, thank you, with both my wives and all our children.

PACKET: Careful, Oldham. You don't want to get a reputation for being a liberal or a softy this early during your tenure on the High Council.

OLDHAM: God grant there might be liberals and softies on the High Council when you get tried for your membership, Floyd.

PACKET: Sitting at this table, I'm Brother Packet. Don't you forget that, Brother Oldham.

YOUNG: Enough of this, we're here to listen to the witness.

WITNESS: You mean you can cut Brother Ebbers off from the church, even though he's dead?

YOUNG: We baptize for and on behalf of the dead, Sister Sorenson. Does baptism for the dead trouble you, or only their excommunication?

WITNESS: No, only . . . all right, I see what you mean now. Only Brother Ebbers was nice.

PACKET: And Brother Ebbers was a viable man, Sister Sorenson. He could have children. Do you know what that means, Sister Sorenson?

WITNESS: I think so.

PACKET: It means he didn't only kill himself, he killed every single male descendant he could have had.

WITNESS: I see.

PACKET: He murdered multitudes.

YOUNG: We're called to be judges in Israel, Sister Sorenson. Unfortunately, niceness is not the question we are commanded to examine. Not for Brother Ebbers, and not really for anyone.

PACKET: Sister Sorenson, did you feel there was anything unusual about Brother Ebbers's niceness?

WITNESS: How do you mean?

PACKET: Well, he was nice enough that you think to mention it. Did he pay particular attention to any of the sisters? Did he pay inappropriate attention to any of the sisters?

WITNESS: Oh no, not at all! Not even when Sally Jensen, she's from up Manti way, made eyes at him. He only tipped his hat, and when she asked if he was married, he admitted he already had wives, and he felt that four was enough.

PACKET: Did he mean that four was enough for any man? Do you think he meant to criticize the Doctrine?[5]

OLDHAM: Kind of a stretch, don't you think, Packet?

PACKET: Brother Packet. Unless you want me to call you John.

OLDHAM: I wouldn't mind it.

PACKET: I would.

OLDHAM: Brother Packet, then.

PACKET: Something caused him to shoot himself. Brother Ebbers was employed and in good standing with the Church. He was happily married, as far as we have been able to tell. He was accompanying the Spring Bridal Train from St. George to Salt Lake,[6] picking up the Brides along the way, and then, apparently with no warning, he killed himself. Maybe he was unhappy with his role in implementing the Doctrine.

WITNESS: I think he only meant it's a lot of work to be married to one woman, and being married to four was a lot more work. At least, that's what I think he meant by 'logarithmic.' I'm not so great at math. I've got a strong memory, though. Won both the spelling and the geography bees last year, over to Kanab.

YOUNG: We've heard good things about your memory, Sister Sorenson. That's why we've brought you here, of all the Brides.

WITNESS: Anyway, it was the kind of thing you hear men say about the Doctrine a lot. Besides, I think he shot himself because of what the woman said.

YOUNG: Let's be clear here. When you say 'the woman,' you don't mean Sister Oaks, your escort, or any of the sisters who were called to be on the Spring Bridal Train, do you?

WITNESS: No, I mean the crazy woman, the one with the guns.

OLDHAM: In the interest of continuing to be clear, there's no evidence that Tamar Johnson is insane.

WITNESS: Well, there's all that crazy stuff she spouted, about how the Goddess has finally revealed herself, and the church wasn't ready for it.

OLDHAM: I agree that's some shocking stuff, but –

WITNESS: And about how the King James translators were just a bunch of liars, because when the Greek and the Hebrew in Isaiah both say that "the" virgin shall conceive, the translators just wrote "a" virgin, which is a made-up lie. And besides, they were just men and protestants, so of course they were going to miss the whole point.

PACKET: See what comes of being liberal, Brother Oldham?

OLDHAM: You're the one who called me liberal, Brother Packet.

I'm just trying to be fair to Brother Ebbers. If we really think his eternal soul's at stake here, shouldn't we be slow to judge?

WITNESS: Also something about obsession with sodomites, but mostly about a bunch of dirty old men just taking advantage of the Sterility Epidemic to marry all the girls they could.

PACKET: Evil speaking against the Lord's anointed. That's been the problem with feminism from the beginning, even before they started talking about Asherah. Evil speaking. At least the Godbeites are civil.

OLDHAM: Maybe. But we're not here to try Tamar Johnson.

YOUNG: In their hearts, the Godbeites are afraid we're right.

PACKET: Did the subject of a prior relationship between Brother Ebbers and Tamar Johnson come up?

WITNESS: They were married. He said they were married, he said he was sorry he'd been such a bad husband, he drove her to oppose and defile the very institution of marriage as well as the Doctrine.

YOUNG: Sounds like Brother Ebbers at least started the conversation with his head on right. Have we established what Tamar Johnson was doing there in the first place?

PACKET: She was there to kidnap the Brides, Brother Young.

OLDHAM: Let's allow Sister Sorenson to tell us.

WITNESS: Well, she didn't say 'kidnap.' She stopped the train with a tree across the tracks. I know, because I was near the front and I saw it. And then she climbed aboard the train with her two pistols and made everyone get off and stand in the tall grass.

PACKET: Wasn't Brother Ebbers armed? Wasn't he there to protect the train? Don't we give our men the right tools for the job? Perhaps he didn't shoot her because of their relationship. Perhaps he was soft.

OLDHAM: A softy, you mean. And liberal.

PACKET: I didn't say a liberal, Brother Oldham. Interesting that you would make the connection.

WITNESS: Brother Ebbers had a rifle. Not like a hunting rifle, one of the ones that shoots a lot of bullets fast.

YOUNG: An assault rifle. An automatic.

WITNESS: Yes. But this is what I was saying about the new girl, you see?

OLDHAM: Tell us more about the new girl, then. What was her name?

WITNESS: She called herself Angie, I never heard a last name. She got on at Mona, and she wasn't on the list, but she said she was so hoping she might get a nice gentle bishop from Salt Lake City as a husband and she started to cry, so Sister Oaks went ahead and wrote her name on the end of the list.

PACKET: Have we identified this girl?

YOUNG: Not yet.

OLDHAM: Did you talk to Angie?

WITNESS: I tried. But she ignored me and kept to herself. Only then the train stopped and Brother Ebbers went to the window with his rifle, and suddenly Angie pulled a pistol out of her scripture bag[7] and pointed it at him.

PACKET: Brother Ebbers surrendered to a girl?

WITNESS: He said 'you don't want to do that.' But she kept her gun pointed at him and he kept his pointed at the crazy woman and she kept hers pointed right back, the whole time.

PACKET: If she didn't kidnap them, what did she do with the Brides? Fully half of them didn't make it to Provo.

WITNESS: What she said was, 'She gives you a choice. You can go to those sevener nutballs if you want, or you can come with, and learn Her ways.'

YOUNG: What's a sevener nutball?

PACKET: Stop laughing, Brother Oldham.

WITNESS: Those were her words, not mine.

PACKET: She means Isaiah 4:1. 'And in that day seven women shall take hold of one man.' Johnson and her Asherah-worshipping harridans[8] deny the obvious, that Isaiah was prophesying the return of polygamy. Hence, we have the Doctrine. A prophecy which has indeed come to pass. Denying the truth of any prophecy is bold, but denying one that has already been fulfilled requires particular courage, wouldn't you say, Brother Oldham? Particular nerve? Particular audacity?

OLDHAM: Particular conviction, maybe. By sevener nutballs she means us, Brother Young.

YOUNG: And half the Brides left the train, as simple as that?

PACKET: Sister Sorenson, the transcript can't hear you nodding your head.

WITNESS: Yes, half of them left.

YOUNG: I'm puzzled. I don't think I have any sense at all why Brother Ebbers shot himself.

PACKET: Disappointment at his own failure, perhaps.

OLDHAM: You said you thought Brother Ebbers shot himself because of what Tamar Johnson said. Do you mean those things about Greek and Hebrew?

WITNESS: No. Well, kind of. I mean, it was all one conversation, and it was long. And there was shouting, and she cursed a lot. He didn't curse, if you're thinking that.

PACKET: Was the conversation too long to remember it all?

WITNESS: Yes, by a lot, and like I said, I have a good memory. But I recall the last bit perfectly. I mean, the gunshot was like a big exclamation mark at the end of a speech, if you know what I mean. I don't think I'll ever forget it.

OLDHAM: Go on, then.

WITNESS: She said 'have you forgotten what it's like, Clayne, to defend the revelation?'[9]

PACKET: Outrageous.

WITNESS: He said back, 'I defended the revelation as long as I could, Tamar. I defended it with everything I had.'

YOUNG: I don't like where this is going.

WITNESS: And he said, 'finally I decided that even if I wasn't sure about the revelation, at least I could defend the church. There's value in the church, the church protects us and does good, even if it makes mistakes.'

PACKET: Closeted Godbeite nonsense. And I quote, 'So then because thou art lukewarm, neither cold nor hot, I will spew thee out of my mouth.'[10] Brother Ebbers is damned by his own words, and by his tepidity.

YOUNG: A man who lacks belief but does the right thing is surely not damned, Brother Packet.

PACKET: This man shot himself!

OLDHAM: Is that all, Sister Sorenson? Did they say anything else?

WITNESS: She said the strangest thing. Crazy talk, like I told you.

PACKET: I think I've heard enough.

OLDHAM: Go on, Lucy.

WITNESS: She said, 'But what happens, Clayne, when one day you look at your life and you realize you've gone from defending the revelation to just defending the church to finally defending the church against the revelation? What then?'

YOUNG: And what did he say?

WITNESS: Nothing. He lowered his rifle. And the crazy woman left, and Angie left with her, and half the girls. Sister Oaks tried to talk to Brother Ebbers, but he wouldn't say anything. He just stared out the window while the train crew dragged the log off the tracks, and then when the train started rolling again, he jumped off and walked away to a stand of juniper. Before anyone could stop him, he put the end of that rifle in his mouth and pulled the trigger.

PACKET: Guilt, I think it's obvious. The man knew his lack of faith had lost half the Brides – how many women is that, sixty? He condemned those girls to an apostate existence, and he felt guilty. Better he had put them on a train to Wendover, where they could have become whores.

YOUNG: Brother Packet, your language!

OLDHAM: You don't know that. You don't know any of that, and you don't mean it. You can't.

PACKET: I'm a judge in Israel, Brother Oldham. The Good Shepherd calls us to cull wolves from the flock.

OLDHAM: Clayne Ebbers is dead, Floyd. He won't be ravaging the flock anytime soon. How about we just let God decide his ultimate fate?

WITNESS: Am I done?

PACKET: You know what I know, John? Ebbers's fate is your fate.

OLDHAM: I'll shoot myself? Charming.

WITNESS: Really, can I go now?

PACKET: He lost faith. He allowed doubt to temper his obedience, and he lost faith. That was why he killed himself, and all the sons
he never had. That will be your fall, too.

OLDHAM: Perhaps he felt he lost his way. Maybe he didn't think
he'd lived up to his own ideals.

PACKET: If he had any ideal other than continually holding fast to
the rod of iron,[11] he belongs in hell.

OLDHAM: Is there any room for mercy in your world, Floyd?

PACKET: Is there any room for obedience in yours?

YOUNG: Thank you for your testimony, Sister Sorenson. Yes, you
can go. Congratulations on your marriage to Bishop Partridge, and
good luck!

END TRANSCRIPT

---

1. Following the fission of the LDS Church into competing factions in the 21st
   century (see notes 4 and 8), the excommunication of the dissenting dead became a
   common tool for delineating orthodoxy in the organization.
2. A "High Council" is an advisory and governing body of men with responsibility for
   a "Stake" (see note 3). In this case, the High Council is acting in an ecclesiastical-
   judicial capacity. Although only three men (Young, Packet, and Oldham) are identified in the transcript, more were undoubtedly present. The High Council meets
   privately and its records are private.
3. A "Stake" is the umbrella group containing adjoining congregations, like a
   diocese.
4. The Church of Jesus Christ of Latter-day Saints (Traditional Practice) is the
   second-largest of the contemporary Mormon groups. Its distinctiveness lies in
   adhering to the LDS Church's twentieth-century rejection of polygamy; the largest
   Mormon church, The Church of Jesus Christ of Latter-day Saints, by contrast,
   returned to the nineteenth-century practice of embracing polygamy (see note 5).
   "Godbeite" is a derisive term the larger LDS faction applies to the Traditional
   Practice group, and derives from a nineteenth-century Mormon splinter group that
   rejected the leadership of Brigham Young and practiced a more all-embracing spirituality.
5. The "Doctrine" is the LDS term for the practice of polygamy, also called "plural
   marriage." More specifically, it is a polygynous marriage in which wealthy and influential men take more than one wife. Generally, this means that late in life a man
   takes additional and younger wives, who are in theory subject to the rule of his
   older, first wife. In the nineteenth century, this left poorer and younger men
   without mate; official LDS teaching is that the advent of the Sterility Epidemic as

God's way of clearing the path for the return of plural marriage and also demonstrating the Doctrine's superiority.

6. "Bridal Trains" are regularly-scheduled trains that collect LDS girls from rural areas and bring them to Salt Lake and Utah Valleys to be married.

7. Mormons often carry their famously multi-volume scripture sets to church meetings and similar events in compact totes. This implies that the gun cannot have been very large.

8. The third group that came from the fission of the mainstream LDS Church following the onset of the Sterility Epidemic is more elusive than the other two. Other field reports describe this group as "feminist", "Goddess-worshipping", and "renegade." We have not identified any land or buildings owned by this organization, but it may be the group known from other sources as "The Church of Jesus Christ, Son and Bridegroom", or "The Church of the Firstborn." As suggested by the transcript, they are understood to acknowledge a feminine divinity, perhaps under the name Asherah. Asherah was classically portrayed as a tree, or a woman-tree hybrid; see note 11.

9. Unclear. In context, this cannot mean the Doctrine. Perhaps a reference to Mormon teaching generally, or the inherited ideas of the Mormon founder, Joseph Smith, or divine revelation as a category.

10. The Apocalypse of St. John, 3.16.

11. 1 Nephi 8.30 (*The Book of Mormon*). The passage quoted comes from a vision in which approaching pilgrim cling to a "rod of iron" in order to traverse a "strait and narrow path" and enter the presence of the tree of life. Packet refers to the rod as an image of obedience. Ironically, the tree of life has often been understood to be an image of a goddess, in both the *Bible* (e.g., Proverbs 3.13-18) and the LDS Church's own *Book of Mormon* (e.g., 1 Nephi 11.3-15).

THE GREATEST HORSE THIEF IN HISTORY

I wrote this story for the Straight Outta Deadwood *anthology. When editor David Boop accepted the story for publication, I thought it would be the first Hiram Woolley tale into print. In actuality, "The Seven Nipples of Molly Kitchen" came out one month ahead of it.*

Like "Molly", this story has its genesis in real—and striking—Utah history. Chief Walkara (sometimes called "Walker" by the Mormon settlers) was a real person, and was a horse thief on epic proportions. With some elaboration, the account of his funeral here is consistent with what eyewitnesses describe—the year was 1855, Franklin Pierce was president of the United States, and in the Utah Territory, a Shoshone chief went to his rest with human sacrifices around him and a letter from Brigham Young in his hand.

Even the tale of Carre Shinob, and the relocated corpse, are actual stories told about Walkara. Hiram Woolley, of course, is a fictional character, but I like to think of him as a possible man, a liminal man, a person standing in one of the interesting hinges of time, with feet on both sides of the hinge. A little like Walkara.

"Sugar beets, is it?" The man standing inside his own screen door might have been fifty years old, a few years older than Hiram himself. He dressed better than Hiram, in a button-down shirt and high-waisted trousers, though the calluses on his hands betrayed the fact that his work, too, included manual labor. His face was screwed into a tight and bitter shield.

He looked angry, but he didn't look like a thief.

A creek splashed over rocks behind the house. In the background, across fields heavy with wheat, the town of Heber lay sprawled across the valley floor. Beyond it stood snow-capped Timpanogos.

"Someone tell you I'm a beet farmer, Mr. McCrae?" When Hiram came to a town giving away food, word tended to spread ahead of him. Elbert McCrae was the last man on his list to visit.

McCrae nodded. "A man can only fill his belly with sugar beets so much."

Hiram nodded. "That's why I stopped on the Provo Bench and traded the beets for bread and beef. Can I come in?"

McCrae hesitated, but opened the door. "The Provo Bench, huh? You know, they call it 'Orem' now."

"After the railroad man. I just can't bring myself to use some of these new names. Slow to change, I guess." Hiram set down the crate of groceries he carried to kick the dust from his Redwing Harvesters and beat more dust from the legs of his denim overalls with his fedora. He gestured at the double A sitting on the gravel drive. "My son?"

McCrae squinted. "Looks Indian."

"He's Navajo." Hiram nodded. "Parents died in a fire, and my wife and I took him in."

McCrae grunted. "May as well bring in the whole family. I do appreciate the groceries."

Hiram beckoned to Michael. The boy slid out of the front seat of the truck and scampered up the porch, slipping in through McCrae's front door in front of Hiram with a wooden crate full of groceries in his hand.

"Thanks for letting in the help, Mr. McCrae", Michael said.

"You ain't that much help", Hiram grunted.

"I drive, don't I?"

It was true. Hiram's fainting spells made him uncomfortable driving more than short distances, so Michael drove. If the state legislature did what it was threatening, and started requiring a license from drivers, would Michael qualify?

Hiram pushed away the thought.

"You drive", he agreed.

They set both boxes on a small table in McCrae's kitchen. The table was just big enough to hold the crates on its white and green enamel top without McCrae raising its wings. "You got ice in that Frigidaire, Mr. McCrae? The bacon is cured, but the beef isn't."

"I got ice. I got food, too, comes to it."

Hiram put the beef in McCrae's large porcelain ice box. There was room for it, so he loaded the bacon and vegetables in as well. Despite McCrae's claim, the ice box held nothing but ice and what Hiram had brought. "I'm glad you got food. And I'm glad I can bring you a little extra, Mr. McCrae. I'm just here to help."

"Report to Salt Lake about my habits, is that it?" McCrae frowned. "How much am I drinking, am I attending church services, what exactly does an unmarried man like me living up in the Uinta Mountains do for fun? Come to meddle in the behavior of the working man?"

Hiram shook his head. "You're thinking of Henry Ford. I don't care what you're drinking or whose company you keep, I'm just here to help. We're all supposed to pitch in. Believe I heard Mr. Roosevelt himself suggest that."

"That's your job, is it? To pitch in?" McCrae snorted.

"It's my ministry, I guess you'd say." Hiram shrugged. "My *job* is to grow sugar beets."

McCrae collapsed onto a soft chair, his bitter energy suddenly gone. "I'm sorry. I just . . . I worked all my life, Mr. . . . ."

"You can call me Hiram. Hiram Woolley. My boy is Michael."

McCrae nodded. "I worked all my life, Hiram. I ain't comfortable taking help."

Hiram sat on the sofa opposite. Michael sat beside him, bouncing slightly and drumming his fingers on his knees. The boy could stand to have his hair cut. For that matter, Hiram probably could, too.

"I don't just bring food", Hiram said. "Sometimes I help solve family disputes. Dug a well over in Price last week. I do what I can to be of assistance, when I don't have to plant and harvest. Maybe I can help you find work, Mr. McCrae."

McCrae stared at the hardwood floor.

"Horse ranching, isn't it?" Hiram asked.

McCrae grunted. "Only ever owned one or two at a time, myself. But until last week, I was foreman on one of the local ranches. You really want to help?" McCrae nodded toward the back door, eastward. "Go talk to the owners of the Flying Z, get me my job back."

Hiram sat quietly, hoping to hear still, small voices of guidance. He didn't.

What to do? He had to help McCrae if he could. But the same neighbors who had sent Hiram to find Elbert McCrae had also suggested that McCrae might be a man who deserved to lose his job.

McCrae stared at him. How long had Hiram been silent? "I was told the Flying Z lost a herd", Hiram said.

"Five hundred head."

"The Oldhams figure it's your fault the horses escaped?" The Oldhams owned the Flying Z.

McCrae laughed bitterly. "Worse than that, Hiram. They think I stole 'em. Thirty years of honest work under my belt and a spotless reputation don't matter, they think I made five hundred horses just disappear. That'd make me the greatest horse thief in history, I expect. And hell, I'd be off in California or Texas, spending the money. Instead, I'm here, knocking door to door and asking for more work."

"You don't look like a guilty man", Hiram agreed.

"And yet they won't hire me back", McCrae said. "Nor will any of the other ranches. And there's no work for me in Heber, not even at the tack and saddle shops or in the slaughterhouse. Everyone figures me for a horse thief."

"I'd like to help." Hiram balanced his sweat-stained fedora over one fist as if it were a hat jack, looking out the window at the bleached blue sky. "You have any idea what happened to the horses?"

McCrae opened his mouth, shut it. He looked at Michael briefly, frowned, and then stood, pacing back and forth. "I don't like to say."

"I'll go talk to the owners of the Flying Z", Hiram said. "Whether or not you tell me anything else. But the more I know, the more I can help."

McCrae stopped his pacing and stared at Hiram. "Yeah", he said, "okay. It was Indians."

Indians? Hiram tried to avoid looking astonished. "The Utes? Uintah and Ouray Reservation? It's been a long time since the Utes rustled any horses."

"I didn't say it was them." McCrae cleared his throat. "And I can't say I really know one kind of Indian from another, begging your pardon, but I see the Utes from time to time, shopping down at Heber, or passing by at the Flying Z. They drive cars, they wear jeans and boots."

"Surprise", Michael muttered.

"The horse thieves looked . . . old-fashioned", McCrae continued. "Horseback. Paint and feathers, the whole thing."

The heliotropius in his pocket, the red-streaked green stone with so many useful properties, lay still; McCrae was practicing no deception. Hiram felt a vague sense of disquiet. "I'll go talk to the owners."

"Of course, we'll give Mr. McCrae back his job", Ada Oldham said. Her husband and co-owner of the Flying Z, Ira, stood with his head and shoulders under the hood of his vehicle, grunting his agreement. "Just as soon as we get back our horses."

"He says he didn't steal them", Hiram said. "I believe him."

"He said Indians in war paint took the horses." Ada wore her hair in a simple bun and dressed in calico. She and her husband were working on their Fargo truck together. The ranch house was two stories tall and must have seven or eight rooms, judging from the outside—the Oldhams were doing well, but didn't dress or act rich. In other circumstances, Hiram would have liked them very much, but now he felt waves of distrust radiating from Mrs. Oldham, and, tightening his own stomach, he tried not to radiate it right back. "You believe that, too?"

"I believe he isn't a liar." Hiram watched Michael bounce from side to side in the front of his own truck, the Ford Model AA. "Is he a drunk?" The former foreman had seemed a little defensive about his drinking habits.

"The man is a teetotaler, as far as I know", Ada Oldham said. "Raised Kentucky Baptist. But really . . . war paint?"

McCrae hadn't exactly said 'war paint,' at least not to Hiram, but there was no sense picking a needless fight. "You got any maps?"

"What kind of maps?" Mrs. Oldham asked. Under the hood of the Fargo, Mr. Oldham banged metal against metal and cursed mildly. "If you're looking for a highway, there aren't any. That's why we came out here to the Uintas to run our horses. Get away from the big towns like Provo and Ogden. Even Heber's getting too big for my John's taste, these days."

"Just horses?" Hiram wondered.

"Also cattle." Ada shrugged. "It was horses that got stolen."

"All the maps you got. The older, the better", Hiram said. "If you had any maps from when you first bought the land, I'd be especially happy to look at those."

"What are you thinking, exactly?" She eyed him with suspicion.

"Mr. McCrae saw something", Hiram said slowly. Then he dodged her question with a slight evasion that didn't quite amount to a lie: "maybe if I look on the maps, I'll see what it was."

"Like a rock formation he took in the darkness for an Indian in headdress?" Mrs. Oldham suggested drily.

"Yes", Hiram said. "Something like that."

"I'll give you all my maps", Mrs. Oldham said. "Only remember, I'm not looking for an explanation. I'm looking for five hundred horses."

"I get your five hundred horses back, will you hire Elbert McCrae again?"

"Of course."

He waited with Michael while Ada Oldham went into the ranch house. The boy looked at Hiram with his dark liquid eyes and smiled. Hiram smiled back and tried not to let the sudden pang of loss, such as came over him every time he thought of his wife, twist that smile into a frown.

"So Mrs. Oldham seems to accept the idea that Indians might be thieves", Michael said. "Only she doesn't believe in the war paint."

That ended Hiram's nostalgia, and he tousled the boy's hair.

Ada Oldham returned; her facial expression was softened. "I only got the one, or at least, only the one I can find."

Hiram spread the map over the trunk of his Double A. Michael climbed out of the truck and looked at it over Hiram's shoulder, standing on the running board and hoisting himself high into the air on the mirror.

"We're here?" Hiram pointed at a rectangle on the map.

"No, that's our neighbors. Our house wasn't built when this map was drawn. We're here." Ada Oldham pointed. "And the horses were penned here."

She pointed at a meandering line. Above it, in a white space, were written the words *Carre Shinob*.

"Carre", Hiram said. "I'm no good with languages, but that looks French to me. But Shinob . . . I don't know. What is that?"

Ada Oldham shrugged. "The man who sold us the land gave us the map, and the map came with those words on it. I have no idea what they mean. The line there is the creek, and that's where we had the horses penned. The space under those words is a ridge above the creek."

"The French trappers got as far south as Utah, back in their day", Hiram said. "Provo's named after one of them."

"I taught a little school, back when I was Miss Halstead", Ada Oldham said. "And I think I remember enough French to know that carré is a square. That long, high ridge looks nothing like a square. But you're welcome to go look around it all you like."

"Bit far from the house, isn't it?"

"You gotta go through Heber. We only moved the horses there this year, it was McCrae who suggested it. He scouted out all our land and said he thought that was the best grass. Used to keep the horses just across the road here."

"Thank you." Hiram handed back the map.

Since they were passing through Heber anyway, Hiram stopped and sent a telegram to his friend Mahonri Jones at the B. Y. High in Provo. Mahonri was a librarian who loved a good riddle, and if his own library didn't have the answer, he could walk up the hill to the University.

As Hiram and Michael bounced up the rutted road between high ridges, nearing the creek where the Oldhams had kept their cattle, the late summer sun began to sink.

"You were in charge of packing the truck", Hiram said to his son.

"We have blankets and water and sandwiches."

"What do we have for light?"

"A flashlight and an oil lantern. Did you pack the gun?"

"Go ahead and check", Hiram suggested.

Michael looked into the glove compartment, finding the revolver and the spare full moon. "Shall I make sure it's loaded? Maybe shoot a couple of fenceposts for good luck?"

"You let me handle the gun", Hiram said. "You're thirteen. You get the flashlight."

The road ended at the gate of a rail fence that abruptly blocked off the canyon. The fresh darkness of mountain evening filled the canyon before them. Hiram and Michael both climbed out of the Double A. Hiram tucked the revolver into the back of his belt, and brought along the oil lantern and a box of matches.

Michael solemnly carried the flashlight.

"Can I climb it?" Michael asked.

"Stay close to me."

They climbed the fence. Oil lantern lit, Hiram took slow steps. He breathed in the pine-scented air and, following the burbling creek, looked for horses. He saw plenty of fresh droppings, green, compact balls of recently-digested grass, but none of the beasts themselves and no gap in the fence through which they might have gone. McCrae was right; the grass here was tall and lush, and the stream looked year-round and abundant. And somehow, the horses were gone.

The ridge staring down from above the canyon was bare of trees for its upper half. In the nearly-moonless night, its bulk was a shadow blocking out the enduring stars of the northern sky. Hiram found himself standing still, staring at the ridge, with the hair on the back of his neck standing up.

He pulled his fedora down tighter and scratched the back of his neck to make the feeling go away. It didn't.

"Michael, does Carre Shinob mean anything in the language of the Dine?"

Michael's Navajo was limited—he'd been a very small boy when Hiram and his wife had adopted him—but he remembered a few words. "The people live really far south of here, Pap."

"I know."

Michael circled his adopted father without slowing down as they talked. "I don't think Carre Shinob means anything."

Hiram nodded. He felt a flutter in his chest, and the hair on the backs of his arms was standing up as well. "Are you tired?"

"It isn't late, Pap."

"Shall we hike up that ridge?"

"We'd see better stars up there." They didn't see great stars anymore on the farm in Lehi; Salt Lake was just too close, and Utah Valley was filling up with farms. But on new moons, Hiram liked to drive Michael out west toward Tooele, where the sky was as dark as it had ever been for Jim Bridger.

They hiked up the slope. As they gained elevation on its flank, Hiram saw that the ridge hunkered down into a saddle and then rose to a final promontory before dropping into the two streams that had carved it.

"Up there." He pointed, and a shiver ran up his spine.

"Pap", Michael said. "I have a funny feeling in my stomach."

Hiram did, too. It was a feeling he'd felt the one time he'd ridden the tilt-a-whirl in Salt Lake, a sensation that reminded him of falling. "We're alone up here", he told his son. "Just in case, let's both keep our lights on. That way we can always see each other."

The night air was crisp in the Uintas, even in August, but the hillside was steep and Hiram was sweating by the time they reached the saddle. He shook sweat out of his fedora, wiped his forehead on the back of a sleeve, and then rolled both sleeves up past his elbows.

Michael stuck close to his side as he caught his breath. The boy shone the watery yellow beam of his flashlight in all directions, but especially up to the top of the promontory.

"There's no one up there", Michael said.

"Right", Hiram agreed. "Let's go have a look."

At the height of promontory was a flat patch of bare earth, bordered by a handful of weathered stones and a few stubborn bushes, barely larger than weeds. In the center of the stones lay a low pile of rocks, oblong in shape, about seven feet by three.

A pile of rocks such as you might lay over a body in a shallow burial.

"What is this place?" Michael's voice trembled.

Hiram shivered, but not from the chill; there was no wind and he was sweating. A sensation like an electric current played along his spine. He wasn't especially sensitive, not like Grandma Nettie had been. The veil had been thin for that old woman, and there were moments when past and present alike, as well as, the movements of spirits and angels, seemed to be an open book, written for her exclusive reading. Hiram didn't have that.

But neither was he an insensate clod. A spirit waited atop this hill.

He stooped to examine the rocks and saw that some had been disturbed. He crouched to poke in the earth where the stones had been removed and found a strange set of objects: a scrap of canvas cloth; a large animal claw with a hole drilled through it; one leather glove with the tips of the fingers and thumb cut off; and a strip of paper. Unfolding the paper, he found an improbable signature: *Brigham Young*.

Hiram stood and took a slow breath. Should he take Michael back to the truck? But the boy was already nervous; surely being left alone in the truck would terrify him, despite his bravado.

Hiram could come back another night, but it was a long drive from anywhere he was willing to sleep, and besides, a spirit that was here tonight might not be here tomorrow.

"Listen, son." Hiram knelt, to be able to look Michael directly in the face as they spoke. "I'm not going to lie to you. I think there are spirits on this hill."

"More than usual?" Michael asked.

Hiram nodded. "But remember, a spirit has no flesh and bone, and cannot hurt you. No matter what it shows you, it can't make you do anything. And if you want it to go away, you can cast it out in the name of Jesus."

"I remember." Michael swallowed. He was a brave boy. Hiram tousled his long hair and Michael smiled faintly.

"I want you to turn your flashlight off, but hold on to it, and keep your thumb on the switch."

"I can do that." Michael turned off his flashlight, and gripped it with both hands. "Are you going to turn off your lamp?"

"No", Hiram said. "I'm going to use it to try to talk to the spirit."

Michael swallowed so hard that Hiram could hear his Adam's apple move. "Why?"

"I want to help Mr. McCrae get his job back."

"You think the spirits might know where the horses are?"

"Yes."

Michael nodded.

What on earth was the scrap of paper signed by Brigham Young? A contract, an old deed to the land? A missionary commission? An order for wheat? Hiram shook his head.

He set the lantern on the ground beside the oblong heap of stones.

"I can tell you're here", he said.

Nothing. The air was still. A hundred yards away though he was, Hiram thought he could hear the bubbling of the stream.

"This must be a lonely place. Don't you want to talk?"

The stars shone down, cold and now queerly unfamiliar, as if Hiram had forgotten his years of star-lore, or had been transported to an alien world under a different zodiac.

"That's my lantern on the ground. I know you can see the flame. If you can hear me, make the flame dance. Don't try to put it out, just move it."

The air was still. Hiram fixed his eyes on the lantern.

"Just move the flame. Just a little."

The flame jumped. As if struck by a sudden gust of wind, the flame snapped sideways for a split second before returning to its normal, upright posture.

Michael jumped, pressing himself against Hiram's side.

Hiram wrapped an arm around Michael's shoulder. "Very good. Now I'm going to ask you questions. If the answer is yes, make the flame move again. Gently, you don't want to put it out." But what to ask?

Michael shivered, and Hiram drew him close.

"Is there more than one of you?"

The flame moved.

"Are there fewer than ten?"

The flame moved.

That was a relief. However much the idea of a ghost discomfited Hiram, the idea of a multitude of ghosts was much worse.

"Are there two of you?" Nothing. "Three? Four? Five?"

The lantern's flame moved.

Strange, though. The heap of stones was the size and shape of the grave of a single person.

"Are you all men?" Nothing. "All women? Both men and women? Men, women, and children together?"

The flame moved.

Hiram frowned. "Are you a family?"

The flame moved.

"Pioneers?" Hiram asked. "Mormons?"

Nothing.

"Indians?"

The flame moved.

Hiram pressed the ghosts in this slow fashion, eliciting additional information. The Indians hadn't died in this spot, but had been moved here. Asking about revolutions of the stars, he thought he got the information that they had been here for seventy years—that made 1865, which was consistent with the signature of Brigham Young, who died in 1877.

He stabbed in the dark, but couldn't land on a question that threw any more light on the paper.

"Two weeks ago, horses were stolen from the valley below this ridge." Hiram paused. "Did you take them?"

The flame moved.

Michael was shaking.

"Will you give me back the horses?"

Nothing.

Hiram took a deep breath. "Will you trade the horses with me?"

The flame moved. The ghosts would trade.

But how to find out what to trade?

"Pap", Michael said softly, a hint of a whimper in his voice, "is that you running your fingers through my hair?"

Hiram's hand was on Michael's shoulder. He grabbed the lantern in his other hand and raised it high; as if disturbed by unseen fingers, the boy's hair moved about on his head.

"Turn on your flashlight", he told his son, trying to keep his voice calm. "We're going back to the truck."

They finished out the night in a rented room in Heber. Hiram was awake two hours after falling asleep, with the peep of the egg-yolk sun through the paper blind. Michael, despite coming down from Carre Shinob trembling with nerves, slept another four hours.

He was thirteen years old, and Hiram let him sleep.

No response came to the telegram that day. Hiram examined the objects more closely. He learned little, except that the glove was not of home manufacture—it had a tag stitched inside it, faded now into illegibility. He bought a pair of long leather shoelaces at the mercantile and threaded one through the claw, which he then wore around his neck, right alongside the chi-rho talisman that protected him from enemies.

The scrap that contained actual legible words—the name Brigham Young—was the least comprehensible thing to him. He considered driving back up the ridge with a shovel and unearthing whatever lay beneath those stones, but if the spirits involved—and there were definitely spirits involved, and not just spirits, but the ghosts of dead human beings—were disturbed, then digging up the grave would only disturb them more.

They had offered to trade with him. No, that wasn't quite right, he had asked whether they were willing to trade and they had indicated yes. Or perhaps, the one of them that was speaking had indicated yes. He shouldn't assume he'd been speaking to the same spirit the entire time, since he hadn't asked.

But then that spirit, or another of them, had ruffled Michael's hair.

Had they wanted to trade for his son? Or had they wanted to take Michael? They had said they were Indians. Hiram and his wife had adopted the boy because he was without family—Hiram had been close to the child's father in the Great War—and because they'd been unable to have family of their own. Not all Indians were happy with white people adopting Indians—did the dead Indians want to take Michael away from him?

Would that involve them killing Michael?

Hiram shook the thoughts out of his head. He needed more information. Short of digging up the grave . . .

"Are you okay staying here tonight?" he asked Michael. "We'll lock the door, and I'll leave you here with milk and Graham crackers and all the pulp magazines the mercantile has? As long as they're not *too* lurid, that is."

"I don't know, Pap", Michael said. "I can handle some pretty lurid stuff."

With the sun still up, Hiram climbed up into the saddle of Carre Shinob. There he built a little fire and brewed himself tea, using a packet he always carried in the Double A, hidden inside a folded state map he never used. His grandmother had called the tea 'the devil's snare,' but she'd taught him to use it. The muddy brown infusion made from the jimson weed opened the mind to the universe. To an unprepared mind, that let in chaos—hallucinations, clowning, madness. To a prepared mind, it could let in revelation.

He put the tea in his thermos flask, just a single cup. It would be enough. He put his hand into the glove, and the claw around his neck. He clenched the scraps of paper and canvas in his gloved hand, and he stood beside the tumulus.

Watching the sun sink, he emptied his mind of all thoughts. He inhaled, focused on Michael's safety, reminded himself that the boy was in a bright room eating Graham crackers and reading detective stories, and exhaled, letting go of that concern. He did the same with thoughts of McCrae's belligerence, the Oldhams' indifference, his own physical safety.

With the stage of his mind empty, he placed onto it the questions he had. Who were the ghosts waiting there? What was their connection with the physical objects he held? Why had they taken the Oldhams' horses? What would they want in return for releasing the beasts?

He drank the tea—hot or cold, it was disgusting, and Hiram wasn't one to sweeten anything with sugar.

Then he lay down on the grave.

It wasn't comfortable, but it was necessary. This, too, was an old technique he's learned from his grandmother. Solomon had practiced it, she'd told him, sleeping in the Temple of the Lord until Jehovah himself appeared. The Greeks knew it, and the old Arabs. Mind open, heart focused on his questions, Hiram Woolley lay on the rocky mound and waited to see ghosts.

He touched the Saturn ring on his finger. It was made of lead, forged by Hiram himself rom a simple mold, and scratched by him with the sign of Saturn while that planet was strong in the skies. Saturn ruled melancholy, and dreams, and insight.

He fell asleep.

Hiram saw a man on a horse. Around his neck, the rider worse a necklace of teeth, claws, and bones. Several of the talons might have passed for the one Hiram had found on Carre Shinob. Two young Indians, a boy and a girl, led the horse by its reins, and the man sat stiffly, staring down at them.

Hiram looked down at himself. Wool trousers, muddy boots that weren't his. But he wore fingerless leather gloves on each hand, gloves he recognized.

Whose eyes was he seeing through? Whose memories were these?

He looked again at the rider, and realized with a shock that the man was a corpse. His legs were strapped to the animal and his back was strapped to a plank that rose from the saddle behind him, the whole arrangement keeping him upright in death. The dead man's fist was clenched around a sheet of paper.

A sheet of paper that had once been signed by Brigham Young? But why would a dead man carry such a thing?

To prove his status? To prove to his ancestors, or to his gods, that he, too, was a mighty chief, a person worthy of a friendship with Brigham Young, famous chief of the Mormons?

It was only a guess, but if felt right to Hiram.

He stood on a high bluff, but this was not Carre Shinob. A wide valley full of yellow grass stretched out to the west. This was not the Uintas, it felt more like Beaver or Parowan, with lower hills and cultivated land.

He heard weeping. There were words, but not in a language he knew.

Looking about, he saw that a man standing beside him also wore a wool suit, and had the craggy face and pale hair of northern European. Everyone else on the scene, maybe as many as fifty people, was Indian. Hiram knew enough Navajo to recognize their dress and a few of their words, and this was another people.

The two weeping children led the horse to a hillside tomb, a small natural cave that had almost been bricked in with stones and mortar. Indian men untied the corpse and carried it inside.

But the glove? It remained on Hiram's borrowed hand, outside the tomb.

And there was no canvas in sight.

Here was only part of the answer to Hiram's riddle, at best.

Brother Morley, the other European man said in an urgent whisper, *you cannot allow this to happen!*

Allow what to happen?

Shut your mouth, Hiram found his body saying. *Do you want another war?*

The other man was sullen, silent.

Then let them have the foolish traditions of their fathers. I will speak my eulogy and keep my vow.

Let them have their traditions, aye, no matter what?

No matter what.

The dead man arranged, the Indians stood in front of his tomb. Two women stood in the open doorway itself, and though the others fell silent, they continued a feverish chant under their breaths.

One of the men nodded to Hiram.

Colorow was a great man, Hiram said. *He made war on the Mericats and the Mormonee, and he was a mighty leader in war. Then he made peace with the Mormonee, and he was mighty in peace as well.*

The Indians nodded, satisfied.

Then the warriors standing to either side of the chanting women stepped forward. With long knives, they slit the women's throats.

Hiram wanted to scream. The body whose eyes he borrowed panted and sweated, but did nothing.

Could this be a lying vision? Jimson weed was called the devil's snare for a reason, and could send dishonest dreams, as well as, true ones.

But no, Hiram had a strong mind, and he was prepared.

And the vision had answered some of his questions.

The killers laid the two murdered women—sacrificed women— inside the grave with the chief's body. As they finished bricking up the opening, the onlookers returned to weeping and song.

Hiram forced himself to keep watching.

With the tomb sealed, the two wailing children were led forward. With a shock, Hiram realized that theirs was not the obligatory crying of a professional mourner, or the general sorrow of someone whose tribe has lost a leader, but was caused by real terror.

They knew what was coming.

Then sacrificers drove long iron spikes into the stone to either side of the tomb. They shut iron collars around the necks of the two children, and then with short chains, they shackled the children to the tomb.

The dead chief's tribe turned and walked away, singing.

The man with the gloves and his white companion went with them.

The cries of the shackled children rose piteous to a deaf heaven.

Coming up out of the jimson weed trance, Hiram felt cold. He ached from the rocks and his blood pulsed sluggishly in his veins, ineffective against the freezing Uinta night.

He couldn't let himself come up, he needed to see more.

He tightened his fists around the scraps of paper and canvas.

More, I need to know more.

He forgot the cold, and sank again.

He found himself under a swollen moon, standing on the same high ridge beside the Indian chief's tomb.

You stood the earlier passage, Hiram was saying. He leaned closed into the face of the craggy blond man he'd seen before. *The earlier passage was worse.*

In that murder, and heathen sacrifice, are worse than grave robbing, aye. The other man was furious. *But don't pretend that what you're proposing now ain't a sin, just the same.*

They're asking us. His brothers. It isn't robbing, it's just moving the dead, to keep him safe, preserve his honor.

Hiram pointed at four Indian men as he spoke. Everyone wore long wool coats, and their exhaled breath puffed up in tiny clouds.

The blond man shook his head, shoulders slumping in surrender, and Hiram and the others got to work.

With slow movements and chanting a song Hiram didn't understand, the six men knocked in the stones that bricked up the chief's tomb. Hiram and his fellow white man stood back, and the Indians crept into the tomb holding a white canvas sheet.

When they emerged, there were three bodies in the sheet.

Them, too? Hiram asked, pointing at two small skeletons lying outside the tomb. Years must have passed, because the flesh had all fallen—or been eaten—from their bones, and the collars around their necks had fallen off, together with their skulls.

The Indians nodded.

Hiram helped gather up the children's bones. Picking up one of the skulls—the boy's?—he found it still covered with a thick mop of black hair. He ran his fingers through it and felt tears trickle down his cheeks.

They bundled all five skeletons into the canvas and then together the six men hoisted the bones up onto the back of a buckboard wagon. Hiram climbed into the seat and took the reins, shushing his uneasy horses.

Where are we taking the chief? he asked.

North and east, one of the Indians said. *Far. A place called Carre Shinob.*

Hiram drove into Heber with ache in his bones and disquiet in his stomach. A chief had died and been buried somewhere in the west, and then reburied here. The man's grave had been disturbed by McCrae and the Oldhams' horses, and his ghost had taken the herd.

He'd give the horses back, but after seeing the man's funeral, Hiram's fear that what the chief wanted in return was the life of his son Michael had only increased.

A light in the telegraph office drew him to park there in the gray dawn light, setting the handbrake of the Double A and shuffling into the creaking wooden building. The clerk's desk was vacant, and Hiram stood gratefully in the heat of a coal stove in the corner, feeling its warmth slowly burn away the frost that had sunk into his bones.

The clerk shuffled to his place behind the desk, blowing his nose through a drooping mustache and into a yellowed old handkerchief. "I got a pot of coffee, if you want some."

Hiram shook his head. "Thank you for the stove, though. I only stopped in because my boy's still sleeping, and I wanted to see if I'd had an answer."

"Oh yeah, you're the fella with the queer words. I gotta say, you look more like a farmer than a . . . whatever kind of man would be sending telegrams like that one."

"I *am* a farmer. Beets. Down at Lehi."

"That explains it. Let me check."

"Thank you."

The clerk dug into his clip-stand of messages and came up with one. "Here you go, came in last night while Jensen was working. He didn't have an address to send it on to. Looks like your answer's just about as strange as your question."

"I planned to come in to pick it up." Hiram tipped the clerk a precious nickel and took the telegram. The telegram was from Mahonri, and it was much longer than the question. Mahonri behaved as if he had an unlimited budget for sending telegrams; since Hiram was the beneficiary, he couldn't complain.

Carre shinob is legendary place where chief Walkara's bones were moved. Walkara also known as Colorow and Walker as in Walker's War. Most famous horse thief in history rustled 3000 horses in California in a single day. What are you doing up there?

"Thank you", Hiram said again, and headed for the boarding house.

"They think I'm crazy at the slaughterhouse", McCrae grumbled. The foreman carried a large bag slung over his shoulder and grimaced from the weight as he climbed the ridge to Carre Shinob.

The bag was full of horse bones.

"Did you tell them you wanted to make soup?" Hiram squinted at the sky. In the evening's last blue-gray light, a sheet of glowering clouds gathered. In the east, over the higher Uintas, he saw lightning flash, and then the ensuing thunder crawled past him.

That should help, if anything.

But the storm made him even more glad he'd left Michael a second night in the boarding house.

"Yeah, I tried your joke. That's why they think I'm crazy."

"Well, if this doesn't work, you don't get your job back, and then I guess you're out of options, and you'll have to leave town. So as I see it, the opinion of the slaughterhouse crew shouldn't worry you much."

"And if I do get my job, I stick around, and I get the reputation of an eccentric who makes horse soup."

"You could have told them the truth", Hiram suggested.

They reached the saddle of the ridge, and McCrae set down his sack. "And what is the truth?"

Hiram set down his sack, which contained wooden rattles, a small hand drum, and a square of sheet metal, bowed over to squeeze it in. "Some would call it magic. My grandmother would have denied that."

McCrae spat thick phlegm into the dirt. "And what would *she* have called it?"

Hiram looked up at Chief Walkara's grave mound. "She'd have said that when you need to get something done, you do what works. A cunning woman or a cunning man is just somebody who knows what works."

"I guess on the whole I'd rather be known as the fella who wants to drink horse soup. Shall we get this started, then?"

Thunder rolled across the ridge, fat drops of rain splattered on their faces, and Hiram nodded. The heliotropius was said to be able to call rain. Sadly, it had no power to *dismiss* rain clouds.

They commenced at the far end of the ridge from the relocated bones of Chief Walkara. With the peals of thunder becoming more frequent, until they almost seemed to roll over the top of each other, the two men inched down the ridge. Elbert McCrae shuffled slowly, shaking his head and trying not to look at Hiram.

Hiram danced, kicked his toes into the softening dirt. He also whinnied and snorted, making all the horse-like noises he could.

McCrae carried the sheet metal, and he flexed and shook it. The sound he made was closer to the thunder's noise than to the sound of actual horses. Hiram beat the drum, shook the rattles, and clapped his hands in turn. It was his best imitation of the sound of a running herd, but it was rude and childish at best.

Would it be enough?

He kept his eye fixed on the tumulus, but saw nothing.

As they climbed toward the site of the grave, McCrae traded the sheet metal for the sack of bones. He shook his head. "That's the weakest damn horse imitation I ever heard, Woolley."

Hiram chuckled. "I'm trying, but I'm more of a mule and truck man, myself."

"A horse sounds like *this*." And then McCrae began to neigh and whinny for all he was worth.

And he really *did* sound like a horse.

They climbed the promontory prancing together. At the top, rain mixed with hail pounded down on them as they trotted three times in a circle around the stones, McCrae scattering the bones from his sack all over the knob of earth.

Then Hiram stopped, and McCrae stopped with him. The foreman wore a surprisingly cheerful grin.

"We brought you these horses, Chief Walkara!" Hiram cried, addressed the low mound of stones.

Lightning flashed, illuminating the top of the hill—it was still empty of life other than the two men.

"We brought you these horses to trade!" Hiram added.

The rain had become entirely hail. Hiram shivered. He felt cold, tired, and suddenly alone. He was too cold from the mere weather to be able to feel whether there were spirits present, and there was no way he could light a lamp in these conditions.

"We give you *this* herd!" He tried one last time. "We ask you to bring back the Oldhams' herd!"

Nothing.

He sighed.

"That's it, then." McCrae kicked at the muddy earth. "Well, foolish as I feel, I appreciate the effort."

Hiram nodded. They trudged down off the promontory Carre Shinob, heading down the saddle toward the valley below.

Lightning flashed.

McCrae sucked breath in past his teeth. "You see that, Woolley?"

Hiram raised his eyes. "What?"

Lightning flashed again. The valley below them was full of horses. Not phantasms, but flesh and blood beasts, huddling together beneath the trees to shelter from the storm.

"He brought them back", Hiram murmured.

Lightning flashed a third time. Hiram smelled horses surrounding him, felt their heat as they passed, and heard the thunderous rattle of hooves on the ridge—and yet the ridge held not a single flesh-and-blood horse.

At the high end of the valley, standing just outside the rail fence penning in the horses on that end, Hiram saw a band of Indians. He only saw them for a moment, but he saw them clearly and he knew their faces. He'd seen them before.

He'd seen their funeral.

But now all five sat on horseback. Chief Walkara faced Hiram with one arm raised over his head, holding a spear in greeting.

Hiram raised his own arm in return, and then the Indians were gone.

The heat, smell, and sound of the phantom horses passed with them.

"I'll be damned", McCrae said.

"I don't think so. Anyway, I hope not."

McCrae took two steps away from Hiram, as if mere proximity would damn him. He cleared his throat. "What do I . . . what do I tell them?"

Hiram felt tired. "Mrs. Oldham said she wasn't looking for an explanation. She just wanted her five hundred horses back. She said she'd hire you right back."

"She'll think I stole them."

"Tell her we found the Indians. Tell her the Indians weren't from around here, but they were famous horse thieves, and we bought the horses back. That's the simple truth, as I see it."

McCrae nodded slowly. "And if she asks what we paid?"

Hiram began trudging down to his truck. "*Then*, Mr. McCrae, I would consider telling a lie."

❀

IN A SECRET ROOM

*I am a member of a convention-based troupe that performs semi-impro-
vised, audience-participation-heavy, game-theater events. The troupe
was founded by James Wymore, and consists entirely of authors: David
J. West, Holli Anderson, Robert Defendi, Craig Nybo, Daniel Swenson,
and Jason King are the other members. We once printed and gave away
t-shirts that said "Space Balrogs" on them. "In a Secret Room" is my
contribution to an anthology we put together, mimicking our most
successful game,* Choose Your Own Apocalypse.

*There's something else you should know, to understand where this story
is coming from. For years, when pitching David J. West's books, I would
tell potential customers that David was actually the mere literary
executor of his more famous uncle, Franklin D. Roosevelt's occultist, who
was found dead, naked, in a secret room in the White House.*

*When it came time to write a story for that anthology, I knew what
story I had to tell.*

"How long will you be gone, Doctor?"

"Don't call me by my given name. It isn't seemly."

Benson looks puzzled. "Your first name is David."

He doesn't say *Christian* name, and neither do I. That's deliberate.

I step into the center of the diagram, painted on the floor with the blood of still-living, flawless goats. The things the Hebrews never wrote down, but passed in secret whispers from father to daughter to son, would shock this world of electric lights and airplanes.

The diagram is painted on the wooden floor of a secret room inside the White House. Built originally for Washington's kabbalist Josiah Seixas, I have rediscovered it by the usual means: saffron-scented incense inscribed with the sign of the intelligence of Mercury, a ring of fixed quicksilver, a dowsing rod. The walls are thick enough to stop the sounds of animal sacrifice, and the door is hidden behind a painting of Lee surrendering at Appomattox. The room is lit with candles. I have layered multiple wards of misdirection to ensure that no one knows of the room's existence other than Benson and me.

"My parents named me *Doctor*, because I am a seventh son. It is one of the sources of my gift, as your gift comes from the vestigial tail amputated at birth from your own coccyx and worn dried around your neck. I call myself *David* in part to appear more mundane. As my apprentice, you must call me *Mister West*."

"I won't always be your padawan." Benson snivels.

I need a better apprentice, and in less pinched times, I'd have one. But first the WPA and now the war effort have sucked up much of the best magical talent, and as Roosevelt's personal occultist, the unofficial member of his cabinet hidden behind the words *and others*, I am in no position to complain about the President's call for resources.

"What in Hades is a *padawan*?"

Benson looks as if he's swallowed a bird. "It means an apprentice."

"You need to stop reading Crowley and the Theosophists", I tell him. "The nonsense they invent to fill the enormous gaps in their knowledge can only obscure the few grains of truth they actually possess. Try one of the Arabs. Abd al-Hazred or, better, al-Jildaki."

"Yes, Mr. West."

"I'll be gone only an hour, as you experience the passage of time.

I'll enter the body of the vagrant I've identified using the Eye, then retrieve my staff and other accouterments from the wall of the boarding house."

This is serious magic, though Benson cannot grasp it. I will travel forward in time and enter the body of another man.

But the challenge is serious. Starting as early as I have, fortunately, if I fail, I have time to try again.

"And with your staff and seals", Benson says slowly, "you will be able to close the gate as soon as it is opened."

He is an idiot, but he's my apprentice. "Yes. That is the best moment, because the Old One's cult will have exhausted all its energy, spilt its precious blood, and taken its one shot. And then I will steal their victory from them."

"And save the world." Benson smiles.

"Yes."

"On December 21, 2020."

"The winter solstice. When the energies of this world are at their ebb, yes. As they are today, on this winter solstice, 1943."

"But what if they kill you?"

I shrug out of the silk robe resembling a long smoking jacket but embroidered ornately with the characters of a forgotten Chinese script, the words telling in poetic stanzas the story of my own life, and hand it to Benson. I am careful not to disturb any of the markings on the floor. This leaves me naked, as the magic requires. To ease my passage through the astral sphere and into a future configuration of the planets, I have also shaved all the hair from my body.

"If they kill me", I explain, virtually certain that I have explained this many times before, "then they only kill a vagrant drunk, and I return here to my time and body with seventy-seven years to marshal my resources and try again. As many as seventy-five more times, if need be."

"What does this have to do with the war?" Benson asks.

"Benson", I say. "Shut up."

Benson retreats to the corner of the five-sided room.

I lie in the center of the diagram. The wood floor of this room is ordinarily cold, since the furnace vents all stay far from it, but the wood now is hot to the touch; if my buttocks had any hair left, the floor would scorch it off. I endure without a murmur. This is the energy of the markings themselves. I can do no magic without a talisman, and here, to send myself a traveler to such a remote day, I have built a talisman the size of the room.

I close my eyes and chant the words. I invoke Jupiter, all the constellations and the great precession, and the *primum mobile* above all.

Abruptly, I am clothed.

I smell smoke and the reeks of urine and cheap alcohol, and a bitter wind digs at my skin through a cloak of rags. I drag myself to my feet, climbing up the brick wall beside me.

"Where you think you're going, Peterson?" growls a heap of rags at my feet.

I have no time for this. I turn and walk toward the boarding house.

I know immediately that this is solstice, in the year 2020. I know it because a cold, sticky mist that smells of bog and charnel fills the Mall. I keep the long grass to my left, circling around it toward where I have hidden my tools, seventy-seven years ago.

My borrowed flesh is stiff, from alcohol and years of abuse, from cold and from sleeping on sidewalks. Ah, well. The Eye shows me what it chooses, and not what I choose. I have selected this body because the Eye told me it would be here. I selected the boarding house for the same reason.

I stagger across concrete steps, and over ragged grass. Winter has left all the trees skeletal and angry.

From deep within the mist comes a rumbling sound, like thunder, only it is a thunder that carries words. I know enough of this language to know I must immediately clap my hands over my ears. I do so, but it is with an effort.

The mist glows red. Where the Washington Monument should be stands instead a ragged circle of inwardly-curving stone pillars. Like teeth.

The red glow illuminates the faces of the office buildings and museums that enclose the Mall. As the Eye had shown me they would be, the buildings are all draped in bright red cloth. For the rite, to welcome the world-ending abomination the cult now tries to bring to Washington, D.C., the buildings have been converted to flags.

Nazi flags. The black swastikas on white circles glare like malevolent, welcoming eyes at the mist, and then the light dies.

The shrill, wet screams of sacrificial victims rise again as the Nazi Anierophants and Oneiromancers pour more human energy into the blasphemous cosmic womb from which they attempt to draw the beast.

I'll say this for them: if the Eye has shown me true visions, the cult at least had the wisdom—or the good taste—to kill all the congressmen and senators first.

"Who goes there?" a voice asks me curtly. "Papers?"

It's a Nazi officer. At least, he's wearing the crisp khakis and the armbands our boys are... were... fighting over in Europe. But his accent is depressingly American. He sounds like he could be from Indiana.

Fortunately, he thinks I'm drunk.

"Papersh." I stagger a bit, slur my words.

"Never mind." The Nazi from the Midwest smiles. "Come with me."

He reaches for me, obviously intending to go heap me on the pile of corpses exsanguinating a squirt of cosmic bread crumbs into the void. I head-butt him right in the nose, and when he drops to the grass, I pounce.

His screams might go unnoticed among the wailing of the doomed and the damned, but I won't take any chances. I grab him by the sides of his head and twist his neck sharply. The loud crack his neck makes as it breaks sickens me, but I have no choice.

The world is at stake.

The red glow returns and the rumble of thunder-speech. I clap my hands to my ears and stagger to the boarding house.

The building has barely survived to this date. It is now condemned, with red tape wrapped around the gap-toothed iron fence warning casual passersby away from the impending demolition.

I am not a casual passerby. I hop the fence—this is harder than I expect in my borrowed hobo's skin, and I fall on my face. Then I push through the front door, sagging off its hinges, and go directly to my room.

I hit the wall switch and a single bulb lights up, swinging from a length of wire overhead. I have seen this very room this morning... this morning, that is, in 1943. My wooden bed is gone, and my table. In their place are a cheap iron bed-frame that is slowly rusting to nothing, and a slat-backed chair that is missing two slats and a leg.

Also, the wall has been torn open.

My vault, my repository. The place where I carefully sealed up staff, seals, ring, and cloak, to arm myself for the battle with the Nazi void demon, is revealed. I reach into the wall and feel around, hoping that I will find my tools, fallen into a shadowed corner.

My hope dies, instantly and brutally.

My things are gone. I am unarmed and defenseless.

"Perhaps you were looking for these", a voice behind me says.

I spin around, forgetting to even play the part of a homeless drunk. I don't know the face of the man confronting me; he might be a university professor, from his tweed jacket and scuffed black shoes. He raises a fire bucket to the height of his chest and overturns it. A cloud of black ashes sifts down, and falling rapidly from the cloud to the floor go shapeless lumps of silver and amber, torn scraps of cloth and leather, and scorched paper fragments.

My tools.

"No", I mutter. I slouch, trying to resume the appearance of a hobo. "I was lookin' fer a.... fer a bottle. Whishky?"

The man shakes his head. "Oh, Doctor West." He drops the bucket to the floor between us with a clank, and then I see the knife in his hand.

Not just any knife. The dull glint suggests meteoric iron, and the scratching hint at antediluvian names of old gods of death: Anubis, Odin, Nergal. I would like time to examine it more closely, but this knife is a tool of death. It may be a thing that can kill me permanently, despite my borrowed body.

I step into the bucket and launch it upward with my foot. The metal catches the professor in the jaw and hurls ash into his face. He staggers away, and I throw myself out the window.

As I am squeezing through, he catches my rag cloak. For a moment, I'm pinned, but then the rotting fabric tears and I'm through, onto the roof over the boarding house's front porch. He lunges after me and I dance away, to the edge of the rooftop, and the knife narrowly misses.

I scoot around the window frame and scramble up onto the roof above my room. My pursuer curses and climbs out after me. This is exhilarating, I can't lose, so long as he doesn't kill me with the dark death-god dagger. All I have to do is break my own neck—the beggar's neck—and I wake up again in my own body, inside the Roosevelt White House, seventy-seven years earlier.

But at the highest chimney of the house, I pause.

The screaming has reached a new feverish peak, and the dull red glow has become a blazing beacon, a reddish sun burning on the Mall as the old year dies.

I see the columns. There are thirteen of them.

And I see the beast moving forward through the columns.

Where the beast comes from I cannot say—there is no visible gate behind it, and it appears to grow larger, or more solid, or more now, as if my eyes are witnessing a dimension of the cosmos they have never before seen, and my pitiful brain struggles to interpret the data it receives. Similarly, I cannot tell how many limbs the beast has or whether it has wings or tentacles. I see obscene fleshy membranes, and eyes on every surface, and mouths opening on hands and feet and belly. I see nothing resembling a head or a face. The beast looks in all directions. It looks at me, and into my heart.

Have I underestimated the challenge?

Should I have brought reinforcements?

The scratching of the professor's shoes on the shingles behind me warns me just in time. I tear my thoughts away from the incomprehensible blasphemy against the order of the universe that now crawls forth onto the Mall, tossing humans into its many maws....

And I duck.

The knife cuts through the air over my head. It misses, and still I feel a burning on my flesh where it almost makes contact. Years of study of the sweet science kick in, and I punch my attacker in his throat.

He falls to his knees, choking. He swings again, and misses.

He's off-balance, clinging to the shingles.

I punch him in the eye, and he goes rolling backward down the roof. His head strikes the chimney beneath him with a soggy thump, and he lies still.

I turn to regard the beast again. Is it walking? Crawling? Dragging itself forward on its elbows? I cannot tell. Perhaps the world shifts, hurling itself and its pathetic, candleflame-lived occupants into the many devouring maws of the beast.

It heaves itself upon the white house, which crumbles to the ground and erupts in sheets of flame.

Still it looks at me.

Shivering, I crouch. Still feeling the eyes on me, I descend the rooftop, hiding from the vision of those many eyes. This is the thing I have come here to defeat, and instead I have lost.

But this is only one round, and I have deliberately chosen a bout that will last many rounds. I have but to kill myself, return to my natural time and body, and try again.

I stop to examine the knife. I do not touch it but crouch over it on the boarding house rooftop. The glyphs are Lemurian and Atlantean, a horrible unlearned mishmash but magically-effective nonetheless. If only I could hide this inside a wall and find it in my own time when I return.... but clearly, I cannot.

Sighing, I stand. The shrieks are unbearable now. Thousands must be dying of slow torture this very moment. Or is the beast itself shrieking? Does its natural song sound like the dying howl of sacrificial offerings?

I will not look at it again. I do not need to.

Instead, I step to the edge of the rooftop and confirm the location of the wrought iron fence. Then I take a running leap and throw myself face-first toward the rusting spikes.

I feel the cold iron enter my borrowed neck and chest.

I awake, in my own flesh. The floor beneath my back and calves has grown cold. The candles sputter, their wicks nearly consumed.

"Benson", I croak.

There is a pause. "Yes?" Benson answers.

I ache. My throat and chest hurt from the wounds my host body has just now died of, seventy-seven years in the future. I sit up, shivering. "My robe. I feel cold."

"You're going to feel colder", Benson says. He stands in the darkest corner of the room, his face in shadow and invisible.

"Impertinent pup!" I shout. "Now, of all times, you would play the idiot? I am done with you!"

I stand, stiffer and more awkward than ever I was in the hobo's flesh, and step toward the hook from which my robe hangs.

Improbably, I strike an invisible barrier.

I look down at the floor, and I see the diagrams I made. New markings enclose the old, and the new markings are wards of imprisonment and enclosure. Roaring wordlessly, I pound the unseen barrier. Stalking the star-shaped perimeter of the diagram, I test it with my fists and feet, shouting every counterspell and sacred name I know to shatter the spell that suddenly binds me.

"I *am* done", Benson agrees. "You see, I *have* read the Arabs. All of them. Many years ago."

I glare at him. "What do you want?"

"You have seen what I want." He steps forward, and in a final flicker of light, I see the light of alien moons within Benson's eyes. Then the candles die and darkness falls. "Everything I want is coming, Doctor. In seventy-seven years."

Doctor.

I have been betrayed.

I roar, but he says nothing more. I hear the secret passage that is the room's only entrance open and shut, without a glimmer of light.

We have all been betrayed.

The world ends in seventy-seven years. I have seen it.

But my world ends now. In darkness, alone.

I sit.

I will meditate to slow my breathing and my heart rate, ease my metabolic processes to a thread, whisper as I have learned to do from the yogins of Calcutta and Mayapore, but it will only delay the inevitable. Only Benson can find me, and Benson is my captor. My body will consume its fat, then its muscle, then its organs.

I will not be found.

My mummified corpse will be crushed to powder by the beast, on December 21, 2020. I have seen it, with borrowed eyes.

I lie on the floor and close my now-pointless eyes of flesh.

Could I have stopped this? Could I have seen the betrayal coming?

What in Hades is a *padawan*?

MAGIC SYSTEMS AREN'T MAGIC

Essay

One of the great things Baen does to promote its writers is to have them write fiction or non-fiction pieces for publication on the Baen website. I wrote this piece, which was published on the site the month Witchy Winter *came out.*

A few initial notes toward more authentic magic in fantasy novels. And an invitation to read Witchy Eye.

When I tell people that I write fantasy novels, more often than not the next words I hear are "what's your magic system?"

This is a ridiculous question. It reflects a state of affairs in which many fantasy writers today are writing "fantasy" novels with *no magic in them at all,* and using artificial constructs euphemistically called "magic systems" or "hard magic" instead. This is a loss to fantasy literature.

Magic is notoriously difficult to define. Etymologically, we get the word from Greek *mageia,* which means the theology of the *magoi,*[1] the dream-interpreting Persian priests said to have called on the infant Jesus.[2] This suggests that as we examine the meaning of the word "magic" more deeply, we're going to find connections with religious practice, spirituality, oracles, and things done by outsiders, that is to say, *people other than ourselves.*

A recent study of Jewish magic by Yuval Harari devotes its substantial first chapter to reviewing academic understandings of what magic is from the mid-nineteenth century to date.[3] Harari characterizes the evolving understanding of magic as moving broadly through three trends, or three kinds of theoretical explanations of magic. There is obviously significant overlap among his categories, and I would suggest we should see a fourth category interwoven with the others. What follows is my synthesis and summary of what Harari claims.

Harari describes early theories as evolutionist, meaning that they identify magic as "a stage in the process of spiritual and cultural advancement that humanity undergoes in the course of its development."[4] Some of these theories find the origin of magic in specific human needs (exorcism of spirits, which are the source of all "physical and spiritual problems")[5] or in posited early beliefs about the structure of reality (in animistic thought, in which all things have individual spirits;[6] or in the allegedly even earlier belief that all things have a collective soul;[7] or in the belief in "the law of participation, which implies a linkage between the individual's personality and things in the world").[8] Other theorists have tried to identify in magic a pre-modern intellectual phase with some relationship to science and religion, e.g.: that magic is the "original form of human thought", preceding religion, which in turn precedes science;[9] that magic is the "first sign of scientific thought", in that it posits knowable laws of the universe that can be manipulated to achieve results;[10] or conversely that the laws of magic have their origin in religion, where they "serve as part of the perception of holiness and holy powers".[11]

Harari goes on to identify as separate trends sociological and anthropological explanations of magic; for simplicity's sake I'll lump these together. Some theorists have found the definitions of magic in the community of users and non-users, for instance arguing that: religion is how we collectively approach the "lofty and beneficent" gods for help, whereas magic is how we individually approach "inferior and negative entities";[12] magical acts are externally or physically identical to religious acts, but are socially prohibited;[13] magic is religion before it gets organized, and lone sorcerers are replaced with a priestly caste;[14] or magic is what is performed by people of low or vague social class.[15] Some writers have argued for a calendrical explanation of magic: religion is comprised of acts that are performed cyclically, and magic is undertaken in response to crises.[16] Recent theorists have argued that there is little or no distinction between magic and religion at all: that all magical and religious behavior exists on "a continuum of ritual behavior";[17] that the difference between magic and religion exists only in the eye of the Western observer;[18] or that the difference between magic and religion is purely a semantic problem.[19]

I would extract a fourth category of theories of magic from Harari's summaries, to wit, psychological explanations of magic. Some thinkers have seen magic as "the emotional reaction of primitive man to the anxiety evoked by the surrounding world."[20] Others have seen magic as a psychological tool, protecting the self or "ego" and thereby developing the institution of the individual,[21] ritualizing optimism to confer hope,[22] or imposing order on the world.[23]

Obviously, we have just begun to scratch the surface of what magic is in the real world. No mention is made in the above summary, for example, of the content of real-world grimoires, of magic as initiatic traditons, of what real-world spells actually look like, of the phenomenon of pseudepigraphy, or many other important and interesting issues.

Nevertheless, Harari's summary suggests a criterion by which we may judge the verisimilitude of "magic systems" or otherwise the magic described in a fantasy story. An authentic magic system would fit many, or maybe all, of Harari's definitions. In other words, an authentic magic system would be one in which academics who are not themselves practitioners, observing magical practice in the story world, could propose any of the foregoing theories to explain why practitioners do what they do.

To make a few more specific points. In an authentic magic system:

   1. At some margin, magic should resemble science, with
      knowable laws and repeatable operations.

2. At some margin, magic should resemble religion. The line separating magical and religious ritual should be difficult to find. One person's magic should be another person's religion.

3. Magic should be connected to social and in-group status (the theology of the stargazers becomes the wizardry of the Greeks).

4. Magic should meet (individual and also collective) psychological needs of those who seek to employ it.

A "hard magic" system certainly could meet our criterion for authenticity. Without conducting any kind of survey, my unscientific impression is that most of them don't, and in fact, don't consciously try. Instead, they are constructed to follow consistent internal logic and provide a system of costs and possibilities for the story setting.

The lack of authenticity in the magic systems of contemporary fantasy is a loss; let's consider again Harari's list. In the real world, magic is intimately connected with the human response to crises (which is to say, growth, heroism, narrative, destruction, change, and initiation). Magic is at some (or all) stages intrinsic to human thought, and it is closely related to human worship. Magic is defined by social lines, and by our perceptions of our own cultures and other cultures.

In other words, magic is tightly connected to the human spirit. Fantasy at its best is the what-if literature of human spirituality, one reason being that magic in the real world is tightly bound to the human soul. Therefore, what-if postulates about authentic magic in a fantasy setting are what-if postulates about our spirit, and the human condition. A "hard magic" system that is rigorous, logical, and consistent, but lacks the ambiguity, sociality, spirituality, visceral psychology, and thought-content of real magic, has taken a long step away from the human soul. To me, candidly, many "hard magic" systems feel like fan fiction for a roleplaying or collectible card game, rather than the mirror to the human condition they should be. Our literature becomes the poorer thereby.

So, Dave . . . what's your magic system?

My Baen series, *Witchy War* (book two, *Witchy Winter*, comes out in

April 2018) is set in an alternate earth in which I've taken Jacksonian America apart and rebuilt it as an epic fantasy setting. Therefore, all the magic as practiced by the characters in the *Witchy War* series comes from real-world magic, either built from the blocks of real-world or in the form of whole real-world traditions.

Sarah Calhoun and other characters in the *Witchy War* series (the monk Thalanes, but also the Yankee chaplain Ezekiel Angleton and the Necromancer Oliver Cromwell) practice a high magical art called many things, but especially *gramarye*. I deliberately emphasize this name for its connection with grammar, and the implication that such magicians construct spells from basic principles. Specifically, they build spells using the laws formulated in the real world by James George Frazer (and in the story setting, by Sir Isaac Newton in his ground-breaking opus, the *Principia Magica*):

> If we analyze the principles of thought on which magic is based, they will probably be found to resolve themselves into two: first, that like produces like, or that an effect resembles its cause; and, second, that things which have once been in contact with each other continue to act on each other at a distance after the physical contact has been severed. The former principle may be called the Law of Similarity, the latter the Law of Contact or Contagion. From the first of these principles, namely the Law of Similarity, the magician infers that he can produce any effect he desires merely by imitating it: from the second he infers that whatever he does to a material object will affect equally the person with whom the object was once in contact, whether it formed part of his body or not.[24]

In other words, Sarah and other gramarists practice magic like anthropologists. This is explicitly a magical approach taken by the educated and upper-class among magical practitioners, including Polite monks (sisters and brothers of the Humble Order of St. Reginald Pole, patron saint of Christian magic) and university-trained magicians, though the monk Thalanes at least expresses the view that all magic is some form of gramarye. Gramarists' spells work because the practitioners have the ability to construct analogies and impose them on the world by force of spirit.

Early on in *Witchy Eye,* the Appalachee Elector Iron Andy Calhoun refers to the Emperor Thomas as a "Chaldee numbskull", which is to say, a devotee of astrology.[25] This is a fair accusation: Thomas has nativities cast, uses judicial astrology (the art of forecasting events and choosing propitious times by studying celestial bodies), and seeks to capture the benevolent influence of the zodiac and the planets by the use of images (when we first see him in a recruiting handbill in Free Imperial Nashville, the image of Thomas's crown "subtly" incorporates the "seal of the planet Mars"). This latter astrological art is not one you see in supermarket tabloids these days, but is taken very seriously by such important grimoires as *The Picatrix*[26] and Henry Cornelius Agrippa's *Three Books of Occult Philosophy.*[27]

The *Witchy War* series includes practitioners of Vodun (voodoo). In *Witchy Eye* we meet Etienne Ukwu, the gangster son of New Orleans's bishop. Etienne is also an initiated houngan, that is to say a Vodun priest (and he has other intimate connections with Vodun divinities, but . . . spoilers). In *Witchy Winter*, when he confronts an initiated mambo working for his enemy, the Chevalier of New Orleans, the accusation that each hurls at the other is faithlessness: the misdeed of being a mere *bokor*, a mercenary practitioner of Vodun magic operating outside the confines of an accepted tradition and without the consent of the loa.[28]

German Brauchers in Pennsland and the Ohio are referred to in *Witchy Eye,* but really come onto the stage in *Witchy Winter*. Braucherei is a tradition of active prayer on behalf of petitioners; *brauchen* is *to try* in Pennsylvania Dutch, and a braucher is willing to try to effect a cure or solution on behalf of another person—provided that the braucher must remain disinterested, so he receives no payment and can't be related to the person he's helping. In *Witchy Winter*, Luman Walters is a hedge magician whose quest for initiation into the secrets of the universe has led him to borrow or steal from many magical traditions, including braucherei. The braucher prayers (formulaic prayers, that sometimes have fixed ritual gestures and may require physical components) Luman knows come from the bestselling grimoire ever written in North America, John George Hohman's *The Long Lost Friend*.[29] Another braucher art Luman practices is the writing of *himmelsbriefe*— fixed-text "heavenly letters" which, written with fine materials and pure intent, are supposed to protect their bearer.[30] Braucherei's strict moral requirements weigh on Luman, and push him to take some large personal risks late in the story.

In the Hellenistic world there existed a cosmopolitan, international system of magic, in which spells and magical words fossilized into existing professional practice and were shared around the Mediterranean. Even relatively insular cultures like the Jews participated in this international system, while omitting certain practices and adding their own contributions.[31] In the *Witchy War* setting, this corpus of magic is identified with the pseudo-pharaonic culture of Memphis and said to have been preserved by the great Memphite wizard Jean d'Anastasi (this is, ahem, one of my little historical jokes). Memphis is Luman Walters's other great source of spells and arcane arts,[32] and although it imposes dietary taboos on him, it doesn't include the moral strictures of braucherei . . . and at least one of those Memphite spells gets Luman into trouble.

Classical shamanism is at home on the steppes of Asia, but features of shamanism appear in magico-religious practice all over the globe. In *Witchy Winter*, the ceremonial misbirth of one man's child drives him to seek a physician. In turn, that healer must first heal himself, and he does so by shamanic initiation, rising on a drum-that-is-also-a-horse out of his body and into the eternal world of the stars. There he is torn to pieces by cosmic ogres and rebuilt with iron bones and a piece of quartz in his head; this rebuilding gives him powers, including the power to return to the celestial world, where he can interact with the spirits of all things, living and dead, and effect powerful healing. In the course of his rebuilding, it is implied that this religious experience dates back to or connects with the lore of the red-headed giants who were among the earliest inhabitants of the continent, and who have now mostly been driven into the north. Note that the words *shaman* and *shamanism* do not appear in the book.[33]

A North American spiritual practice said to have shamanic features is the Midewiwin medicine society of the Ojibwe. The Midewiwin know healing songs, and at key points in the year enact important rituals in their lodges that are designed to fill their spirit pouches with beneficent power.[34] Midewiwin medicine men appear briefly in *Witchy Winter*.

Finally, as in the historical real world, in the *Witchy War* setting, there is a fine line between Christian practice, scripture, and liturgy, on the one hand, and magic on the other.[35] Examples in *Witchy Eye* include: corn reading, the practice of reading passages of the gospels to fields of grain in order to drive away malevolent spirits and permit the grain to grow better; a curse pronounced by the Bishop of New Orleans, complete with the shaking of dust from his shoe on the cursed party;[36] and an instructional illusion spell formed of the stained-glass windows of a cathedral. A particularly fun example for me from *Witchy Winter* is one cleric's conversion of a funeral mass into an attack spell, complete with hostile psalm passages, a voodoo doll in the casket rather than a corpse, and a crowd chanting *kyrie, kteinon* ("Lord, kill!").

This doesn't exhaust the forms of magic that are referred to or appear in the *Witchy War* series. Lullian Alchemy gets a nod, for instance, and there are rune-carving vitki priests in the Germanic northwest of the Empire, and there is a deck of Tarocks that shows extraordinary properties. But I've tried throughout the series to build "authentic" rather than "hard" magic, because I believe that authentic magic connects more meaningfully to the human condition. And connecting to the human condition (in the context of a rollicking adventure tale) is what I think fantasy literature should be all about.

1. Liddell and Scott's Greek-English Lexicon, s.v. "mageia".
2. Matthew 2.
3. Harari, Yuval (2017). *Jewish Magic before the Rise of Kabbalah*. ISBN 978-0-8143-3630-4. Detroit: Wayne State University Press, pp. 15-67.
4. Ibid o. 15.
5. Ibid p. 20.
6. Ibid p. 18.
7. Ibid pp. 29-30.

8. Ibid p. 53.

9. Ibid pp. 21-23.

10. Ibid p. 18.

11. Ibid pp. 34-45.

12. Ibid pp. 32-33.

13. Ibid pp. 35-38.

14. Ibid p. 38.

15. Ibid p. 58.

16. Ibid p. 63.

17. Ibid p. 64.

18. Ibid p. 65.

19. Ibid p. 65.

20. Ibid p. 24.

21. Ibid pp. 26-28, 39-43.

22. Ibid pp. 45-50.

23. Ibid p. 59.

24. Frazer, James George (1963). *The Golden Bough* (abridged). New York: Macmillan Publishing Company, p. 12.

25. I have found a useful handbook for getting into the basics of astrology to be Frances Sakoian and Louis S. Acker, *The Astrologer's Handbook* (New York: Harper-Collins Publishers, 1973). You're going to want to have a good handle on naked-eye astronomy before you even start, or it will be hard going. An excellent historical survey is Nicholas Campion, *A History of Western Astrology* (2 vols., New York: Bloomsbury Academic, 2013, ISBN 978-1-4411-2737-2 (vol.1) and 978-1-4411-8129-9 (vol.2)). The classic and highly influential early modern work is William Lilly's *Christian Astrology*, a three-book work first published in 1647. Lilly was the great English astrologer of his day. My edition is William Lilly's *Christian Astrology* (2 vols., Bel Air: Astrology Classics, 2004).

26. Greer, John Michael and Warnock, Christopher, translators (2015). *The Illustrated Picatrix: The Occult Classic of Astrological Magic Complete in One Volume*. ISBN 978-1-312-94181-6. Renaissance Astrology, pp. 84-132.

27. Tyson, Donald (editor) and Freake, James (translator) (1993). *Three Books of Occult Philosophy Written by Henry Cornelius Agrippa of Nettesheim*. ISBN 0-87542-832-0. Woodbury: Llewellyn Publications, pp. 375-411.

28. I've found accessible discussions of voodoo thought and practice in: Mambo Chita Tann, *Haitian Vodou: An Introduction to Haiti's Indigenous Spiritual Tradition* (Woodbury: Llewellyn Publications, 2012, ISBN 978-0-7387-3069-1); Kenaz Filan, *The Haitian Vodou Handbook: Protocols for Riding with the Loa* (Vermont: Destiny Books, 2006, ISBN 1-59477-125-1); and Kenaz Filan, *The New Orleans Voodoo Handbook* (Vermont: Destiny Books, 2011, ISBN 978-1-59477-435-5).

29. Hohman, John George with Harms, Daniel (editor) (2012). *The Long-Lost Friend: A 19th Century American Grimoire*. ISBN 978-0-7387-3254-1. Woodbury, Llewellyn Publications.

30. Bilardi, C.R. (2009). *The Red Church, or the Art of Pennsylvania German Braucheri*. ISBN 978-0-9820318-5-8. Sunland: Pendraig, pp. 307-315.

    Herr, Karl (2002). *Hex and Spellwork: The Magical Practices of the Pennsylvania Dutch*. ISBN 1-57863-182-3. York Beach: Red Wheel/Weiser, pp.75-105.

31. Bohak, Gideon (2008). *Ancient Jewish Magic: A History*. ISBN . Cambridge: Cambridge University Press, pp. 291-350.

"To take a modern example, the charm against the Evil Eye will contain the name of Christ or of a Saint in a Christian charm, the name of Muhammed in the Muhammedan, and that of an angel or a mysterious name of God in the Jewish formulas, though all the rest would be identical." M. Gaster. *The Sword of Moses: An Ancient Book of Magic, from an Unique Manuscript.* Lexington: Theophania Publishing, p. 6.

32. Luman's mental "grimoire" is drawn from Hans Dieter Betz, *The Greek Magical Papyri in Translation*, Chicago: The University of Chicago Press, 1986.

33. The single must-read book on shamanism is Mircea Eliade, *Shamanism: Archaic Techniques of Ecstasy,* Princeton: Princeton University Press, 1972.

34. See Frances Densmore, *Chippewa Customs,* St. Paul: Minnesota Historical Press, 1979, pp. 86-97.

35. A ground-breaking and influential study of this subject is Keith Thomas, *Religion and the Decline of Magic,* London: Penguin Books, 1971.

An interesting book to read while considering the subject is Reginald Scot's *The Discoverie of Witchcraft*. Scot's aim is to end the persecution of witches, and it seems likely he didn't believe in the reality of the magic he was documenting at all. Nevertheless, to expose the very idea of witchcraft as his peers understood it to ridicule, Scot documents many instances of Christian prayers or artifacts being put to magical ends. Reginald Scot, *The Discoverie of Witchcraft,* Mineola: Dover Publications, 1972.

36. Matthew 10:14-15.

DEI BRITANNICI

A Prologue to Witchy Eye

This short story is a prequel to the Witchy War, *describing an incident referred to in the series. It is also the elaboration of a pun: in real life, John Churchill's father Winston tried to win his way into the restored Cavalier court by writing a flattering work of genealogy entitled* Divi Britannici. *In the* Witchy War *setting, Winston instead wrote a book called* Dei Britannici, *reconstructing a pre-Christian British pantheon, and ultimately inspiring his son's bold actions described in this book.*

Edward Grant in real life was a very good friend of mine, our neighbor in Surrey. He was an accountant, a cleric in Aldershot, a rambler, a reader of naval catalogs, and, although I didn't think of him as my father, I did think of him as our son's English granddad. He said of himself that he was a pagan at heart, in reference, I think, to the great emotional value he attached to the changes of the seasons and the natural world of which he was a part.

"Please," Father Edward Grant pleaded. "I believe this may be vital."

The cold October rain skipped right past Grant's tall boxy hat and poured down his neck. He shivered, despite the heavy cloak. He'd ridden a long way, dressed in priestly black in the hope that if he met Cromwell's men, their respect for clergy might give him some protection.

"The general be in council." The guard's face was stony, but then relaxed, ever so slightly. He and his fellow soldiers wore Churchill's red and white, faded and stained almost gray. "I wot who you be, Father. I were born and raised in Aldershot. St. George's Road, just up the 'ill from your church."

Grant seized the guard's hands. The other man's skin felt hot to the touch, the priest was so chilled from his two days' ride over the North Downs and into the Weald. "Daniel!" he cried. "You're the butcher's son, I know you! I baptized you, Daniel!"

"Aye, you brought me to salvation, Father, but this ben't the right moment for such recollections. I be on duty."

The other guard, who hadn't spoken, stepped forward and put a hand on Father Grant's shoulder.

A breeze blew open the tent flap behind Daniel for just a moment, and Grant caught a glimpse of long curly white hair. Not the powdered white of an aristocrat's periwig, but the glossy white of a man whose natural hair had turned that color prematurely, and framed within the silver curls, pale ivory skin.

"Sir Isaac!" Father Grant tightened his grip on Daniel's hands, hearing the younger man's knuckles pop. "Sir Isaac Newton, I see him in there in the council." His mind raced.

"Aye, Father, he were invited to General Churchill's council of war, and you were not."

"Only do this, and I will leave." Grant shuffled back half a step, mud sucking noisily at his heels, but retained his grip on Daniel's hands. "Only give Sir Isaac a simple message. If he is not interested, I will go away."

The second guard grunted his disapproval, but Daniel nodded. "Aye then, Father. What be the message?"

"Tell Sir Isaac someone has stolen the Aldershot parish register. Sir Isaac, you understand. Sir Isaac must hear the message."

The two guards looked at each other skeptically.

"I am not mad," Grant said. "You know me, Daniel, I baptized you." He sobbed once, saying the word *baptized*. Then he sniffed deeply, feeling the rain and chill begin to settle into his lungs. "You know I am not mad."

"I wot you *were* not mad, Father." Daniel took a deep breath. "And therefore I shall bear your message. Stay here."

Daniel pushed the priest further back. With an effort, Father Grant relaxed his hands and let Daniel go. The young guard from Aldershot stooped to enter the tent.

The second guard snarled, tilting his pike forward slightly in a threatening manner. "I be no Aldershot man, and I ken you not, sir. Keep your distance."

Sir Isaac Newton exploded from the tent and into the rain. He was not dressed for the weather, in his white shirt and breaches, but he plunged past the guard to grab Father Grant by the shoulders in a close embrace. He smelled like man who had not bathed in many days, and his fingernails were stained odd colors—alchemy, no doubt.

"The parish register of Aldershot!" Newton gasped. "Stolen! Are you certain?"

"I . . . I am the parson, Sir Isaac," Father Grant stammered. "The lock was shattered with a musket ball, and nothing was taken but the register. You understand why I have come straight here, I think."

"Damn it! Damn us!" Sir Isaac spun and dragged the priest with him toward the tent door. "Damn *you*!" he cried to the guard. "Damn the delay! Damn it all!"

He pulled Father Grant into the tent.

The interior was lit as well as warmed by torches, and further warmed by a small fire. All the flame left the tent smoky despite an open flap in the tent ceiling that let in a constant spatter of rain in exchange for some of the fumes. Standing around a light table bearing a map were men Father Grant didn't recognize, other than Daniel the butcher's son and, from his paintings, General John Churchill. The famous war leader had a shopkeeper's face, but enviable hair, long, black, and thickly curled. He looked much better groomed than his wizard.

"Sir." Father Grant executed his best bow, holding his dripping hat to his chest and keeping it there.

"My sergeant here says you've come to report a stolen register of baptisms," John Churchill said.

"Aye," Daniel said.

"And burials and weddings." Father Grant nodded. "Though it's the baptisms in particular that concern me."

"And my thaumaturge Isaac is thereby distressed, though I do not for the life of me see why. Still, he is my wizard, and what is the point of having a magician in your company if you ignore his advice? Also, I find that the most surprising things become matters of life and death when one battles the Necromancer and his forces."

One of the other men in the tent pressed a warm goblet into Grant's hands. It smelled of wine and he gratefully took deep gulps, breathing as much as tasting the spices.

"It's the Aldershot parish, John," Isaac Newton said. "Aldershot."

"A third of our men here today are from Aldershot," Churchill said.

"Stolen," Newton continued. "The church was broken into and nothing was stolen but the register."

"They left the pyx and the chalice," Father Grant said. "Pure silver. They left the poor box. So not ordinary burglars. Not looters."

"And if Aldershot, why not Farnham?" Isaac said. "Why not Haslemere? Do you understand, John?"

John Churchill removed an octavo volume from his coat pocket and ran his fingers over the spine and cover. Father Grant caught a short glimpse of the book's title and author, stamped in gold on the front: *DEI BRITANNICI, WINSTON CHURCHILL*. John's father, a scholar whose researches into the ancient Britonic and Saxon religious practices of the island had earned him first censure, then praise, and ultimately a reputation for being a heretic.

"I am *beginning* to understand," John Churchill said.

"I do not," Daniel said, somewhat indignantly. The others ignored him and he kept his place.

"It is contagion." Newton paced the tent in an erratic pattern, wheeling and retracing his steps, changing his angle radically with each turn. In his movements, he resembled nothing so much as a bee. An enormous, silver bee. "A person, having once been in contact with the Aldershot register—and at such a fragile and energy-ridden moment as baptism, at that!—must always be in contact with that register, from the point of view of a practitioner of gramarye. It's an act of genius, if cruel genius. Do you think he has read the *Principia*? Good god, did I inadvertently teach the Necromancer his craft?"

"*I* have read the *Principia*," Father Grant said. "It is how I saw the problem."

"There you have it, Isaac," Churchill said. "If you gave the Necromancer this foul idea, then you also planted the seed of our salvation in the heart of this good parish priest."

"Begging your pardon, Sir Isaac," Grant added, "but in addition to neatly demonstrating the principle of contagion, might this not also be an example of the principle of sympathy?"

Newton stopped pacing and fixed Father Grant with a piercing eye. "How so?"

"The man's name is like the man. Therefore the man's name *is* the man. Especially at baptism, where the child is remade in a new image. What one does to the name, one does to the man. Or am I mistaken in my understanding?"

"It is indeed I, then, who have done this to us." Isaac Newton's eyes brimmed with sudden tears.

John Churchill snorted. "Oliver Cromwell was forty years on this earth before you ever saw your mother's breast, Isaac. What on earth do you believe you can have taught him about magic?"

Father Grant, shocked by the sight of tears, struggled to recover. "Indeed, he may have come to similar conclusions from reading Albertus Magnus. Or Cornelius Agrippa, or other books. I once spent an hour in the library of a London Jew, who had the most astonishing texts."

Churchill clapped his hand on Newton's shoulder, nearly knocking the other man down, but he turned his attention to Father Grant. "Is Albertus Magnus part of your lectionary cycle, Father? That seems rather off the beaten path."

Father Grant looked down at his hat. "I aspired as a younger man to wear the red. To be an adept of the Humble Order of St. Reginald Pole. Only I hadn't the talent for it."

"That's too bad," Churchill said. "I'd trade a lot for few more solid Polites."

Isaac Newton straightened his back, his grief falling off him like red leaves blown off by an autumn storm. "But this parish priest had done you better service than many a wizard would be able, John. Thanks to his warning, we have a chance."

The flattery from Sir Isaac, his participation in the discussion with such eminent men, and the danger he knew loomed over them all boiled together in Father Grant's veins and thrilled his heart. "A nighttime raid?" he suggested. "Have you men bold and able enough to creep into the Necromancer's camp and steal back the register?"

John Churchill blinked at him. "Is that where the book is, then?"

Grant faltered. "I don't . . . I thought . . . ."

"They could be anywhere," Sir Isaac said grimly. "For all we know, he has the register of every parish in Hampshire locked up in the Tower of London and is there preparing to incorporate them into some unhallowed spell."

"What is his intent, do you think?" Churchill asked.

Isaac Newton's expression was grave. "I *hope* it is merely to *kill* all your soldiers, John."

Daniel the butcher's son gasped audibly.

"Quite," Churchill agreed. "I'd rather have them dead than raised against me as more of those rotting Lazars."

"A counter-spell!" Father Grant suggested. "We gather the men in a church until the danger is passed, and we ward the church, further, against the Necromancer's black art."

"Isaac's black art, you mean." Churchill chuckled. "No, I think not."

"How would you know when the Necromancer had tried his spell and failed?" Newton pointed out. "Even assuming I could create a counter-spell that would defend against such an attack. It is I, who am to do this, is it not? When you say *we*, father, do you not mean *Isaac Newton* shall do it?"

Father Grant wanted to apologize for his presumption, but what came out was a mumble, incoherent even to himself.

"What about silver, John?" Newton asked. "How much have we got?"

Churchill shrugged. "This army marches more on paper redeemable with the Knights of St. John than it does on specie, Isaac. I doubt I have enough coins to give each man a silver shilling to clutch."

"And that might not be enough to protect them, in any case." Newton frowned.

"I have a different idea." Churchill's eyes gleamed.

"Tell us," Father Grant said.

"I have a conceived a scheme that should save the men of Aldershot," Churchill said, "as well as any other men whose baptismal records Cromwell has stolen. And it won't exhaust my wizard or cost me silver. And indeed, it should allow us to lay a trap for the Necromancer's men."

"It certainly sounds good, John," Newton said. "What other miracles might it accomplish, this plan of yours?"

Churchill smiled slyly. "It will make of Father Grant here a sort of magician."

"No," Edward Grant murmured. An uneasy feeling pinched his stomach. "I don't see how that could possibly be true."

"Father Grant," Churchill said, "I think you are the only man who can save the Aldershot lads from the Necromancer now."

Grant's knees trembled. He drained the last of his goblet and set it on the table. "What do you need?"

"Sergeant," Churchill said to Daniel, still standing in the door of the tent. "I need you to round up every stray animal in camp. Let us spare the horses, if we may, but every other animal. I mean every cow, goat, dog, cat, rat, and mouse you and your men can find. If it were less cold, I'd set you to trapping snakes as well. My orders, no exceptions, any man resisting is to be knocked unconscious. Am I clear?"

"Aye, sir." Daniel offered a weary salute and exited.

"And me?" Grant asked. "What do you need me to do?"

"First," Churchill said, "I need you to steel your conscience."

His sobs long since exhausted with the rainfall, his eyes red and his heart black, Father Grant crouched in the gorse thickets on a ridge overlooking Churchill's camp. With his travel cloak wrapped around him and his hat pulled down low, he should be invisible from the valley, a black blotch against the dark green gorse. Dawn was near. At the edge of camp, the horses grazed where they had been picketed, blissfully unaware anything had happened.

Churchill's men lay strewn about camp. Some were on cots, others in tents, some on the ground beneath trees, others slumped forward at watch posts. The fires, hammered by rain until midnight, were now almost extinguished.

At the far end of the valley, the sound of marching.

Unnatural marching; too regular, too wooden.

The horses heard it first, and responded. They pulled at their pickets, they whinnied in protest.

Father Grant, alone in the gorse where John Churchill had left him, forced himself to watch.

The men of Essex and Kent, the Roundheads, came into view first. They wore the Necromancer's black and brown. They carried muskets over their shoulders and bandoliers of cartridges over their chests. Their marching was disciplined enough, but it was human.

Behind the easterners came the Models.

They were the height of men, and some had faces painted onto their knob heads. Garish red devil faces, or crooked crimson grins under green hair, or bright yellow circles with black dots for eyes. Some also had black uniforms painted on their wooden bodies, but many were unfinished, showing garishly what they were—wooden puppets, the height of men, holding spears. Age, weather, and battle had chipped and splintered them, leaving many of them as spiny as hedgehogs.

Puppets without strings.

Murderous, man-sized marionettes.

It was the Models, walking on broad wooden feet the size of tree stumps and stepping forward together, as perfectly synchronized as a clock, that made the unearthly sound of the Necromancer's advance. Their joints clicked as they walked, and the movement caused their the wood of their long limbs to creak as well, like a forest in the wind.

The Roundheads reached the first watchmen, still at the edge of camp. They rolled the guards onto their backs, and then a collective cheer went up from Cromwell's army.

Several of the soldiers bayoneted the already-dead men, to be sure.

Father Edward Grant had saved Daniel and the other Aldershot lads from that fate, at least.

The other Roundheads broke rank and ran forward to loot the camp.

The Models stopped where they were. Controlled by the Necromancer, or by one of his sorcerous lieutenants, they had no lust for booty like that which drove their mortal colleagues.

Grant felt sick to his heart.

The Roundheads rushed forward. Most threw their muskets into the grass, anxious not to be burdened and slowed down by the cumbersome Brown Besses in their race to get their hands on silver rings, gold teeth, pay packets, even fresh food.

The Roundheads flooded into camp, and a sudden horn blew.

At the horn's signal, every man of Aldershot and every other man in Churchill's Hampshire Corps sat up, took aim, and fired. A ragged *BOOM* rang out over the valley, wreathing the scene in blue smoke at the exact moment that a crescent sliver of orange sun rose in the eastern sky.

Roundheads fell on all sides.

In Edward Grant's ears, the booming of the guns sounded like the ringing of the bell. Once for each man in the camp, and the last time for himself.

Stunned, disbelieving, most of Cromwell's men only stopped their efforts to loot and stared instead. Churchill's men fired again; each had lain within reach of as many loaded muskets and pistols as possible.

John Churchill's men rose with pikes, bayonets, and swords, and charged into the unresisting Roundheads. In Grant's mind's eye, the book of the Gospels slammed shut. Again and again, once for each man who fell.

"Pikemen, form up!" Churchill strode from his tent with a pistol in each hand, hair flying behind him. It made a grand entrance, and for good effect, he fired the pistols at the Models.

The Models charged.

"Fire!" Churchill yelled.

He did not mean *guns*. As the Models crashed into the pikemen and slowed, becoming entangled with the long spears and halberds that tried to push them away, another dozen men charged from Churchill's tent. Daniel the butcher's son was one of them, and they held bottles in their hands. The bottles were stopped up with oily rags, and the rags themselves were burning.

In a frayed wave, the bottles hurtled through the air. Maybe half of them missed, but even those that struck the ground shattered, splashing the Models with flaming oil. The direct hits were even more impressive, coating the Models in some cases nearly from ball-like head to clomping foot in sheets of flame.

Some flaming Models managed to crash through the pikemen. If anything, the Models were more terrifying when aflame—their mere touch wounded, and one of them scooped up two of Churchill's men, one in each arm, and hugged them screaming to its chest as it collapsed, all three of them destroyed by the fire.

All three, snuffed candles.

But mostly, with Cromwell's musketeers fleeing, Churchill's men had only to hold back the Models while they burned down to cinders.

When the last Model was a heap of embers, Father Edward Grant staggered down through the gorse.

All night long, one at a time. He had asked each man in camp his full Christian name, and then by bell, book, and candle, he had excommunicated them. He had started with John Churchill, who'd done it, he said, to set the example, and he'd done it holding his father's book. Isaac Newton followed, then Daniel the butcher's son, and last of all Father Edward Grant.

Whose name, after all, was also in the Aldershot parish register.

Paradox. He had excommunicated himself, and God must have accepted it, because Father Edward Grant yet lived. But that was not blasphemy enough. Saving his own life by renouncing heaven was not vile and venal enough for this black night, no.

To know for certain when the spell had been cast, John Churchill suggested, and also to give the Necromancer the impression that his magic was succeeding, Isaac Newton added, they had agreed it was important that *something* die.

After excommunicating each man, therefore, Father Edward Grant had baptized an animal by the same name. Cats, dogs, mules, vermin. Baptized and then penned up, tethered, or caged, and last of all to receive baptism had been a scrawny brown mouse christened and baptized Edward Grant. In that one final case, Grant had baptized the mouse first, hoping he might still then have the authority to do so, before excommunicating himself.

He shook at the memory.

The animals had died one at a time, simply dropping in their tracks. Churchill had organized his battle plan and given his men orders, then sent Grant up onto the ridge to be out of harm's way.

Now, as Grant staggered down the hillside, cold and bone-tired, feeling a fever begin to burn up his forehead, Churchill strode forward to meet him. Daniel the butcher's son followed a few paces behind.

"Father!" Churchill called, opening his arms to embrace him.

Grant accepted the embrace, reciprocating it but little. "No," he said, "I am no father. Indeed, I am not Edward Grant." He reached into the pocket of his coat and took out the little brown mouse, stiff and cold. "This was Edward Grant. Father Grant, Christian."

Churchill looked at his face carefully. "Maybe. But if so, then you are Edward Grant, magician. Edward Grant, hero. Edward Grant, the man who saved England."

Grant was too numb to respond. Instead he staggered on. "I must gather the animals up."

"Why?" Churchill asked.

"They died Christian beasts. They deserve Christian burial. God forbid one of your men try to eat a baptized sheep. In the eyes of God and the church it might be cannibalism."

"I'll help you," Daniel offered. "I'll dig a grave for each, if you like."

Churchill chuckled uneasily. "Of course."

Grant took a few more unsteady steps.

Then he collapsed, but Daniel caught him.

Churchill called again. "You really have saved England, you know!"

"You've saved me," Daniel whispered. "You brought me to salvation again, Father."

"Have I?" Grant stopped, not looking back but gazing on the camp, where Churchill's men now looted the bodies of the Roundheads for their bits of silver and copper, their weapons and ammunition. He looked up into Daniel's face, blunt and honest and wearing a look of mixed pride and surprise. "Perhaps. And have I also damned England? Have I damned you, Daniel? Have I damned us all?"

THAT STATE OF AWFUL WOUNDEDNESS

I wrote this to be exhibited at BYU's Harold B. Lee Library. I was privileged to be co-curator of the exhibit, which commenced in December 2020, and was called A Desolating Sickness: Stories of the Pandemic.

"Do you think maybe the flux is punishment for the war?" Gibbs searched Hiram's face.

Hiram's bones were heavy and his eyes dry as dust. When he closed them, he saw Yas's eyes, open in death. Hiram hadn't been able to save his friend. "I'm inclined to think that the punishment for making war is that you have a war."

"So the flux is just one more thing God sees fit to dump on us, eh?"

Hiram stood inside a Catholic church, leaning on a crutch. The building's walls were cool white plaster, and a row of columns supporting tall arches marched from Hiram's position toward a stained-glass window at the back of the church, above an altar. Hiram could read neither Latin nor French, so none of the chapel's many inscriptions or engravings meant anything to him. He could understand the stained-glass image, though: Christ in a red robe, Christ floating above the ground, was the returned and resurrected Lord, Christ come back to usher the world into its state of millennial peace.

The image made him smile, despite everything.

Gibbs lay on the stone floor beneath an arch, a short stack of personal effects beside his head: spectacles with a cracked lens, a razor, three books. The army didn't have enough cots, so in this church-cum-field hospital, the patients lay on thin mattresses, covered by greasy wool blankets. A second man lay on his own mattress beside Gibbs. He faced away from Gibbs and Hiram both, into a dark corner of the church. Between the two mattresses lay the second man's possessions, including a pen, tattered blue notepad, and a single book.

"Are you a *Mormon* chaplain?" Gibbs asked.

"I'm just Mormon," Hiram said. "A doughboy like you, I expect. Father Raphaël asked me to talk to you."

"Father Raphaël thinks I'm mad at God," Gibbs said.

Hiram shrugged. "Sometimes . . . that's understandable."

Gibbs pointed at Hiram's crutch. His hand trembled. "You came over from the wounded hospital."

"I got shot." Hiram tried not to think of the mob of German cultists, foaming at the mouth, and Yas Yazzie's last moments, lying on frozen mud.

"They have you across the street?" Gibbs asked. "In the library?"

"No books there now," Hiram said. "I don't know, might have been a library once."

"I'm not mad at God," Gibbs said. "There's no God to be mad at."

"Ah." Hiram shifted position on his crutch, wishing he had a stool to sit on.

"Neither will the Lord suffer that the Gentiles shall forever remain in that awful state of blindness." Gibbs smiled, showing a missing tooth in the front of his mouth. "That's what the book says, isn't it?"

"First Nephi, thirteen." Hiram nodded.

"Well, I'm not blind anymore," Gibbs said. "And I guess that means I'm a Gentile."

"That ain't even it." The man in the other mattress stirred. The blanket fell away from his face, revealing a pale and sweaty cheek. "You're quoting it wrong."

"That's Nuttall." Gibbs laughed. "Now I not only gave him the fever, I can't even quote the Book of Mormon right."

"Neither will the Lord suffer," Nuttall recited from his pallet, "that the Gentiles shall forever remain in that *state of awful woundedness*."

Hiram scratched his head. "I seem to recall it the way Gibbs does. Though I'll admit, I've been shaken up and knocked around a bit recently, so maybe I'm remembering it wrong."

Nuttall forced himself up onto one elbow, grabbing his book from the floor and handing it to Hiram. He shook violently and coughed from the effort; by force of will, Hiram managed not to turn away, but he touched two fingers to his chest, reassured by the feel of the cool iron disk of his chi-rho amulet against his skin. He took the book and examined it. Its spine announced that it was the BOOK OF MORMON; its cover was brown leather, stained dark by years of handling. Inside, the text was not divided into numbered paragraphs.

"Grandma Hettie's *Book of Mormon* was an old one, too," Hiram said. "Before Orson Pratt broke it up into verses." He turned to the title page and found: PRINTED BY E.B. GRANDIN, FOR THE AUTHOR. *1830*. "First edition."

"It was my great-grandfather's copy." Nuttall fell back on his mattress, shivering. "He gave it to me when I shipped out."

Hiram had to find First Nephi thirteen by his memory of the text; the chapter divisions were not the ones he knew, either. There it was, at the top of page 31: "Neither will the Lord suffer that the Gentiles shall forever remain in that state of awful woundedness," he read.

Gibbs rose almost to his knees to force a different *Book of Mormon* into Hiram's hands.

This one had the familiar chapters and verses, and Hiram found the passage quickly. "I'll be hog-tied," he said. "Awful state of blindness."

"Two *Book of Mormons*," Gibbs sneered, "and no God."

"I didn't give you the flux!" Nuttall snapped.

"It was you, visiting that whore Angeline, or it was God." Gibbs laced his fingers behind his neck and stared at the ceiling, a sour grin on his face. "Take your pick."

"You had symptoms first!" Nuttall spat as he accused Gibbs, and Hiram clenched his teeth together to avoid lurching back.

"That doesn't mean anything, you idiot."

"And she's a fine girl!" Nuttall collapsed onto his blankets. "We just talk."

Hiram looked at the two books again. "Why are they different?"

"Because it's all nonsense," Gibbs said.

Nuttall was slower to answer. "Because . . . because someone thought he knew better than the book, and took it on himself to fix the words."

Hiram scanned the rest of the page. "It's the fact that the plain and precious parts of the Gospel of the Lamb are missing. That's what causes the . . . the woundedness."

"Or the blindness!" Gibbs snapped.

"Shame to have two Mormon fellows from the same regiment quarreling," Hiram said.

"Same town." Nuttall's voice sounded wet around the edges, as if he had been crying. "Grantsville."

"I'll read a verse or two," Hiram said softly, "if you don't object."

"Trying to change my mind?" Gibbs asked.

"It won't work," Nuttall said.

"The only mind I ever really try to change is my own." Hiram said nothing for a moment, and when neither soldier answered, he read, from Nuttall's copy. "I looked and beheld a tree; and it was like unto the tree which my father had seen; and the beauty thereof was far beyond, yea, exceeding of all beauty; and the whiteness thereof, did exceed the whiteness of the driven snow. And it came to pass that after I had seen the tree, I said unto the spirit, I behold thou has shewn unto me the tree which is precious above all. . . . And the angel said unto me . . . Knowest thou the meaning of the tree which thy father saw? And I answered him, saying: Yea, it is the love of God, which sheddeth itself abroad in the hearts of the children of men; wherefore, it is the most desirable above all things."

He stopped reading, and silence filled the church. Down the row of columns, Hiram could hear the gentle tread of Father Raphaël's feet, and the soft cries of a man deep in the grip of fever.

Yas had had no time to cry for himself.

Hiram hadn't wept for him, either.

"I might pray," Hiram ventured, "for all of us. If you don't stop me, that is. We're abroad, and we could stand to have the love of God shed in our hearts."

They didn't stop him.

KUNG POW CHICKEN FOR PYGMALION

I met a Canadian publisher at WorldCon in Reno, back forever ago. His press planned to produce a Wuxia anthology and he invited me to submit. I was in the middle of James Clavell's Asian Saga *as my top-of-the-toilet-tank books, so I found my story in the space between the British Empire and the Middle Kingdom—two very chauvinistic societies, horns locked with each other.*

Or at least, a steampunk version of that space.

The twin mouths of the riot gun gaped in Jerry's face.

Diu nei lou mou on all foreign invaders and the fornicating worms that serve them, he thought sourly, but he grinned his best nervous, sweaty grin and held up the paper bags.

"Food, heya?" He shook the bags around under the nose of the tall Anglo gunman. The smell of the food, and especially the chili-laden chicken, cut through the fish and oil stink of Aberdeen Harbor. "Szechuan food? Very delicious! Hot and sweet!"

"Who are you?" The big man eased his gun a few degrees away

from Jerry. His voice sounded hoarse and grinding, like he might be sick. With his free hand he patted Jerry down, checking for concealed weapons. As if Jerry was some *lan yeung* barbarian, weak enough to need to carry around a gun. All Jerry had on his person was the food, a stack of napkins in one back pocket and a bundle of chopsticks in the other.

"Jerry Xu," Jerry grinned even broader. "Delivery boy, Chow Fat's Heavenly Szechuan Palace. This is *Sea Witch*, heya?"

Professor Pevensey would be horrified to hear me butcher the English language like this, Jerry thought. Well, *diu nei lou mou* on him, too, and all the rest of the *ngong gau* lecturers at that flyblown dungheap Cambridge, and every other Englishman. Jerry liked waist-coats, modern plumbing and public house darts, but mostly he was glad for his English education because it made him a better servant to the Dowager Empress and the Middle Kingdom.

He understood his enemy better.

The big man took the bags from Jerry's hands and took a step back. "Stay there," he ordered Jerry in his low rumble, and he foraged through the greasy paper with his nose like an animal. The barbarian was gigantic, and he looked ridiculous. He had a thick English mustache that looked stiff as a brush, and a bowler hat, and a tweed sports jacket. He was overdressed for the hot, sticky climate, unlike Jerry, who wore simple black trousers and the white restaurant tunic, with the palace-and-dragon sign stitched over the breast in gold thread.

The Englishman moved funny, too. He jerked a little with each motion; Jerry wondered if he might be constipated. Too much bad English food, all bread and pie and cheese and lager. Nothing tasted like anything at all on an English table, except pickled onions.

And the *mo lei tau gau* Scots were even worse.

"You try, you like very much," Jerry promised. He had to force himself to speak pidgin English. It was a little embarrassing, but it was the price he had to pay to protect the Middle Kingdom.

Besides, there was no one here to hear him except the idiot giant, who probably thought all Chinese spoke like mentally defective children.

The big man squinted at Jerry.

"Go on! You try! Very tasty," Jerry assured him. He carefully avoided looking past the guard at the *Sea Witch*, though he was anxious to get aboard and learn the secret technologies of her masters. He'd waited nearly a week for the *ban tsat* Englishmen to send out for food, and now that he had his shot, he wasn't going to bungle it.

The deck of the *Sea Witch* was swamped in shadow. There were gaslight poles on the quay, and light leaking from windows in the *Sea Witch's* hull, and light on ships elsewhere in Aberdeen Harbor, but if there were working lights on the *Sea Witch's* deck, they had been left off. Even through the shadows, though, Jerry could see the tall pipes rising out of the ship that marked her as a steamer. That was not so unusual anymore, but she also carried built into her hull mysterious guns. Informants, dirty louse-ridden English seaman in need of more money for drink and whores, had called them *railguns*. They had said that the guns worked by magnets, like some children's toy or a back-street healer. They could fire a projectile over great distances, the *tsat tau* traitors claimed, and didn't even require gunpowder.

The same *cau hai* informants had also told Jerry and his superiors that there was something else aboard the *Sea Witch*, something that they couldn't explain or identify, something called the *Pygmalion*. Of course, Jerry knew the story of the Cypriot king who fell in love with a beautiful statue and whose prayers to Aphrodite brought her to life. Still, that knowledge didn't help him puzzle out what the *Sea Witch's Pygmalion* might be.

Jerry speculated that it might be a perfume, or some other technology that would make a man fall in love. Industrialized seduction would be a very powerful weapon, indeed. Jerry imagined Chinese soldiers marching against shattered English positions only to be struck by a Love Gas, or a Love Ray, to then lay down their arms and rush to beg the nearest English woman for affection. Or Englishman. Or even the nearest inanimate object—the original Pygmalion had fallen in love with a statue, after all.

And these days, when everything human was being reduced to gears and pistons, a love weapon seemed almost reasonable.

Pygmalion was a tantalizing code name.

The English had brought these secret items to Hong Kong, their stinking offensive toehold in the throat of the Middle Kingdom. It could only be because they planned to use them against the Dowager Empress and her people. Use them for their own purposes or maybe sell them to accursed rebels or criminals like the Heaven and Earth Society or the *so hai* White Lotus.

So Jerry had come to spy and to steal; and if he could not steal, then to destroy.

The big *quai loh* looked into the bags uncertainly, so Jerry took matters into his own hands. He slipped a pair of chopsticks into his hand and used it to dig out a couple of pieces of spicy chicken. He popped them into his own mouth.

"Mmmm, good!" he smiled and rubbed his belly. *Diu nei lou mou* on this stupid man for making me wait, he thought, then caught himself. Patient. Must be patient.

The tall man still looked perplexed. Or maybe curious. Jerry shoveled a mouthful of the Kung Pao chicken in his direction this time, and the big barbarian took it, chewed and swallowed.

"Good, heya?" Jerry asked.

The tall man smiled. "Good," he rumbled. Then he frowned a little. "Hot," he added. "Sweet."

"Yes," Jerry agreed. Now let me take the food belowdecks, you gigantic hairy *quai loh* idiot.

The barbarian took the chopsticks out of Jerry's hand and turned. "Hot and sweet," he groaned again. He walked away across the *Sea Witch's* deck. As he walked, he took another bite of the Kung Pao chicken.

"Hey!" Jerry yelled. "You gotta pay, yes? Cash money!"

A curse on all Englishmen and their tasteless food, Jerry thought grumpily, but at least it was working in his favor.

"Follow me," the big man wheezed.

Another Englishman detached himself from the shadow of the steamer's deck. "Where are you going, Pygott?" he asked. He held a riot gun, too.

"Taking this food down below," Pygott explained in his creaking voice. "And this Chinaman." He jerked an enormous thumb over his shoulder at the gangplank. "You watch."

The huge brass steam funnels of the *Sea Witch* loomed overhead as the barbarian led Jerry into the wheelhouse. He noted the steering wheel, locked in place while the boat was moored to the quay, a compass and a thicket of levers and switches that controlled the steamer, and speaking tubes that connected the wheelhouse to other parts of the ship. There was a panel to one side that was covered with a brass lid and locked shut with a heavy padlock. Might be the controls to the so-called *railguns*.

Steps led down beneath the wheelhouse, through a narrow staircase lit with electric lights in spherical glass bulbs. The big barbarian Pygott turned and clomped down the steps, taking another bite of the chicken.

All gods bear witness, Jerry thought with glee, I'm in. He kept his face fixed in the stupidest coolie grin he could manage and he followed the big Englishman.

Pygott's steps were awkward, clumpity-clump. Clumsy oaf, that's what England got for feeding her sons nothing but milk and beef. They grew too big and too hairy and they stomped around like pasty white mastodons.

Halfway down the stairs, Pygott took another mouthful of the Kung Pao chicken. At this rate, it would be all gone before Jerry got a meaningful look around. Maybe they'd send him back for more.

At the bottom of the steps was a steel door with a shuttered peep-hole at eye level. Pygott raised his arm to knock on the door—

and his arm became spastic, flailing bat-like against the metal—

rat-a-tat-tat... tat... tat-a-toom!

Pygott jerked back away from the door, falling partly on top of Jerry in the process and knocking him to the stairs. Pygott was surprisingly heavy.

"Diu nei lou mou!" Jerry shouted, and then clamped his mouth shut. "I mean, take care!" He forced a chuckle. "You are very big man, you crush me!"

Pygott yanked himself to his feet again with one hand on the wall. He still held both paper bags clutched in his other fist. "I'm always careful," he murmured. This close, Jerry decided that the Englishman's voice didn't sound like grinding at all; it sounded like a violin or a hurdy-gurdy, like a rosined bow or wheel rubbing against strings.

Also, now that Jerry could see him in the light, Pygott didn't look very good. He had a waxy complexion and his eyes looked glazed and the muscles of his face didn't move very much, even when he talked. Jerry thought the man looked sick. Or maybe he was an opium fiend.

And he stank, but not the usual flyblown rotten meat and unwashed armpits stink of Englishmen. He smelled like oil.

Maybe he was a well-bathed mechanic, Jerry thought.

"Maybe chilies too hot for you, heya?" Jerry laughed. *Ham gaa caan*, you stupid clumsy ogre. *Diu nei lou mou.*

"Hot and sweet," Pygott agreed. Even his breath stank of oil, through the spicy Kung Pao cloud.

The peephole opened. "Crikey, hit's Pygott! An' hit's got... 'e's got *food.*"

The door opened and Pygott lurched through.

Jerry followed, pulling the wad of napkins out of his back pocket with one hand and the bill in the other. "You pay in yuan?" he asked, waving the bill. "Or shirring?" he deliberately slurred his Ls into Rs for the benefit of the stupid *quai loh*, and for his own amusement.

Pygott shut the door with a heavy *clank*.

The space behind the door was some kind of secure chamber. Jerry's trained and educated eye noted immediately that the walls and both exits were built of steel and held together by heavy hex-shaped bolts. A periscope with twin handles and a viewing plate dropped from the ceiling above, along with several speaking tubes that must connect to the wheelhouse. Seats were steel stools, bolted immovably to the floor. A Winchester rifle leaned against the wall in the corner. It looked like a Model 1876, Jerry thought. Forty-five caliber shells, a serious man-stopping firearm.

To Jerry's left and right were large cylinders mounted on trestles that had hatch handles at their low end and rose at a gentle incline up through the wall and ceiling behind Jerry. Wooden crates beside the low end of each tube were labeled *SHELLS*.

Guns, he thought. This must be the gunnery room, and those tubes were the *cau hai* railguns.

Three people stood in the room, not counting Pygott. There was a chubby, heavy-jowled man in top hat, evening coat and monocle; a man wearing smoked spectacles whose long hair hung down his back in a powdered queue; and a woman in a black corset, flat bonnet and scarlet wasp-waisted skirt, who held a half-opened green fan in each hand.

"Get him," Spectacles said quietly.

Pygott grabbed Jerry by the arm with one hand.

The big oil-reeking dungheap foreigner was much faster than Jerry could have guessed. Jerry didn't try to resist; he was outnumbered four to one, and he wanted more time to look around. He wanted to get a better look at the guns, and maybe figure out what the Pygmalion device was.

He grinned big and stupid.

"No credit," he said. "Everybody gotta pay when food is derivered!"

"Mr. Xu," Smoke Spectacles continued.

"Jerry," Jerry grinned. "Prease, must pay now."

"Lieutenant Xu Hao Dong—"

They were on to him; Jerry didn't wait any longer.

He elbowed Pygott in the chest—

boom!—

Jerry's elbow hurt.

Pygott looked at him, unmoved. Jerry punched the big man in the chest with his other hand—

boom!—

stomped on his instep—

clank!

Pygott still didn't move, and Jerry finally realized why the big barbarian smelled so much like oil.

Jowls laughed, a thin and rasping sound. "Now 'e gets hit, dunne?"

Corset snapped open one of her fans and Jerry saw that it was made of steel, with sharp tips; a kung fu fighting fan. "Shall I commence with a little recreational vivisection?" she asked Smoke Spectacles. She had a voice like a serpent, greased and cunning. "Or do you want to give him a chance to open up to us emotionally first?" Her *quai loh* face was enormous and sweaty and Jerry thought he could have shoved his finger right into any one of her vast, grease-filled pores. Jerry had put up with such women in the public houses of Cambridge, where alcohol dulled his reactions and made even kidney pie acceptable, but in the belly of the *Sea Witch* her hugeness and ugliness made her terrifying, like some *yaoguai* devil. He half expected her skirt to fall away and reveal an enormous snake's tail.

"There's nuffink says a man can't open up emotionally *after* 'e's been cut, izzere?" Jowls sneered.

"Interesting observation." Spectacles chewed his lower lip and arched a single provocative eyebrow in Jerry's direction.

Jerry tugged at Pygott's arm, trying to throw the barbarian over his shoulder. Nothing. The dung-eating mustache-faced thug didn't move. He seemed to weigh a ton, and trying to throw him was like trying to throw a brick wall.

"Hot... sweet..." muttered Pygott, the Pygmalion device. His head bobbled and twitched a bit from side to side on his thick neck. Jerry thought he caught the whiff of burning oil, and it seemed to be coming from Pygott's sportscoat.

Jowls and Corset moved in closer. Corset snapped open her second fan and she flourished them both in front of her big, ugly *quai loh* body. Jowls pulled a gun from inside his coat, a silver Colt 1851 Navy revolver with its long octagonal barrel.

No more time.

"You can't shoot me without caps on your gun," Jerry forced himself to laugh.

"Huh?" Jowls looked down at his pistol in surprise—

Jerry punched, not at Pygott, but at the bag in his hand—

his fist smashed through the bag and hurled a meteor shower of sweet and spicy chicken and chilies into the Pygmalion device's face—

"Sweet!" Pygott moaned; he staggered back, releasing Jerry—

Jerry spun and ducked, under the razor swish of a fighting fan that would have decapitated him. He grabbed for chopsticks in his back pocket.

"Damn!" cursed Spectacles, and grabbed for the rifle.

Jowls raised his pistol once more, realizing he'd been tricked.

Corset slashed again, at Jerry's chest—

Jerry caught the giant barbarian harlot's wrist in a forked pair of chopsticks, pushing the lethal steel aside, just enough to slice his tunic but not his flesh—

still spinning—

he slapped the napkins in his other hand against Jowls's face and pushed—

bang!

Jowls fell backward, blinded, and the 1851 Navy's bullet went wide.

Zing! Zing! Jerry hoped he wouldn't get hit by a ricochet.

"Pygott!" Spectacles roared, pumping the Winchester.

"Hot!" Pygott bellowed as he lurched across the room.

Bang! Jowls was still firing from the floor.

Zing! Zing! Ricocheting bullets swarmed around the inside of the steel tank room.

Jerry spun beneath a fan, ducked under the Winchester and then pushed the gun's long barrel up over his head—

chang!

Corset's other kung fu fan skittered off the rifle's barrel and missed Jerry again. Sparks arced down from the contact onto the back of Jerry's hair and neck and he gasped from the quick pain. Corset stepped aside, Pygott charged—

Boom!

Spectacles fired the Model 1876. The bullet hit Pygott in the chest and he staggered back, arms windmilling aimlessly through the smoke-burned air. He stepped on Jowls, right in the chubby man's belly.

"Oof!" Jowls grunted.

Bang!

Zing!

Jerry spun Spectacles by the barrel of his rifle, tossing the long-haired dirty barbarian into his gigantic-pored slut and yanking the Winchester free. While she batted him aside and they both tangled up Pygott's thundering steps, Jerry kicked open the hatch of the nearest railgun.

The inside didn't really look like a gun at all. It looked like an empty tube with twin tracks running up the inside of it. Jerry ripped the lid off the crate of SHELLS—

kicked back with both feet like a mule to push the *quai loh* fan woman off-balance again—

whipped out a shell—

shoved it into the railgun and rammed the barrel of the Model 1876 in front of it—

then spun around again, a set of chopsticks in each hand, and lunged to the attack.

Bang!

This time Jowls hit Jerry, in the thigh. Jerry slipped and almost fell, just as a storm of bladed green fans crashed down upon him.

He was off-balance and sliding; he'd never catch the attack in time.

Jerry threw himself to the ground and rolled.

"Blast 'im!" Jowls hollered.

Jerry knocked Corset in the knees and she tumbled over him, falling to the ground. As he rolled, he looked for his other adversaries. Spectacles had yanked the door open and was charging through it, back up to the wheelhouse. Pygott was a chaotic flailing terror of enormous fists and feet; his hat had been knocked off, his face smeared with oil and chilies and thick fumes billowing out of his sportscoat.

Bang!

Jowls missed, and Jerry had had enough of the man in the top hat. He finished his roll with one arm extended, hammering down and pounding two chopsticks through Jowls's throat as hard as he could.

He heard the dull wooden *snap* as the chopsticks punched all the way through the foreigner's neck and broke off against the steel of the floor. The Colt 1851 Navy *clattered* heavily as he dropped it.

Jowls gurgled and died.

Jerry spun on his shoulders and kicked with both feet again—his injured leg was slower and weaker, but the kick was still enough to push Corset back again. Her bonnet finally fell from her head as she flew backward, but one of her whirling fans nicked Jerry on his good leg, below the knee.

"*Diu nei lou mou* on all greasy barbarian whores!" Jerry shouted.

He somersaulted backward and staggered unsteadily to his feet, pulling Pygott's bowler hat up with him as he did. He ducked under a drunken punch from Pygott and kicked open the hatch of the second railgun—

and Corset charged him again.

He threw the bowler hat.

It wasn't much of a weapon, but it was flat-brimmed and relatively aerodynamic. The hat sailed straight for Corset's face.

She cringed back—

Pygott lurched by, flailing blindly and teetering from one foot to the other—

Jerry grabbed Pygott's arm, tucked himself low under the big automaton's center of gravity—

and threw him head-first into the railgun.

THUNK!

Bull's eye. Pygott jammed his own head deep into the railgun's open hatch.

The sound of the collision was huge in the steel room.

A steel fan sliced along the ribs under Jerry's shoulder blade.

"*Diu nei lou mou*, you goat-fornicating wanton!" he hollered, and fell forward.

Swish! The follow-up attack sliced another hole in Jerry's tunic and parted his skin, but it was a narrow cut and he threw himself at the stairs. On the way he grabbed Jowls's pistol.

He felt the next attack coming by the timing more than anything else. Halfway up the stairwell he spun back and kicked with his less-injured leg, following with a slash of chopstick fist-fangs.

He missed, and missed, and then he was dragging himself back up the stairs on the palms of his hands, thrashing down at Corset as best he could with legs that throbbed and ached with every movement. Thank all gods for adrenalin, he thought.

"There's the Chinaman!" "Get him!" Jerry heard as he tumbled backward on the wheelhouse floor. He had no attention to spare to see who was shouting. If Jowls had kept his pistol fully loaded, Jerry had one shot left.

He pointed the gun at Corset and squeezed the trigger.

She ducked.

Click.

Diu nei lou mou on all chickenshit barbarians who are afraid of their own gun going off in their pockets, he cursed mentally, and flung the chopsticks at Corset.

She deflected them easily with a fan and charged.

Jerry slammed the door shut, its mild *bang!* lost in the sounds of booted feet rattling around the deck of the *Sea Witch*. He flipped the empty pistol around in his hand and smashed its grip down like a hammer on the locked wheelhouse panel.

He was vaguely aware of sailors surrounding the wheelhouse, holding rifles and harpoons.

Clang!

The lock fell off. Underneath was a smooth plate, neatly bisected. Each half of the plate contained a matching set of simple controls, with levers to change the elevation and direction of the respective gun, and a button labeled *FIRE.*

Fire erupted up Jerry's spine as a steel fighting fan cut into his flesh. He fell forward—

onto the panel—

and punched both buttons.

K-k-k-k-rang-ng-ng-ng!

Jerry had expected the sound of an explosion, and instead there was an enormous tearing sound. The *Sea Witch* jumped, like a horse with a nail suddenly driven into its hoof, and when it landed, it didn't land level.

Corset hit the floor hard and bounced once. Seamen stumbled as the deck under their feet bucked.

Jerry, already pressed against the panel, was the only one in sight not to lose his balance. He threw open the wheelhouse door and lunged for the railing.

"Stop him!" he heard Spectacles shout.

Bang! Bang!

Then Lieutenant Xu Hao Dong hit the water and was out of the reach of the filthy barbarians.

He surfaced fifty feet away in the darkness, laughing despite the oily slick that the water of Aberdeen Harbor left in his mouth. He laughed harder when he saw the hole the size of a dinner plate in the *Sea Witch's* hull.

And he laughed hardest of all when he dragged himself by the strength of his arms out of the water and flopped onto the wooden planks of the quay. He laughed because he found himself lying on top of Pygott's mustache, still attached to the rest of Pygott's lower face. Jerry picked up the fragment of Pygmalion and examined it under the gaslights.

He marveled now that he had missed the fact that Pygott's face was metallic. The jaw was cleverly hinged and the skin was mysteriously elastic, but it didn't look human at all.

But the brassy lips of the detached mouth smiled at him oddly, and were pursed together as if Pygott might have been blown to smithereens in the act of once again declaring the Kung Pao Chicken "sweet."

And the mouth and chin and mustache were all shiny with oil and chilies.

ARISE THOU NIARLAT FROM THY REST

Nathan Shumate invited me to submit a short story for his ground-breaking Space Eldritch anthology. This was my first attempt at Lovecraftian fiction (I wrote three more for Nathan, all in this volume), which is much darker and more fatalistic than what I generally write. Also, this was my first work composed with Scrivener, a piece of writing software with which I ultimately wrote several short stories, but which has never (to date) captured my heart, despite some excellent functions.

Jack Kale was something of an homage, a reference to a character created by my friend Erik Holmes for his novel, Sword of Worlds. It's also a reference to the kinds of characters Erik created for roleplaying games we played in our youth: competent, tough, no-nonsense, unreconstructed. It is no comment at all upon Erik that I used Kale to communicate an idea about bigotry: that its innate presence in our makeup is due to a low-level survival advantage it confers, but that higher-level success requires us to overcome it.

"Is this enough blood?"

Sa-Niarlat, born Senwosret, high priest of the venerable complex of Huut-Niarlat, gazed down from the height of the valley temple. Once, the plains behind him and across the river's gorge had been lush and wet with rain. There had been no valley temple then, and no need for one. Men had traveled freely on roads that cut through meadows and forests to bring them to the temple overlooking the river. Sa-Niarlat knew, for he had seen it, lying in utter darkness in the god's heka-barge and breathing in the greasy yellow fumes of durhang.

There had been sacrifices, yes, blood shed under the eyeless gaze of the god. And the sacrifices had been effective. Blood had whetted the god's appetite, and his saliva had watered the plains and raised the emmer, the einkorn, the barley, and the sheum that had given life to tens of thousands.

Now, below the gates of the valley temple, angry men took each other's lives in tens of thousands. The incense-stink of hot blood filled Sa-Niarlat's head with giddy delight. Almost, it gave him visions.

When the new gods had come, the plains had dried up; there had not been enough sacrifices to water them and the god's presence had withdrawn, into the void and his state of black, blessed rest. Other sanctuaries to the god had been burned but not sacked, their treasures left to rot and tarnish as cursed. The sands had come and covered the land. The roads had been lost, and the river had replaced the road. Then the valley temple had become necessary, a gate at the river of the level that opened into a passage sheltered by long sandstone walls leading up to the temple at the bluff behind it.

The valley temple had become necessary, and the deception. Sa-Niarlat, who rejoiced in a name bearing his god's blessing and the glorious titles Helmsman of the God's Black Barge, Feeder at His Father's Teat, and Lector of the Black Book, passed before the world as the humbler, poorer Senwosret, Keeper of Secrets of Sebek the Crocodile.

It was Sebek's image that adorned the valley temple, in two immense statues flanking the valley temple's gates, and in plaster-and-paint murals within it. To a careful observer with an eye learned in the ancient signs, the statues and murals would have revealed something else: a Sebek hexed and impotent, a puppet, and behind him, a true, ancient, and hungry power, waiting with cold thirst for a sacrifice large enough, satiating enough, to bring it and its blessings back to its ancient lair.

But there were few such eyes that might see the statues and murals, and fewer still that were not themselves adepts of the temple. Most of the traffic through the valley temple, up the long passage and into the Forecourt, consisted of supplicants of the crocodile, and they had no idea who really heard their prayers.

Heard them and laughed, hungry, and waiting to make his black return.

Of the temple's staff, the large majority did not know whom they truly served. Even Pa-Ankhi, Captain of the Gate, the burly Asiatic at Sa-Niarlat's side.

"Enough blood for what, Pa-Ankhi?"

The soldier gestured below. The last of the temple's defenders outside the walls were subdued. Screaming men were dragged beneath one of the statues of Sebek even as the attackers threw ropes around the monument. Dozens of arms gripped the ropes and pulled, chanting effeminate Theban hymns in unison.

The screams ended in a single wet thump.

The temple would fall, Sa-Niarlat saw. The fire-eyed zealots of Thebes would desecrate the god's earthly darkness, the valley's last hope of fertility and abundance would disappear, and the sands of the infinite desert would well and truly come. Sa-Niarlat and the god's other disciples had not yet amassed enough heka, the vital power-within-the-blood, and did not have a large enough flock of sacrifices, willing or unwilling, to supplement. The god was too far away, and Sa-Niarlat could not summon him.

Unless...

Sa-Niarlat reached within his robe and laid his hand on the obsidian knife that always lay next to his skin.

"Enough blood to convince you that I was right, Keeper of Secrets? That your mysteries are not worth the price it would take to preserve them? That you should have cooperated with the priests of Amun, and permitted them into the sanctuary of Sebek, as all the other priests have done?"

The Asiatic leaned forward and spat over the parapet at the jeering Thebans. When he turned back to face Sa-Niarlat, the high priest slashed him with the knife across his throat.

"Ia Niarlat!"

Pa-Ankhi sank to the stone with a look of surprise on his face.

"No," Sa-Niarlat told his dying Captain. "There has not been enough blood. Not yet. Not nearly."

Blood.

He wiped with numb hands at the crystalline firmament in front of him, looking for a revelation in all the red globular brilliance. He found a face.

Did he know the face? He couldn't be sure. It was a woman's, not particularly pretty, but somehow dear to him. Or hated.

No, not hated. The face he loved was meat, the meaningless face of a cow.

He realized that he was floating.

But he... *he*... who was *he?* He realized in a moment of total loss that he had no idea.

Worse, he had a terrible feeling that there might be more than one answer to the question.

Who are we? he thought, mind flailing.

A shriek stabbed his ears.

The woman behind the crystal firmament opened her eyes. She stared at him through the firmament, slapping long nails against the clear barrier that restrained her.

He smiled, feeling turmoil within himself he couldn't identify. In his hand he found a stone.

Raising it behind his head, he smashed it down on the crystal. The force of the blow pushed him backward, away from the woman. The sack of blood.

She screamed again.

Captain James Rodriguez sat up and smacked his face into the lid of his Hypnotube.

"Ouch!" He tried to rub his nose but couldn't reach it in the narrow slot that carried him while the *NACSS Temerario* traveled in Nullspace. He heard the soft hiss and felt a gentle sucking at his hip and then a hypodermic needle jabbed him.

"Edison!" he cursed.

The Hypnostasis emergence procedure had gotten garbled. He was an experienced Nullship pilot, and had been through Hypnostasis many times. At the end of the voyage, the ship injected you with a stimulant that slowly brought you up, and by the time you were awake, the Tube was open.

That was true whether the ship's systems woke you up because you had reached your destination, or because some combination of data gathered by the ship's sensors triggered emergence.

James caught his breath.

The hypodermic had jabbed him when he was already awake.

So what had brought him out of Hypnostasis?

James put his fingers to his hip and probed. He only felt one tender spot. Could the hypodermic have poked him twice in the same point? And what side effects would a double dosage of the emergence cocktail have?

He shook his head. He'd ask Chaz. In any case, the *Temerario* was a long way from the nearest Terran system, and it was a bad thing if any of its systems was malfunctioning. The North American Confederacy's colonizing ship had left the fringes of Terran space behind at its last entry into Nullspace, twenty-five hundred hypnostatic souls aboard and bound for a recently terraformed Class M planet owned by the Confederacy. Captain Rodriguez was to christen the planet (*Wellman's World*, and when asked by the curious to explain the choice, he shrugged the blame off onto the inexplicable whimsy of bureaucrats), deposit the colonists, remain in orbit until they had shelter and a Nullspace Communicator in place, and then return.

In and out, a freight run, nothing to write home about. Certainly not as glamorous as the actions against pirates James had flown as a young Navy officer, or even his later Customs work shutting down smugglers making the lucrative Mars Run through the asteroid belt of the Terran Home System. Though if the *Temerario* were malfunctioning, this freight run might be about to get significantly more exciting.

But really, all the Hypnochamber had done was garble up its awakening sequence slightly. There was nothing to indicate that anything had gone seriously wrong aboard ship.

He forced aside the nagging question of what had awoken him.

The Hypnotube *chunked* cheerfully and its lid split down the middle, parting and sliding open in both directions. The inrushing canned air of the ship's Hypnochamber made James realize how much worse the Hypnotube air smelled. It was the stink of his own body, too much, too close, and too long.

He threw one leg out of the Hypnotube, then the other.

The light in the Hypnochamber was amber. He raised his head enough to poke it out of the Hypnotube and look around; the other Tubes were open, but the rest of the crew lay still asleep. They'd been injected like James, but were waking up at the normal, gradual rate. The *Temerario's* captain relaxed, just a little. There was no indication that the ship's malfunction, if there had even been one, had been anything other than limited.

He pushed with elbows and shoulders and forced his body out of the Hypnotube in a ragged lurch.

James shook his head. Maybe it was the dream that had woken him. You weren't supposed to dream in Hypnostasis. He never had, and he'd never heard of anyone else doing it, either. And what in the name of Leibniz kind of dream had that been, anyway? So much blood. Actual spilled blood was a rarity in Naval warfare, mostly seen in boarding actions, which were uncommon—space was large, and ships shot at each other over great distances. A Navy man saw gore mostly in accidents, or dirtside brawls.

A wave of dizziness and nausea swept over James. He thought he smelled blood for a moment, and hot sand. The tight Ultraceramic walls of the Hypnochamber swung around him like the enclosure of a

G-force training simulation. He sucked in the plastic-tinged air of the
Temerario's recycling tanks, feelings its stale tang tickle his lungs.

Amber light meant that the *Temerario* had terminated Hypnostasis
early for some reason, so James touched the interactive wall panels to
find out why.

Or he tried to touch them, anyway, and discovered that he couldn't.
His right arm hung numb and useless at his side.

"Newton," he cursed, and used his left. He shook his arm at the
shoulder as he worked, trying to get blood to flow back into it. Must
have cut off circulation, wedged into the Tube like that, he thought.
Or maybe this was the result of getting the emergence injection twice.

The touch panel lit up under his fingers, in Basic Mode. He tried to
direct it to activate Standard Mode, but the icon remained stubbornly
inert as he punched it over and over again.

"Chaz," he said, and because the computer didn't answer to its
nickname, he shouted it: "Chaz!"

Nothing.

"Computer. Ship's computer, *NACSS Temerario*."

Still nothing.

He growled under his breath. Fine. He could do this; it would just
take a little longer.

Dredging more complicated procedures from his memory, procedures designed for emergency situations in which the higher functions
of the ship's computers had been disabled—usually by power loss—
James asked for more information.

He would have liked visual representations of the data, schematics
he could rotate to view at any angle, colored spectographic reconstruc-
tions. Instead, he got line after line of numerical data. His eyes blurred
trying to read it, his head hurt, and his breath came short. He leaned
against the bulkhead, smelling again the unexpected combination of
heated sand and blood. Far away, he thought he heard screaming in a
language he didn't understand. Olfactory hallucinations, he thought
grimly, and now auditory.

James sighed and ran the fingers of his left hand through thinning
hair, letting his senses drift back to normal. He'd ask Chaz for a sedative, he resolved, just as soon as he was sure it was safe to do so.

He forced himself to look at the numbers again. It wasn't immediately obvious to him what they meant. Gravity. Gravity and mass, as if there were a planet, he thought. Only there was no planet. Wellman's World was still lightyears away. From James's recollection of the time-adjusting star charts and data over which he'd pored back at Dunsany, he thought the nearest significant mass of *any* sort should be lightyears away.

But there was something. If it was an asteroid or similar mass, it had moved awfully fast to get into the *Temerario's* path, which had been carefully charted through empty space. If it was a ship... James looked at the data again and blinked... it was *enormous*.

"Sandhu..." He turned back to the Hypnotubes to see if the *Temerario's* science officer was awake and functional yet.

Blood.

There was blood spattered on the floor of Hypnochamber, and the rest of the crew was gone.

Except one. One of the Hypnotubes had someone in it.

"Vito?" The Tube belonged to Vittorio Moroni, the ship's medical officer.

James stepped closer, feeling a knot of dread in his chest.

Vito looked peaceful. He might have been still in Hypnostasis, but for the fact that his throat was slit and blood soaked the blue tunic of his uniform.

"Vito!" James reached for his fellow-officer's corpse, again instinctively using his right hand—

which didn't respond.

James looked down at his own hand, biting back a curse.

The hand was red with blood.

"Hop to it, doc!"

Jack Kale roared like an angry ape as he threw his heavy shoulder against the door. The howling on the other side was inarticulate, deprived of consonants, and mad. The door shuddered, nearly throwing Jack to the floor.

The frayed veteran of the Great War and sometime private man of violence threw aside his Thompson. Without a loaded drum, the gun was useless, anyway. He drew his service pistol, a battered but meticulously cleaned and oiled M1911, and jerked back the slide.

"I *am* hurrying."

"I'm saving two shots for us, professor!" Kale yelled. "No way I'm having my liver plucked out on some ginny altar!"

"They're not Italians."

"No? Coulda fooled me."

"Did they seem particularly Italian to you when they were eating Carver's intestines?"

Kale snorted. "Put garlic on it, and a wop'll eat anything."

Randolph Choate nodded his retreat from the argument, trying to ignore the tumult and focus. Lemurian was hard to read in the best of circumstances, with its obscure determinatives and its recursive ergative syntax. It was harder when a bloodthirsty mob of worshippers of a dead god wanted to distract you.

Or sacrifice you to their blasphemous anthropophagous deity, as they had done to so many others. The kidnappings, the newspapers' 'mob violence,' the rash of murders and the warehouse fires on the Miskatonic—all sacrifices, all feeding and summoning the god.

He blinked away a sheet of orange. The colors in Randolph's vision were beginning to bleed into each other, fade, and sometimes shimmer. Objects telescoped closer and further away as he looked at them. He wasn't sure how well his mind was holding together, at this point. Too many revelations. The truth was dangerous, and an open mind was a vulnerable one.

The god was emphatically not dead, he reminded himself. Remote, perhaps. Trapped, hopefully. Dangerously close to emerging. The stars pointed to it, with their conjunctions in forgotten constellations. The ancient Lemurian prophecies were emphatic, and the enthusiastic activity of the cultists certainly suggested they thought something was about to happen.

The mob hit the door again and one of the hinges burst free, pinging across the room and disappearing in darkness.

The basement of the Burroughs manor was lit only by the kerosene lamp Randolph held over the stone tablet in his hand. Kale had brought a flashlight, but, as Randolph had predicted, the electricity in the device had begun to fade as the Gate opened. Even the lamp guttered, as if an unfelt wind sucked at its flame.

The cold, dark thing on the other side drank in the power and grew. Power and blood, Randolph thought. On some level, the same thing, as the ancient Hebrews had well known.

Carver had been right; the museum had been easy to rob. Randolph only wished he'd foreseen that the Burroughs Coven would be after the same tablet. He didn't know what he would have done differently, but something, he was sure. He would have proceeding more cunningly, and Carver would not now be dead.

Carver had made a sacrifice, Randolph thought. A choice, a hard choice, showing willingness to give life for the greater good. It was up to his friends to make the journalist's death meaningful. Also Delilah's, he forced himself to articulate in his mind, and he willed himself not to think of the writer hanging herself by the neck from the hotel balcony after reading a mere Latin paraphrase of the very tablet he now held in his hand.

The lamp illuminated the tablet and picked out in yellow a ragbag of details in the basement. Randolph couldn't explain them all, or interpret them. The two chipped and eroded statues of the Egyptian crocodile deity Sebek, for instance, that squatted on either side of the black, lichen-crusted wall seemed out of place, though the Egyptian incantations scratched about their bases were appropriate enough. *Niarlat live, Niarlat watch, Niarlat come*, over and over. *Arise thou Niarlat from thy rest* was as eloquent as the graffitoes got. Between and before the statues lay a broad, low altar of stone, and the lamp cast enough light for Randolph to see the runnels carved in its surface and in the floor, leading away into dark, unpenetrated corners of the hall.

The air was damp and cold from the proximity of the Miskatonic. Randolph squeezed his fingers into fists to force blood into them and ran a chewed fingernail under a row of elusive characters.

"Blood," he said out loud. "Blood opens the gate and awakens the monster. Enough blood, and the right incantations. Blood there has been." He peered into the darkness between the Sebek-idols. "And if the gate opens? What closes it?"

"Toldja we shoulda brought dynamite!" Kale skidded six inches away from the door as a force on the other side pounded into it, then fought his way back, the hem of his stained trench coat flapping around his ankles. "Or a cement truck! Fill this whole damn cellar with wet cement, it'd take the ginnies twenty years just to dig it out, much less fill it with blood."

"If only I had a time machine," Randolph lamented. "I could have driven here in a cement truck."

"If you had a time machine," Kale grunted, "we coulda gone back to when this Niarlat's ma was pregnant, and whacked her." He pronounced the name in a way that rhymed with *beer hat*.

"Niarlat, you mean."

"He and his ma got the same name? That's messed up. No wonder he's so pissed off."

Randolph found the line he needed, and reread it. An incantation, a hex that would damage the gate, and maybe destroy it altogether.

As Jack Kale spewed a stream of obscenities directed at all of America's immigrant communities, he read it again, to be sure he'd understood.

"Jack," he said slowly. "I'm going to have to leave you for a few minutes."

"*Leave?*" Jack snorted. "Where you going? There ain't but the one door—" he grunted, slamming his full weight against the door in question, "and that way is suicide."

"There are two exits from this place." Randolph sighed.

Both doors might be suicide. It was a hard choice, but he had to respect Carver's sacrifice. Whatever the cost, he had to stop the black god.

The sun edged towards the Akhet, and beyond the line of the horizon the darkness of the Duat, to be caressed in the sacred, penetrating embrace of the god. Almost, salvation could be called. Sa-Niarlat climbed down from Pa-Ankhi's roan horse at the pylon giving entrance to the Forecourt. A young initiate, head shaved but the tattooing not yet begun, took the animal's reins.

"Master," the initiate whimpered, brown eyes liquid with despair, "we're all doomed."

"Child." Sa-Niarlat smiled benevolently. "Though the time is not of my choosing, I believe I must now teach you the sacred knowledge of the Dark Chamber."

"Will you take me into the Inner Court?" The boy's chin trembled. He was a merchant's son, an innocent, an idiot, a beast. He was blood only, worthless for any other purpose.

Sa-Niarlat shook his head. "Kneel."

The boy knelt, and Sa-Niarlat chanted a quick hymn to the god. The boy's brow furrowed at the words he didn't recognize, words older than Narmer, older even than Huut-Niarlat itself.

"What sacred knowledge?"

"You already possess this knowledge," Sa-Niarlat said. "My errand is only to point it out."

The boy frowned. "What knowledge?"

"We're all doomed."

The knife flashed black in the reddish glow of the sun sinking into the western desert, and the boy fell to the sand.

The horse, an animal trained for war, snorted patiently. Sa-Niarlat killed it too, mingling its blood with the boy's. Hot red liquid spurted over Sa-Niarlat's sandals, and he let it, reveling in the feeling of warm, sticky toes.

Below, the sound of the valley temple's gate crashing to the ground came as a muffled, faraway *tumph*. One gate opened, Sa-Niarlat thought, with satisfaction and sacred, ecstatic despair. Soon he would open another. Men and horses flowed into the opening, singing a song Sa-Niarlat did not know and did not fear. His god was coming, and his god would silence the squealing of the piglets of Thebes.

The Keeper of Secrets carried the dagger openly in his hand as he strode into the Forecourt. Papyrus columns bordered a square space that was open to the sky. On the inward-facing sides of the pillars were carved and painted the stories of Sebek familiar to his worshippers.

On the reverse sides of the columns, facing into the shadowy, star-speckled passage that surrounded the court, were more surprising images.

Adepts and initiates gathered around Sa-Niarlat. The true ignorant followers of Sebek stared in awe at the weapon in his hand, no doubt imagining that he had bloodied it in defense of their blind and impotent crocodile idol.

Those who had been to the Dark Chamber merely looked at his red footprints and nodded.

"Brothers," Sa-Niarlat addressed them. "Children. It is time."

"Gabe! Sandhu!" James banged on the intercom panel, but no one answered.

Wait... were they dead? Someone was dead, he dimly thought, but he couldn't remember who. He had heard screaming. Was it someone far away, maybe? Someone a long time ago? Someone on a hot, sandy beach?

His face itched. His heart screamed dully into his throat. Was it the *Temerario's* passengers? He remembered something wrong with the ship's Hypnostasis system. Had Chaz murdered the entire population of Wellman's World?

Who was Chaz?

Maybe the science officer and first mate weren't answering because they had been killed on burning sand, their blood seeping into the path of the oncoming Theban horde, a warhorse sacrificed on top of their bodies.

He shook his head, snapping the fog back into the corners of his consciousness. Nightmares. He'd never heard of the emergence cocktail having side effects like this, but then he'd never heard of anyone overdosing on it. "Tesla!"

Something had gone wrong in Nullspace. There was something... he tried to remember... *outside* the ship, and it had made things go wrong. He was jumpy, sick. Crazy? Overdosing. In Basic Mode, Chaz wouldn't dispense the sedative that James desperately needed, because

James couldn't remember how to give it the right instruction. Especially not in this state; the more he tried to focus, the more vague the details of Chaz's operation became.

But he remembered this: the bridge had an emergency kit, a physical box bolted under the captain's chair that could be accessed without any assistance whatsoever from the computer.

He lurched into the passage outside the Hypnochamber.

Had he killed someone? How many people? He felt numb.

The passage was lit by the white emergency strip at floor level. Even the ceiling emergency strip was dead, which meant something had really leeched their power. James racked his brain, trying to think of phenomena that could have done this. Had he mischarted their course, and flown them through a star? But Gabe had checked his figures, and besides, if that had happened, they'd be dead and atomized, or in a bottomless wormhole of their own creation, or... he racked his brain, trying to remember all the nightmare scenarios the astrophysicists had played out for his Nullspace Navigation classes at the Academy. They were terrible, but they all resulted in destruction or isolation, permanent exile from physical reality. None of them led to drained batteries.

The lift didn't respond.

Behind the lift's tube and all along it ran an emergency ladder. Even without the lift, the entire ship was accessible. Downward lay the twenty-five hundred Tubes of the colonists, as well as the escape pods and most of the functional parts of the ship. Engines, life support, the minimal weaponry that the ship carried, mostly to deter the pirates that travelers outside of Terran space occasionally encountered. Upward lay the bridge.

James grabbed the rungs of the ladder just as the *Temerario's* artificial gravity gave out and *up* and *down* ceased to exist. He didn't really notice the sudden weightlessness, though. He was anchored to the rung, and besides, he couldn't take his eyes off his hand.

It was covered in blood, and held a large, black flake of stone. Like a caveman, he thought. Like a caveman, slaughtering animals to eat. Or sacrificing to his ancient beast-headed gods.

He felt a warm feeling in his heart at the thought, and smelled sand again.

He flexed the limb's muscles. His arm was strong. That seemed wrong to him, but he wasn't sure why.

Launching himself with toes against the rungs of the ladder, James ascended towards the bridge.

Blam! Blam! Blam!

Jack Kale leaned away from the door with one foot jammed under it, his M1911 punching thumb-sized holes through the wood. If the door were bigger, and there were more room on the other side for the cultists to mass together and pool their efforts, Randolph guessed that they would already have trampled his brawny friend into the mud and be in the room.

As it was, Kale looked exhausted.

"I could use a hand here!" Kale shouted. "Like a magic sword! Or a big fighting wolf! Or grant me three wishes, so I can wish these freakin' ginnies into guinea *pigs!*" He leaned into the door again to eject his clip, then rummaged for bullets in the pocket of his trench coat. "Ain't you supposed to be a wizard?"

"You're no fencer, Jack. What would you even do with a sword if you had one?" Randolph dug into the deep pockets of his coat, looking for the things he needed. A tallow made of human fat, with its wick fashioned from a grave shroud that had wrapped the same corpse. A ball of his own hair, carefully collected over weeks. A knife only ever sharpened on flint. Chalk he had dug from the earth himself. Other collected oddments he shoved aside, not needing them for the conjuring he planned.

"I'd stab me some ginnies, is what I'd do. It's a sword, whaddya think I'd do with it?"

"Touché."

Randolph Choate was not so naive as to believe in anything like white magic, any more than he believed in fairies, angels, happy endings, or beautiful women who were attracted to gangly professors of Hellenistic esoterica. Magic started at gray, and shaded quickly into a blackness darker than most people could imagine. Randolph tried his best to stay in the gray.

Whenever possible.

He knelt and wedged his hair under the door. The muttering on the other side didn't sound human, but like a muffled and half-heard argument among goats.

Curiosity stopped him for a moment to listen, and he would have sworn that the *sound* of the chittering, howling voices on the other side was *pink*.

Pink soft, pink warm, pink inviting. Come join us safe join us lovely join us pink pink pink.

He tore away his attention. He was, he knew, running out of mind.

Time, blast it. He was running out of *time*.

He jammed the candle under the juddering door and chalked four Lemurian glyphs on the crumbling gray cement of the floor. Then he cut himself, and bled onto the spell-contraption.

"Jiminy," Kale muttered. Randolph ignored him.

He felt strength ebb from his body as he chanted the words of the spell. This exercise had seemed like a game, back at the University. Now, any minute he could gain in holding back the horde was a minute more he had in which to defeat their god.

Not defeat. Thwart, misdirect, close the path before. It was the gate that was his target, not the Sleeper in the Void. Anyone foolish enough to attempt to defeat the great Resting Niarlat of the Abyss deserved what he got.

A tiny part of his mind saw his flowing blood and felt there was something... mistaken... about it. An error.

The door stopped shaking. *Thumps* and *crashes* from the other side suggested that the parties that wanted entrance continued to pound on the door, but it now held firm as if it were a stone wall.

Randolph stood.

He turned and headed for the idols. "It won't hold long."

"Thanks. Hey, uh... you're still bleeding."

Randolph held up his hand and looked at the gray ichor running from his palm. He smiled, ignoring the failure of his eyes. "I've never

known a magic spell that was ruined by the addition of a little blood."
He continued towards the gate, limping from exhaustion and pain.

"I'd feel a lot better if you'd tell me what you're doing."

"I'd feel a lot better if I knew."

He knelt before the gate. Unsure what to do about the statues of Sebek, he knelt between them rather than in front of them, to face the darkness beyond rather than the idols themselves.

It was a scientific operation, he told himself. It was taking local action in ways that produced remote effect, according to known and predictable patterns, following the scientific, procedural instructions on the Lemurian tablet. You could call it magic, if you liked, but that did nothing to change its essential character.

And it definitely wasn't *prayer*.

Pretending he wasn't lying to himself, Randolph Choate began to chant.

He couldn't wait until the god arrived. If the god arrived, it brought utter ruin with it.

He had to go where the god was, and lead Niarlat astray.

"This is astonishing."

Gabe yanked the emergency kit from underneath the captain's chair. In the sudden aftermath of gravity loss he yanked too hard, and sent himself gliding across the small bridge, thumping into one of Chaz's inert panels. The emergency kit banged him in the chest, and droplets of blood from the wounds he'd sustained trying to save Vito's life scattered in a fine red mist about the bridge.

He was painfully aware that between him and his wife prowled his batshit-crazy captain, with Vito Moroni's blood on his hands. This was supposed to have been Gabe's last haul with the Navy. At Wellman's World he retired, so he could farm and Annie could teach school.

"I'm interested in two things right now," Gabe grunted. "If you can get the power on again, great. If you can help me subdue the captain, great. Anything else, right now, fails to make my give-a-damn list."

"I think it's a wormhole," Balbinder Sandhu said, ignoring Gabe. "But there's something inside it. Something huge."

"Huh."

"And maybe organic."

"Congratulations. You've discovered space whales."

Sandhu missed both the joke and the irritation in Gabe's voice. Gabe undid the latches on the captain's emergency kit, scattering tubes of antiseptic cream, painkillers, and adhesive bandages in all directions around him in a slow-moving cloud.

He grabbed the stungun.

Gabriel Goldman had just watched Jim Rodriguez slaughter his own medical officer like a farm animal. Not *watched* as a passive bystander; Gabe had tried to intervene, and for his trouble had been beaten and cut by his captain, who somehow had a big bit of sharp stone in his hand, like volcanic glass.

And...

Gabe felt dizzy. He sucked canned air into his lungs and drifted, thumping his skull gently against the bulkhead. The gray light of the bridge faded to a dimly-pulsing black and he struggled to hold onto the stungun.

It was the sudden shift to zero-g, he thought as he fought back from the brink of unconsciousness. And the Hypnostasis emergence cocktail still coursing through his veins.

Gabe caught himself against an inert computer panel and shook it off.

"What have you got there?"

Gabe grunted. "Glad you can tear yourself away from the screen, Bal. It's the stungun we came for." He held up his hand with the stungun in it—

only it wasn't the stungun.

It was a stone tablet.

The tablet was the size of Gabe's two hands put together and worn smooth all around its edges. Glyphs that might have been little letters and might have been little pictures marched up and down both sides in columns, surrounding two different central images. On the obverse side was what looked like an opening between two doorposts. The space between the two posts was carved out and flakes of some ancient paint lingered in the depression. On the reverse was a... a monster.

Gabe shook himself, feeling an uncomfortable tingling in his spine. Monster? Why a monster? Tentacles for a head and three arms and legs didn't make a creature a monster. It was just a nonhuman life form, unknown to Lieutenant Gabriel Goldman, despite his long years spent getting to know the worst bars in every ragged port of known space. But there was something about the image that was troubling. Wrong. It seemed different each time Gabe blinked, and the shape of it... didn't work. The geometry of it was tangled. Things that necessarily had to be behind were before, and vice versa.

A thing of too many dimensions. Gabe shuddered. Just looking at the images made him feel... uncomfortable. Out of place. Wrong.

"That's doesn't look like NACSS issue," Sandhu said. It might have been a joke, but there was a strong note of fear in his voice.

Thud!

The sound came from the emergency ladder.

Gabe had a moment of panic, but then found he did have the stungun after all, in his other hand. Where had the tablet come from, then? Had it been inside the emergency kit? Was that someone's idea of a joke? Or was someone in the crew hiding it?

But who would have access to the bridge? For all his war stories about busting tariff runners above Mars, was Jim Rodriguez an antiquities smuggler? It made no sense at all. Even if he was, there was no one on Wellman's World to smuggle antiquities *to*.

It didn't matter now. Gabe pushed gently off the wall and drifted parallel the opening of the shaft.

Jim Rodriguez banged his way bridgeward in the ladder's tunnel. He didn't move like the trained and experienced astronaut that he was, though. He moved like the worst of dirtsiders, like an untrained bear, slamming his elbows and head against the walls and muttering words Gabe could hear but didn't understand, or even recognize. It might have been the same gibberish he'd been shouting when he'd slit Vito's throat and tossed Gabe across the Hypnochamber.

It wasn't just the words that were wrong, though. His voice sounded raspier than it should, and deeper.

"Stop right there, Jim!" Gabe called. He tucked the queer stone tablet under one armpit and aimed the stungun at his drifting captain.

He felt dizzy again and sucked air through his teeth. Sandhu watched at his shoulder.

The *Temerario's* captain shouted his strangled, violent babble again.

"Full stun," Sandhu suggested.

"That your scientific opinion, Bal?" But Gabe had already set the stungun to its maximum setting. At that level, in the best of circumstances, he'd only get off a dozen shots before the energy cell gave out. Given that the something seemed to be draining the power out of the ship, he had no confidence that the 'gun's wasn't also depleted.

Jim shook his fist, spraying blood around the ladder tube, and kicked himself forward.

Gabe hit the fire switch. Golden light flashed in the bridge and in the ladder shaft, and the beam hit Jim—

who kept yelling.

"Again!" Sandhu yelled, pointlessly. The science officer pushed off a wall to throw himself out of the captain's irregular, tumbling path.

Gabe fired twice more, and then he depressed the switch a fourth time and nothing happened.

Jim hurtled out of the shaft in his direction, swinging the object in his hand. The object with which he'd killed Vito, some kind of caveman knife. He still moved like a lubber, showing no sign of his zero-g combat training, which was a blessing. Gabe twisted to one side, the knife narrowly missed him, and he threw his captain against the wall.

Jim hit hard, and for a split second as he impacted into one of Chaz's larger interfaces, all the lights of the bridge snapped on, as did the viewscreens. Gabe saw the impossibly dark black of deep space, the distant twinkling of remote stars, and a thing.

And then the thing was gone. And then it was there again.

It looked like a pit...

...deep... as infinitely deep as the space around it, but in a different direction.

Motion within the pit—a maw—tentacles?

His mind couldn't process what he saw. He felt a ball of ice in the pit of his stomach.

"Help me..." Jim Rodriguez moaned. His voice was streaked with despair, but it sounded like him again.

Gabe jerked his eyes away from the viewscreen. He found he was breathing hard and sweating. "Chaz," he said. "Distance to anomaly?"

"Ten thousand kilometers and closing." Chaz's voice crackled, its North American Standard accent thrown off by the warble.

Sandhu cursed in Punjabi.

"Degree of magnification, Chaz?"

"Zeeeerooooo." Chaz's voice slowed and dropped in pitch. The lights snapped off, and the ship's computer's voice disappeared with them.

Gabe slammed the nearest panel, then kicked it, trying to resuscitate the computer again. Nothing.

"Not enough power," Sandhu said, reading the minimal data that still marched down the dark viewscreens.

"No kidding." Gabe kicked the wall, knocking himself away from it.

"Just about everything we have left is going into life support."

"I'm siiiick," Jim Rodriguez groaned. "Help me."

The *Temerario's* captain trembled, pawing at the bulkhead. He reached out to his science officer with quavering fingers.

"Dammit, Jim," Sandhu whined. "I'm an astrophysicist, not a doctor!"

"My head..." Jim rubbed his temple and squeezed his eyes shut, curling slightly towards a fetal ball as he did so.

Gabe mentally cursed the stunner. Was it broken? Was the cell so depleted that the stun had been ineffective? Or had Jim Rodriguez just shaken off three stungun blasts, any one of which should have dropped a horse in its tracks?

And was it the monster outside that was drinking the ship dry? The same monster that was incised into the stone tablet with the glyphs?

But that was ridiculous. That was impossible.

"Okay," Sandhu agreed. "There's a sedative in the kit."

Gabe laughed, looking at the medical supplies drifting all around the bridge. "Good luck finding it."

Jim whimpered. "The dreams," he said. "Sand and blood."

"There it is." Sandhu dragged himself along a wall towards a spinning sliver, just above Jim's shoulder. Gabe wouldn't even have spotted it in the gloom, barely relieved by a single guttering emergency strip, but it certainly might be a hypodermic. "Got it."

Jim lashed out. His motion was sudden, swift, and sure, and the blow sent Balbinder Sandhu spinning away in a graceful backwards arc, head first, arms out to his side, and fat globules of blood trailing behind him.

Throat slashed open.

"Ia Niarlat!"

The same kinetic energy sent Jim spinning back the other way, into the far corner of the bridge. He hit the bulkhead flat against his back and bounced.

Gabe almost jumped at him then, but in the strangeness of the moment he hesitated. Then Jim regained his balance. The captain glared at his first mate and co-pilot with a malevolent sneer. "Sand and blood," he hissed.

Sandhu's body struck the bridge's main viewscreen in a splatter of red.

Gabe hurled the useless stungun at his captain, gripped the stone tablet tightly in one hand and kicked himself into—*down*—the ladder shaft.

He had to protect the passengers.

"Sand and blood!"

Sa-Niarlat led the entire staff of the temple across the Inner Court. Those who had never seen it before might have stared if they'd had more time; here the papyrus columns were identical to those in the Forecourt, only rotated one hundred eighty degrees, so that the esoteric versions of their tales faced the viewer, and the exoteric versions were turned to the walls.

The esoteric tales were still lies, of course. But they were lies that taught in the direction of the glorious black truth.

The Inner Court had a ceiling, and on it were carved and painted stars. Sa-Niarlat looked back to see some of the Sebek worshippers staring upward as they walked, trying to puzzle out the constellations that were represented. Sa-Niarlat had done the same thing as a youth. Only later, after many sacrifices, had he learned what those stars really were.

He stopped at the Veiled Passage and turned to face the temple staff. The crashing sounds of the Thebans hammering at the doors of the Forecourt were still audible after priests closed the Inner Court's doors.

"The time has come for your ascension to the god's great bark," he told them all.

"Sebek will save us."

"If he does not, we will swim with him in the waters of the sky."

Sa-Niarlat nodded piously. "We will swim with the god," he agreed. "One at a time," he told a Brother of the Dark Chamber, and he ducked to pass through the veil. "As initiates."

He wandered along the row of tombs, trailing blood in his wake, looking into the frozen faces of the dead.

Not dead, something told him. Sleeping, behind plates of glass. He asked himself how he knew that, and found he had no answer.

If they were not dead, he wondered, then why was he flying?

And where did all the blood come from?

He looked into the crystal shroud of one of the bodies and saw that it had been scratched repeatedly with a sharp tool. Long, deep gouges criss-crossed the window, marring the dull light that flowed around the sleeper's face and up into his hand as he traced them with one fingertip.

In the tomb beneath his fingers, which was not a tomb, the dim light illuminating its occupant flickered and died, and then the gouges were no longer visible.

The air felt thick in his lungs. Because it seemed like the right thing to do, he took the stone in his hand and began scratching at the crystal. His stone blade cut deep grooves, but he slammed it with too much force and it flaked, shooting splinters of black glass tumbling in all directions, slicing into the flesh of his own cheeks and forehead.

Under his hands, the tomb shook violently.

A portion of his heart exulted.

Jack Kale finished reloading the drum of his tommy gun and spat on the floor.

The door rattled. The huddled masses yearning to eat his flesh on the other side of it yelled their crazy gobbledygook and howled.

"Go to hell," he told them, and mimed shooting through the door. He held his fire, though. Every second the door could buy them was time for the professor to do his professorish bit. Jack didn't really believe in magic, but he'd seen old Choate stop the door from caving in, and he'd seen him drive away that scaly flying thing with some weird words and the wave of a bit of chicken guts, so who was Jack to judge?

Anyway, whatever it was, Jack's job was simple. Watch the door until it burst open, and then blow as many foreigners to kingdom come as he could manage.

Better light wouldn't hurt. "Professor? You still using that lamp?"

No answer.

Jack tiptoed over the scabby wet cement to Professor Choate. The gaunt old guy lay on the floor, tightly clutching the bit of stone they'd lifted from the museum to his chest. His lips moved and Jack could hear mumbled words, but he couldn't make them out over the howling of the wops. Anyway, Choate wasn't talking to Jack.

He also didn't seem to be using the lamp, so Jack stooped to pick it up.

In the illumination cast down by the raised light, he saw that there was something under the professor.

Not an object, he realized, but an image. That crazy old ginny

Burroughs—Burroughs was an Italian name, wasn't it?—not only had statues of giant crocodiles in his basement, he'd painted a picture on his basement floor.

Jack squinted. Through the lichen and the damp it was hard to be certain, but as best as he could make it out, the painting was of some kind of boat. It was curled up at the front and the back, and it had a canopy on its deck like a tent, and a bunch of bald men pulled at its bank of oars, rowing the boat through a field of stars.

Jack snorted,

"Ginnies."

Randolph Choate blinked and tried to focus. He was seeing through a veil of aqueous humors, he knew, his own perceptive and elective faculties—he hesitated to call them his soul, for the metaphysical and even theological implications of the word—using another man's eyeballs.

He hoped, at least, that his vessel was human.

He looked down, flexing muscles and feeling relief that what he saw were indeed forearms and hands.

But he was flying. Gray walls, featureless but for the rungs of a ladder, flashed before his flooded vision.

He realized he had no sense of up and down. Was this the void? He had expected to find himself in coruscating energy, or the cold depths of space, not a tunnel. Was this hell? Randolph's stomach fluttered, and he thought, for a split second, that it had been too long since he'd been to church.

Not hell, though. Far too prosaic for hell. And yet he was within a tunnel, and moving.

In a cloud of dark mist. Blood?

The vessel struggled to resist. Randolph felt his arms flap spastically, grabbing at the rungs. He missed the catch, but snagged himself and threw off his trajectory. He bounced against the passage wall, spun, hit again, and lost his grip on the Lemurian tablet.

The tablet spun away from him in the weightless void.

Randolph clamped his will hard on the vessel, forcing the enslaved jaw and tongue to utter another Lemurian incantation. The spell took effect and the vessel relaxed; control became easier. With more grace, though not much, he caught himself on the ladder. Flailing in a passage too small for his purposes, he struggled to force the body around and return to where he'd lost the tablet.

The tablet was gone.

Then Randolph saw an opening in the side of the shaft. It was as large as a doorway, and he hadn't seen it because he'd been flying so quickly without gravity. This void, this strange hell-though-there-was-no-hell, was a warren. He pushed himself through the opening and found the tablet, spinning like a top in mid-air.

The vessel seized control of itself. It kicked off one wall, throwing Randolph against the facing surface and slamming his head against it. The wall was made of something that looked like china but felt like metal, and Randolph hurt.

Randolph willed his mastery over the vessel's vocal cords. He chanted in Lemurian again, trying to subdue the vessel. He needed the vessel's body, to get him into position to misdirect the rising demon. And if he couldn't even control the host, how was he to stop the dark god?

The vessel's hand gripped the vessel's throat, trying to squeeze the incantation into silence. Randolph chanted faster, batting at the vessel's free arm with the one he commanded.

The force of the struggle spun him around in the air, and as his vision began to grow dim he saw words clearly stenciled on the wall: HYPNOSTASIS.

The characters and the roots were Latin. Was the word English?

"Stop!" he croaked. "I've come to help!"

It was a gamble; he knew nothing about the person whose body he inhabited.

But the hand eased off, and then the vessel reached over to steady their shared body by touching the wall.

Randolph relaxed his control over the vessel's muscles, clinging tightly with his will to the thread of energy that bound them together. He saw more of the chamber now. It was vast, it curved out of Randolph's sight in two directions, and it was full of steel and glass tubes. Tubes the size of coffins. A red-black cloud of globules slowly spread out into the room from the space Randolph and the vessel occupied together.

"Who are you?" the vessel asked. It was accented strangely, but it was English. "Are you some kind of... what *are* you?"

Randolph took over the talking by a brute exertion of his will. "Randolph Choate. I'm a man. I'm a Virginian, I teach at a university in Massachusetts. I'm here to stop the monster."

"Jim?"

"Niarlat."

Randolph waited through a prolonged silence. He began to wonder if his spell had damaged the vessel's cognition.

"Jim said that name when he... killed people. Niarlat."

"Is Jim an immensely large creature with tentacles for a head?" The conversation was draining on Randolph. He wanted to get it over with, find the dark god and confuse its path. "What powers does Jim serve?"

"Jim is a spaceship captain. He's human. As far as I know he serves the North American Confederacy. But there's a monster outside. I... I can't really describe it."

Randolph considered. He didn't know what *outside* meant in this context, but he didn't want to take the time to find out. The void, he assumed. And he knew the image of the ceremonial bark on which his body lay in the basement of the Burroughs manor was a sort of spaceship, if by spaceship the vessel meant the sort of thing that emerged from the fevered imaginations of Jules Verne and H.G. Wells.

"What's your name?"

"Gabe. Lieutenant Gabriel Goldman."

"Take me to the monster, Lieutenant."

"Uh... that's not possible. Anyway, it's a bad idea, and it would take too long. We'd have to suit up, and that'd take an hour. The monster's outside the ship."

Randolph considered. "Then take me to Jim."

"Jim's dangerous."

"So am I, Lieutenant." Randolph took control of one arm long enough to reach out and grab the spinning tablet. "So am I."

Sa-Niarlat knew the way, and those who would follow him did not. It didn't matter; the way was a straight corridor, with no turns or exits but the door at the end, and the lambs could not get lost.

He had come down this corridor the first time on hands and knees as a young man. He remembered now with a thrill the black terror of that moment, believing still that he was an acolyte of Sebek, though an acolyte who understood that Sebek was a hungry god who sold his blessings to man for blood. He remembered being seized at the door-way, held, threatened, and then cut—

but only enough to make a personal offering to the god. Lying on the runnels, feeling the blood drip from his neck, he'd thought himself doomed. Instead, he'd been dragged to his feet and taken aboard the god's bark, to learn the first oaths of the prow, the mast, and the helm.

He kicked aside his sandals in the darkness, hearing them thud softly against the stone wall of the chamber. With his feet bare, he could tell where he was by the patterns of the channels carved into the floor. He positioned himself beside the entrance into the Dark Chamber, knife in his hand.

He lit no torch. No man had lit a torch in the Dark Chamber, the mooring quay of the god's astral bark, since the first stones of its ceiling had been laid, millennia earlier.

He breathed deep the thick and clotted air. Traces of durhang, and the rich loam of blood.

Sa-Niarlat heard the shuffling scrape of hands and knees patting on sandy stone. He knew from the volume exactly how far away the first lamb was. He knew from the runnels under his toes exactly where to stand, and where to thrust his hand in the darkness, and where to slash with the knife.

He held back the lamb's head to open the throat wound as wide as he could, and thrilled to the feeling of hot blood over his bare feet. He heard with tremulous joy the soft splash of the same blood spilling into the pool in which the bark rested.

Before the second lamb could overtake the first, he dragged the exsanguinating body itself to the lip and threw it into the pool.

"Ia Niarlat," he whispered throatily, his body gripped with lust.

None of the lambs struggled. He had not struggled, when he had been the lamb, but then his sacrifice had been one of consecration and devotion, requiring his whole soul but only a little blood. These lambs served a different purposes. These lambs sacrificed in order that the god's bark would float.

"Why is everything pink?" the vessel Lieutenant Gabriel Goldman asked.

Stop wasting my energy with useless queries. "Because my grip on my sanity is tenuous at best. Apparently the eyesight is the first thing to go."

Gabe chuckled. "*You're* crazy? *I'm* the one talking to a voice in my head."

"Touché, Lieutenant."

"Call me Gabe. Since we're sharing the same body and all. Seems too personal to stand on rank, doesn't it?"

"As you say, Gabe."

"We should be armed. There's twenty-five hundred people sleeping on this ship, including my wife, dammit. I'm their only defense against a crazy guy with a rock."

"We *are* armed."

"I forgot, I'm a crazy guy with a rock, too. What are you going to do, Choate... what am *I* going to do... throw it at him?"

"I'm going to read it."

Randolph didn't know whether he'd be able to read anything. The passage spun and bucked in his visual field. Through the glass panels of the tubes nearest the vessel, he saw pale, ghoulish faces, faces that might have been human. He was afraid to look closer.

"This is all so totally wrong."

"Please." Randolph relaxed, focusing just enough to stay attached to Gabe. "You are a man of earth, yes?"

"I'm a North American."

"That... *thing*... outside your *spaceship* is going to North America if we don't stop it. To a small town in Massachusetts, as it happens. It will kill your twenty-five hundred sleepers first, with as little remorse as if it had swatted a fly. I need to see the thing to stop it, or at least its summoner. Maybe, in his presence, I can cast... I can do what I must."

"Summoner?"

"Jim, I think." It was just a guess, but it was the best Randolph had. "Please."

"Okay," Gabe agreed. "But he's armed, and I'm not, and I'm pretty close to vomiting."

Randolph felt sick, too. His vision swam completely away from him for long seconds.

The vessel Gabe maneuvered himself into the shaft and looked along it. Randolph relaxed; the spinning and the shifting of colors continued, but when he let Gabe be in control it was better. Gabe was comfortable in this unreal environment, and with a flick of his wrists, sent their shared body sliding along the tunnel.

Another man's face appeared at the shaft opening. With him came a swarm of blood droplets, and an obsidian knife glinted in his hand. Randolph almost shouted a warning, but he realized that Gabe must see the other man, too, and he conserved his energy.

Still, Gabe slid towards the end, and the other man seemed to be gathering his body to pounce, raising the knife—

closer—

Randolph tried to seize control, but the vessel Gabe shut him out with an effort that made them both gasp—

the raised knife—

the slash—

at the last second, Gabe grabbed a ladder rung at the lip of the shaft and caught himself. The other man, who must be *Jim*, attacked the empty space where he expected Gabe to be, and missed. In the weightless void, the energy of his blow turned his motion into a forward leap, his face slamming into the floor and his body rebounding and spinning away from the shaft.

Gabe snapped his wrist and slid smoothly out of the tunnel. The chamber they entered was shaped like a gumdrop or a mushroom cap. A cloud of garbage drifted about in the air.

Jim crashed into the wall. He lost his grip on the obsidian flake, which whizzed away from him into the junk. He grabbed a ridge in the wall paneling and stopped his motion.

Gabe reached out and snatched the knife from the air. Randolph felt heartened, though he knew that this defeated Jim was only a mortal servitor, a cultist, or maybe even a vessel like Gabe.

"Come easy, Jim," Gabe said. "I'll give you a sedative."

Jim nodded slowly, then let himself drift away from the wall. He reached out a hand submissively to Gabe.

Gabe tucked the tablet under his arm and grabbed Jim's hand.

Excruciating shock torture spasms electricity blood's on fire—

engulfed in the sudden onslaught of pain, Randolph struggled not to lose consciousness.

Choate spasmed. White foam spewed from the professor's lipless old mouth and his knees slammed repeatedly into his own chest.

Jack dug into his pants pocket, then shoved his wallet into the professor's mouth. Choate was already on his side, so he wasn't going to drown in his own... foam.

"Easy." Jack patted Randolph Choate on the shoulder.

CRASH!

Behind him, Jack heard the door give way.

He turned and opened fire. *Rat-tat-tat-tat-tat*, the tommy gun chewed into the foremost members of the rampaging mob.

Funny, Jack thought. They didn't really look like ginnies. They wore suits and frocks, and except for the bloody and totally messed-up state of them, they might have been the kind of people who'd get invited to Burroughs Manor for dinner.

Until Jack mowed them down. Then they looked like oversized rag dolls, banging into the walls and dropping to the ground. Their blood ran across the floor in straight lines, like it was pouring into tiny irrigation canals. Which, Jack realized, it was.

Jack walked slowly forward and dropped every one of the creeps in the basement with him and then the first few in the hall. As the tommy gun ran dry he hurled the kerosene lantern into the hall for good measure.

The crazies ran away. Not so crazy that they liked being on fire, at least, Jack thought with some satisfaction.

"How do you like *that?*" he yelled after them. "Screw with the troll, you get the horns! I mean *bull!*" Jack faltered. "Screw with the bull, I said. I meant. Ah, hell."

He picked up the door and grunted with the effort it cost him to shove it back into place, kicking aside the body of a man in a priest's collar. It only occurred to him as he snapped the door upright that he had thrown away the light, and would be plunged into total darkness.

Only he wasn't.

The thing the professor was lying on—the picture that looked like a boat—glowed a smoky green. And above the professor, also glowing in dull green, the ceiling of the basement was spangled with dots that might have been stars.

He gripped the stone fiercely, wondering what it was and dimly remembering that it was something important. His face burned, and the skin of his hands.

The god, the god was coming.

What god?

He looked into his left hand and saw that he held a severed woman's head. He thought the sight should shock him, but it didn't. He pulled the head to him by the hair and looked into its eyes as it bobbed around, floating with him in space. Just a thing. Just a head. Just a blood head thing blood.

Blood flowed through the air around him. His arm burned, and looking down at it, he saw that the flesh of his forearm was slashed open. He looked up, and the lights shut off completely.

In the darkness, he screamed.

The first Brother of the Dark Chamber announced his approach with a hymn. Now that the slaughter of the lambs was done, the blood pounded less in Sa-Niarlat's ears and he could again hear the sounds of the Theban army above.

"We are doomed," he said joyously to the Brother, "but it is the god who dooms us." He crossed the plank bridge to the god's bark and stepped unerringly to his position at the helm.

The deck beneath his feet rocked slightly and the rudder felt like gnarled and carved bone in his hands. The hymn grew in intensity as more Brothers entered the room, and spread in physical space as they arrayed themselves out around the edges of the pool, chanting together.

Niarlat, live
Niarlat, watch
Niarlat, come
Arise thou Niarlat from thy rest

Overhead, dim lights swirled into being. They were stars, and Sa-Niarlat instantly recognized the constellations.

The stars were in the same alien pattern as the stars in the ceiling of the Inner Court. You could not see such constellations in the skies above Huut-Niarlat.

Sa-Niarlat joined the hymn.

Niarlat, live

The stars seemed to rise into the distance above his head, to become true astral bodies, cold and unimaginably remote. Sa-Niarlat's heart again roared like thunder in his own hearing, joy exulted his frame.

Niarlat, watch

The boat under his feet began to glow. Sa-Niarlat had chanted this hymn in this spot a hundred times before. He had smelled the blood of sacrificed lambs and the hot sand upon which it spilled, seen the stars above show their light. The boat had always remained inert. His eyes drank in the details; the leather sail, the railing around the deck of long bones and skulls, the lichen-encrusted twisting mast, like an olive tree or the split tentacles of the god himself.

Satisfaction.

Niarlat, come

Blood, thick in his nostrils. His own death was imminent, but it had always been inevitable. He had been marked as a sacrifice to his god many long years ago, and the knife at his lamb-like throat had only been stayed for a time, to permit him to complete greater service. This was his moment. He would feed the god not only his own soul, but the soul of every Theban at the gates and every Sebek worshipper who fell to a Theban sword. The blood would summon the god, open the door for him. The impatient and foolish Thebans were creating a mass sacrifice to their enemy on a scale that the god's own priests, in hiding for centuries, had not been able to achieve.

Was it enough blood? Sa-Niarlat's god was a thirsty god. Then Sa-Niarlat's heart skipped a beat as the deck of the bark rose into the air.

Arise thou Niarlat from thy rest

James ripped his hand away from Gabe and bit his own lip.

He'd been yelling something, but they were words he couldn't make out or control.

This is madness, he thought. The white-jumpsuit boys in the Academy and the NACSS claimed that Nullspace was safe, but there were always whispered stories that suggested otherwise. Crewmen who murdered mates in their sleep. Cannibal ships. Captains who willingly flew their own ships into stars.

Space-sickness, they said. Cabin fever. Fables.

Or an overdose. His hands trembled, and he couldn't remember from one moment to the next where he was or what he had done. Wasn't that what an addict experienced? He'd been injected twice with the Hypnostasis emergence cocktail, hadn't he? Hadn't he? Was he the galaxy's first emergence cocktail junkie?

Maybe. An *emerger.* He shuddered and laughed. They'd study his case in the Academy.

But maybe not.

James felt another person inside him. Sometimes his body did things, and it wasn't him giving the orders. But that was a crock, he knew; he was dodging responsibility for... for something. Had he killed people? No, the other person inside him had.

But the other person could only be James himself.

James laughed, trying to exorcise his unsettled, whirling sense that everything was shattered. Instead, he heard his own cackle and cringed.

Had he always had a split personality? he wondered. He didn't think he'd experienced missing memories before this fateful trip, but he didn't know how much he could trust his own mind. Maybe he'd forgotten his prior forgetting.

He cackled again.

Something inside James grabbed him and impelled him forward awkwardly. His arms flailed, and though it seemed a directionless movement at first, it ended with the obsidian flake in his hand. Images of burning white sand flashed through James's mind, and men on chariots with spears and shields.

A ship. A ship that flew.

Murders.

"Blood and sand," he gasped, and then spat out an incomprehensible stream of gibberish.

He bounced off a bulkhead, and the Other inside him relaxed his grip. James swooned and nearly fainted at the sudden absence, but steadied himself by inhaling big gulps of air.

He tried to throw away the stone, and found that the one part of him the Other still held tightly was James's weapon hand.

"Sagan," he muttered.

Gabe anchored himself to the captain's seat and stared at James.

"I'm sorry," James told his first mate. His entire body shook with the effort. "I need... relieve me of command."

Gabe shouted a series of nonsense syllables back at him, and the Other seized James's jaw and shouted back.

Darkness filled the bridge, though the emergency lights seemed to be burning as bright as ever. James felt his body wracked with pain like a thousand hot needles stabbing him. Gabe writhed, let go of the captain's chair, and drifted.

His arm, the arm James had touched, withered and aged before James's eyes.

The Other kicked his feet against the bulkhead and made James lurch forward. He spun slowly head over heels forward, stone knife slashing. I have to stop the Other, James thought. Even if he is me. I can't let him—me—kill Gabe.

Gabe shouted more nonsense. Then: "Stop! Jim, stop!"

James collided with the captain's chair and the Other caught himself. Gabe cowered before him. I must stop him, Jim thought, and didn't know who *him* was.

The Other raised his weapon in James's hand.

"No!" Jim howled, and made his final move. He seized control of his weapon arm—

twisted the blow as it fell—

and slashed his own wrist.

In this queer weightless void, blood didn't spill or flow. It exploded out of a body in heartbeat-powered jets, each burst articulating into a swarm of discrete balls like a barrage of shotgun pellets.

Jim stabbed the obsidian knife into his own arm and bounced away shrieking. The blood that squirted from his veins was blue. For a moment, Randolph wondered whether the man was inhuman, but then the blue became a colorless gray, the chamber rippled before his eyes, and he remembered that he was losing his mind.

"Jim!" shouted Gabe the vessel.

"Leave him!" Randolph barked through the same lips. "We have no time!" He wondered if Jack Kale had already joined Carver in death, and then he wondered if the word *already* had any real meaning in this context.

He didn't let himself think about it.

Jim drifted towards the shaft, convulsing. Some of the curses that came from him might have been Egyptian. Others sounded like a history of science lecture alternating with gibberish. "Kepler! Feynman! Franklin! Hawking! Darwin!"

Randolph noted distractedly that the man's voice modulated back and forth between a strained tenor when he spoke English and a growling, raspy baritone when he spewed out Egyptian.

"Show me the monster," Randolph said. He felt like throwing up. The wall of the spaceship slid away from him and rushed back in irregular contractions. "The beast... outside this... craft." He relinquished control, struggling just to stay awake.

Gabe pushed to a panel in the chamber's wall and pressed buttons. "There it is."

Randolph looked and guffawed. "That's not a beast. That's a row of numbers."

"That's data. Look." Gabe pointed their shared finger at a number that rapidly decreased. "That's our distance. The wormhole, and the thing inside it, are getting closer."

"I can stop it." Randolph said the words though he didn't know whether they were true. "I can turn its path aside, but I need to see it. Is there a vantage point?"

Gabe laughed hollowly. "You open the door for a vantage point, you, me, and everyone else on this ship dies instantly."

"A window?"

Gabe pressed buttons. At the shaft entrance, Jim thrashed and screamed, throwing out drops of blood like a centrifuge.

"There's not enough power." He pointed at another number. "I can't get the visual up without shutting off other systems."

"Shut off other systems."

Gabe tried. "I can't." Randolph felt sweat beading on the vessel's skin. "There's too little juice in the system. To turn on the visual, I have to shut down life support for the rest of the ship."

"Do it."

"I'll die. *You'll* die... if you *can* die."

Randolph thought of Delilah, swinging slowly by a knotted hotel sheet in the rain. The face of Mr. Burroughs himself, smeared with Carver's blood and belly fat as he ripped out a length of intestine with his teeth. "I can die. Do it."

"There are twenty-five hundred people down there!"

Randolph considered for a moment. The vessel Gabe, he remembered, had mentioned his wife. Small wonder he was distraught. "Is there enough *juice* to withdraw from the... *wormhole?*"

"Maybe." Sullen and defiant. "Maybe we can make one push, and get out of this thing's way."

Randolph looked for the right words to say. He would have sighed, but he lacked the energy to be that much in control of Gabe's body. Instead, he drifted as he ordered his thoughts. "In the United States," he finally said, "there are one hundred twenty million people. The earth with her billions is at risk. Twenty-five hundred lives are a terrible loss, but they are twenty-five hundred doomed lives anyway. You and I, Gabe, must make a choice. I am sorry that your wife is with us, because it means we must make a choice for her, too. It is a hard thing, and I resent that it is our fate, but there is no avoiding it."

Gabe said nothing.

"I too am tempted by this will o' the wisp hope, but I cannot take the risk of being deceived. Much blood has already been shed," Randolph added. "To make the sacrifice worth it, you and I must choose to shed a little more."

Silence.

"We sacrifice twenty-five hundred," Randolph said. "We save the earth."

"Schrödinger!" Gabe pushed off from the bulkhead and glided to the shaft opening, where Jim tossed and turned in the air. He'd stabbed himself again, and yowled like a cat on fire.

"Blood and sand!"

"Goodbye, Jim," Gabe said. He hooked a foot into the struts of the captain's chair, grabbed Jim by the ankles and pushed the other man head-first into the shaft. Jim drifted away, shouting nonsense.

Randolph was impressed with the ease with which Gabe moved in the void. He continued to be impressed as Gabe punched the glass from a small panel he hadn't noticed and yanked the lever inside. With a muffled *thump*, a plate snapped across the shaft opening from where it had lain hidden in the shaft wall.

"Mechanical trigger," Gabe explained. "Explosive-powered. It's an emergency system, uses no power. He won't bother *us* again."

Unspoken: Jim was now locked in the same part of the spaceship as Gabe's wife. Randolph felt a heavy, heavy weight upon his soul.

They returned to the wall panel. Randolph sensed tears on the vessel's cheeks and his vision threaten to dissolve into tatters of blackness and static.

"Thank you."

"What are you going to do?" Gabe asked.

"Tangle its path. I can't kill this thing. Nothing can kill it. I don't even know if it is alive, in any sense of the word you and I would understand. But I think I can keep it from its destination, send it somewhere else."

Gabe nodded. "You ready to kill twenty-five hundred people, Choate?"

Randolph hesitated. "Yes."

Gabe touched the panel again. Nothing changed that Randolph could detect with his wrecked vision, but Gabe's shoulders slumped.

"Now what?"

"Now we run out of oxygen. A few minutes at most, I guess. But you'll have more power for other ship systems." Gabe laughed hollowly. "At least only one of us is breathing." He touched a spot in the wall. "We'll last longer."

The panel filled with an image, and Randolph shuddered.

It rocketed away from him and then lurched back, blurred, shifting in color and spinning, but Randolph recognized the thing on the screen. He knew the writhing tentacles, the mouth, the body in too many dimensions. He knew this beast from the Lemurian tablet. He knew it from other ancient images, and he knew it from his nightmares.

Niarlat-Hetep, the resting Niarlat, Niarlat in his prison.

Arise thou Niarlat from thy rest, he thought. This was Niarlat's rest, a light-shot, trembling, extradimensional cocoon in the vast darkness of outer space. Here it had lain for eons, and from here madmen sought to bring it to earth. A golden-black, coruscating ribbon of light and void crossed the vast nothingness of space, between the cocoon and the spaceship. It was as if a great cone of the void had been seized and twisted into a hank of cosmic rope, an umbilical and a highway for the dark god.

That ribbon, Randolph saw, was the gate. His spell in the basement of the Burroughs Manor had been successful, and had brought him here, into the very path of the god.

"Curie."

And before Randolph's eyes, the crackling energy around the colossal elder god split and dissipated. Niarlat stretched, snapped its vast tentacles in the void, and began to move. Like a swimming jelly, it devoured the darkness with swallowing movements of its tentacles and dragged itself forward, up the ribbon of light and darkness towards the spaceship and an ignorant humanity.

Randolph seized control of the vessel Gabe. He was weary and he could barely see, but if he didn't act now, the thing before his vision—the thing towards which he was rapidly hurtling—would devastate the earth.

He couldn't hurt the elder god, but he could tie a knot in the path at its feet.

Randolph tightened his grip on the Lemurian tablet and began to chant. The tentacles snapped through space at a speed that Randolph would have thought impossible had he not seen it, rushing towards him in the viewing screen. Or was it only Randolph's withering sanity that made it seem so?

He resisted the temptation to chant faster, knowing he would only garble the difficult language. He heard a soft banging and scratching sound and realized that Jim was outside the emergency gate, pounding on it with fist and stone.

The tentacles hurtled nearer. The gold streaks in the ribbon glowed brighter and the black was blacker still, and the ribbon seemed taut and full.

Randolph Choate chanted firmly and clearly, articulating each syllable for his dead friends, and for the entire human race. He felt his soul slipping away as he chanted, and he realized with a moment of awful horror that the spell was stealing it. The enchantment by which he would entangle the gate was killing him.

He persisted. He would make the sacrifice, for Delilah, for Carver, even for Jack Kale.

He could do it, he knew. He bit off the last syllable with his teeth, and then he *had* done it. In his view, the shimmering ribbon twisted, an elbow of ninety degrees kinking suddenly into existence. The gate was entangled, the path dragged aside. Whatever Niarlat did, it would not reach the destination its cultists imagined.

Randolph looked up at the viewing screen at the dark god flying in his direction, feeling life, time, vision, and mind all slip away from him. As Niarlat grew closer he felt his own breaths coming harder; this was it, asphyxiation, the end he had chosen. The heart he shared with Gabe raced. The angle of the viewing device changed perceptibly as Niarlat changed its angle relative to the spaceship, and for the first time Randolph saw the long knobbly body of the vehicle in which he rode the cosmos. It look like a string of silver bubbles against the black.

Silver bubbles full of people. Full of people, full of blood. Blood was power.

A horrible doubt seized Randolph Choate.

"Planck."

Niarlat smashed into the hull of the spaceship. Tentacles grasped and tore, shattering the craft. Sudden motion spun the conical chamber violently, slamming Gabriel Goldman's body against the bulkhead.

The viewing screen went blank. Randolph's vision began to follow.

In the last horrible second before it all left him, he wondered what he had done.

The ground trembled.

"Earthquake, really?" Jack shook his head. When it rained, it really hit the fan.

The stone crocodile statues on each side of the professor teetered back and forth too much for him to be comfortable, so he picked up Choate's unconscious body and slung it over his shoulder. The professor was still foaming at the mouth, but he was still breathing, too, so Jack wasn't too worried. Also, he was muttering in his sleep. It didn't sound like American, but half of what old man Choate said didn't sound like American, even when it was.

Jack set the professor on the floor again when he was sure he was out of danger from the statues, and turned his attention back to the rattling door. It would have been nice if the earthquake had killed the crazies outside, but no such luck.

"Ginnies."

He pointed the tommy gun at the door and got ready to fire.

BOOM!

A sound like thunder exploded into the basement of the Burroughs Manor, and the air became thick with dust. Dust, Jack thought, and the smell of blood. Only the dust smelled wrong. It smelled like hot sand, of all things. For a second, he thought the earthquake might have toppled the house above him, but that was ridiculous—whatever sand there might be on the grounds of the Burroughs Manor, it wouldn't be *hot*, not at this time of year.

He turned to check on the professor and discovered something much more unexpected.

A boat.

A frickin' boat, with oars and a sail and everything, sitting where the picture of the boat had been. Its mast was jammed up into the ceiling, bringing down cement dust, and its gunwales had knocked over the two crocodile idols.

If he hadn't moved the professor, Choate would have been smashed flat.

The door shook, its planks groaning.

Choate coughed, spitting out dust, and sat up.

"Oh, good, you're back. Everything go according to plan, professor?"

Choate grinned. He had a stone in his hand, but it wasn't the one Jack remembered. It was chipped and flaky, like a big old Indian arrowhead, and he didn't see any pictures on it. Maybe the ship had knocked this rock out of the wall, he thought. Maybe this arrowhead was one of the piles of junk and trinkets the professor always seemed to be able to produce to work his mumbo jumbo.

Jack turned back to face the door again, away from the professor, and aimed his tommy gun. "We saved the day, then. There's still nutjobs outside the door, but don't you worry about it none, the tommy'll take care of 'em."

He heard Choate climb to his feet, spit, clear his throat, and spit again. Then, just as the door rattled hard because something on the other side slammed into it, Choate spoke. Only it didn't sound like Choate; the voice was deeper, and more raspy, like the voice of a dedicated smoker and drinker.

And the words it said certainly weren't American.

Jack was glad to have the professor back, anyway. He didn't like being alone in the basement, with the shadows and the statues and the stars glowing on the ceiling, and however queer the bag of bones got with his bits of string and foreign jabber, there was no denying that Randolph Choate could *do* things. Things that really ought to be impossible, like jamming the door shut with a ball of hair.

"Ia Niarlat," Choate said, behind him.

"Yeah," Jack chuckled without enthusiasm. "Let's get 'em."

THE REDEMPTION OF EGGBERT BAILEY

This is the second short story I wrote for the Simultaneous Times *podcast. If you're ever in Joshua Tree, stop by the Space Cowboy book-store and check it out.*

"It's gone," Hackett said. "I'm a little surprised to see you."

The usual gleam was absent from the pawnbroker's eye and the deep lines of his face drew up together in a funereal array under his shock of silver hair.

Eggbert Bailey ran his eyes across the shelves behind Hackett, seeing neat displays of pistols, swords, knives and medals. Had Hackett been a soldier once himself? He seemed to favor them.

"You weren't burgled," Eggbert said.

Hackett shook his head. "Your ticket expired. Another customer bought the medallion."

Eggbert growled. "Of all the objects to acquire. A trinket."

Hackett nodded slowly. "I'm sorry. It's hard to lose things. Even things that look as if they have no value."

No value. Eggbert Bailey looked down at his rumpled gendarme's uniform, then out into the chaotic early evening street of the *Vieux Carré* beyond Hackett's windows. He'd had a mission once, and a purpose in life. He'd traded them for a sergeant's pay and mere survival. And with the Chevalier running short of cash, even those were now in question. "It had value to someone. Enough to buy it from under me."

He laughed. The laughter hurt.

"I have other medallions I could offer you," Hackett said. "Even other medallions with Franklin's Shield on them. Though . . . if I judge right, it isn't the mere symbol that matters to you."

"You're a kind man," Eggbert told the pawnbroker slowly. "I took the loan, and I knew the risks. Now I will pay the price."

They both nodded and Eggbert stepped out onto the boardwalk, into the drifting smoke and the tangy smell of liquor. Gendarmes of the Chevalier should be on watch in this free-living quarter of New Orleans, thick with criminals, but they would mostly be derelict in their duty. The industrious among them would be pursuing side employment—the more honorable shaking down delinquent borrowers with threats of broken legs or standing bodyguard to one of the city's still-liquid merchants and the less honorable simply committing robbery. The unambitious gendarmes would be drinking and cursing the Chevalier's failure to pay them. A few, especially the Choctaw and Bantu men with families living inland, away from the city, had already abandoned their posts entirely, becoming phantoms in the Chevalier's service, mere names on the roll.

Mere names. Ghosts.

Men without missions.

Soulless men.

Eggbert Bailey sighed. Should he turn to robbery, and risk being hunted down by his own men? Take on private work? But work as a gendarme had given him anonymity and a place to hide, from Jackson's enemies and allies alike. Not to mention the risk of being hanged or shot, once the Chevalier got his financial affairs in order.

Perhaps the loss of the medallion was no loss after all, a mere trinket, as he had told Hackett. And he had scraped together the money to reclaim it—he had a sudden strong urge to trade the silver in for a night of alcohol-fueled oblivion.

"Pardonnez-moi." A low voice spoke from Eggbert's left. "Excuse me."

Eggbert turned. The speaker was a fat Creole in white sleeves and a black vest, sweat running down his face despite the cool spring air. He craned his neck to look up at Eggbert, as most men had to do.

"I'm not on duty," Eggbert said. "You can just say hello."

"Ah, *duty*." The Creole's eyes gleamed. "It is so excellent that you should immediately resort to such a word."

Eggbert frowned. The briefly-seated former Bishop of New Orleans, Etienne Ukwu, was a gangster whose men wore black waist-coats and white shirtsleeves. Was this Creole offering employment? The Chevalier had driven the Bishop from his seat in the St. Louis Cathedral, replacing Ukwu with his own puppet. Now Bishop Ukwu stalked the streets of New Orleans, consecrating the host in hiding or preaching from street corners and then fleeing the Chevalier's men. "I'm not looking for work."

"No. You are looking for . . . this." The Creole held out a sweaty hand, and in it lay Eggbert's Franklin medallion, the one given to him by Andrew Jackson himself, the night before Jackson's final battle. "They call me Monsieur Bondí."

That's not what I came here for, Eggbert wanted to say. Instead, he just looked at the dull gleam of the tin amulet. It was a cheap decoration, a thing a man might buy for himself on any street corner. Hackett had loaned him more than its monetary value, so Monsieur Bondí had in turn paid too much.

"What do you want?" Eggbert asked.

The Creole pressed the medallion into Eggbert's hand. Eggbert meant to resist, but instead his fingers snatched the familiar cool metal like a starving man snatches bread.

"Men of purpose," Bondí said. "Men of heart."

Without consciously willing it, Eggbert followed the sweating man. Bondí led him down the boardwalk and across a muddy street. In the center of the crossroad stood three pillories, and in them hung men: Des Chutes, Moreau, and Parkinson. All three were gendarmes and decent men, and Moreau had a family. Now all three had welts showing through shirts that had been whipped to rags, and eggshell and scraps of tomato in their hair. A motley gang of young boys were now throwing stones.

What had the three men done to deserve this fate?

Two sad-faced, pimpled youths, uncomfortably stuffed into uniforms too large for them, stood guard, and did nothing to interfere.

Dereliction, desertion.

The Chevalier's army was enormous in the muster-books, and unable to come to the field. The Chevalier filled the ranks with informers, but soon there would be no one left to hold the whip and only the Chevalier's own spies to punish.

A smaller, more loyal force would have been more powerful.

Eggbert and Monsieur Bondí sat down at a table in an Irish tavern, one of the drink-houses belonging to the Kennedie brothers. The Kennedies made their real money as fences. Eggbert closed his fist around the tin disc.

"Your master is the Bishop," he said.

Bondí nodded. "You are observant."

"You don't look like a leg-breaker. Or a priest."

"I am an unworthy devotee of St. Bernardo of Pacioli."

"An accountant." Eggbert laughed. "And how you do account me, then?"

"I account you a leader," the Creole said. "You are respected. You earned your way up through the ranks. You respect yourself. You respect your fellow gendarmes."

Eggbert searched the room for any sign of listening ears and saw none. "They deserve better."

"They deserve a better master. And a good captain."

Eggbert squeezed the medal until it imprinted the image of its rim in his flesh. "And I am a mere sergeant."

"Good men get promoted." Bondí smiled.

Eggbert shook his head. "Are you suggesting . . . rebellion?"

Monsieur Bondí leaned forward over the table. "I am suggesting that the Chevalier of New Orleans has pawned his men, and has let his ticket expire."

Eggbert Bailey took a deep breath. "Keep talking."

THIRSTY BONES

I wrote this originally for a quarterly magazine of fantasy and horror content that was planned to launch just as soon as it completed its kickstarter. It looked great, and I had an idea, so I wrote the story as soon as I was invited to contribute.

Naturally, the kickstarter then failed.

But then Joe Monson invited me to submit to a horror-themed anthology to benefit the Life, the Universe, & Everything *symposium. I've been an attendee and supporter of* LTUE *for a long time, and a big fan of Joe, so I sent the story to him.*

"You were right." Dick Jenkins looked mildly surprised and deeply bitter. "Bones."

"I didn't kill your brother." Alf Shaw's good eye and his voice were sour.

"Blessed are those that hunger and thirst after justice." Hiram Woolley set aside the Mosaical Rod, ignoring Shaw's look of skepticism, and peered down into the pit. It was shallow, a square trench hacked out of the tawny orange clay. At one edge, white bone protruded jarringly into view.

A human skull.

In the center of its forehead, a hole.

A warm breeze rose from the valley behind Hiram, scattering red sand over the skull and bringing the scent of juniper to his nose.

"Don't you mean righteousness?" Shaw grumbled. "The beatitudes, right? It's hunger and thirst after *righteousness*."

"Come to think of it, you're right." Hiram raised his hat, letting the warm breeze dry some of the sweat on his balding scalp. "Only I heard my Bible from Grandma Hettie as a boy, and she sometimes quoted it funny. Comes of her reading it in German, I guess."

Jenkins shouldered forward and looked into the hole. "That's my brother, I'm sure of it."

It almost certainly was, since Hiram had found it with a hazel Mosaical Rod carved with the name *Tommy Jenkins* and bound with a rubber band to a faded photograph of the man. Hiram felt uneasy—his service in the war hadn't inured him to the awe and dread of death, but the opposite.

"Might be." Hiram squinted at the Henry Mountains, white-shouldered with snow. "Hopefully we can find water in the wells, now."

Somehow, he doubted it. That had been too simple.

"Most likely an old Ute body, anyway," Shaw said. "Or Navajo, they ain't too far away. Always finding arrowheads and old corn cobs around here. These ain't gonna give you a lick of water, I don't know why I ever went along with this. Angeline was here, she'd tongue-lash us all senseless."

"He walked right to the spot," Jenkins said. "Are you saying it was coincidence? Or that this sugar beet farmer knew the body was here to start with?"

"Even if that is your brother," Shaw bulled ahead, "that don't mean his body is what's dried up all the wells."

Both men's tempers were running high, and the peacemakers were blessed, too. "In any case," Hiram said, as gently as he could, "we have bones to deal with."

Shaw grunted, Hiram stuck in his shovel, and the three men quickly unearthed the skeleton, laying it alongside the pit.

The corpse lay close enough to the surface that its flesh had been eaten away by bacteria. Stubborn tufts of long red hair clung above the temples. Hiram stretched his back and looked down both sides of the ridge on which they stood, at the Shaw farm and the Jenkins land. They were far from any trail, and the body might have spent seasons exposed up here without being noticed. If the corpse did belong to a Ute, it was a Ute who'd worn denim jeans. Strips of the fabric clung to the skeleton's legs and pelvis, and corduroy patches stitched together and faded almost to white suggested what might once have been a jacket.

"Thirty years." Jenkins sucked air in past his teeth. "My brother wore a coat like that."

"What, a patch coat?" Shaw grunted. "We all wore patch coats and we all walked on rag rugs. I grew up poor, same as you, and this skeleton ain't got enough of a face to tell who he was."

"My brother disappeared, Shaw. I say this is him."

Hiram felt uneasy in his stomach. He leaned on his shovel and snaked his spare hand into the pocket of his overalls, wrapping his fingers around the cool stone of his heliotrope. The stone had the power to warn him of deceit, but now it lay still and innocuous.

"Your brother telegraphed from San Diego. He didn't *disappear*, he *left*."

"*Someone* telegraphed from San Diego, and then we never heard from Tommy again."

"And you inherited your daddy's farm!" Shaw snorted. Both farmers were heavy men, red from working in the sun, but Shaw was the beefier of the two. He mopped the back of his neck with a handkerchief, sweating from the exertion of the conversation. "Maybe it was you that killed him, and then lied about a telegram. Hell, I never saw no Western Union slip!"

All three men wore overalls, long-sleeved shirts, and hats. Hiram's was a fedora, Jenkins's was a black, broad-brimmed affair that looked vaguely old-world to Hiram, and Shaw's hat was woven of straw.

"Anyway, this isn't some old Indian skeleton," Hiram murmured.

"That is a bullet hole in its head. Whoever it is, might be recent enough there's a murder statute would stick."

"I could get the sheriff." Shaw's facial expression was dubious. The sheriff was a two-hour drive away. "Or we could just say a few nice prayers and bury him again. The skeleton won't know the difference, anyway, whoever he is."

"Couldn't *you* do something?" Jenkins asked Hiram. "I mean, to know who killed him?"

"We're trying to unblock your wells," Hiram said. It was only after he'd dug deep enough and seen water recede from before his feet three times in both men's wells that Hiram had become convinced that there was a supernatural cause for the water's failure. It was then that the story of the missing Tommy Jenkins had come out.

"But don't you think it was the murder that dried up the water?" Jenkins insisted.

Shaw snorted.

Hiram had thought the disappearance—the *murder*—might be connected, but now he wasn't so sure. The skeleton looked so . . . normal. Peaceful.

Jenkins softened his voice. "We'll get the sheriff, of course. But if you wouldn't mind . . . looking into it a bit first?"

Shaw chuckled and shook his head. "If either of you goes around telling anyone I committed a murder thirty years ago, on account of this witch found an old skeleton with his divining rod, I got a lawyer in Fillmore who will eat you both alive."

"I'm not a witch," Hiram murmured. "I just . . . know how these things work." At the mere mention of the word *witch*, his hand reached for the protective chi-rho amulet that hung under his shirt. With two fingers, he pressed the metal disk to his chest, taking comfort in its cool familiarity.

"I heard tell the body of a murdered man bleeds again in the presence of his murderer." Shaw jeered and gestured at the skeleton. "Look, Dick, it ain't bleeding! I must be innocent!"

Jenkins said nothing.

Hiram turned to Shaw. "You don't mind if we go lay him out in your barn for a bit, do you? If the presence of the body is causing trouble with the water, maybe removing it to the barn will help." This bit of misdirection was awfully close to a lie, for Hiram's taste.

Jenkins looked disappointed. Shaw looked smug, and nodded. "Just don't tell Angeline. She won't want to know there was a dead body that close to her potatoes."

While Shaw fetched a tarp, Hiram considered. Could he get to his Ford Model AA truck and get the bottle of powdered egg white and mercury out of his toolbox without attracting notice? He doubted it. Not that he couldn't practice his craft in front of these men; they had both watched him make the Mosaical Rod and follow its guidance to the buried corpse. But for the trick he had in mind, it was best if the tested party were taken by surprise.

He'd have to improvise.

They shifted the skeleton carefully onto the canvas tarpaulin that Shaw brought back.

"What's he got clenched in his fist?" Jenkins asked.

"Dirt," Shaw muttered.

"There's a glint of silver there. Hold on." Jenkins brushed at the skeletal fingers and the dirt they clutched until he found a silver flake, the size of a fingernail.

"What is it?" Hiram asked.

"Junk." Shaw stood and hefted one end of the tarp, above the skeleton's head. Hiram lifted the other, at the feet end, and they began to walk to the barn.

Jenkins followed, examining the flake.

"You got a name on that bit of metal?" Shaw asked. "Or maybe it says 'Alf Shaw killed me,' writ out there on gold plates so we know it's God's own truth!"

"There's no writing," Jenkins said. "I don't know what this is."

In the barn, they laid the skeleton on a work table, shifting aside some half-cut lumber and tools to make room for the body. While Shaw adjusted the bones, catching the skull before it rolled off the table, Hiram found what he was looking for: a long iron nail. Concealing it in one hand, he took the bloodstone into his other.

"You didn't kill this fellow, did you, Mr. Shaw?" he asked.

"I sure as hell did not," Shaw said.

The bloodstone didn't contradict him.

"What about you, Mr. Jenkins?" Hiram asked. "Did you kill this man?"

"How about it, Dick?" Shaw demanded, bearing down on his neighbor.

While the two men glared at each other, Hiram scratched the Eye of Abraham into the wood of the barn, gazing across the skeleton at the two farmers. The nail's tracks in the wood were subtle, leaving the eye and the symbols surrounding it visible only if you were looking for them.

The Eye was supposed to be drawn with egg white and mercury, but Hiram found that, in many things, a chaste and sober mind and true intent made up the deficit of a missed technicality here or there.

"I didn't kill my brother!" Jenkins snapped, his red face darkening.

"He didn't ask about your brother, Dick! He asked about this poor bastard. You kill this fellow or not?"

"No!" Jenkins shrieked, then stomped off the corner of the barn. Shaw stood beside the table, puffing and squeezing his fists.

Again, the heliotrope told Hiram nothing.

"Is there some reason Mr. Jenkins might think you'd kill his brother?" he asked Shaw. "Is there bad blood between your families?"

Shaw hesitated. "It ain't that, not a feud or anything." The big man pawed at the dirt with the toe of his Redwing boot.

Hiram watched the faces of both men. In the presence of the Eye, a guilty man's tear ducts should flow. Both Alf Shaw and Dick Jenkins looked agitated, upset, off-balance, and even angry, but neither man was crying.

Dick Jenkins took deep breaths, steadying himself. "Tommy was in love with Angeline. With Alf's girl."

Shaw laughed. "Maybe. Only *she* wasn't in love with *him*. She was in love with *me*."

"Her *father* was in love with you, Alf Shaw. Her father loved your land, three times as much as he loved our land, because that was the ratio of the acreage."

Shaw looked to Hiram and shrugged. "You see? And so I'm glad there's a hill between us. But Angeline was engaged to me, and I guess poor Tommy ran off to San Diego. Or maybe he died up on the ridge of a broken heart, if this really is him."

A female voice cut through the conversation, strident in tone. "What are you men doing in here?"

Alf Shaw turned to meet his wife. Angeline Shaw wore pretty calico under her denim house dress, and she had a black wire egg basket in one hand. She was stick thin had a creamy complexion, with a nose sharp as a carrot and glittering eyes.

With tears in them.

"You did it," Hiram said.

"What?" She looked distracted, surprised.

"Angeline?" Alf's voice rose in a questioning pitch. "Tell him that's nonsense. You didn't do anything."

Angeline looked right past her husband, and the color drained from her face. "Tommy." She swallowed, and dropped the egg basket.

"Good god." Dick Jenkins inhaled deeply, and let his breath out slow.

"Angeline?" Alf pressed.

She ignored him and walked toward the body. At each step, her eyes watered more. Tears began to run down her softly-wrinkled cheeks.

"Why did you kill him?" Jenkins asked.

"She didn't!" Shaw roared.

Hiram pointed to his written sigil. "This is the Eye of Abraham. The eyes of the guilty water in its presence."

"YOU HAVE A SKELETON IN HER BARN!" Shaw bellowed. "*That's* why she's crying."

Angeline Shaw seemed not to hear her husband. "How did you find him?"

Not *where*, but *how*.

"I have means," Hiram said.

"Why did you do it?" Dick Jenkins's eyes were filling with tears now. "He loved you."

Angeline seemed to grow paler by the second. "He was going to ruin everything. He was going to tell."

Tell what? That Angeline loved Tommy? But many marriages had gone ahead despite similar impediments. That Angeline wanted out of marrying Alf? But she hadn't, if she'd killed Tommy to be able to marry Shaw.

"You had already married Tommy," Hiram guessed.

She shook her head. "But I was carrying his child."

Alf Shaw staggered and fell, like a brained beef. Dick Jenkins's chin dropped to his chest and his hands fell to his side, twitching.

Angeline stopped at arm's length from the skeleton, staring at it but not touching.

"Where's the baby?" Hiram asked.

"Safe," she said.

"Safe from Alf? With foster parents?"

"And safe from you, and from everyone. Safe from all the bitterness and the terrible choices of this horrible life." The tears and mucus flowing down Angeline Shaw's face muffled her voice. Her face looked nearly translucent.

"You killed the baby," Hiram said.

Nothing.

"Did the baby ever get a name?" Hiram asked. "From a preacher, or a county clerk, or someone with authority?"

Angeline Shaw shook her head. "But I called him *Robert*."

It would have to do.

Hiram had an idea. "You buried him with a locket, didn't you? A silver locket?"

She only glared angrily.

Alf Shaw was climbing to his feet again. The Shaws and Dick Jenkins all looked too shocked to cause each other harm, so Hiram stepped out to his truck for another hazel stick. Returning, he found them standing where he had left them, staring at each other with wounded eyes.

With his clasp knife, Hiram quickly carved the name *ROBERT* into the bark of the rod. Before she could react, he stepped in close to Angeline Shaw and plucked a long gray hair from the back of her head. Taking a hair—bright red—from the skeleton, he wound them around each other.

"What are you up to?" Alf muttered.

"I think there's one more thing to do before we solve the water problem." Hiram notched the hazel rod with his knife and pinched the wound hairs into the notch, tying them neatly into place with a square knot while singing Psalm 130, "Out of the Depths," using Grandma Hettie's melody.

He held out his hand to Dick Jenkins, and the farmer knew what he wanted without words. Jenkins handed over the silver flake. Hiram cut a second notch into the wood and inserted the flake into it, all while continuing to sing.

Then he swung the completed Mosaical Rod experimentally—and felt a tug.

"You'll be walking a long distance, witch." Angeline Shaw's voice had lost its stunned, dreamy quality, and regained its knife-like edge.

"It wouldn't be the first time." Hiram tipped his fedora and left the barn.

The other three followed him, Dick Jenkins at his shoulder and the Shaws farther back. Hiram kept the rod loose in his hands so that it could move of its own accord and let it play back and forth in an arc.

Consistently, it led him back up the ridge.

"Fool," Angeline Shaw spat.

Hiram reached the trench from which they'd recovered Tommy Jenkins's body and picked up the shovel he'd left there. He kept walking, following the tug of the Mosaical Rod.

"Miles and miles away, and you're going in the wrong direction." Angeline's voice was ugly.

And then the Rod pulled straight down.

He walked a few steps away and tried the rod again, following its tug to the same point. When a third experiment got the same result, he set the Mosaical Rod aside and put the tip of the shovel into the orange soil.

Angeline Shaw laughed. "You're not even a *good* witch!"

"Cunning man," Hiram said. "I'm a cunning man, if you must talk about me that way. Not a witch."

But was she right? Had her eyes watered, after all, only because she had seen the body of the lover she'd murdered? Had Hiram led himself to an empty spot in the desert, imagining tugs upon the rod?

The third time he sank his shovel into the earth, he struck a box. Kneeling, he scraped away the rest of the soil with his hands, lifted the box, and stood. It was round, wrapped in fabric, and beneath the sand and soil it was a turquoise green.

"Hat box," he said. "From the Z.C.M.I. up at Salt Lake City. I guess you were a fancy young lady."

Angeline's sneer and all the cruelty and rage had left her face, and was now replaced by fear.

"This isn't where you buried the box," Hiram suggested.

She shook her head faintly. The breath-powered rise and fall of her chest was almost imperceptible.

Caked dirt glued the lid onto the hatbox, but with his clasp knife Hiram managed to pry it away. Within, lying on crumpled yellowing tissues, was a tiny human body. It was large enough to have fingers and toes, and its head was swollen and huge. A silver locket was wrapped around its neck and shoulders like a boa; the locket's hinged door had been snapped off, revealing a picture of a young man who resembled Dick Jenkins. The child's arms were stretched out over its head as if it were pointing at or reaching toward something.

It wasn't rotten, or desiccated. The flesh looked firm and moist, almost alive. Slick, even, as if still wet with the creative waters of birth. There was no visible injury on the child's body. Had Angeline Shaw drunk some toxic herb to rid herself of it?

Not *it*, but *he*. The child was a boy.

Hiram followed the line of the baby's arms; they pointed toward the spot where he had excavated Tommy Jenkins's body, only an hour earlier.

"Almost," he said softly to the little corpse. "You almost reached him."

"What?" Angeline Shaw tottered forward several steps. "What's in there?"

"Robert." Hiram stepped toward her, holding the box so she could see within. Both Alf Shaw and Dick Jenkins held back, masks of uncertainty hiding their red faces.

Angeline looked into the hatbox at the child's body.

Robert's eyes fluttered open.

Angeline stared, her eyes making contact with the baby's. She released an unnatural groaning noise, a sound that came from her belly, and staggered back. Clutching at her throat, she fell to the earth.

Her husband and Dick Jenkins both knelt beside her, trying in vain to get Angeline Shaw to breathe again. Hiram looked down into the hatbox, searching for judgment or condemnation. He was just in time to see the baby Robert's eyes close again.

And then, as if it were being burned in a fire, the body crumbled rapidly into dust. All that remained was a withered trail of ash, coiled in the shape of a question mark, and a broken silver locket.

"For they shall be filled," he said to himself.

He said the healing charms he knew to help Angeline, but they were in vain. Then he said a short prayer over her body as Alf Shaw and Dick Jenkins sat in stunned defeat to either side of her.

The wells would be full now.

TWENTY-FIVE DOLLARS AND NO RESIDUALS

The early bluesmen liked to tell stories about themselves and the devil. They encouraged stories about them selling their souls, they gave them-selves titles like "The Devil's Son-in-Law" and "The High Sheriff of Hell." This was advertising; it told listeners that what they were about to hear was scandalous and exciting.

The following is my own take on inventing a blues ghost story. Jace Killan invited me to participate in an anthology called Cursed Collectibles, *and this is what I produced for him.*

A feller comes in the door, *ring-ding-ding*. He's a man I've been looking for a long time, but of course I don't tell him. Better it's a surprise.

The honking of cars and the growl of a bus rise in volume with his opening of the door, and then fall again when the door shuts. The city outside is so unreal at this moment, it might as well be heaven.

"I'm looking for old wax cylinder recordings." The man is white, he's thin in the face and in the hands, but has a safety belt of belly fat around the waist, bobbling above his canvas belt. Liver spots on his forearms, wisps of white hair drifting around his skull. "I heard you might have some."

He doesn't look at me. He looks up over my head.

"Some?" I chuckle. I force myself *not* to put my hand into my jacket pocket, though the man's arrival makes me feel drier and lighter and emptier than ever, so empty I think that if the door opened again and a breeze brought in another whiff of that diesel smoke, it might just take me on out the back door with it. "I'd specialize in the things, if I didn't think that much specialization would put me out of business. Gotta sell vinyl, eight-track, cassette, and these days, I sell a lot of CDs. Kids got no respect for the tangible manifestation of music."

"No respect at all." The feller's smile is way too broad. He's humoring me.

"No respect for the artistry of arranging a series of tracks into a definite order, though really that went out when they created random-izing order on CD players. You ever listen to Sergeant Pepper in random order?"

"It's shit."

"That's generous. An album is more than just a collection of songs, it's got a logic and a narrative of its own. 'Best of' compilations are worthless nonsense for the same reason." His smile is faltering. Maybe I'm laying it on too thick. "Anyway, you didn't come to hear me complain. You looking for a particular cylinder?"

"Really, I'm looking for masters."

I gotta be real careful now, not to give anything away, not with my words, not with my face, not with any surprise hand movements. "I got a few of those, not too many. You're talking about real collector's items."

"Specifically, I'm interested in any master cylinders recorded for Lethe Records, by an engineer named Louis Shaker."

"Shachar," I say, and regret it.

"You know the man."

I shrug. "You ain't the first person as come in here looking for Lou Shachar masters."

"Oh really?"

Now I really need to play dumb, before the sweat starts trickling down my forehead. I laugh. "Third or fourth, maybe? Last guy came in here, oh, two years ago, I finally asked him what gives." This is all invented, nobody ever came in here before looking for Shachar masters. Gotta be careful not to over-egg the pudding.

"What did he say?"

"He said, believe it or not, that there's a story about Lou Shachar's masters. They say that any time he first recorded a bluesman on wax, he took that singer's soul. Put it right into the cylinder."

The feller hesitates a bit too long. Yeah, he's the one I been waiting for. Then he laughs, too. "So all that crossroads at midnight stuff, Robert Johnson, Peetie Wheatstraw, whoever. Only instead of a man meeting you at the crossroads, it's the company engineer who takes your soul."

"I reckon that's about the size of it. Folks want to own a bluesman's soul. Can't say I see why, but there's no accounting for folks. Maybe they're doing black magic with it."

"Maybe they just like the way it sounds." The feller hitches up his pants. "Or maybe it's Woody Guthrie-style agitation codswallop, same kind of nonsense as is in 'Sixteen Tons.' You know why the big mining companies really had company stores, don't you? So the men wouldn't drink their whole paycheck, and their wives could have store credit and get what they needed. My name's Gary."

"I'm Charlie."

We shake hands.

"I have a collection of Shachar masters," Gary says. "There's one in particular I'm looking for."

"Complete your collection, eh?"

Gary shrugs. "I've heard rumors that Big Al Dixon once recorded with Shachar, and I read a few months ago in the catalog of an estate sale that that cylinder was sold by some collector's grieving children, in a lot with a bunch of other old music. Got there too late and no record of who bought the lot, but the sale was in town here, so I figured it's worth checking in at the vintage shops."

"Vintage shops." I chuckle. "I like that. Sounds better than 'junk' or 'second-hand'."

"These things aren't junk."

"Yeah." My eyes tear up slightly. "You know, I heard Big Al play. He could barely hold his guitar, I doubt he knew what chord he was even on. But he sang like a foghorn, and it was worth it, just to see a man that big blowing through such a tiny mouth harp."

"I read he was a bully," Gary says. "Beat his women. Cut his manager once with a razor. The kind of guy you can really believe he sold his soul."

"Or had it stolen," I say.

Gary puts his hands in his pockets and nods. "You got such a master, by any chance?"

"I got no masters." I lean forward, resting my elbows on the counter. "Over on that wall are all the cylinders I got. Take your time, but I know my stock by heart, and I got no Al Dixon."

Gary nods. "I believe you. Thanks, anyway."

"Tell you what," I say. "I come across an Al Dixon master cylinder, how will I let you know?"

Gary produces a card. I'm hoping for an address, but all it has is a name, *Gary Buchanan*, and a phone number. Not even a job title, just name and phone. The phone prefix makes it a local number, at least.

Well, that'll have to do.

"What do you think it's worth?" I ask.

"For resale, I don't know," Gary says. "Maybe not much, but I already admitted I'm trying to complete my collection. Tell you what, you get me the Big Al Dixon master, recorded by Lou Shachar, and I'll give you a thousand dollars."

I whistle. "A thousand bucks for a soul? Back in the day, the going rate was twenty-five dollars and no residuals."

After Gary leaves, I close the store and clutch the cylinder with both hands. Touching the wax, feeling the grooves cut by that madman Shachar all those years ago warms me. It's the *only* thing that makes me feel warm these days, winter and summer alike. It makes me feel full, too, it's a blanket, a mistress, food, and drink, all at once.

It's like heroin was to me, back in the day.

It's my soul, dammit.

Too bad I didn't get an address, that would have made the whole thing easier. I try the Internet, but I'm not good at that stuff, even when I can talk one of the kids at the library into helping me, and this ain't something I can get a kid involved in. I peck out a few searches, get no results, and give up.

I'll just have to let a little time pass.

How long is not suspicious? It takes me three days to prepare, in any case. I've got a master cylinder for another record company, not one that sold race records, it's a klezmer band, but physically it looks just right, the same size and color as the blanks Shachar used.

I have a teakettle, since tea is most of what I live on these days. I boil water, and carefully steam the label off the klezmer cylinder. Then I steam the label off the Big Al Dixon master—the song is "King Snake Stomp," which back in the day, really made the folks get up and shake it—and with a little yellow paste and a brush, I put the Big Al label on the polka-playing Jews.

That takes me three days of my spare time, after I lock up. But three days is too soon, Gary'll never believe I just stumbled across the master, right after he came looking, so then I wait.

Just to be sure, I start carrying both cylinders with me. Sometimes I forget I've switched labels, and mistakenly grab the klezmer. It feels cold and inert to me, which is always an instant reminder.

Feeling the cold wax reminds me of that room, 211 in the Grand Hotel, on the other side of town here. To keep down the room noise, Shachar put the mic in the corner, and I huddled over it on a wooden, slat-backed chair, big fingers crawling up and down the guitar strings and harp rack gouging a hole in my neck. Shachar threw the hotel room mattress over the door to muffle sounds from outside, and told his two men not to breathe.

We were only going to get one take, he warned us, over and over again.

Thirty seconds in, if you listen to the master, you can hear one feller sneeze. Shachar was true to his word, we cut it in just the one take, sneeze and all, and that was it.

A season passes. Summer's gone—I don't miss it, I feel cold, regardless—and leaves drift down the September sidewalks when I decide it's time to call Gary Buchanan.

I've found a Big Al Dixon- Lou Shachar master, I tell him. The store's closed, maybe I can deliver it to him.

He gives me an address. I can't tell whether he's surprised.

I don't recognize the address until I get to the building, and then I remember it. It's an old warehouse squatting on a bluff over the river. It stares at me as I come up the brick lane, between a meat-packing plant and a machine shop.

This was Lethe's warehouse, back in the day. I came here, the day that old mambo looked at the lines of my palms, checked the dregs in a cup of John the Conqueror Root tea to confirm, and told me I had *already* lost my soul. I knew immediately what it must have been.

So I came here, but I got nothing for my trouble, and Lou took back his promise to make more recordings, to boot.

Twenty-five bucks for three minutes' work felt like a lot of money, back then. And I had no idea what residuals even were.

I'm only carrying the one cylinder inside my jacket pocket. Not that I've left the other behind—I never do that—but I've got it taped inside my thigh.

I walk bow-legged, anyway.

The door is buckled with age and the river's humidity, but its locks and knob are new. I knock and yell. "Mr. Buchanan!"

A dog barks, but not inside the warehouse.

Buchanan lets me in. He's practically salivating.

"Do you have it with you?" he asks. He's still looking over the top of my head.

"Like I promised." I hand the cylinder over.

He gives me a thick envelope. I put it into my pocket. Not counting the cash might look like a show of trust, but really, I don't care about the money.

Hell, if he *did* cheat me, I wouldn't want him to realize I found it out just now.

He holds the cylinder in both hands and smells it. "You can practically taste that chopped chord on the backbeat, can't you?"

"If you're gonna listen to it now, I'd be pleased if I could hear it with you."

He hesitates. He isn't sure he wants me to stay, which makes me more certain that I *do* want to stick around, but I'm not going to blow my chances by saying anything. I just hang on my own grin and wait.

"Come upstairs," he says.

Upstairs is an office space at the top of a metal staircase, with windows overlooking the entire floor. The door here is new and solid and Gary Buchanan works through three locks with separate keys.

While he's unlocking the door, I count at least two security cameras.

Inside, the room is not what expect. I imagine office furniture as I walk in, but what I see is two tables, one with master cylinders standing on their ends in rows like chess pawns, and the other with an old player-recorder, the kind that makes cylinders and can also run them back.

"Hell of a place to keep a collection," I say. "You think every one of those cylinders is worth a thousand bucks?"

"This is Shachar's office," Gary says. "That's his machine."

"I heard he recorded in hotel rooms and bars," I say.

Gary nods. "And brothels and riverboats and restaurant kitchens. And once in a restroom in the state capital building."

"I guess you don't want to listen to your music in a restroom, though, that it?"

Gary takes a deep breath while he thinks about his words. "In affairs such as this, things that appear to be of no consequence can matter immensely. Continuity of place. Sustained contact in the past."

"My line of work, I've talked to more than one sound nut," I say. "Excuse me, I meant *audiophile*. Never heard anyone say 'sustained contact in the past' mattered. I ain't confident I even know what you mean."

He gets a look in his eye, and it's the first moment I'm sure Gary Buchanan plans to kill me. "Would you like me to show you what I mean?"

I make a show of indifference. I scratch my nose with one hand, and shove the other hand into my pants pockets. I cut the bottom out of those pockets, so I can reach the other thing I've taped to my thigh, which is a long razor.

Long and sharp.

"Sure," I say.

He plugs in the machine and it comes to life with a slow buzz. I know that buzz. It had a microphone jacked into it when I first saw it, but this was Lou Shachar's machine when I first met him, when we first did business.

Gary puts the cylinder on the spindle and touches the needle to it, stepping back as the speakers crackled with lively sound.

His grin of anticipation collapses into a flat line as fiddles, horns, and a drum kick out in a raucous version of "Hava Nagilah," the musicians barely managing to hold themselves to the same tempo all the way to the end of the recording.

"That isn't it," he snarls.

He checks the label, I worry the concrete floor with the toe of my shoe. "It's Big Al Dixon on the label."

"Does that sound like Big Al to you?"

I hand the cash back over.

He stares at me without taking it. He's thinking, do I kill this old fool from the vintage music shop?

"Tell you what," I say. "I want to earn back that thousand bucks. Give me a couple weeks, I'll call everyone I know in the valley. Second hand shops, collectors, everything. If I can get my hands on that cylinder for less than a thousand bucks, I'll bring it to you here. And if the price is higher than that, I'll tell you where you can find the cylinder yourself. Deal?"

He takes back the envelope.

In this case, no need to wait. I come back the same night.

I bring tools from the hardware store—crowbar, drill, screwdrivers, hammer—and a mask of Winnie the Pooh, together in a grip bag with the master cylinder. I wrap the cylinder in a rag to protect it. Halloween's coming, you can buy stuff like a mask in the autumn without anyone asking awkward questions.

I walk, and I put on the Winnie the Pooh mask when I'm half a block away. This part of town is quiet at night, there's no one to see me.

The locks on the outer door are solid, but it opens outward, so it's got hinges on the outside. That's easy, I just rip the hinges out of the wood with the crowbar.

I creep up the stairs by the moonlight coming in through gaps in two of the walls. I'll be on the cameras, but that won't matter, not with the mask. I don't notice until I get right to the top of the stairs that Gary Buchanan is there waiting for me.

With a pistol in his hand.

"I couldn't be sure," he says, looking over my head.

"Sure of what?"

"Dammit, Al," he says, "one mask wasn't enough. What made you think throwing a second on over the top would help anything?"

I'm quiet for a minute. What's he talking about, two masks? Finally, I strip off the Winnie the Pooh head and toss it to the warehouse floor. "I just came to . . . I just came . . ."

"You came to listen to your own master," Gary says. "I can't let you do that."

I put my right hand in my pocket. I still have the razor taped there, just in case. I force a laugh. "Okay, you got me. Look, I *do* have the Dixon-Shachar master. Tell you what, you let me listen to it with you, I'll give you the cylinder. Let's call it five hundred bucks, instead of a thousand. Fifty percent discount for your trouble."

"I can't let you listen to it."

"You were going to before."

"I could tell what you'd given me was a fake. If I let you listen to the master, on the very machine that recorded it, the spell will be undone, and you'll get your soul back."

Exactly. He has me dead to rights.

"I'm going to do something else," Gary says. "I'm going to free the boy."

"What boy?" I laugh.

"You don't know?"

I shrug and chuckle. "Just you and me here, Gary. It's always been just you and me. Gary and Charlie."

He reaches to the wall and flips on the light switch. As the overhead fluorescents flicker into activity, he holds up a silver tray. It's been polished to a degree you rarely see in silver, so it's reflective, every bit as much as a mirror.

He holds it up to my face . . . and I see the face of a young man.

A white kid, really, still has freckles. Maybe twenty-five years old, twenty-six at the most.

I touch the face. "Damn." I had forgotten. How long have I been in the young man's body? I remember him coming into the shop now, saying he was traveling across country in his grandpa's car and was looking for any old eight-tracks I had around. I remember me—in the body I had borrowed before—giving him a cup of tea.

"I'm going to take you out of that boy, Al," Gary says. "I'm going to take good care of you. You can sit right on the shelf with Robert Johnson and Peetie Wheatstraw and Doug Sims. And don't worry, I'll listen to you from time to time, when I need to, or when the mood takes me. There's no music like . . . soul music."

"Damn you," I say. "A pun? Really? At a time like this?"

I tear the razor from my thigh and step forward.

Or rather, I try to step forward. But I fail. I can't move. My feet are rooted to the metal of the staircase. Looking down, I see chalk markings on the metal. They weren't there this afternoon, I'm sure of it. There's a circle, and two triangles making a six-pointed star, and a bunch of queer markings like you might see embroidered into the wall of a gypsy's tent.

I can't move my feet.

I swipe at Gary with the razor, but he's planned for that. He steps back out of my reach and I miss.

"I'll shoot you," I growl.

"No, you won't," Gary says. "Big Al Dixon beat women. And he cut men with a razor or he kicked them, but he never carried a gun."

"Asking for too much trouble, black man carrying a gun," I grumble. I regret that policy now. I regret not having a pistol in my pocket tonight.

Gary starts chanting. I don't know the words, they ain't English.

I raise the razor to my own borrowed throat. "Stop, or I'll kill the kid."

"Now *that* I believe," Gary says. Then he sprays mace into my eyes.

Or rather, he sprays mace into the eyes of the kid, which feels like it's over my head, because I'm really in the wax cylinder inside the grip bag, as much as I am in the seventeen-year-old with freckles. But I feel the mace, it catches me by surprise and I drop the razor.

"Twenty-five dollars!" I roar through my tears and through the fingers over my eyes. "How would you feel? Wouldn't you want to go free? Wouldn't you fight to get back your soul? I was tricked by the record company man, and I didn't get the kingdoms of this world—I got twenty-five dollars!"

Gary finishes his chant and picks me up. I'm just in the master cylinder now. The kid in whose body I spent the last two years—before him there was another young man, and before him another—runs away, weeping. Gary lets him go.

Gary hefts the cylinder thoughtfully. I'm screaming, but he can't hear.

"Twenty-five dollars," he says, "and no residuals."

SEED

I think this might be the first thing I published that offended people. It certainly wasn't the last, ha!

But to those reviewers who thought this story contained inappropriate content, I would say that it was not written out of any prurient interest, but to the contrary. Authors are not supposed to explain what they meant, but I will say that in this story I was trying to find my way toward an increased understanding of the fall of man. I don't think it makes much sense to think of Eve and Adam's fall as being driven by sex —in the narrative, it's explicitly about knowledge.

I think the fall might have something to do with language.

Her lover caressed her from the inside. Her skin tingled from the energy, ancient and primal, that welled up within her, coursed through her sinews and transformed her entire being into one vibrating Pythagorean string, a perfect single note of husky alto joy. She screamed, feeling her lover between her teeth, under her tongue, behind her trembling eyeballs. She did not dare breathe, *for fear the wind in her lungs would cause her to explode, and then her lover stroked her with his fingers.*

No, not his fingers.

Not fingers...

Sapient Metic Fallows awoke in her bunk, awash in sweat.

The zero-G safety straps she had clipped over her before taking a couple of hypno tablets and drifting into merciful voidsleep chafed, grinding the salt of her own sweat back into her skin. She freed herself with a flip of the fingers on the straps' latches and bounced slightly off the sleeping shelf, pushed into the gravity-less space of her tiny quarters by the equal and opposite reaction to the working of her stubby fingers against her own chest.

Fingers.

Did she miss sex that much? She shook her head to no one and peeled off her one-piece sleepfilm garment in a slow forward roll, tumbling directly into the corner of the cabin that was her ultrasonic shower. No, if sex had been that interesting, she never would have left Tertius, would have taken a planetside job somewhere. The Fleet employed plenty of people in Requisitions, Supply Chain, Maintenance, Interstellar Comms, Strategy, Intelligence, and other functions, and she could easily have found a berth. Einstein, she cursed to herself, if she'd really been that interested in sex, she could have taken a job at Harbor Hospitality Services, and had all the sex she wanted. There were plenty of men—and women—who liked a stubby body like hers.

No, she had insisted on entering the Sapient Corps because knowledge was much better than sex. It gave you similar power over others, but left you feeling cleaner. So she had said goodbye to her companion of two years... she strained now to remember his name as she splayed and parted her thick brown hair to let the ultrasonic beams pound her scalp clean... Brion, that was it, and taken to the void.

She heard a soft *thud* in her quarters and froze in place. A footfall?

Her back was to the tiny cramped space, and prickles crept slowly up her spine. The fact that she was drifting in zero gravity made it worse. It made every goosepimple feel like the physical touch of an unseen intruder. She forced her mind through the obvious paces, like a child convincing itself to walk into a dark room: she had been alone when she had gone to sleep; her door had been locked; she hadn't unlocked it. She was alone.

She tried, but could not by the sheer power of her mind force the muscles in her back to unknot. At least she managed to keep her back turned. The thought that someone was watching her shower was distracting, made her feel warm and tingle in ways she couldn't quite consciously describe.

She heard the footstep again—

pushed off the indentation around a hatch in the wall—

and spun around.

Nothing.

Her quarters were empty.

Maybe, she thought, she could get Doctor Plectrum to have the ship increase her dose of downer, the libido suppressant administered to every crewperson of the Fleet's voidgoing vessels. This wasn't her first troubling dream of the voidjourney. Metic snapped off the ultrasonic beams and frowned, wishing they had a *COLD* setting and actual water, like you could find in a Hospitality Bath, or the oldest buildings on Tertius. She felt clean but still troubled, flushed, uncomfortable.

She itched inside, and had no way to scratch.

Metic checked her wall comms unit as she slipped into her black sapient's trousers and tunic and found a blinking orange bridge summons, priority *PROMPT*. That was it, she told herself. She had heard the summons activate, and in her distracted, nearly-daydreaming state, she had convinced herself it was a footfall. But the thought didn't let her force a sigh of relief through her lungs.

She exited into the ring-passage outside her quarters and headed for Captain Charamander's Briefing Room.

She returned the crisp salutes of two passing engineers—like most of the Femship *Atalanta's* officers, Metic bunked alongside the crew—and continued towards the central lift. The engineers were both pretty, prettier than she was, and the fact that their hair was dangerously close to being on their collar and therefore longer than the Chastity Regs permitted suggested awareness of their own charms, and perhaps a touch of vanity. Metic was not bothered by this, but she was bothered by the fact that she noticed their attractiveness, and that the fire in her belly continued to smolder. She was not a sapphic—could *not* be a sapphic, and travel the void in any of the Fleet's ships, all of which were sex-segregated for the same reason that the crew's rations were tampered with.

The Fleet made plenty of mistakes, but it knew this one true thing about human nature: that there was no such thing as safe sex. Any sex was dangerous, but especially sex in the cooped-up interior of a void-ship, isolated, deprived of the space and means to vent rage, envy, possessiveness, and the other brutal passions of the dark underbelly of the human soul. A lovers' tiff with a blaster in the middle could easily mean a ruptured hull and the death of hundreds of valuable personnel, a waste of millions of hours of expensive training. Sex in a voidship was a breath away from violence and catastrophe, so the Fleet went to great lengths to be sure its voidships were chaste. Such sapphics and thebans as undoubtedly slipped through the Fleet's screening kept their heads down and their couplings discreet. The others waited for planetside R&R or home leave, and were grateful for whatever it was the ship put in their food.

The lift door hushed open and shut to admit her, the interior lit up in recognition of her rank, and Metic grabbed another rung just in time to steady herself as the lift shot bridgeward. A minor shift of physical orientation prepared her body for the onset of the voidship's artificial gravitational pull.

She tried not to think of any similes to describe the action of the lift, and in a few short seconds the subtle stasis fields that prevent the lift's passengers from braining themselves when it decelerated took hold of her, the lift stopped and hushed open, and Metic Fallows, Sapient First Class, Lector of Xenoarchaeology and Ancient Terran Languages, pushed herself out onto the bridge level of the *Atalanta*. The light gravity, set by Fleet protocols at 0.75 Tertian, pulled her to the corrugated floor.

"Sapient Fallows," the Watch Ensign, a pretty girl whose name escaped Metic's memory, recognized her. "You're wanted in the briefing room."

Metic spotted the bawdy possibilities inherent in the words *you're wanted*. As required by the Chastity Regs, she ignored them. It wasn't hard for her, she tried to tell herself. She wasn't interested in sex. Even her recent dreams were... were nothing, a physiological phenomenon, nothing more.

She nodded thanks to the Watch Ensign and entered the briefing room.

"Sapient." Captain Sarit Charamander whirled in her high-backed, heavy-armed chair to face Metic. Sarit was a cinnamon-skinned woman in a gold Captain's tunic whose tall, lean body seemed a strange mismatch for a full-cheeked, almost *plump* face. As if by way of a fierce statement of adherence to the spirit above and beyond the letter of the Regs, Captain Charamander kept her head shaved.

Metic saluted, and only then noticed, hanging above the oval table in the center of the Briefing Room, the image filling the vidscreen. It was a planetside landscape of pink stone, carved by wind or water into twisted columns and narrow ravines and striated with dark green streaks. Something deep within her, something that coiled around the base of her spine, trembled at the sight. It might be the perspective, but the pink stone seemed to lean at impossible angles, in directions that hinted at a tangled, physics-denying spatial labyrinth the eye couldn't quite catch. Metic squinted, but still couldn't quite manage to follow the curves.

"We're in orbit," she said, half-intending a question. "Did we detect a distress beacon?" She knew something was out of the ordinary because the *Atalanta* had been traveling for Calidia, a world known to her from her studies as principally tropical in climate. The *Atalanta* carried medication and other supplies for the Calidian Provisional State, the rowdy little potentate that ran the planet these days and was more or less a friend of the Fleet and the Federation, and in exchange the Calidians were to let Metic examine a set of recently-discovered ruins, allegedly replete with some sort of mummified, semi-anthropoid life form. This was what Sapient Metic had come for; this was why she had left what's his name. Brion. Knowledge.

The image Metic saw on the screen could not be the Calidia she had read about in preparation for their arrival.

"Yes," Captain Charamander said. Her face twitched, betraying something that gnawed at her, maybe something she didn't want to admit; Metic was not a sapient-heurist, but some lies were more obvious than others. "The crew is not generally aware of the contents of that beacon."

Metic now looked around the table and found faces she knew. Doctor Plectrum sat with a straight back, a curious half-smile on her lips and her iron-gray hair plastered in tight ringlets around her temples. Lieutenant Lillian Chatterjee was short and pale, her skin an almost unnatural gray-white, like an albino's. Her eyes gleamed with enthusiasm, as they always did. Lieutenant Chatterjee, Metic remembered, was a communications engineer; she and the doctor wore the blue uniforms of bridge officers. Commander Wyot Thulliver was a tough-looking woman, with a face like a boiled ham and an apple-shaped body broadened in the shoulders by exercise and combat. The *Atalanta* was not a fighting ship, but Commander Thulliver was first officer of the ship's complement of rangers, professional scouts and soldiers trained in planetside operations, guerilla warfare, wilderness survival, and extreme environments. With Commander Thulliver was her aide, Lancer Elsa Durmont. Lancer Durmont was slender woman whose poise reminded Metic of a Tertian cat, about to spit its venom in your face or flee, and you couldn't know which until it made the first move. The rangers wore their ready-for-action browns.

"We're going planetside," Metic murmured, and she sat. "Is there a message?"

Captain Charamander remained standing, her feet shoulder-width apart and her hands behind her. "Message?" Metic read curiosity and amusement in her eyes, along with something else... that thing the Captain didn't want to talk about. "Why should there be a message?"

Metic controlled a pang of irritation at the Captain's heavy-handed attempt to play games. "Unless you have sealed orders I'm unaware of, we're off course. This means that something unexpected has happened. We're in orbit around a planet you think may contain hostiles."

"May," the Captain acknowledged.

"Hence the rangers who will accompany your landing party. Lieutenant Chatterjee will keep you informed. My presence might indicate ruins, but if we were going down to look at an empty archaeological site there would be no need for the doctor. Therefore I infer that we are going down to look for known or suspected populations that may be ill. And *either* these populations inhabit an archaeological site, *or...* and I think this is more likely... they sent a message and you'd like me to help you understand it." Metic folded her hands on the table in front of her and tried not to look smug. Whatever power her knowledge might give her, it was unwise to cross the Captain of a voidship in her own briefing room.

Commander Thulliver cracked open her boiled ham and emitted a bark that might have been meant to express humor. Grudgingly, Captain Charamander followed with a single raised eyebrow and a head-shaking grin. Two finger taps to the so-discreet-as-to-be-practically-invisible controls on the edge of the table's surface changed the visual on the Briefing Room's vidscreen.

The image that appeared was shadowed and streaked with bolts of static, as if the video had been captured in a cave using old or homemade equipment, and in the midst of an electrical storm, to boot.

"Look behind the man," Captain Charamander said softly. Metic squinted at the screen.

Partly cloaked by the shadow and the distortion, a man's face and shoulders jerked into view. His mouth opened, and with jerking, exaggerated movements of his jaw, he spoke.

"This is a distress call. Voiddate eleven seven fifty-four, dot seventeen, dot thirty-two. I am Captain Jade Worthing of Fleet Homship *Actaeon.*"

His voice sounded wrong, grating and scraped. Metic ignored the sound and focused on the image; behind Captain Worthing was a pink stone wall, and on it, scrawled in a brown paint, were large letters.

VENTUM CAVE, Metic read.

The transmission continued. "*Actaeon* and all his crew are stranded on this uncatalogued planet, coordinates to which I transmit in the data band accompanying this message."

Captain Worthing leaned forward and Metic saw there were more letters behind him, splashed in the same big hand. *SEMEN IN VENTO LATET.*

There was more. Worthing's motions were exaggerated and jerky as he clutched at the blue tunic of his Fleet uniform. "We have limited supplies and request the assistance of any Fleet voidship within range of this transmission. Captain Worthing out."

"I read the words 'wine cave,'" Lieutenant Chatterjee blurted out. "*Ventum* has to be 'wine' or 'vintage.' They must have encountered a local population, one that's technologically advanced enough to ferment wine."

Metic was so surprised at the outburst it was all she could do to raise an eyebrow. Doctor Plectrum snorted. Feeling flushed and surprised, but also excited at the obvious mystery, Metic took a moment to gather her thoughts. A mystery meant knowledge, unknown things to discover.

"*Ventum cave*," she said, pronouncing the words carefully, "is Latin, an old Terra Prime language from the pre-Industrial Age, and has nothing to do with either caves or wine. It means 'beware the wind.'"

"I know what *Latin* is."

The communications engineer looked like a whipped dog, so Metic smiled at her by way of a comforting gesture. "Good guess, though."

"And the rest?" Captain Charamander still stood. She shifted from one foot to the other as she spoke.

"'The sperm lies hidden in the wind,'" Metic said, and then felt her face burn. Doctor Plectrum looked at Metic with cool, wide-open eyes and not a hint of a smile. Lieutenant Chatterjee blushed, which, given her complexion, made her look like a beet. Thulliver and Durmont both began to laugh, the low, insinuating chuckles of professional soldiers.

"Not sure that's the right place to hide it," the ranger Commander grunted, "but I guess I'll defer to the sapient."

"*Seed*," Metic corrected herself stiffly. "'The seed lies hidden in the wind. Beware the wind.'"

Her correction only made the rangers laugh harder.

The restraining harness clicked softly as Metic anchored herself into her seat, tightening each strap in turn over her exosuit with careful attention.

"You well?" Doctor Plectrum asked, buckling herself into the adjacent seat. *Atalanta's* dropship was a small voidcraft, seating a pilot and up to six passengers in tight rows of two. A bay beneath their feet, visible through the steel webbing of the craft's floor, held its ordinary provision of emergency supplies, along with extra water, rations, and lightweight blankets.

Metic shook her head slowly. "I think I need more downer. I've been... having dreams. Feeling..."

"Excitable?"

Metic nodded.

"*More* downer?" Plectrum looked intrigued. "How recently have you had these dreams?"

There was nothing to blush about, Metic told herself. Plectrum was her physician. This was a medical question. "Recently. Last sleep cycle."

"You're not alone." Doctor Plectrum lowered her voice. In the fore of the dropship, Lieutenant Chatterjee ran through pre-ejection procedures, sharing all the vessel's analytics with *Atalanta's* bridge over a comms link. The rangers had not yet boarded. "The sheer number of voidgoers sharing your complaint is making my sickbay look like the galaxy's slowest bordello. Never has the wisdom of the Fleet's policy of sex segregation been more apparent."

"Is the ship's synthesizer broken? Maybe it's stopped lacing the rations."

Doctor Plectrum sighed. "*Atalanta* has been dispensing triple the standard dosage of downer into the rations of every single woman aboard her for three weeks. I know this because I instructed the ship's computer myself, and I know it because I have been testing random samples of the rations daily. The good Femship has done her job, and by rights we should all be as cold as Belorian Ice Sloths. Instead, we burn."

"Beware the wind," Metic joked, and immediately regretted it. It shouldn't amuse her that her rations were being altered without her knowledge. "It seems a little presumptuous for you to experiment on the crew."

Plectrum stared at her coldly. "I don't experiment. I try to heal. Only in this case, what I'm instructed by the Fleet in its infinite wisdom to try to cure is arguably the fundamental drive of our species, the great motivator and the mechanism of genetic hygiene, the obsession that has not only led to our greatest crimes but has also fueled our artistic triumphs."

Metic blinked. "Sex?"

"Sex. You are what you are, my dear sapient, because your ancestors for millions of years have been violent, sex-obsessed maniacs. The inability of homo sapiens to keep it in his—*and her*—pants has driven genetic diversity, protecting us from the risks of becoming a monoculture and defeating uncounted parasites along the way, while the sexes' respective attractions to the best of all possible mates, by hook or by crook, has spread the best genes far and wide throughout the pool. Don't they teach you these things in the Sapient Corps?"

"I'm a xeno-archaeologist. And a linguist."

"And a human. Which means that just underneath the skin, you're a sex fiend anxious to come out and party."

Metic wanted to change the subject, but the material at hand didn't allow her to change it very much. "Do you think our landing on this planet has something to do with... with the burning?"

"Void and Nebula," the doctor cursed. "I hope not."

"But you wonder," Metic insisted. "And that explains your presence in the landing party."

Doctor Plectrum didn't respond to the suggestion. "Let's find these poor stranded Homshipmen. If we're lucky, maybe the Captain will authorize a little improvised planetside R&R here and now and we can cure this shipwide sweet tooth with a candy binge."

Metic almost laughed. "And if we're not lucky?"

"If we're not lucky, I have the authority under the Chastity Regs to declare a libidinal emergency and prescribe the R&R myself."

The clump of boots on the dropship's ladder announced the boarding of the rangers.

"Safety restraints, everyone," Lieutenant Chatterjee called.

Metic's chanted march through Belorian prospective mood conjugations couldn't quite distract her from thinking about Doctor Plectrum's tirade about sex. Worse, she continued to feel a presence at her elbow, or just behind her. A sexual presence, though it didn't quite feel *male* to her. *You are not alone*, the doctor had said, and the words hung in her consciousness and mocked her. She told herself she was grateful the restraining straps wouldn't let her turn around and look.

What did snap her out of tangled, conflicting lines of thought was a sudden string of curses from Lillian Chatterjee.

And then a violent impact, as if she had been punched in her entire body by a fist the size of a tree.

The rangers were out the shuttle door while Doctor Plectrum was still shaking Metic out of the shock that enveloped her. When Lancer Durmont shouted the all clear, Metic followed, wobbling. She wore a blaster on her hip, and though she had completed the required minimum training with the weapon at the Academy—and the required minimum was extensive—she was unaccustomed to the weight, and felt like she was hunching sideways as she walked.

"What happened?" she asked.

"Crash." Doctor Plectrum's matter-of-fact monosyllable rang like a gong.

Lieutenant Chatterjee had brought the dropship down in a roughly circular canyon with high pink and green walls, but it had grazed the cliff face on its way down—Metic could see the charred pink where the collision had happened—and then landed on its side. The dropship was wrecked; Metic was no engineer, but she could see that two of the three rocket engines the craft used to propel itself back off the planet were crumpled and useless.

The planet didn't care. The sky overhead pulsed a shiny indigo through the visor plate of Metic's exosuit, lit by the system's tiny but brilliant yellow sun. The atmosphere of the planet, like its gravity, registered well within human comfort range, but Captain Charamander had ordered them to take no chances.

Metic heard the shuttle door shut behind her. "I'm sorry," she heard Chatterjee mumble behind her. The sapient spun around, half expecting to see the young engineer shaking her hair free in the atmosphere, but instead saw Chatterjee brandishing a handheld sensor. "There's no wind."

"Nothing to be afraid of then, is there?" Doctor Plectrum muttered. She didn't sound convinced. "Have you informed Captain Charamander of... the *nature* of our landing?"

Lillian looked away. "The dropship's comms unit is totaled," she said. "I can't raise *Atalanta* on it, and our suit units aren't powerful enough."

Doctor Plectrum pointed at the nearest wrecked engine. "This thing isn't taking us back, that's for sure."

"Which way to the coordinates of *Actaeon*?" Metic asked. "They may or may not have a functioning dropship, but we know their beacon works. If we find them, we can reach *Atalanta*."

Chatterjee consulted the sensor and pointed. "Up on that butte," she said, her voice coming in crisp and clear through the earpiece comms unit in Metic's exosuit. "Or behind it."

Lancer Durmont pulled backpacks out of the shuttle hold and distributed them to the landing party. Unlike the others, the two rangers did everything with a weapon in one hand, and Metic noticed that as the Lancer worked at the packs, her Commander stood careful watch, scanning the canyon walls intently with her blaster carbine held at the ready.

"Look at this, sapient."

The voice belonged to Doctor Plectrum, and Metic turned to see what was so interesting. Plectrum stood beside a boulder twice her own size, kicking it with the booted toe of her exosuit. Thick flakes of pink dust scuffed away from the boulder as she hammered at it, drifting down to settle on the ground.

Not dust, Metic realized. Some kind of plant life—fungus, or lichen, or dried algae. It flaked off the stone in thin rings.

"The stone isn't pink at all," Doctor Plectrum said, once she had exposed a face-sized patch of it. "Or green, either. It's a very boring brown."

"Newton." Lieutenant Chatterjee whistled, a sound that the

exosuit's comms unit turned into a piercing shriek in Metic's ear. The Lieutenant looked around at the canyon walls. "You mean all of that...?"

"Yes, she does," Commander Thulliver barked. "She means that all of that, under the cake frosting, is really a very boring brown. Let's not forget our mission, or the chain of command. Lancer Durmont will lead out and I'll bring up the rear."

The Lancer marched briskly towards the butte.

Metic shrugged into her backpack and followed, but before she was out of sight of the shuttle she turned back for a last look. Wisps of the pink vegetation Doctor Plectrum had scraped off the rock drifted slowly upward in the air, diffusing into a pinkish mist that couldn't obscure the shuttle, but gave it a fleshy organic halo, like a pink dandelion blown into a cloud by a child's breath.

Beware the wind, she thought, wondering who had written that message and why. *The seed hides in the wind.*

Lancer Durmont disappeared into a narrow ravine up ahead, just as the sun passed out of view and the canyon plunged into late afternoon shadow. Metic stopped, staring at the ravine mouth.

"What is it?" Lieutenant Chatterjee asked as the engineer and the doctor came up behind and joined her in her hesitation.

Metic stared at the ravine and shook her head, unable to quite put a finger on the source of her unease.

"Look too much like forbidden fruit?" Doctor Plectrum chuckled.

It did; the ravine walls were pink, though streaked through with dark green, and a shiny sort of pink at that, a pink of flesh and secrets. It might be a trick of the light, an illusion created by the last movements of the sun's rays on the canyon walls, but the pink looked to Metic like it was even *moving*.

"Pretend you're delivering a baby," Doctor Plectrum suggested. "Or administering a pelvic exam." She kept marching.

Lieutenant Chatterjee stayed by Metic's side. "Is it too terrible?" she asked, and there was a faint sound of strain in her voice.

"You're the sapient of a Federation Femship!" Doctor Plectrum called back through the comms link. "You cannot let yourself be defeated by imaginary pudenda!"

Metic spurred herself forward, only a couple of steps ahead of Commander Thulliver. Plectrum was right; there was nothing here to fear. The *Atalanta* had come to an uncharted planet, of which there were many. The Femship's crew would rescue the stranded crew of another Fleet voidship, which was, if not strictly routine, neither particularly frightening nor at all heroic. Unrelated to the shipwreck and the rescue, Metic and some of the Femship's other crewmembers had been feeling a little more... *aroused* than they should. This might be a malfunction, or an unexpected side effect of an undetected illness in the ship's crew, or even a prank. In the end, it was nothing. *Atalanta* would rescue her brother ship, and then carry her sapient on to examine Calidian mummies.

And the reports she would file from Calidia, and the papers she would write afterwards, would make Metic Fallows a household name. Not that she wanted the fame, no—she just wanted to be the *one who knew*.

She entered the ravine without looking up, and for the first time she drew her blaster.

Lancer Durmont tried half a dozen ravines before finding one that led to the top of the butte. By the time the party had explored multiple dead ends and wound its way up through the narrow crevasse to its further opening, the sun had set. Metic emerged from the chasm sweating inside her exosuit and knocking free small clouds of pink with each kick of her foot or scrabbling for a handhold, only to see that the butte was broader than she had realized, and taller, too. Above them it rose again, a butte upon a butte, its great shadow blocking out the light of two moons and myriad stars in unfamiliar configurations. This close to the looming bulwark of stone, the shape seemed wrong. It blocked too much light, it menaced the tiny Terrans on its gnarled and jagged hump with sullen, silent hatred, and its vastness and proximity denied Metic of even the simple escape of looking away. Everywhere she turned her eyes waited black walls, and underneath night's cloak she knew lurked the fluttering, twisting, slimy pink with stripes of green. Even the unfamiliar stars, usually a source of novelty and wonder even to experienced void travelers, stared at her with troglodyte resentment and willed her to leave.

"We make camp here," Commander Thulliver ordered. Metic's flesh pulsed against her will with every syllable; she told herself the warmth of her body was fatigue, and resisted looking at the other women.

Lancer Durmont set up an exotent of interlocking plastic rods and tiles while Lieutenant Chatterjee tried again to reach *Atalanta*. Even at the higher altitude, though, the exosuit comms units were simply inadequate.

The party 'ate,' if that was the right word, by attaching ration tubes to the chest-mounted feeding ports of their suits and loading the condensed, sweetened contents into the recycling systems of their exosuits. Metic ached to peel off the suit for comfort, and to get away from her own smell, but knew she shouldn't. *Ventum cave.* Even if there wasn't much *ventum* to speak of.

Metic lay down to sleep inside her exosuit, wishing she had even an ultrasonic shower and a sleepfilm garment instead, and turned the audio of her exosuit's comms unit way down. Lieutenant Chatterjee lay between the sapient and the doctor. Metic looked at the milky-white opaque ceiling and tried to empty her mind, grateful at least that hers was the only body she could smell. Lancer Durmont joined them, and Metic drifted into restless dreams.

A man's voice, dark and muddy, croaked into her ear as she slept. "I crashed the dropship because I was distracted," it said. In her dream, it seemed to Metic that the man's voice came out of Lillian Chatterjee, only Lieutenant Chatterjee rose swaying above Metic like an enormous, lust-scorched worm, her entire length scabbed pink.

I know, Metic said. She didn't know how she knew.

"I was distracted," Lillian continued, "by thoughts of *you*. Surely you must have noticed."

In the darkness Metic awoke, sweating, and pulled her hand out of the grip of Lieutenant Chatterjee. If she was awake, the comms engineer gave no sign of it, and Metic soon plunged back into fits of sleep punctuated by the crisp sounds of footsteps outside the exotent.

In the morning, Commander Thulliver lay sleeping inside the shelter and Lancer Durmont was gone.

Elsa Durmont had disappeared, but not without a trace. There were scorch marks from a blaster on nearby stones, black scars where pink and green alike had been burned away and the boring brown rock beneath revealed and defiled. And there were tracks.

"Something took her." Thulliver pointed. "That way."

The pink was disturbed in ragged furrows that skipped from side to side but led to the corner of the butte where the stone rose again.

Metic felt tired.

"We'll get her back," Thulliver growled. She checked the power level on her carbine and began marching up the scuffed trail.

"We don't know what might be out there!" Metic called after the ranger Commander.

"No." Thulliver got smaller and smaller in Metic's vision, but her voice came just as clearly through the exosuit comms. "But we know it has our Lancer."

"It survived laser blasts!" Chatterjee objected.

Thulliver sighed. Despite her brisk walking pace and the restricted flow of oxygen she had to be getting through the exosuit's recycling systems, her breathing was almost perfectly normal, as if she were at rest. "As far as I can tell," she said, "Lancer Durmont missed her shots."

To Metic Fallows, sapient and unriddler of the secrets of dead civilizations, that fact offered more mystery than it did answers. Lieutenant Chatterjee looked at her with helpless eyes and began to round her lips as if to whisper—

but then caught herself, maybe realizing that the linked comms units of the exosuits made private conversations impossible. Doctor Plectrum moved first, breaking the stalemate to push on after the ranger. Metic followed, and she thought she heard the faintest sound of a whimper over the comms as Chatterjee rushed not to be left behind.

"Don't worry," Commander Wyot Thulliver grunted from the head of the procession. "We're still going to find *Actaeon*, too."

"We have to," Metic whispered.

The scuff marks led them in a trail around the rough, broad ledge of the butte, and when they turned inward and upward again, something in the terrain stopped Metic. She looked, looked again, and then called out.

"Wait!"

"What is it, sapient?" Commander Thulliver pronounced Metic's title with an audible sneer.

"Look." Metic gestured with both hands. "Look what you're standing on."

Thulliver looked down, and then above herself at the pink stone. "Looks like a defile to me. I think it will lead to the top. That's clearly where the trail goes."

"Hooke's eyes," Doctor Plectrum swore. She saw it.

"What is it?" Lieutenant Chatterjee sounded forlorn at the realization that she was missing out.

"It's a road," Metic said. "A road bounded by columns."

She was sure of it. The columns were hard to see because many of them were worn down to stumps, like the rotted and missing teeth in the head of a poor Backworlder who'd never seen a dentist, but a few of the columns still rose up and in, two of them nearly touching, as if the road had once passed through stone rings on its way to ascend the mount. Or immense ribs. Even the worn stumps were still symmetrically spaced enough that, but for the fuzzy pink carpet that obscured everything, Metic was sure she would have seen them sooner for what they were.

"Hawking's hangnail," Thulliver snarled, "are you going to get all hot and bothered for crumbling ruins *now*?"

But the truth was that the realization that the landing party stood on an old, lost road, of a civilization that might be utterly unknown to Metic and to Terran civilization in general, didn't get the sapient hot and bothered. In fact, she realized with restrained delight in a corner of her brain, it was the first time in days—maybe even weeks—that she wasn't thinking about the inflamed cravings of her body at all. She tried not to notice her relief, for fear that the simple act of acknowledgement would bring her attention back to her flesh and its desires. Cold imagination flooded her mind like brilliant light, building the lost columns to their former dimensions, developing wrinkles in the defile ahead into neatly-carved steps.

She had to look.

She brushed pink and green fuzz off the rock. As she did, the green fell away and hit the ground like a picked scab. The pink did not. It clung to her fingers, and she saw as she looked closely at it that the pink substance looked like a mass of ropy worms. Worms that wriggled, ever so slightly. Not enough for her to be sure they were actually moving, as opposed to responding to breezes Metic couldn't feel through her exosuit, but enough to wrap neatly around her fingers. She shook them off and scraped more handfuls away from the rock, hurling the pink mess into the air around her and behind her until she had cleared a patch of stone.

Which was covered in glyphs.

She gasped, and Plectrum and Chatterjee gasped with her.

"What is it?" Wyot Thulliver asked. "More Latin?"

"Better." Metic traced swirls, lightning bolts, and arrows with the tip of her exosuited finger. There were even figures that were clearly depictions of some kind of animal life, though the forms were hunched over, vaguely reptilian, long-tailed, and six-armed. A burst-like image, she thought, might be the sun, and she wondered whether the arch-bound road might have a solar alignment. A few measurements taken with her handheld ought to give the *Atalanta's* computer enough data to detect any such connection. Collections of dots and dashes might be numbers, and she wondered if they could contain astronomical data. She'd need to run long-term visible star simulations, forward and back, once she got back to *Atalanta*.

She looked up and down the road. With Elsa Durmont missing, it was a dereliction of duty, not to mention unkind, to think of leaving the landing party to the search while she paced off and recorded distances or extrapolated ancient constellation movements. She indulged herself in a few seconds of the fantasy anyway before saying any more. "Something new. Something we can't read. Yet."

"Oh yeah, that sounds much better." Thulliver snorted. "My Lancer's still missing. How about we hold the reading lessons after we get her back?"

Metic followed the ranger Commander reluctantly up the highway of ribs. Beneath her feet she could feel the broad firm steps she had imagined, obscured from view by drifts of pink stuff, pinned and bounded by the green clots. It killed her to walk past column after column, imagining as she did that they must all be covered with glyphs. Traces of a new civilization, glimpses of an ancient world, an unknown tongue. A dead language? A lost race? She imagined four-armed saurian sages, gracefully trundling down their primeval road to greet the rising of a benevolent solstitial mother with wordless baritone polyphony.

She almost tripped over a stair. Or did the race survive, here in this impossible, horrible landscape? Had the creatures that had built the arch-bound road and covered its columns with glyphs also taken Lancer Durmont? Had they captured—or done worse to—the crew of Homship *Actaeon*? Were they the 'wind' she was warned to fear? Were they not four-armed, but perhaps winged? Involuntarily, she cringed and looked up at the sky.

Fear banished the images of ancient civilization from her mind.

In their place, the burning of her body returned.

The stair was long because the steps were low, and to ascend to the height of the mound the road turned and wound up around its outer edge. Their progress slowed and the breathing of three of the party, at least, became labored. The booted feet of the ranger Commander before her kicked up a cloud of pink fiber, and as Metic marched directly into it her legs became ever more coated in pink strands, like spun and colored sugar at a country fair. She ignored her new layer and looked up at the mountain above them. What might have seemed, before she noticed the arches, mere outcroppings of rock or shallow depressions in its face now appeared to her as ledges, windows, parapets, arrow slits.

And on those ledges, in the shadows of those depressions, she saw movement.

"Stop."

"Let me guess," Thulliver snorted, "you've found an alien latrine."

"A garbage dump would be more useful," the sapient inside her forced Metic to mutter. She pointed up at the depressions. "Something's up there. Moving."

Thulliver scanned the wall wordlessly. The ranger adjusted a knob at the side of her exosuit helmet as she did so, and it took Metic a moment to remember what the knob was—Thulliver was adjusted the magnification power of her faceplate. Feeling slightly foolish, Metic touched her knob as well and zoomed in on the wall.

Close up, she could see even more clearly that the parapets had not been her imagination. There were narrower stairs and ledges than the one on which the *Atalanta*'s landing party trudged, stairs and ledges with superior vantage points. These were siege defenses, she realized. Defenders with the higher ground could hurl stones, or garbage, or flaming objects, down on any invader approaching by the main road. The existence of such defenses told her more about her six-limbed saurians... theirs had not been an entirely peaceful world.

No sign of movement, though.

"We have to recover Lancer Durmont," the doctor said. "But let's not forget that our mission is to find Homship *Actaeon* and its crew. Movement might be them."

Commander Thulliver shifted her grip on her carbine, holding it ready to fire up the wall. "Lieutenant Chatterjee. A flare, if you please."

Chatterjee fumbled with the pouch at her thigh and extracted a flare. The device was self-igniting and easy to spark; the comms engineer snapped off the tip with her hands and pointed it skyward, launching a bright green flare up into the indigo sky.

With a jolt, Metic realized it was afternoon again already.

They waited.

There was no response to the flare.

"Right," the ranger hissed through her teeth. "Keep your eyes open."

The winding stair ended, just beneath the top of the butte, in a cave. This time Commander Thulliver snapped and fired one of her own flares, hurling a green spark into the yawning abyss. The witch flame struck a wall and burned, illuminating a cavern like a gaping maw, with a stair that ascended at the far end into a hole in the ceiling. More siege defenses, Metic thought. The fitzing light of the flare turned the pink carpet green, and the stripes of green into bands of deep black.

Without detecting anything that might be a word, Metic thought she heard voices. A fist squeezed her heart.

"Come on," Commander Thulliver said. "Let's not wait until the flare burns out."

Metic followed the ranger up a long, steep flight of stairs, passing through an infinite void before emerging in the center of a square plaza. The curving columns of the avenue of rings were here repeated, leaning outward, away from the plaza and then curving up and back as the stone supports in the facades of crumbling walls. Metic's blood pounded in her ears and she deliberately put her blaster back into its holster, afraid that in her enthusiasm for the potential discoveries she might be tempted to scour away the pink scum with firepower.

"Leibniz's knuckle," Commander Thulliver ground out between her teeth. "Durmont!" she barked into the exosuit comms unit. "Where are you?"

"What happened to the trail?" The doctor's voice had a strained sound to it, but her faceplate was turned away and Metic couldn't see her expression.

The pink fuzz-scum-slime covering the ruins of this lost citadel atop the mountain was intact on the walls, still pinned by the striated bands of dark green, but the pink ground covering was severely disturbed.

Metic's heart skipped a beat. "Is this city inhabited?"

"No way in Newton's bunghole," Thulliver shot back.

"Maybe it's the crew of *Actaeon*," Lieutenant Chatterjee suggested.

"It better be." Thulliver marched forward, leading with the muzzle of her carbine. "For their sake."

"It's getting late," Doctor Plectrum observed. "And we left the exotent set up below."

"We left in pursuit of a kidnapper," Thulliver growled.

"A kidnapper who works at night." The doctor pointed at the deepening indigo of the sky. "Which is fast returning."

Thulliver opened her mouth as if her next move was to bite the doctor's head clean off her shoulders. Metic shoved her body between the two women.

"Where is *Actaeon*?" she asked Chatterjee. "It's as good a place as any to look for Durmont," she said to placate Thulliver, and to the doctor, "and we can find shelter there."

Lillian Chatterjee consulted her handheld sensor before pointing. "Two hundred meters."

Metic briskly walked in the indicated direction, calculating that her departure would force the others to follow, and cut off any more argument. And if she was wrong, at least a little distance would get her out of the shouting match.

She turned at a strange angle from the plaza, following a road that went where Chatterjee had pointed without being quite straight or direct. The way turned, the footing underneath slanted now this way and that, and Metic felt she was in a carnival attraction; a mirror that showed her as tall and thin would not have been out of place. For stretches, the darkening sky disappeared as her way cut through the middle of a crumbling building like a tunnel, and the echoes of her feet and her breath sounded like other feet and the breathing of other lungs in the darkness around her. She pulled her blaster again, not quite meaning to, and tried to visualize again the peaceful sun-worshipping lizards of her imagination.

Which, in her heart of hearts, she knew to be complete fiction. What *was* real was the fear in her heart and the burning in her loins.

And then she came through the tunnel and saw *Actaeon*. "It's here," she announced. She stood still to get a good look at the voidship.

Homship *Actaeon* had crashed into a many-storeyed warren of a building. Scorch marks all around told Metic a story of thrusters being fired to lessen the impact. Multiple weaving paths trodden among the pink and green worked their way through the rubble around the vessel.

The crew of *Actaeon*, Metic thought.

Or paths left by creatures that met them here.

"Hello, *Actaeon!*" she called. Anyone in an exosuit with a working comms unit, or anyone monitoring standard Federation channels inside the voidship, ought to be able to hear her. "Hello, *Actaeon*, this is Sapient Metic Fallows of Fleet Femship *Atalanta*. Repeat, this is Femship *Atalanta*, here to assist."

Silence.

And then the wind picked up. She couldn't feel it, but Metic could hear the wind whistling past the helmet of her exosuit, and she saw a furred fringe of pink lift off the ground around the margins of *Actaeon* and disintegrate into the air.

The seed hides in the wind, she thought. What seed? What wind? Who would leave that message? Her mind's eye flashed a thousand solar cycles, ten thousand, maybe, into the past, and she imagined a wind battering into pieces the civilization that had built this odd, crooked city. Had the wind brought the seed? Was the seed the pink fungal worm that covered everything... or was it the green? Or both?

A footfall in the darkness behind her.

Metic spun and fired—

and missed disintegrating Lillian Chatterjee by the narrowest of margins. The red blaster bolt flashed past, the comms engineer ducked, and a chunk of stone and pink fungus collapsed out of the ceiling where Metic had shot it.

In the tunnel, something scuttled away.

Metic and Lillian Chatterjee stared at each other with wide eyes.

"Report!" Commander Thulliver snapped over the comms.

"My fault," Metic admitted. "I'm sorry, I got jumpy, I... thought I heard something."

"You did." Lillian grinned weakly. "You heard me."

"I see you," Thulliver said. "Hold your position."

The Ranger and *Atalanta's* doctor jogged out of the dark tunnel double-time, both holding their weapons ready.

"What kept you?" Metic joked.

Thulliver frowned. "I thought I saw something moving, but I was wrong. A trick of the light."

A wave of yearning swept over Metic, bearing on its crest the powerful impression that someone waited for her in the darkness. Not Elsa Durmont, but someone else. Someone... more grand, more powerful.

Metic's lover.

Nonsense!

She shook her head to clear it, looked at Lillian Chatterjee, and saw that the comms engineer's face looked stricken with lust. Maybe it was the same expression she herself wore, she thought, chuckling grimly under her breath.

She needed to get a dose of downer that worked, as soon as she possibly could.

"Speaking of light," she said, "can we agree that we should get inside *Actaeon* and look for survivors?"

"If I had a dozen rangers," Commander Thulliver muttered, "I'd turn this rock jumble inside out tonight."

"But you don't," Metic said. "You've got a ship's doctor, a linguist, and a communications engineer. And we'll keep looking if you want, but we're all so tired we're seeing things, and our mission was to come here to find the crew of *Actaeon*. If they're inside," she shrugged and pointed, "maybe in the morning they can help us look."

"Yes," Lillian Chatterjee said, and she almost sounded like she was crying. "Let's get in out of the wind."

Metic looked at her sharply.

"Fine," Thulliver agreed. "Into *Actaeon* it is."

Actaeon's emergency lights were on. Given their nuclear power source, Metic thought, they'd stay lit and glowing softly blue like this for thousands of years before eventually fading out. The blue lines lay tangled like long phosphorescent snakes along the broken, jumbled passages that cut through the hulk. Given the materials it used to build, the Federation would leave great ruins for the scholars of some future civilization to explore.

"Chatterjee!" Commander Thulliver snapped. "Comms! Find us anyone on this vessel!" Thulliver stationed herself, carbine ready, in the two-abreast crack through which the landing party of *Atalanta* had come through *Actaeon's* hull and watched the descending darkness outside.

Chatterjee found a comms panel and spoke into it. "Attention, crew of Homship *Actaeon*. This is Lieutenant Lillian Chatterjee of Femship *Atalanta*. Please acknowledge."

Silence.

Thulliver growled, still staring outside.

"Log?" Doctor Plectrum asked.

"Downloading it into my handheld now," Lillian answered. "Encrypted, of course."

"What about a personnel list?" the doctor pressed. "And a deck map. We can go look for *Actaeon's* officers."

"How about the ship's supply of downer?" Metic interjected. The question caught even her by surprise, and she stammered to justify it. "I... I wonder if maybe *Actaeon* had been experiencing anything unusual."

Lillian pressed keys on her handheld. "No downer," she said. "And no record of when it was all dispensed."

Doctor Plectrum glared at them both. She opened her mouth—

and Commander Thulliver fired her carbine. The red blaster bolt threw smoke and a crimson flash into *Actaeon's* corridor. Thulliver cursed. "There's something moving out there."

"Have you tried the infrared optics?" Lillian suggested.

"Shut your igorant facehole, you whiny little sapphic!" Thulliver snarled. The unexpected ferocity of the attack knocked Metic back on her heels. "I'm using the infrared *now*. Whatever it is I'm looking at isn't *showing* on the infrared."

"Maybe it's the wind." Metic meant her comment to be calming, to defuse the tension. Instead, it brought to her mind's eye the Latin warning behind Captain Worthing.

Conversation dropped to nothing.

"Personnel," Doctor Plectrum repeated herself softly after a few moments, and Lillian Chatterjee jumped to comply.

"Sharing now," the comms engineer said.

Metic's handheld beeped at the reception of data and she looked down at the device. Someone had written a warning in Latin, and there was an obvious candidate for at least an initial query. She tapped in a few characters to search the file for the name and qualifications of *Actaeon's* sapient.

Albert Degas, she read immediately. *Terra Prime History and Literature*.

"*Actaeon's* sapient," she said out loud. "He left us the message. *Beware the wind*, that came from him. We've got to find him."

The ship's deck map showed clearly where Sapient Degas's quarters were, but reaching them was more of a challenge. The first route the landing party attempted ended in frustration, a corridor crushed out of existence by the weight of the voidship's hull. Some scrambling up over ruined bulkheads and sliding on their bellies brought *Atalanta's* landing party to the indicated spot.

As she slid last out of the crack giving access to the corridor where Degas had his quarters, Metic heard scuffing, rasping noises behind her.

"Hello?" she called. "Sapient Degas?" Nothing. "Albert?"

"It's probably nothing," Lillian said worriedly.

Commander Thulliver harrumphed. "You go ahead," she instructed the others. "Find your sapient." With hands and hips she forced her body up a crumpled slope of wreckage and wedged herself into a position above the crack through which they'd come. "Whatever's following us, I'll wait for it here."

"Maybe it's just the wind." Metic could see the strain of Lillian's smile through her visor.

Thulliver squinted down the sights of her carbine at the crack beneath her. "That joke wasn't funny when the sapient said it," she grunted. "Newton knows your sense of humor isn't any better than hers."

"Come on." Metic took Lillian by the hand. The comms engineer put up no resistance, and *Atalanta's* doctor followed close behind.

Two corners, and then a stooped-over shuffle through a corridor whose wall—which would have once been its ceiling—sagged dangerously low brought the women to an opening that Lillian's handheld identified as the quarters of Sapient Degas. The door was gone, and scorch marks and fragments of twisted metal clinging inside the doorframe suggested it had been blasted out of existence. The corridor stank of rot and the chamber, lacking emergency lighting, yawned like an abyss before them.

Metic became aware of the sweat drenching her body inside the exosuit as it seemed to all freeze at once. She shivered, licked her lips, and drew her blaster.

"Degas?" she called.

No answer came, and she stepped inside.

Infrared optics in her visor showed her nothing, so she switched them off, pressed herself against the wall with her weapon ready, and waited.

"Metic?" Lillian called from the corridor.

Her eyes adjusted, and Metic realized she was not alone. The other occupant of the room, though, was still. Still, dead, and headless.

"I need light," Metic said. It had been no more than a half-formed thought, but Lillian Chatterjee stepped into the room behind her and struck another flare.

The corpse sat on a voidchest. In its hand—in *his* hand, Metic forced herself to think—he held a blaster, dangling from a single finger through the trigger guard. Scrawled on the floor in dark letters was another message. Again in Latin.

"What does it say?" Lillian Chatterjee crowded against Metic's back.

"Commander Thulliver," Doctor Plectrum said behind them, speaking into her exosuit comms unit. "You should come see this."

SUB VESTIMENTA ARCANUM, she read. "Under clothing, a secret," she translated.

"Too damn right," the doctor muttered.

Lillian's breathing was loud over the comms unit channel. "What does that mean?" she asked.

Metic hesitated, torn. This had to be Degas. Had he written a message before someone killed him? Before he killed himself? She clutched desperately at the mystery, at the intellectual challenge, willing it to drive the lustful thoughts of falling clothing and the taut skin beneath it from her mind. It almost worked.

She reached forward and touched Degas's corpse—
which lurched forward onto her.

Lillian screamed, Doctor Plectrum cursed, and Metic Fallows fell to the floor with a moldering headless corpse on top of her. She kicked, spat, dragged herself out from under it... and in the act of pushing the body from her, her fingers found what she was looking for.

Through the thin fabric of the dead sapient's tunic, the outline of something hard and square.

Metic stood, trembling from an adrenalin rush.

"Get hold of yourself," Doctor Plectrum grumped, grabbing Lillian Chatterjee by the shoulder and shaking her. Lillian screamed again, high pitched and frantic.

Metic rolled the corpse onto its belly and reached under its tunic—it had to be *it* again, she couldn't bear the thought that she was touching a dead person, so the corpse had to be a mummy, a relic, an impersonal thing—you're an archaeologist, get hold of yourself—
she grabbed the book.

It was a plain brown notebook, untitled. She flipped through it and saw lined pages full of cramped handwriting. The words were not corpses, were not people, missing or dead, so she sank herself into them, trying to shake off the many cloaks of discomfort piled about her neck and shoulder by immersing herself in knowledge, only it turned out the writing didn't contain knowledge after all.

Lillian Chatterjee continued shrieking.

The book contained art. Notes on literary motifs, snippets of poetry, fragmentary half-ideas that might be seeds Degas hoped one day to germinate into a novel.

Doctor Plectrum injected Lillian Chatterjee with something through her exosuit, and the comms engineer collapsed.

But the last several pages of the notebook were different. They were filled with Latin.

"Thulliver!" Doctor Plectrum called. "I've had to sedate Chatterjee. We need your help!" There was no answer, and *Atalanta's* doctor stepped out in the corridor, drawing her own blaster.

"Sub vestimenta arcanum," Metic muttered, squinting to decipher the ancient language. "A secret. Fear the wind. The seed is on the wind."

Another message from this same dead man. A warning, and a clue, maybe a clue written in this book. So what had happened to *Actaeon?* What had happened to Degas himself, and who had killed him?

A cold, irrational, but unshakeable certainty seized her.

Degas had killed himself. He had left a warning about the fate of *Actaeon*, and he had killed himself.

Shuffling steps in the corridor jerked Metic's attention from the notebook. She pointed her blaster at the doorframe and very nearly pulled the trigger when Doctor Plectrum squeezed into view.

If Plectrum noticed her near extinction, she pretended not to. "Thulliver's gone," she panted.

Lieutenant Chatterjee's flare snapped once and burned out.

"Bohr, Bohr, Bohr," Metic muttered. The blue emergency lighting gave her enough illumination to read by, but only barely. Her eyes ached.

Lillian Chatterjee slept under a low table in the corner of *Actaeon's* galley, still sedated. Doctor Plectrum sat perched on a metal stool beside the table. She held her blaster in her hand and kept herself alert by deliberately swinging her aim back and forth between the two gaping entrances to the room. Metic ignored her, and the wreckage that was the voidship's kitchen and dining room, and tried to read.

It was hard going. Where the handwriting was clear she could decipher it easily. The opening words were *SCRIBO MEA MANU FRATREM INSANITATEM ET ABYSSI ARCANA TIMENS*, which she deciphered easily. "I write with my own hand, fearing the madness of my brothers and the secrets of the deep," she translated aloud, as a check on her reading.

"Cheerful," the doctor sighed. "It's enough to make me pine for a saucy limerick. Or, all things considered, maybe a chaste one."

Something had happened to Albert Dugas. When he had been writing poetry, he had written in a bold, clear hand, with large, circular capital vowels and plenty of space around each word. It was the handwriting of a man who self-consciously wrote to be read, even in his personal notes, someone who expected that an editor or a biographer or both would pick their way along his trail of breadcrumbs in search of literary and anecdotal diamonds. When he had begun writing in Latin, without warning or preface, he had done so in handwriting that was cramped, hurried, and slanted. It was the twisted calligraphy of someone slashing out notes by handlight under a blanket, barely punctuated, the scrawling of a madman. And as he went on, he got worse.

"Commander Thulliver," Doctor Plectrum said, testing to see whether the ranger's exosuit comms unit would pick her up, "Lancer Durmont." There was no answer. There hadn't been an answer the previous twenty times, either.

HOMINES ARDENT, she read. *The men burn*. Unintelligible lines. More lines she could read, few and far between, but as she sank deeper into the reading the Latin language fell away and the words burned themselves directly into Metic Fallows's consciousness.

The four-arms knew this.

The summit temple records the final defeat.

Gupta is a madman. He didn't go first, but he went furthest.

Women. It wants women.

It reads our minds. It speaks to our minds. It controls our minds.

Beware the wind.

I cannot let myself be taken.

And finally, after two pages of completely unreadable blots, a single word scratched out in gigantic letters across half a page: *FUGITE.*

Flee.

She heard a footfall outside the galley and dropped the book, fumbling it to the floor.

Silence. Metic looked over to Doctor Plectrum to find that the older woman had dozed off, slumped improbably against the galley wall without having fallen from the stool. Her snoring and Lillian's rasped gently out of sync, dissonant pitches and competing rhythms, a slow tenor and a quick bass.

"Thulliver?" Metic called hesitantly. There was no answer. "Durmont?"

Silence.

Metic shivered violently, a spasm crossing her back and prickling the skin between her shoulder blades. A terrible hunch gripped her and she reached up to her exosuit helmet to switch the comms unit from broadcasting to other exosuits on the network to external-audible mode. She picked up her blaster.

Her voice felt tiny in the silence, but she cleared her throat and called out. "Who's there? This is Sapient Metic Fallows of Femship *Atalanta*. Are you a crewman of *Actaeon*?"

A voice rattled into the galley from the corridor beyond. It was a man's voice, dry, sad, and remote. A voice she knew. A voice she had heard before, speaking from a Lillian Chatterjee-faced, worm-bodied creature of her own dreams.

"We're afraid," the voice said.

She hesitated. "Of what?" she asked.

"We're afraid you won't like us."

A pause.

"We very much want you to like us."

Metic pointed her blaster at the entrance from which she seemed to hear the voice most loudly. "I'm pretty friendly," she said. The muzzle of her blaster trembled, even though she supported her aim with both hands. Her breathing was shallow, and a tremor swept her legs and pelvis. "Why don't you come in and introduce yourself?"

The voice didn't answer.

"Is that Worthing?" she called out. "Gupta? Someone else from *Actaeon?*"

No response.

Metic crept forward. The blue emergency lightstrips burned a halo in the air around her, imprinting brilliant streaks in her peripheral vision. She swam through her own sweat, tip-toeing around the galley, pressing her shoulders against the wall through her exosuit, her own breath loud in her ears. Strings in her thighs trembled and sang.

She forced herself to ignore the wild reactions of her flesh and think through her situation. If she called out again, she knew, the man would hear she had moved. She gripped the blaster with both hands, counted to three, and leaned gun-first into the corridor.

There was no one there.

She didn't let herself sleep, and the dreams came for her anyway. The tickling itch of sweat drying under the exosuit became an unbearably sensuous tickle, a feather-stroking of the intimate secrets of Sapient Metic Fallows's body. She clamped her hands to the floor away from her body and steeled her mind, marching through verb conjugations and reciting Homer to herself out loud by memory. It wasn't the Chastity Regs that motivated her now, but the terrible sense that someone or some*thing* had turned her body against her. The clanging epic dithyrambs rocketed off the inside of *Actaeon's* hull and struck her with full force, but in vain—no amount of Greek or Hittite or Belorian could distract her from the steadily growing sensation that she was naked, was being touched by unseen fingers, and was watched by a thousand eyes.

She burned.

She should wake the others, she thought. The doctor, at least. But she feared to, and she didn't quite know why.

Ventum cave. Semen in vento latet... semen in vento... semen...

She feared the unseen hand, and she craved its touch, wanted it all for herself. Did the hand belong to the voice? To the man who wanted to be liked?

Or had it been a man? Had there even been a voice at all, or was the voice as illusory as the fingers? Answers, by Edison! She wanted answers.

"Amo, amas, amat..."

The summit temple, Degas had written. The answers were at the summit temple.

An image of a pink spire filled Metic Fallows's mind and fire raged in her blood. She squeezed air in and out of her lungs through gritted teeth, forced open heavy eyelids, and chanted.

When the first sliver of daylight crept down the blue-lit tunnels of *Actaeon*, she trembled, and this time not from lust.

"Get up," she croaked. When the other didn't stir, she kicked over a stool.

The *CLANG* knocked Doctor Plectrum off her perch. Lillian Chatterjee jerked upright so fast she banged her faceplate against the underside of the table.

"Thulliver?" the doctor asked, groggy.

Metic shook her head. "We'll find her. In the meantime, we've got someplace to go."

"Where?" Chatterjee sounded drained and distant.

"The summit." Metic had prepared her lie. "If I were trying to get above this stuff, and get comms reception, that's where I'd go. The highest point."

She would be the *one who knew*, she told herself. The *one who knew* had power. The one who had power would not be controlled.

She turned her back on the other two without looking at their faces.

The pink landscape mocked her, an army of wagging tongues.

Metic ignored the taunting and marched up. Like Xenophon, she thought grimly, slowly losing my troops.

The summit temple could only refer to one building, she guessed. It had been invisible from the lower slopes of the butte, and she had failed to notice it in the darkness the night before, but emerging from *Actaeon* it was unmistakable. On the highest spur of the butte, glowering down at them and ringed by outward-thrusting stone slivers, buttresses that buttressed nothing, was an enclosure made of arches, like an old Terra-Prime cloister from the medieval era, or like a huddle of massive pink-encrusted trilithons.

The burning had become an ache, as if a fist inside her was grabbing her most tender parts and twisting them into a knot. A hungry knot.

She could not ignore the feeling, so she marched. A trail rose up in zigzags from the pink-scabbed city, clambering the sides of the butte up towards the summit. Metic wondered if the man she had talked to last night might be watching from the peak. If he were armed, she was exposed on the trail, and he could easily pick her off, even with a weapon as primitive as a dropped rock.

She wondered what he looked like. Was he handsome? Tall? Did he have the ugly face of a warrior? The high forehead of a ship's captain? The gentle hands and whisperlike touch of a doctor, stroking, stroking?

Then she wondered if the man even existed at all.

"I don't feel good," Lillian Chatterjee muttered.

"Suck it up," Metic muttered back. *You little sapphic*, she wanted to mutter, but she was afraid if she voiced the reality of Lillian's obvious attraction to the sapient, even inside her own head, the aching lust of her own body would drive her to respond to the Lieutenant's feelings. She softened her voice. "We'll rest at the next switchback." The whisky-and-lust huskiness in her own words embarrassed her.

"Yes sir," Lillian mumbled. Then she threw up.

The sound of retching and the splash of vomit against the inside of the exosuit's visor burst loud over the comms unit. Lillian staggered backward, a yellowish-pink soup sloshing visibly around her face, and she crashed into Doctor Plectrum.

They fell down the slope together, tumbling like kittens, and when they struck a column in their path and stopped it was with a loud *CRACK*.

Lillian continued to vomit. Metic lurched down the hill with long steps, scuffing bare long patches of rock where her heel dug away the pink covering. She grabbed Lillian by the shoulder and jerked the comms engineer forward, trying to push her face down so she wouldn't swallow or inhale her own bile.

In the moment of turning Lillian Chatterjee over, Metic saw clearly the mass of the comms engineer's vomitus. It was a yellow slime, thick with wriggling pink worms.

She pushed Lillian down with a hand on the girl's shoulder. "Get it all out!" she barked, shaking the crewwoman of *Atalanta*. Even splashing around in vomit, the sight of Lillian's body writhing on the ground caught Metic's breath short. Her mind's eye flooded with obscene images, she was gripped by a raging desire to hurl herself upon the engineer and slosh about like a rutting pig in the frothy puddle of vomit.

She jerked her eyes away. Who's the little sapphic now? Metic felt sick, and still aroused.

Doctor Plectrum stepped closer, boots crunching on the ground. "Look." The doctor pointed at a spot beneath Lillian Chatterjee's arm.

A neat hole was punched through the exosuit, a neat hole with the cauterized crisp edges characteristic of a blaster bolt's work, exposing beneath it the skin over Lillian's ribs. Skin that should have been ivory-pale, warm, and supple.

Metic staggered back, shaking her hard and trying not to join Lillian in vomiting. Lillian Chatterjee's skin was crusty with interlocking pink rings, rings that burrowed into the skin, absorbed it, coated it, turned Lillian Chatterjee's body into a single massive scab. Lillian flailed on the ground, pounded at her exosuit helmet with both hands.

"It's my fault," Metic hissed, remembering what she thought had been a near miss the night before. "I almost shot her. But this..." This was worse.

"It was an accident," Doctor Plectrum said.

Metic looked at the doctor and hissed again, wordlessly. She now saw the source of the loud cracking sound—Plectrum must have struck her exosuit's visor against the rock when she landed, and it was now missing a chunk the size of a human thumb.

"Beware the wind." Metic made connections out loud. "Degas was trying to warn us. The seed is in the wind. The seed... it took *Actaeon*."

Lillian ripped off her helmet and spat writhing worms all over the ground.

"We don't know what this is," Doctor Plectrum said, her voice shaking. "We don't know what happened to *Actaeon*."

Lillian staggered to her feet, stumbling away from the other women. A wordless shriek of pain burst from her. Pain, Metic thought, or desire.

"It killed them." Metic knew it had to be true, though she couldn't explain how or why. "Whatever it did to them, it's doing now to... to her." She jerked a thumb at Lillian Chatterjee.

"What's the matter!?" Lillian howled. "What's wrong with me?" She staggered sideways and turned to face Metic. The skin of her face writhed with worms, puffed, blistered, split, oozed. "Why don't you want to *take* me?"

Metic bit the inside of her own cheek. Her body pulsed, her stomach churned, and she *did* want to ravish the scabby pink comms engineer. "Stand down, Lieutenant," she said calmly. She had the presence of mind to draw her blaster and point it at the ground between the two of them. She had never killed anyone, never even shot anyone... not *deliberately*, she thought, avoiding looking at the hole she had burned the night before in Lillian Chatterjee's exosuit.

"Stand down?!" Lillian hurled the words like a weapon. She threw back her shoulders, looking taller with each sentence she shouted. "I will not! *You* stand down!" She towered over the sapient and the doctor. What in Tesla's name? She *was* taller. "*Lie* down, and I will fill you with my seed!"

She leaped at Metic.

The attack was lightning-fast, and only the fact that Metic had already drawn her weapon saved the sapient's life. Lillian Chatterjee hit the ground in a smoking ruin, the scabrous disaster of her face forever charred clean by the blaster bolt, her neck reduced to a smoking stump. Pinks worms wriggled from the stump of her neck and dropped to the ground about her.

"Hooke," Doctor Plectrum muttered.

Metic trembled. "It's worse."

The doctor laughed, a single jagged sound like the bark of a Luathan sand-sloth. "How could it be worse?"

Metic kept her blaster in her hand. "Check your visor."

Doctor Plectrum ran her fingers over the plate until she found the hole. She poked a finger into it and her eyes widened. She stared wordlessly at Metic.

"There's no guarantee what happened to her will happen to you," Metic pointed out. She wobbled on legs that felt like water.

Plectrum exhaled slowly, unlatched her exosuit helmet, and pulled it off. She tossed the headgear aside and scratched her head vigorously, prying free iron-gray curls that had been plastered down by sweat. The gesture made Metic's own scalp itch with envy, and then a sympathetic itch ran down her entire body like an arpeggio played top to bottom on a harp.

"No," the doctor agreed. "But it's likely. Aboard *Atalanta* I'd have my diagnostic tools, pharma-synthesizers, cryostasis chambers. I'd stand a chance."

"Down here..." Metic didn't know how to finish her own sentence.

"Down here," the doctor did it for her, "when I go crazy, you shoot me."

Metic jammed her blaster into its holster and turned away. The slow, moist fire engulfing her frame hid her tears from her until she tasted their salt as they puddled in the corners of her mouth.

She stepped over the smoldering ruin that had been Lillian Chatterjee and continued the climb up to the summit.

The outward-lurching buttresses made a crown, Metic decided, as she trudged upward. A grand pink head, noble, virile, topped by an ancient crown. Indomitable, alluring, wise, invisible eyes keen with insight.

As she shuffled among the columns, though, the crown faded and was replaced by so many hostile fingers. Fingers... some memory stirred in her, throbbing and breathless, but she couldn't quite hold it. Instead Metic stepped closer and stared, letting the images sink in and exploring the nearest column with her gloved hands. The stone had at one point been scraped clean—she could see the marks of a blade—but it was furring again with the pink fungal worms, twitching in a breeze Metic couldn't feel.

The stone was covered in markings; Metic's heart throbbed dully within her, some delight at potential discovery making itself heard through the pounding drums of lust. Glyphs, pictures of the six-limbed creatures again, twisting, sinewy images some of which might have been stars, or plants, or body parts, or other unknown creatures. The glyphs were cut deep, weathered around the edges, and speckled in their depths with flakes of some clinging paint. She tried to imagine her baritone sun-worshipping lizards, ambling down their grand avenue at the solstice, and couldn't.

Scratched alongside the glyphs were more Latin characters.

Metic squinted, stared. Tried to force the characters into words, and here and there succeeded. *SEMEN* recurred over and over, usually near a stylized spiral image. *VERMES*, *worms*, sometimes near the same spiral and sometimes near clusters of short, wiggling lines. The word *SEX* threw her off until she realized it was the Latin number *six* and referred to the alien creatures whose images were so prominent on the columns.

She squinted harder and tried to force the words into sentences. And failed.

Degas had been here. A hot fist of jealousy clenched around her heart when she realized that he had somehow deciphered some of these glyphs, had learned to read a previously unknown language that belonged to an apparently dead sentient race. It was a feat she herself would pay almost any price to replicate, she thought.

Degas's own price had been madness and death.

And it looked like the madness had dragged down whatever he had learned with him into his solitary suicidal grave.

Madness. Lust.

The men burn.

"There's nothing here," Doctor Plectrum said.

"There's knowledge." Metic didn't look away from the column. "I thought you wanted knowledge."

Metic's head spun.

Madness. Lust. Knowledge.

The doctor panted. "About people. About *us*. What is this?" She joined Metic at the column. "Worms? Fungus?"

"Knowledge. Truth about the universe in which we live, and the fate of this planet."

"If I have anything to say in the matter," Plectrum said, "the fate of this planet will be to catch a series of *Atalanta's* nukes. Even if I'm standing in the blast myself. We should go back to *Actaeon*, try to get communication working. We need to get out of here."

A man's voice croaked from behind one of the columns. "We cannot allow that. We *will not* allow that."

Madness. Lust. Knowledge. Sex. Madness.

Metic knew the voice, and its dark timbre made her shiver.

"Who are you?" she called.

Slow scuffing footfalls scraped a robed and hooded figure into view. He was a tall man, Metic thought, and for a moment she imagined that the figure would throw down his robe and turn out to be a six-armed reptile, seven feet tall.

But that was ridiculous.

"We... *I* am Salazar Gupta." The voice rolled from the shadowed recesses of a baggy, all-concealing hood. "I am... I was a physicist. We are... something... else... entirely."

His voice held a lascivious curl to it, a flippant, ironic, note of seduction. Metic's breathing came so shallow she wondered whether she was getting any oxygen at all. She felt light-headed, and then she knew.

She *knew*, but there was no triumph in it.

"You are telepaths," she said. "You've been harassing us in our sleep." And in our waking. Madness. Sex. Knowledge.

"We are *a telepath*," said the hooded figure calling itself Salazar Gupta, "or perhaps an empath, but neither term is really sufficient."

"You've invaded our dreams."

"I would have said your *loins*. Your lust does not reside in your dreams, Sapient Metic Fallows."

Doctor Plectrum stepped forward, shoulder to shoulder with Metic. Metic heard rasping breaths and couldn't be sure whether they came from *Atalanta's* medical doctor or *Actaeon's* physicist. Or both.

"What do you want from us?" the doctor asked.

A silence followed. A thin cloud of pink spores drifted over the summit; Metic wiped her visor clean with one hand and shuddered; Doctor Plectrum's face began to look pink-furred.

"We are the original inhabitant of this planet," Gupta said. "Eons before you warm-blooded bags of blood and mucus dragged yourselves from the juvenile primordia you once knew as Earth, we came here. We came here from the stars."

"Orion's belt," Doctor Plectrum quipped. "He wants to tell a story." She leaned forward slightly in her stance, as if the pink spores were heavy and dragged her down.

Gupta laughed. "*He.* Very good. He. That is what is at issue. You are an impatient race, a quivering horde of upstart flesh, and if you must cut to the chase, as you so quaintly and unintelligibly say, then that is what we want from you. To be *he*. And *she*."

"I like stories," Metic said. "Tell me what you mean."

Gupta nodded, a low bow that nearly bent him double and only served to emphasize again how immensely tall he was. The bow also brought him forward a step, and Metic struggled to keep her hand off her blaster. She felt dizzy. She wasn't quite sure how, but she had arrived at a dead end. And Gupta's rasping, gravelly voice struck a physical chord in her, a low note that continued to resonate long after the man's... the creature's... every word.

"You human beings were not yet alive in any sense in which you would recognize the word when the Sixlings came."

"The lizards," Metic hazarded.

"They had warm blood. And they fled an old world, a world on which their god had arisen to crush his worshippers, who in their age and their wisdom longed for the nothingness of the abyss. Those who escaped came here, took from us our world, and for a long time enslaved us with their cruel technologies."

"The green lichen," Doctor Plectrum hazarded. The sound of her voice snapped Metic out of a deep reverie—she had forgotten she was not alone.

"The green lichen. They made it, from life forms they had brought with them, and they sprayed it on us. It bound us to stone and locked us into a long and dreamless sleep." Gupta's voice drew Metic in. In its somber tones there were piping discordant notes, as if he had scarred his vocal cords with smoke and alcohol and then swallowed a whistle to boot.

"Something woke you." Plectrum scraped at her face and arms, wiping away the accumulating pink fuzz.

"The Sixlings brought with them their own death. Not all of their party were rebels against their god, and some of the worshippers saw in us a way to achieve the destruction they desired. They found us down in dark caves, out of reach of the lichen that was our nemesis, and they freed us into the air of this world."

"This is Schrodingered beyond belief," Doctor Plectrum snorted. "You're Salazar Gupta, and you were not living in a cave beneath this pink planet eons ago."

"*I* am Salazar Gupta," the still-faceless man agreed. "*We* are... nameless."

The word hung in the air a long time.

"You destroyed the civilization of the Sixlings." Metic felt a small tone of sadness amid the intense fascination as her mind flooded with images of peaceful six-armed creatures being encrusted, scabbed over, and devoured by the pink worms. The image cranked her arousal to an even higher pitch. She wanted to throw herself among the pink-flocked aliens of her imagination, naked, wild, and free, in an orgy of violent self-satisfaction and death.

"As they wished."

"As *some of them* wished," Doctor Plectrum corrected Gupta. "That's a serious difference. Still, you win. We're leaving now, and you can keep this useless rock."

"I cannot allow that. We *need* you." Gupta said the word need with fiery lust in his voice. "We *want* you."

"The lichen," Metic guessed. Her mind raced. "It hadn't gone anywhere, so once you devoured the Sixlings, you and your predator settled back into permanent stalemate. You're not dead, but you're pinned by the green stuff, you can't go anywhere. Except maybe the parts of you that are still deep underground."

Gupta exhaled, a dry, gritty cackle of satisfaction. "We have been waiting a long time for you, Sapient Fallows."

"Leibniz," Doctor Plectrum cursed. "Sexual reproduction. That's what this is all about. You can't get around the lichen and it can't get around you because you both reproduce asexually. All of your... spores... worms, whatever, are genetically identical, and so all of them are identically vulnerable to the lichen. You need something to break out of the stalemate."

Metic's heart twisted into a hard ball. "And that something is sex?"

She heard a whimper from a different direction, and though the sound was soft it nearly made her jump. She turned and saw *Atalanta's* rangers. Durmont and Thulliver both limped into her view, dragging bodies across the pink-furred stone that at first appeared to Metic to be horribly mutilated.

When she realized what she was really looking at, she nearly broke into tears.

Lust. Sex. Knowledge. Madness.

The women dragged themselves forward on all fours, laboriously because their bellies had swollen to vast proportions. Gone were Elsa Durmont's cat-like poise and the apple-torsoed solidity of Wyot Thulliver. The gross distortion of normal human dimensions threw Metic off for a moment, but when she had gotten over the general pallid frog-like appearance of the two rangers, who both seemed to be naked and encrusted from head to toe in patches of pink, she realized their true state.

Madness. Her mind revolted. Was this the end of knowledge?

Her body burned.

They were pregnant. Or at least, they were in some state that caricatured pregnancy, that bloated their bellies, slowed their movement and threw off their balance.

"Metic Fallows," Commander Thulliver said. Her lips flapped loosely over her words and slurred them. Her voice had gravel in it, and a high-pitched buzz. "What a pleasant surprise to see you here." Pink worms fell from Thulliver's mouth as she spoke.

Salazar Gupta scraped another step closer.

"No," Metic whispered, but her heart said something different. Madness. There was no knowledge that did not end in madness. Sex. Lust. Madness.

Cold death the only alternative.

"No!" Doctor Plectrum barked, with considerably more conviction.

"This is so much better," Elsa Durmont muttered, thick, pink drool sliding down over her chin and onto her bare, bloated breasts. "I don't burn anymore."

Gupta straightened his back in a movement so swift it sent Metic and the Doctor both staggering back in surprise. The same movement whipped back his hood and tossed aside the folds of his robe, revealing a body that was as misshapen as it was tall. He curved through his spine, and his flesh bloated, scabbed and knobby around bones that had elongated and become thicker. Even his head, with worms dripping from its eye sockets, no longer looked quite human, though the festering eyes gleamed with a light that Metic recognized and desired. It was not the light of lust, much less love, but the light of knowledge. Madness. Knowledge.

Metic spun, weightless and disconnected. She didn't know which way was down.

Salazar Gupta the giant worm stroked his own pink, rugose flanks with long-fingered hands. "You may view this body as a curse," he whispered, a hoarse urgency in his voice. "But is not every body a curse?"

"No!" Doctor Plectrum snapped.

"Yes," Metic whispered. She burned, and sweat dripped down her skin inside the exosuit. Knowledge. Lust led to sex led to madness led to knowledge madness knowledge madness.

"And think what is to be gained." Gupta smiled, crooked, twisted, toothless. "Immortality. And knowledge."

"Yes," Metic whispered again.

"You will be Queens Consort. You will be *us*. You will live forever, and your children will be a new race of gods. With the gift of your loins, and the seed of the man Gupta and his comrades, we will escape the hold of this Sixling curse and retake our place as ruler of this world. Indeed, with your vessel *Atalanta*, we need not be limited to this world, or to any world."

More scraping footfalls among the pillars dragged more misshapen giant man-things into view. Metic looked upon them and wanted them, not for their flesh, but for the fleshlessness that union with them promised, the sensuous knowledge madness life and immortality that they could give her. They nodded heavy heads in her directions on long necks like flower stalks.

This was not madness. Knowledge was illusion. Madness was illusion. Sex was life was existence was knowledge madness knowledge madness.

Sex and life were all there was.

"Yes!" she cried.

"No!" A blaster bolt flashed past Metic, and Elsa Durmont exploded into charred flesh and a floating cloud of pink. To her horror, Metic could discern little creatures in the carnage, creatures that were not quite worms and not quite human fetuses either, but some horrid-fascinating thing between, something with a tail and arms and an eyeless face.

She staggered back and grabbed for her own weapon. The once-men-now-gods of Homship *Actaeon* reared back shrieking, and then pounced forward.

Doctor Plectrum fired again, and Commander Thulliver's howl of pain was cut short as her entire body above the bloated belly burst instantly into a cloud of ash. She toppled sideways in two pieces, and the pool of viscous red fluid that pooled around her body swarmed with more of the same little creatures.

The god-men of *Actaeon* sprang forward, nails extended like daggers.

Doctor Plectrum swung around to face Metic. Her face was scabbing around the eyes, nostrils, and mouth, and her expression twisted into something that might have been self-loathing, or fear, or hatred. She raised her blaster at Metic—

but the sapient pulled the trigger first, and the bright flash of energy ripped through Doctor Plectrum, tearing her in half.

The doctor hit the ground.

The god-men paused.

Metic felt tired. And uncertain. And afraid.

But she looked up about her at the former men of *Actaeon* and felt the desire of their collective flood into her. She dropped her blaster to the ground.

They sighed, a chittering, gurgling sound of relief.

Metic stepped over to the ruined bodies of her fellow crewwomen, bent, and scooped up two of the animalcules thrashing about in their conjoined gore. The things were perfect, godlike in their staggering inhumanness, something she might have seen on a Mesopotamian façade or in the oldest writings of Tibet, little devil-angels. Tentacles at their sides probed the fabric of her exosuit, thin but strong tails wrapped around her fingers, and long-tooth mouths mewed tiny, demanding cries for tribute.

"It is a hard birth, as births go," Metic Fallows, Queen Consort, said.

With one trembling hand she undid the clasps holding in place the helmet of her Exosuit. The air was thick and warm with love, and with the scent of scabrous, bleeding, love-loathsome, and lustful flesh of divine-demonic beings. The only true knowledge.

"But it is only the beginning."

Raising her bloody, screeching step-children to her lips, Metic kissed them both. Then she set them on the ground, and waited patiently to receive the seed of her many husbands, the seed of her self, the seed of her new *we* that would live forever and know the only thing there was to know.

PUT UP A SIGN

I wrote this short to be performed as a play, with music, on Jean-Paul Garnier's excellent podcast, Simultaneous Times. *This is the first time the story appears in print.*

"**Y**ou ought to put up a sign," Luman Walters grumbled.

The watchmen, Youngstown German brawlers with faces like undercooked pork rumps, ignored him. He said it again, *auf Deutsch* this time—his German was pretty good—and they shoved him into the hard, wooden chair.

Luman winced, and the vicar's grin got wider. The priest stood in the corner of the room, florid and satisfied. The man had stumbled across Luman in the act of reading the gospel over a client's field and had immediately summoned the watch.

The town official—burgermeister or alderman or whatever he was —put round spectacles over the ridge of his thin face and gazed at Luman with dispassion. "Should we also put up a sign saying, 'do not kill anyone'? Perhaps also 'no stealing within the bounds of this town' and 'do not burn buildings'?"

Luman admired the withering scorn of this village headman, but he also didn't have any cash to pay the fine. All his ready money, specie and notes, went to Helga to pay her father for the lessons in braucherei that he was ostensibly teaching to her, but on which Luman eavesdropped.

The old man was blind.

And Helga was bored, and threatening to quit. She'd demanded more money, and now if Luman didn't come up with six shillings by the end of next week, his studies in German magic would be over. He also worried Helga might tell her beefy male cousins what Luman had been doing, and then he'd end up tarred and feathered and ridden out of town on a splintery rail.

He winced again.

"I'm not sure that 'do not practice magic without a license' falls into quite the same category as arson," Luman suggested, trying to sound inoffensive and puzzled. "And I didn't realize that Youngstown licensed wizards, in any case."

"The issue is not lack of a license." The burgermeister's smile was lopsided, like the drawing of a child. "And this is not Youngstown. If you look out the window, you can see the walls of Free Imperial Youngstown. You can just *barely* see them, as the town is eight miles away. You are in the village of Hubbard. And the issue is that you practiced magic *at all*. The village council of Hubbard has imposed a very strict ordinance: no charms, no wizardry at all, within a mile of Little Deer Creek or Mud Run."

The priest cracked his knuckles. "And you, my young friend, have been ensorcelling crops right along Little Deer."

"*Ensorcelling* is an awfully big word for a bit of corn-reading," Luman protested. "And I didn't do anything your parishioners didn't ask me to."

"Didn't *pay* you to do." The priest's face was sour. "Simon Magus. And I have heard rumors of money-digging."

"Luman Walters." Luman sighed. "Please. And anyway, this town *has* a wizard."

The priest's back stiffened. "We do not."

Luman furrowed his brow. He didn't want to display too much

knowledge. "I heard . . . some of the people I helped mentioned a hexenmeister. Herr Hoffmann."

"Herr Hoffmann is no sorcerer," the priest growled. "He is a man of great faith, and his prayers and traditional medicines are highly esteemed for their effectiveness."

Luman bit his own tongue to prevent himself from shouting: *that's the same thing!*

"*Herr Hoffmann* is a respected member of the community," the burgermeister said. "*You* are a vagrant. Do you think, in any case, I could give you the same leeway and consideration I would give Herr Hoffmann?"

Well, there it was.

"How much is the fine?" Luman asked.

"One crown."

Luman's shoulders slumped. "I'm a little cash-poor. I don't suppose I could spend an afternoon in the stocks or something, rather than pay a fine?"

"I could put you in the gaol," the burgermeister said thoughtfully.

"For how long?"

The crooked smile returned. "Until someone paid the fine."

That would be never. Luman's father had driven him from the farm for taking up wizardry rather than the plow, and he certainly wasn't going to pay his son's penalty. And there was no one else.

"There is another possibility." A wet-lipped grin nearly split the vicar's face in two.

"You shouldn't pay this man's fine," the burgermeister said.

The priest quickly shook his head. "But I was thinking, perhaps instead of a fine, he could confess in church. I could make an object lesson of him."

"That would be humiliating." The burgermeister squinted at Luman.

The priest nodded. "So humiliating, he might have to leave town afterward."

Luman hesitated, but only briefly. "Please," he said. "Not that. Anything but that."

The burgermeister and the priest laughed.

Luman stood to one side of the pulpit, beneath a stained-glass window. The image in the window showed Adam and Eve, clad in furs, fleeing Eden across a barrier of thorns and thistles. A wooden placard hung by rough twine from Luman's neck, with writing in three languages:

Zauberer

Lukwetatku

Sorcerer

He wasn't sure what language *lukwetatku* was in—one of the Haudenosaunee tongues, maybe? Some kind of Algonk? There were Indians in the congregation, and faces that looked as German as strudel, but the vicar's sermon was in English.

"By the grace of God as brought by His Son," the priest said, winding to a close, "we no longer hang witches."

A few faces in the crowd looked disappointed at the news, but most nodded piously. Several looked at Luman with curiosity; in particular, a row of older women sitting together on a pew just in front him.

Older women alone. Likely widows, mothers and grandmothers. Familiar with women's ways of doing things, and if they didn't have men in their houses, they might need work done.

Luman smiled at the widows, trying to look harmless, wise, and professional at the same time. It wasn't easy, but this was a face he had practiced many times.

Several of the widows smiled back.

"But if we suffer this witch to live, giving mercy that we too might receive mercy, then at least he will confess his sins." The priest turned and looked at Luman expectantly.

Luman cleared his throat. "I am a wizard." He felt brazen saying the words out loud; he was no gramarist, had never even been to one of the big colleges of magic, in Philadelphia or New Amsterdam, had never been inducted into the mysteries of St. Reginald Pole. He was a self-taught hedge wizard at best, trying to scrape together enough magical art to make his way in the world.

The priest rapped his knuckles on the lectern. "More. More detail. Make a confession."

Luman raised his eyebrows, but nodded. "I read the gospel over Frau Schulz's corn," he said. "And worse . . . I took money for it." He sneaked a sideways look at the vicar, and found the priest nodding in satisfaction.

"How much money?" a widow in a dark green kirtle asked.

"Tuppence," Luman said. "But even performing magic for small amounts of money makes me no better than Simon Magus."

He tried to look dejected.

The widows hung on every word.

The priest nodded. "More!"

"I dug for money in Herr Becker's forest. We found a grave site, a Firstborn burial in jars, with gold and iron coins. And Herr Becker paid me, too."

"More!" the priest insisted.

"I was paid a one-twelfth share." Luman tried to look ashamed. "It came to three or four crowns at the moneychanger's."

Several burghers in the congregation elbowed each other and nodded.

"Anything else?" the priest asked.

"I dowsed for water," Luman said. "One shilling. I healed cows of the murrain, one penny per cow, a shilling minimum."

"Did you write Himmelsbriefe?" a widow with a red kerchief binding her hair asked. "Heavenly letters, for protecting a house?"

"Heaven help me, I did," Luman said. This was a lie, but he'd watched Herr Hoffmann show Helga how to write them, and had copied out Hoffmann's original, so he was confident he could write a Himmelsbrief. He thought about what he ought to charge. "Two shillings, plus the cost of the fine ink and paper."

"That's enough!" the priest barked. "So you see, this man is a confessed wizard." He smiled at greasily at Luman. "And will you be leaving Hubbard now?"

The entire congregation looked at Luman Walters, interested in the answer.

"I will," he said. "Though I will spend the rest of this day here in the chapel, meditating on the seriousness of my sins."

Many heads nodded.

The widow in the red kerchief had a small purse open and was discreetly counting the coins inside.

And, Luman thought, he would keep the sign.

THE DEAD WHO CARE

I wrote this story for the anthology Parallel Worlds: The Heroes Within, *a collection curated by L.J. Hachmeister, which found me shelved alongside such luminaries as Jody Lynn Nye and Jim Butcher. Hiram Woolley is a cunning man, which is to say, fundamentally, a healer. And a ghost is a person badly in need of healing.*

H iram saw the man standing beside the road from a long distance away, first as a smudge of gray, but then as a tall fellow, thin like Hiram himself, in a frock coat and a short top hat.

It was odd that the man stood beside the road out here, in the dark deserts of eastern Utah. The nearest town was an hour's drive, and Hiram didn't see a car or a horse. The Model T's lights showed sagebrush, tall grass, and talus slopes, all chalked white by the spell of the electricity.

What the man wore was stranger still: he was dressed in a dark blue frock coat, such as would have looked old-fashioned, quaint, or overly formal before the war. Now it looked like an echo of a world long dead, as did his hat.

Hiram almost drove past, leaving the man to his fate; after his defeats in Cameron, he was in no mood to be company to anyone. But the stranger waved his arms to flag Hiram down and Hiram abruptly thought of the tale of the Good Samaritan.

Grandma Hettie hadn't raised Hiram to be a Levite.

Taking a deep breath, he stopped the car.

In the pocket of his army coat, Hiram had his service pistol. Traveling these desert roads alone, it didn't pay to be defenseless. The stranger didn't look like a robber, anyway.

The man in the frock coat reached for the handle of the car door, then hesitated. His face was poorly illuminated standing beside the car, but he looked middle-aged, thin as Hiram himself. He was clean-shaven and pale, like a man who worked indoors, and had a long-bridged nose that ended in a bulb, like an onion. "Can you give me a ride?" the stranger asked.

"As long as you mean me no harm," Hiram said. His response was no trivial word game; the Model T was protected by a lamen, a paper talisman that Hiram himself had made and tacked to the floorboards underneath the seat, and Hiram didn't want to say anything that would lower his defenses.

"I mean no one any harm." The stranger smiled. "My name is Asael Johnson. I need a ride to the meadows."

"Asael. *God's healer*. That's an angel name."

Johnson's face brightened. "Do you know Hebrew, then? You don't look like a rabbi."

"I don't know any Hebrew. I barely know English." Hiram laughed. He wore denim overalls under his soldier's greatcoat, and a fedora on his head. "I'm Hiram Woolley. I'm a beet farmer now, I guess, and I'll take you to where you want to go."

Johnson stepped into the Model T. As Hiram put the motorcar into gear and lurched forward again over the gravel road, he had the uneasy sensation that he hadn't seen Asael Johnson either open or close the car's door.

"That's quite the coat you're wearing," Johnson said.

"I fought in the war," Hiram said.

"A lot of men died," Johnson said. "You're lucky you came home."

Hiram nodded. His best friend, Yas Yazzie, hadn't been so lucky. Hiram blinked away sudden tears and tried not to remember Yas's last moments, kicking his life out in a frozen ditch as the wolf-men on their trail howled for blood.

He tried not to remember his own failure, too. Yas had had a child on the way, and he had made Hiram promise that if he didn't make it home, Hiram would see to it the child was taken care of. That was what Hiram was doing down in Arizona—for two years, he'd kept on eye on Betty Yazzie, making sure she had work and enough money. With her death, Hiram and his wife Elmina were trying to adopt the boy.

Michael, a big-eyed, staring toddler.

Hiram had come down to talk to tribal elders as well as the judge. He'd thought he'd be able to bring the boy back with him, but the foster parents in Cameron were objecting, and trying to adopt the boy themselves. Goodman, that was their name. The Goodmans wanted to keep Michael. Hiram had appealed to the elders to intervene with the judge on his behalf, but they had been reluctant. What made one set of white Mormon adoptive parents better than another?

The elders hadn't intervened, the judge had sided with the Goodmans, and Hiram had driven north, empty-handed. He had tried. He had failed, but he had tried to keep his promise to Yas.

Wasn't that good enough?

"The best men died," was all he said. He cleared his throat, suddenly thick with phlegm.

"Good men died," Johnson agreed. "Good men lived, too."

"What town did you say you needed to go to?" Hiram asked. "Meadow?"

"It's not a town. Mountain Meadows."

Hiram's breath stuck in his chest. "The massacre site?" He hadn't realized this road passed the location of the 1857 mass murder. "Someone lives there?"

"One man."

Hiram's sense of unease grew. Keeping his right hand on the wheel, he sneaked his left under the loose collar of his shirt and gripped the iron of his chi-rho medallion. "You have to be careful at a place like that. There are dead who linger."

"The dead who care." Johnson smiled faintly.

"Unfinished business." Hiram wasn't sure why he was still talking. "Vengeance. Justice."

"Mercy."

Hiram took a deep breath and drove a few minutes in silence. "You're wearing quite the coat, yourself."

"I was a doctor," Johnson told him. "This was my coat for formal occasions. It was a common enough sort of coat at the time."

Asael Johnson was a ghost.

Hiram was giving a ghost a ride in his car. He took a deep breath.

"And is tonight a formal occasion?" Or had Asael Johnson died at a dinner party? If the man had been killed at Mountain Meadows, surely he wouldn't have died in evening wear.

"I suppose it is. I will need your help, of course."

Hiram nodded slowly. What help could the dead man need from him? "Because I was a soldier?"

"No, I don't need help for that."

The words didn't put Hiram's mind at ease. Could he say no to whatever the ghost wanted? Of course he *could*, and then he'd have to be prepared for the ghost's reaction. Some ghosts threw things. Others caused people to die of heart attacks, and pure fear. Could Asael Johnson grab the steering wheel and drive Hiram off the road?

Hiram slowed down, just a bit.

But ghosts lingered on earth because they had unfinished business. Business of a passionate nature, business important enough to stick around for, which often meant they were murder victims themselves, intent on avenging their deaths. Ghosts were the dead who still cared about what happened on earth, and needed to set something right.

Something the living *couldn't* fix or *hadn't* fixed.

Maybe Hiram could help Asael Johnson resolve his unfinished business in a way that would minimize the mischief.

"It's horrifying what was done to those people." Hiram offered. "They were innocent."

"There was a lot of fear in the air at the time." Johnson nodded. "The Mormons were polygamists who had tried to flee the country because they didn't quite fit in and talked about building their own kingdom in the Rocky Mountains. The federal government thought the Mormons were in revolt and the Mormons thought the federal government was out to get them. Then the Baker-Fancher wagon train came through, announcing that any Mormons who were sick of Brigham Young's rule could take refuge with them and be escorted safely out of the state. There were rumors that members of the Baker-Fancher party had poisoned Mormon wells, and that they had killed Mormons in Missouri, back in the 1830s."

Hiram's own father was a polygamist who had never quite fit in, taking additional wives even after the Church had publicly disavowed the practice. Hiram had only learned about his father's other families when Abner Woolley had abandoned him and his mother and gone to live in Mexico. "There were provocations, all right. Those don't justify murder."

Johnson smiled. "I was not killed at Mountain Meadows, if that's what you're guessing."

Hiram felt cold. "Am I guessing?"

"If this were an old riddle game," Johnson said, "or part of a fairy-story, you'd get three guesses. If you guessed the answer in three, you'd get a prize of some sort. A magical power, a wish granted, a secret treasure. And if you didn't get the answer in three guesses, something terrible would happen."

"I would lose the princess."

"Or you would die."

The Model T struck an unseen stone or root, leaping into the air and landing with a hard rattle. They rode in silence for a minute. Hiram's heart clubbed his lungs and he tried to control his breathing.

Hiram forced himself to think. The ghost of a dead man—a man not recently dead—was coming to Mountain Meadows, to meet another man. A living man, it seemed. The dead man hadn't been murdered in 1857, but had unfinished business with the living man.

Who could the ghost be?

The current year was 1921; sixty-four years had passed since the massacre. That meant that the living man could have been an adult at the time, now in his eighties or nineties. A perpetrator?

But Asael Johnson had said he hadn't died at the Meadows. Could Johnson be a relative of one of the victims, come to avenge the death of a loved one on an old murderer?

What consequences would Hiram suffer if he guessed wrong?

"I died of a heart attack," Johnson said.

"Unexpected?" Hiram asked.

Johnson nodded. "I was visiting a patient. My patient suffered from gout, and after giving the man his bottle of Haycock's Celebrated Gout and Rheumatic Pills, I stepped into St. George Boulevard and dropped dead without a word."

"There are worse ways to die."

"You have seen many, I expect."

Hiram nodded.

"I have seen quite a few, myself." Johnson paused for a moment. "William McKinley had just been elected president."

Hiram thought. "Nineteen hundred, then."

Johnson nodded. Jackrabbits hurled themselves across the street in the glare of the headlights. It occurred to Hiram that he couldn't smell the dead man at all—he smelled his own sweat, and the oil and exhaust odors of the Model T, but not another human being.

"You were forty years old?" Hiram wasn't sure that a ghost retained the last appearance it had had in life, but that seemed reasonable, especially in light of the fact that Asael Johnson was apparently wearing the clothes he had died in.

"Forty-four."

Forty-four. That would make the year of his birth 1856. That very nearly ruled out revenge for the murders as Asael Johnson's reason for continuing; he would have been an infant at the time of the massacre, so he would only have known any dead kin as stories told to him later.

Hiram doubted anyone could work up enough passion to continue as a ghost over the murder of someone they didn't personally know.

On the other hand, there had been small children in the wagon train.

"You know," he said, "Brother Brigham taught that a child under the age of eight isn't accountable yet for sin."

Asael Johnson laughed. There was wind in the sound, and a faint echo followed after it. "Yes. So did Joseph. But they got it from Mormon, you know. 'Behold, I came into the world not to call the righteous but sinners to repentance; the whole need no physician, but they that are sick; wherefore, little children are whole, for they are not capable of committing sin.'"

"You were raised Mormon," Hiram said.

"I feel a second guess coming on."

"Maybe." Hiram shrugged. "There were children in the wagon train. The Mormons and their Indian . . . allies . . . ?"

"Accomplices?"

"That's fair. The Mormons and Indians killed all the adults, but they let children live. Because Brigham taught that children weren't responsible, weren't guilty. And whatever the wagon train had done—if they had poisoned wells, if they had killed Mormons in Missouri, whatever—the children didn't deserve death."

"What are you saying, Mr. Woolley?"

Hiram was still formulating his thoughts. "The Mormons took those children home and adopted them. Or they tried to, anyway, but when the Army came through and heard that there were surviving children, they forced the Mormons to give them up."

"Are you suggesting I was one of those children?"

Hiram considered. No, that didn't make sense. Those children were returned to kin elsewhere, and would have been raised anything in the world other than Mormon. A one-year-old boy exposed to Mormons for a few weeks would not remember a passage from the Book of Mormon on child baptism decades later.

"There were rumors of other children. Jacob Hamblin had adopted Indian children . . ." Hiram suddenly found himself tearing up, thinking of Michael, Yas's and Betty's boy he and Elmina had tried to adopt. What had Hamblin's son been named? Albert, he thought. And if Hiram failed to keep his promise to Yas and abandoned Michael, would Yas return as a ghost to haunt him? Surely, Yas would have enough passion to be able to do that. And Yas had been one of the most spiritually powerful men Hiram had ever known.

"Yes?"

Hiram cleared his throat. "Not all the children were accounted for. There were rumors about why not. Some said that Jacob Hamblin's adopted Indian children killed some of the wagon train children, or some other Indians killed them. Others said that some of the Mormons simply hid the children from the Army and raised them as their own."

"This is your guess, then," Asael Johnson said. "That I was the child of one of the Baker-Fancher party. That my parents were killed in the massacre, and that I continue on the earth until I have my vengeance?"

Hiram gripped his chi-rho amulet. "Yes."

"Wrong."

Hiram exhaled slowly, his chest tight. What, then?

"But you are getting closer," Asael Johnson added. "Much closer."

The Model T knocked around the ragged edge of a gentle, oblong hill, and a single light drifted into view. It was yellow, the warm light of an oil lantern, and it was a short distance from the road.

"Is this Mountain Meadows?" Hiram asked. "Is that the man you've come to see?"

"Yes."

Lost in his thoughts, Hiram nearly missed the turnoff. Slowing and turning left from graded gravel onto rutted red clay, he startled a small herd of pronghorn antelope. Their white rumps bounded away into the darkness like bouncing balls in retreat.

Hiram parked at the house. It was a sagging, hand-built shack of red stone, with a bleached-white wooden porch slouching even further on one side. The shack was large enough to contain two rooms at most, and the light seemed to come from the back room. There was a hint of an outhouse beyond the structure. Hiram aimed his headlights at the front porch and set the hand brake.

What was the connection between Hiram's ghostly passenger and this rickety cabin?

"Is this man one of the murderers?" Hiram asked. "Did he pull the trigger at Mountain Meadows?"

"Is that a guess?" Asael Johnson's voice was hollow and gloomy.

Hiram shook his head. "Just a question."

"He wasn't," Johnson said. "He moved here later."

What kind of man moved to a massacre site? A morbid man? An obsessed man? A grieving man? An angry man?

A man who wanted never to forget?

"He's dying now," Johnson said. "Old age."

Who was Asael Johnson? The man in the cabin was old, but he wasn't one of the 1857 murderers. And nevertheless, the old man had moved to the massacre site to die here alone. And Johnson was the right age to be one of the wagon train's children, only he wasn't.

And now the two had unfinished business.

"If you have no more guesses to make," Asael Johnson suggested, "perhaps you'd like to knock on the door."

Hiram shut off the car and stepped out. Circling the Model T and stepping onto the porch, he felt cool sweat trickle down the small of his back. He thought of exorcism techniques, and prepared to shout the sacred names and secret words he knew that might chase the ghost away.

The door was a slab of bleached wood, hanging ill-fit in the roughly rectangular doorway. Hiram smelled the exhaust of the Model T and the crisp tang of sagebrush. He knocked.

There was no answer.

Hiram turned back to the Model T and found Asael Johnson standing beside him on the porch. The ghost had taken its hat into its hands, which prompted Hiram to do the same. His hair was beginning to thin on top, and the chill night on the sweat of his scalp was shockingly cold.

"This wasn't your home, was it?" Hiram asked.

"Never."

Hiram knocked again.

This time, he heard a groan within. Asael Johnson watched him intently. Hiram touched his chi-rho amulet through his shirt and overalls, but resisted putting his hand on the revolver in his pocket. The hammer was on an empty chamber, so he'd have to pull the trigger twice before the weapon would shoot.

Hopefully that would be unnecessary.

"I'm coming in," he called in a loud voice.

Then he opened the door and stepped into the cabin.

The front room held a three-legged table with a scarred and stained white linoleum surface, a cast iron stove throwing an ebbing wave of warmth against Hiram's legs and belly, and a small bookshelf. A rag tie rug lying in the center of the floor had been walked almost to ribbons. The light from the second room was strong enough for Hiram to see photographs in cheap frames standing in a row along the shelf, beside a small stack of books.

Lots of photographs.

"Hello?" Hiram called. There was no answer. He stepped into the center of the room; turning, he saw Asael Johnson, standing motionless on the porch outside. Johnson's face held no expression. Why was the ghost waiting?

Then Hiram saw a sheet of paper tacked over the doorway. The light was too dim to read the words, but stepping close, Hiram would make out the astrological signs and the columns of Hebrew characters that told him what the sheet was: a lamen, a paper talisman much like the one protecting Hiram's car.

Asael Johnson wasn't coming in because he *couldn't* come in. The lamen stopped him.

This was why Hiram had been brought to this place.

But he wasn't ready to play his assigned role quite yet. He wasn't sure he *should*.

He lingered to examine the photographs. They were family pictures, mostly, of different families, all old and yellowed with time. They wore nineteenth-century clothing, bonnets and corsets and frock coats and top hats.

The photographs were *almost* of different families. As he looked from one photograph to the next, Hiram realized that he was seeing seven different families, all headed by the same man.

The realization hit him like a punch to the stomach.

Was Hiram's own father living a shack like this, somewhere in Mexico, his bookshelf cluttered with portraits like these?

Hiram stepped away from the shelves to catch his breath.

"Hello?" he called again, and stepped into the second room.

This room was smaller and held nothing but a bed and a lamp. The lamp was a brass oil lamp, sitting on the wooden floor, its flame turned down low. The bed had once been a four-poster, but one of the posts and the canopy were gone, the bed sagged toward one corner, and it was heaped with ragged wool blankets and furs. For a moment, Hiram thought he was alone, but then he saw the face.

It protruded from one end of the pile of coverings, shrunken and shriveled like an old apple. The face was a man's, pitted and gaunt with age, and only a few wisps of hair clung to the mottled dome of his skull. The pile of blankets rose and fell slightly, and then the man opened his eyes. Blue irises swam in glistening rheumy pools, wandering slightly.

This was clearly the same man sitting as the head of the family in each of the photographs.

And he had a long, onion-shaped nose.

And then Hiram understood.

"Are you a doctor?" the old man asked.

"No," Hiram admitted.

"I've been praying for a doctor."

The old man closed his eyes. Was he dead? But no, the heap of furs and wool rose and fell again.

He walked to the door and stood just inside it, meeting Asael Johnson's gaze. Johnson's eyes were full of tears, glittering like the old man's.

"Well?" Johnson asked.

"This is your father," Hiram said.

He paused, but Johnson said nothing.

"Your mother was one of his wives. Maybe his first or second, when he was a young man. And she didn't want to live in Utah anymore. Maybe she was the first wife, the wife of his youth, and when he proposed taking a second wife to her, she rebelled. Or maybe she found she no longer believed. Or she didn't believe enough to live in the desert, deprived of the conveniences of civilization. And she heard there was a wagon train coming through, offering asylum for Mormons who wanted to flee."

Asael Johnson was a mirror image of Hiram Woolley, in some ways.

Johnson looked down at his feet.

"She took you with her and joined the Baker-Fancher wagon train, heading to California and a new life. Only she was killed. And then you were taken in by a Mormon family and raised as one of their own. And when the Army came through looking for taken babies, they were looking for children who had been with the wagon train. They had a list, I guess, and you weren't on it, so you just disappeared. You were raised with the name Johnson, as a Mormon. Probably somewhere not too far from where your father lived."

"That's your guess?" Johnson looked up, face expressionless.

"At some point, the old man figured out what had happened, because he moved back here. Maybe hoping to find you and your mother. Maybe afraid of your ghosts. Maybe just feeling guilty."

Johnson said nothing.

Reaching up, Hiram pried out the four tacks pinning the lamen to the wall and then took the written amulet down and folded it into quarters. "How did you find out? Did you know, in life?"

"Yes," Johnson said. "My dead mother came to me."

"In waking?"

"In dreams. I wore a Saturn ring, and it brought her to me."

"You never contacted your father in life?"

"She didn't want me to. She wouldn't tell me his name, and I couldn't discover it from the records."

Hiram thought of Yas, and his promise. He thought of Michael, staring up at him with big brown eyes. He thought of the Goodmans, who worked hard and meant well, but had known neither Betty nor Yas Yazzie.

"Will you stay?" Johnson asked.

"No." Hiram tucked the lamen into his pocket. "Whatever healing is going to happen here, you don't need me to witness it."

Johnson entered the shack and Hiram exited. His boots crunched loud on the sand and pebbles as he walked to the Model T, which started on the first try, still warm from being driven earlier.

He turned the car around and drove back to the main road. There he hesitated.

God's healer. The whole need no physician, but they that are sick.

Yas Yazzie would care. So would Betty.

Hiram took a deep breath, and turned the car back, toward Cameron, and the tribal elders, and Michael.

SEVEN STARS

I tried to force Nathan Shumate's hand with this story; he had published Space Eldritch *and* Space Eldritch II *and* Redneck Eldritch, *and some of us were trying to pressure him into doing a volume called* Frontier Eldritch. *To goad him, I went ahead and wrote this story. It didn't work. Then Lyn Worthen happened along, though. She was looking for stories for her anthology* Mirages and Speculations, *and I asked if a bit of western horror would be acceptable. It turned out the answer was yes.*

I am fascinated by the Divine Feminine; this should not surprise long-time readers, who may be accustomed to finding me exploring that power from the point of view of curiosity, attraction, or even reverence. The following is a horror story in which the Divine Feminine appears as malevolent force.

June 14, 1881
Seven Stars Church
Miskatonka County
New Mexico Territory

Dearest

This place would be an Eden, if only there were water. It will be an Eden, if I can bring it about by any means mortal or divine, and you will be my Eve.

Your uncle's memories and the map he drew me were together an unfailing guide. The church lies in the dry hills above a high valley. Cattle roam the hills and the valley both: sour-eyed, long-ribbed kine such as Pharaoh must have dreamed in the second week of years. If these be the herd, I shudder to imagine the herdsmen, whom I have not yet met. At the sight of me, I believe I witnessed one of the cows running a scaly gray tongue over sharp teeth, as if in anticipation of a meal. I gave Jenny my heels (gently, mindful of the kindness implied by God's consignment of dominion over the beasts to Father Adam), rode into your uncle's canyon, and found the church.

It is not set in what you would call a cheerful locale. The canyon ends in a box of sheer walls, and though the sandstone is mostly an orange color in the lower parts of the arroyo, by its end they have become streaked with dark red and black. Indeed, the shade of the walls was a strong indication to me that I was in the place your uncle remembered, the church in which he took sanctuary from coyotes.

I have, Dearest, seen no coyotes.

I have written above that there is no water. This is the natural man's pessimism, and I must correct myself. As I write this, saddle thrown over a fallen log for a desk and Jenny yanking mouthfuls of long yellow grass from the sandy soil, a thin trickle pours down the sheer cliff behind the church and wends its dogged way halfway down the canyon, at which point it gives up the ghost, finally disappearing in the sand. So you see that Divinity has a thought for me, and I have a source of water that will provide for both me and the mule, at least for now.

Later—perhaps tomorrow—I shall find a way to the top of the cliff and explore what the source of the rivulet may be. If it be a spring, then my source of water is assured. If, as I suspect, this water comes from the still-melting snows of the highest peaks above me, then something dramatic shall have to be done to secure water for the summer. We shall perhaps have occasion to see whether miracles have ceased.

There is, I should mention, a well. At least, there is a broad shelf of rock split by a gap large enough to admit a small boy, and stained as by the continuous outflow of water. There is no flow of water now. Beside the well lies a heap of stones, twelve cracked and sharp-angled chunks of sandstone—almost, as it were, a parody of such altars as Abraham must have used—and upon the altar, that is to say, upon the heap of stones, I found a curious thing.

It is also of stone, the length of my forearm, and carved either by a madman or by an idiot. Its features are wrong, with no eyes, a jagged mouth, and teeth like broken fangs. I believe it is meant to be a woman, given the features its maker hacked into its body, though those features are sharpened, overwrought, and angry-looking. It is a ghastly work, apparently of the same stone as the cliffs around me, and when I first picked it up, it felt—would you credit it?—cold and wet.

I wondered briefly if the thing might be valuable to a university or a collector, but quickly concluded it could not. The object is not art, but a gruesome joke at art's expense, so I threw it into the tall grass away from the church.

Before the sun sets, I must tell you about the church itself.

The slabs—no, they are pillars—are thick and rough. Almost, I would wonder if they were made by man at all, except that they rise to support a lintel over a doorway. The stone is a different stone from the canyon walls. It is green, a yellow-green, as of slow, algae-filled water, or... well, Dearest, the similes that occur to me are mostly distasteful, so I will spare you.

———

I have marked the page above with a line to show that I have put down my letter and had a conversation with a queer person. He rode slowly into my canyon camp, looking at the ground like an Apache hunter and holding a repeater rifle across his saddle. He was thin as rawhide leather and looked just as rough, with a shapeless hat low over his eyes, a loose waistcoat hanging from his shoulders, and long white mustachios, like a mock Spaniard in a two-penny melodrama.

I rose and introduced myself. He looked at me for long seconds, spat into the sand, and then began to speak, in a manner so profane and distasteful I can barely bring myself to even represent what he said, much less reproduce it.

"You don't look like one of them dadgummed inbred motherbothering sons of leeches."

I hardly knew what to say to that, but managed to agree.

"You know you ain't safe up here. Not alone, not if you was with the entire territorial bothering delegation and the dadblasted Texas Rangers to boot, every one of them armed with a Henry and a full belt of grenadoes. I seen you ride in, tinhorn and stupid, and I don't want to see you bothering killed. Sun's still up, time for you to get on that mule and hit the dadgummed road."

"I have a divinity degree from Harvard," I said. This, of course, to clarify to him that I was not stupid.

"You had a gun, it'd be a sight more bothering useful."

"If I had a gun, I couldn't in clean conscience call myself a man of God. Are you Christian, Mr.—?"

The rider stared at me with big eyes, their whites made yellow by debauched habits and their overhanging eyebrows snarled in a thicket of graying wire. Finally, he spat again. I could smell the sharp tang of the tobacco under his lip. "Anders. Cass dadbothering Anders. And no, not really. Not such as ever got dressed up of a Sunday and went to no bothered-up church."

"Good. I've never been able to abide people who dress up for church. Our Lord cared nothing for fine dress, but loved tax collectors and courtesans."

Anders squinted at me. He rested his left hand on his saddlebow and I saw that across the back of his hand he bore a tattoo. It didn't look like a sailor's ink, but more like an astrologer's—Anders bore a quavering, shapeless star on his person, and though I saw it but a moment, I had the impression that at the center of the star danced an eye, or a flame. "I reckon you just bothering called me a whore," he said. "Or a tax collector. And I ain't sure which is worse."

"They are equally precious in the eyes of God," I said.

Anders shook his head. "I guess it'd be one blazes of a sermon. But if you want to live to preach it, get the blazes out of Miskatonka. I sure as ordure am."

And with that, Mr. Anders turned and rode off.

I beg forgiveness for simulating such crude and violent turns of phrase, Dearest. These are the men among whom I now live. When our church is freshened and full of parishioners, and you sit at the head of the pews, they will no doubt be more civilized.

The church! I had forgotten. But it grows dark.

———

I have lit a fire now, with gnarled strips of dried wood from the tangled groves that scratch at the canyon walls all along their base, so I can finish the letter.

Above the doorway rests a ponderous lintel of the same green stone, and carved into the lintel are seven stars. They are quite distinctly seen even from the ground, fifty feet below, as they have been filled with a dark substance like paint or tar. They must have been painted long ago, because much of the color has flaked out, but enough adheres to clearly show that the shapes are stars. Seven stars, each star seven-pointed, and I am reminded of St. John's seven stars, and seven spirits. Strange-looking though this place might be, and gloomy though its airs, a certain spirit hovers above it. The same spirit, I am confident, that hovers over all creation.

Within the entrance is a single long room, more narrow than I would have chosen, but possessing its own windows in the form of straight slits that rise up to the ceiling or the upper walls, variously, letting in bold and irregular bolts of light during the daytime. Filled with rows of benches—or, in a pinch, logs for pews such as Enoch and his flock must have rested up in face-to-face worship of their God—it will make an adequate, and maybe even a superlative chapel. The darkness filling the upper space of the chapel is sublime and terrifying, as the darkened Holy of Holies of Solomon's church must have been. I am not one for incense, Dearest, as you know, but I can imagine the heady effect that a brazier of scented coals might have in such a space.

Enough. Left to my own urges, I would consume the entire night in writing to you. In the morning, I must consider water—perhaps, Mosaically, I shall strike the rock and make water spring forth by the power of my faith. More likely, the Jenny and I shall go exploring. I shall post this letter to you at the soonest opportunity.

Yours in faith.
Charles Broadhammer

P.S. Do you know, I meant to hurl that nasty statuette into the tall grass, but I suppose I must have forgotten to do so? As I lay down on my saddle blankets, I saw it crouching at the edges of the firelight, staring at me with those horrid eyes. I tried to sleep regardless, but, feeling spied upon, I eventually rose and threw the ugly thing away as I had first intended. Now, no doubt, I shall sleep soundly.

———

June 19, 1881
Sabbath
Seven Stars Church
Miskatonka County
New Mexico Territory

Dearest

I ask forgiveness for the too many days that have lapsed since I last wrote. I still carry that first letter about with me, in the pocket of my frock coat, and when I am at last able to post it I see I shall post two letters together. I would have written sooner, only I have been tired. So tired.

I have not struck the rock and produced water. But I did, as I said I would, mount Jenny and follow the trickle of water further up the mountains. I had to retrace my trail nearly to the mouth of the canyon to find a place with sufficient footing for the mule to ascend, and even then the trail across the top of the canyon was intermittent and precarious. There are snakes, as long as a man, that hiss and rattle and flick their long tongues. I do not know how Eve could be seduced by such a loathsome creature, and I am grateful that Jenny remained imperturbable in their presence.

Above my canyon (I call it mine, though it remains your uncle's claim, and who knows who built that church in the first place?), I followed the water through a broad saddle, and eventually came to a cliff wall, orange- and brown-streaked. My stream, I could see, neither gushed from a spring nor dripped from melting snows, but oozed out of the mother stone itself, under a shaggy crown of water cress.

I let Jenny free to drink from the stream, and pressed my own face up against the stone to suck the water as it came to the surface.

"I am Electra," said a voice behind me.

Even choking, Dearest, I kept my sense of humor. "I am grateful, then, not to be Agamemnon."

Turning, I saw two of God's less comely children. The woman was short, bony, and dressed in rags of wool and homespun cloth. She only had one arm, and one eye, and she had been the speaker. Her own hand held a large jug.

The man beside her was taller, but equally lean. He lacked a leg (from the knee down, he was peg-legged as any pirate), and one ear, and he learned on a battered single-shot rifle, grinning to reveal a mouth consisting more of gap than of teeth. "Al Sione."

"Mr. Sione," I said, "ma'am, I see I am not the only one in this country who thirsts."

I stood aside, but Electra made no move to fill her jug.

"We're all thirsty," she said. "Been a long time since they was water."

"We give what little we can," Sione said. "We give, She gives. The Apaches have got wary."

He pointed, and then I saw that the rivulet of water passed by several radiating branches in its course. With a fuller stream, it would have fanned water out in multiple ditches, spreading across the saddle in various directions.

"Do you farm?" I asked them. "Or keep herds?"

"Try," said Electra.

You can see, Dearest, that they supplied little grist for decent social intercourse. I smiled and tried harder. "Are you married?" I asked them.

Sione laughed, a sound like a cat scratching wool. "Not us," he said. "You'se the married one."

He pointed again, and this time at Jenny. I saw now a strange thing, and somewhat vexing. Jenny's saddlebag bulged near to bursting, and the reason why was in plain view—in a fit of absentmindedness, I had packed and brought along the ugly figurine, the head of which protruded above the dried beef and fruit and Lucifer matches packed against emergencies, staring eyelessly at the pale sky.

"I am not yet married," I said to them proudly through my bafflement, "but I shall be. I am engaged, to a fine young lady of Philadelphia society. Miss Lucinda Ellenmoor."

"Ellenmoor," Al Sione groaned.

"Like that miner," added Electra.

"Yes," I agreed. "Her uncle Heywood staked a claim to the canyon below us. He made his fortune here."

"He's sent us other miners," Electra said. "As he agreed."

I thought Sione looked at her sharply, but he said nothing, and who knows what strange fancies pass through the minds of such wretched hill folk?

"I am not a miner. I am, as it happens, an ordained minister, and Uncle Heywood had given me permission to use his land to start a church. For the shepherds and cattlemen and farmers of the county. I could marry you, if you wish."

"He don't like you much, I guess," Sione said. He scratched the air again with his laugh.

"He respects me," I said, not at all defensively. "We are to be family, and whatever the general resemblance he may claim to find between preachers and bats, he and I have an understanding. He made his fortune on this land, and I shall make mine as well, only mine shall be a treasure in heaven. Where Uncle Heywood returned to civilization with baskets full of gold, I shall return laden with the saved souls of men."

"Souls," Electra mouthed. Her voice was deep and gravelly, and if I shivered at the strangeness of it, I positively jumped at the sudden

THUD!

that I heard next.

Jenny snorted and cantered several paces away from the water.

Behind her, in the sand, lay the statue. It had landed upright, and I will confess to you, Dearest, that I gasped and clutched at my own breast. My heart hammered at twice its usual rate for long seconds after I realized that nothing had happened.

The statue had slipped from the saddlebag where I had placed it, that was all. But you know, Dearest, the emptiness of the country out here, and stubborn strangeness of Electra and Al Sione (I think of them as the Siones, whether they be lawfully married or no), gave a large and surreal cast to every experience I had. For a moment, buttons clenched in my fist and the cloth of my shirt stretched tight against my shoulder blades, I would have sworn the little idol was mouthing words at me.

I will not tell what word I thought I heard, for you would think me an imbecile or a child. I shall tell you someday, when you are here and we are married, and these encounters are far behind us and rendered ridiculous and charming by inexorable time.

"They'll come, you being here," Al Sione said to me.

Electra only laughed, like a crow.

"Come to church," I said. "This Sunday."

"There's a wedding in the offing, you can expect guests," Sione said.

And thus, without answering my invitation, they left.

———

I awoke this morning lying on the pile of stones, my face wet. I have dreamed wild dreams, Dearest, of an iron-black sky heavy with rain, a rain that falls out of my own ribcage.

———

I am writing this on the evening of the Sabbath day. Given the encounters I have had this week, I had thought it possible—I will not say *certain* or even *likely*, but possible—that I might see parishioners in church today. I have seen no one. They may yet arrive, but given the pink and purple that now streaks across the sky from the west, I may perhaps be deluding myself. Still, I can finish this letter to you.

———

I rode down out of the canyon two days later to find the county seat.

I do not believe the town has a name. If it has a name, it may be the same as the county—Miskatonka, but that it an ugly, barbarous, godforsaken label dragged, no doubt, from some Indian patois and worthy of being eventually forgotten in favor of a more Christian title. I do not hope for *New Jerusalem*, the capital city of the *Territory of Palestine*, but a name such as *Progress* or *Labor* or *Fraternity* would roll off my tongue with more joy than the guttural *Miskatonka*. Such a name would say something, at least, about the inhabitants of the place, or it might inspire them with ideals, encourage them to reach for something better.

For the people of Miskatonka, scarred, shuffling, mongrels that they are, desperately need motivation to reach for something better.

Miskatonka squats on a dirty creek flowing down from the same mountains in which I found Uncle Heywood's canyon. As your uncle suggested, it has no existing church. The absence of a house of God is striking, given that Miskatonka appears to be a prosperous town. It boasts a bank, an undertaker, a saloon, a hotel, a dry goods store, a carpenter, and several sturdy homes.

I tapped the shoulder of a passing gentleman after dismounting, intending to inquire after the post office. As he turned to face me, the grotesque deficiency of his face nearly caused me to drop Jenny's lead.

The man had no nose. The scar in the center of his face was raw and red.

I stifled an unworthy exclamation, smiled, and made my inquiry.

The gentleman, who worse a silk waistcoat adorned with a gold watch and ivory buttons, looked me up and down. "You are the preacher," he said. "In the old ruins up in the canyon."

You know my manner of dress, Dearest — I choose not to identify my profession by a uniform of any sort, and clothe myself simply, so I was surprised at his intuition.

"I am."

"My name is Merope," he said. "I am a member of your flock."

He smiled, but the absence of a nose gave his face the appearance of a death's head, and I fear I must have shuddered.

"Merope," I said, recovering myself. "Is that an Italian name? Catholics will of course be welcome. God loves all His children."

"*If she loves any,*" Mr. Merope said. It was a strange thing to say, but his manner of saying it was even stranger, in that he spoke the words slowly and distinctly, as if to avoid any accidental shibboleth. A mariolater, I must imagine.

"He, you mean," I said. "And He does."

Merope only smiled and pointed at a long, narrow building behind the bank. "That's the county building, preacher," he said. "Such officers as this territory has do all their business there."

I thanked him with a polite tip of my hat. As I led Jenny past him, I called out what I intended as a final friendly reminder of Sunday services: "I'm thinking of calling it St. John's!"

"Seven Stars!" Merope laughed, a sound that was unexpectedly low and ugly, like a belch. "Whatever you call it, the thing is itself. You are welcome, preacher. It has been a long dry season, and we are in want of flesh."

Then he turned and was gone, around the corner of the undertaker's.

I confess I stared after him. Mr. Merope would not be the first believer ever to connect the power of faith and rain — Elijah sealed the heavens, after all, and St. James, the brother of our Lord, was also a man whose word could open the clouds. But it was a strange thing to hear in the New Mexico Territory.

And what did he mean — *we are in want of flesh?*

I unburden myself to you, Dearest. I should not. It is only that the night about me is dark, clouds covering the moon, and I am disappointed. No doubt the Italian gentleman merely meant that his cattle suffered from the drought.

The county building contained, as far as I could tell, but two rooms: a courthouse, which brooded empty and silent; and a jail, where two men sat at a table dealing cards and a third slumped under a blanket behind bars.

I smiled as I entered, resting my burden on a counter that ran beside the door. "Hello, gentlemen," I greeted the two men. "I've come here in the hope that you can help me. Would you tell me how to post a letter to Massachusetts?"

The seated men turned to look at me, and I started.

"Great Goodness!" I cursed. "Is this whole county mutilated?"

I report my outburst in shame, and by way of confession.

One of the two men playing cards entirely lacked ears, having knobby piles of scar tissue on each side of his head instead. The other had only one arm. Both wore tin stars on their chests. Neither showed the slightest perturbation at my outburst.

"The preacher," said the man with one arm. Then he nodded. "My name's Celaeno."

"Bridegroom," said the other.

"Mr. Celaeno," I said, "Mr. Bridegroom."

They chuckled at that, and I flushed. "I ain't the bridegroom," said the man with no ears. He pointed at the burden I'd laid upon the bar. "You are."

I looked down, and I'm damned — forgive me for writing this word, Dearest, but no other will do, I'm *damned* — if I hadn't brought the hideous little statuette all the way into town with me. I laughed off my nervousness: "You do my fiancee wrong, gentlemen. She is a lovely woman of good pilgrim family. This is but a... but a..." My words failed me.

"Taygeta," said the earless man. "Name's Taygeta. We been waiting for you."

"Ain't no post as such," said Celaeno. He pointed with his thumb at a leather bag hanging from one rafter. "Stage comes through, we give 'em the bag, they ride it on to Albuquerque."

"When do you expect a stage?" I asked.

"We don't," Taygeta said.

At that moment, my profound disappointment was shattered by an eruption of shouting.

"Preacher! Dadgummit, preacher, you dad-bothering idiot!"

The man in behind the cell bars threw off the blanket covering him and shuffled to his feet. It was Anders, the wiry, profane vagabond who first met me at St. John's, though in the moment I struggled to recall his name. I've only been able to write it now because I've gone back and consulted my earlier letter to you, still, obviously, in my possession.

"Run!" Anders shouted.

"Sir." I tipped my hat to the prisoner and then looked to the two jailers for an explanation.

They spoke at the same time. "Rustler," said one. "Murderer," said the other.

"I suppose he will hang?" I asked.

They nodded.

"Only God can offer you absolution," I said to the prisoner. "But I would happily hear your confession, and that might bring you ease of conscience."

Anders foamed at the mouth and hurled himself against the bars. "Forget about me!" he howled like an animal. "I'm bothered, anyway! You just bother on off out of here! Now!"

I picked up the the idol — it is, after all, a curious thing, and might look very well above our hearth one day — and Anders flung himself against the iron a final time. As he fell, exhausted and raving, I saw that his left arm ended now just above where his elbow had once been, in a ragged bloody bandage.

———

I have nothing else to report of the week, Dearest. I bought supplies. I explored, but met no one and found nothing else of interest. I prepared for the Sabbath assiduously, as a responsible man of the cloth must. I wrote out in longhand on several of my precious sheets of paper a sermon. When no one came, I delivered it anyway, to the rocks and the tall grass. It was a good sermon, about the importance of sacrifice, and about Queen Helen's sacrifice, and the death of the King, and the importance of rain for a parched land.

The rain begins to come down heavy, now. I shall sleep in the church tonight.

Or perhaps on the stones. They are surprisingly soft to the touch, now that I have cleared away the bones, and the rotting arm with the star tattooed onto the back of its hand.

I didn't give the sermon only to the rocks, of course. You were very attentive, sitting in the front row in the light of the disappearing moon, watching me with your big eyes.

Yours
Charles Broadhammer

――――

Midsummer
The Blasted Land

Dearest

Lady Lady Lady. Vision of darkness and blood, water from the rock, the Abyss made present, Queen of the red star. I bow and I weep. This is a last missive, a proclamation. The day grows long! The sun is too hot, and must be made to withdraw. Withdraw and bless this land with flowing blood. Water. Sterope and Maia, I have met the last. Sterope with her eyes ripped out and cast into the dry womb of the earth years ago, with her gift of black vision. Maia, no tongue, no tongue. Sterope proclaimed my wedding. Maia brought a small sacrifice, a gobbet of flesh, just enough to feed the springs until the wedding. They say I knew the giver. It is a withered arm, and paltry. You are nothing if not patient. Nothing if not generous. I live for your soft bed of water and stone and for your relentless embrace.

At dawn I ride Jenny, Jenny is the mule, out of the temple and down the valley. I am received with thorns and shouting. This is as it should be, I am the Bridegroom. They bow as I pass. They show their beautiful gifts from you, the knobs and the furrows and the protruding bone. I kiss them, a blessing.

The Seven Stars receive me on my return. I am undressed, bathed, made ready. You watch. You are the Lady of the All-Seeing Eyes.

Night comes, and the wedding.

You are beautiful, my Queen.

――――

June 23, 1881
Miskatonka County
New Mexico Territory

Mr. Heywood Ellenmoor

This year's Bridegroom had letters on his person on the day of the Wedding.

Given your feelings for him, we thought you'd be amused.

Seven

RECORDING DEVICES

I have long been interested in folklore, and the preservation of traditional songs and stories. One of the interesting challenges in reading the work of someone like Elias Lönnrot, Wilhelm Grimm, or Joel Chandler Harris is the question to what extent the recorder altered the work he was purporting merely to transcribe (there's an interesting book about Grimm on that subject by G. Ronald Murphy, called The Owl, the Raven, and the Dove).

A related challenge is to what extent the technology of recording alters what is recorded. The reason we hear all those blues recorded by guys like Alan Lomax in the 1930s as three-minute songs is not because that's how long the songs actually were; when performed, they were meant to be danced to, and they were much longer. Rather, the three-minute limit was imposed by the length of the wax cylinders on which the folklorists recorded, and that technological limitation of the 1930s continues to affect how we listen to music today.

So this is a Lovecraftian horror story, about recording devices and their limitations.

The old man's gnarled right hand stopped, springing into the air above the trembling banjo strings and freezing in clawhammer shape, index ever so slightly extended and thumb to the square.

The short sustain of the banjo meant the strings sang their final chord with power, but briefly, and then fell still and silent.

John Hanks reached over to stop the recorder and set the microphone down. He leaned back on the three-legged stool next to the open trunk of the 1937 Ford that held the bulky recording device and wiped sweat off his forehead.

The musician's name was Roscoe, wasn't it? Suddenly he wasn't sure. He'd recorded the songs and playing of so many of these hill folk that their faces and names were starting to fuse, Earl and Sunny and Andy and Roscoe. John's eyes and ears itched, and he rubbed them.

"Thank you, sir." He'd just avoid the name entirely, it wasn't worth wasting any time on it. "You sure that's the last one you know?"

The old man's head swiveled on his neck. His jaundiced eyes, punctuated with glittering dark irises, pierced through the trees surrounding his dog trot cabin and seemed to search out the entire knob of rock that in this part of the world passed for a "mountain."

"Waall…" The banjo player popped his neck by cranking his head in a circle and licked his lips. "Not all songs is proper to sing. Not in public. And some songs just en't proper at all."

John restrained a sigh. Instead, he dug into the cash in his waistcoat pocket and pulled out thirty-five cents. "There you are, Roscoe," he said. "Seven songs and tunes I haven't heard before, a nickel apiece."

"Name's Earl." The banjo player looked down at the dull change in the palm of his hand: two dimes, three nickels, ten pennies. "I got another, I reckon. It's gettin' dark, though."

John patted the microphone. "The folks hearing the recording will see you just as well in the darkness as in broad daylight," he cracked wise. "And if you're worried about me getting back down the… mountain," he swallowed the word in one bite, "the car's got headlamps."

"It en't that. It's only… iffen." Roscoe licked his lips again. No, Earl. "I need the money. Nickel goes a long way these days."

John let him think about it. Some of these old folks up in the hills couldn't wait to get someone to listen to their treasure trove of nursery rhymes, blues, ballads, and hymns. Others acted like they were sharing the most precious thing in the world, and had to be bribed, coaxed, reassured, and sometimes even tricked.

"You jest gonna record it on that... what'd you call it?"

John nodded and grinned. "It's a mobile recording device." The recorder was a chunky machine that ran off the Ford's battery and turned sound waves into grooves in a wax cylinder by way of a hand-held microphone. It was state of the art, or at least as state of the art as you could reasonably be expected to drag up into the *hollers* of Appalachia.

"It en't dark yet," Earl decided. "You hold a red an' a white thread side by side, an' iffen you can't tell the difference, it's dark. En't that what them old presters used to do? Let's git this one down, an' fast." He leaned over his banjo to whisper to John, and his voice dropped an octave. "An' I en't singin' the words, not to *this* song, nuh-uh. But I'll play you the tune, an' I wager you en't heard it. That worth a nickel?"

"Has it got a name?" John turned on the recorder and held the microphone up to Earl. Still plenty of juice in the battery, he was sure —he had no desire to spend the night in Earl's dog trot.

"No, it en't." Earl squinted. He must know, from all the tunes he'd already recorded that afternoon, that John wanted some kind of label, a way to catalog any piece of music. "But it's a tune as old as the hills." As he said it, he was adjusting the tuning on the banjo. At first, John thought it was just tuning up, but then he saw and heard Earl drop the second string an unnatural amount, and when the wiry farmer ticked the strings off one after the other with his fingernail, the resulting chord sounded... off. Modal, but beyond modal. Microflatted. Intervals all wrong. Unearthly. "Old as the hills," the old man repeated.

"Let's hear it."

Earl played.

True to his word, he didn't sing. His tune was long and discordant, a double drone that must have been some sort of diminished fifth by way of interval, or maybe a diminished sixth, but it seemed to John that the distance between the drone notes grew and shrank as the sound moved through time. The drone was accented by choppy bits of melody on the first, third, and fourth strings, shreds of sound that seemed to John like voices.

Not human voices. And not singing.

Old Earl's drone felt like the thrum of earth moving through infinite time in mist and darkness, and as John's eyes seemed to fill with those mists, he would have sworn he saw standing stones jutting from the mists, and heard voices shrieking in joyous celebration. Only the voices weren't human—they sounded more like birds, but not any bird he'd ever heard sing before.

John wanted to rub the hallucination away from his face, but he had to hold his position very carefully or he would fail to capture the sound on the recorder. His eyes and ears itched and his legs felt asleep. Too much time sitting on this stool.

The banjo shrieked again, or was it a bird? Or was it Earl?

Or was it John?

The tune stopped, abruptly.

Darkness had fallen. Darkness as Earl himself defined it; John could no longer tell the white stripes from the red in Earl's old cotton shirt.

"The nickel," Earl said.

John fumbled for the coin in the darkness. "You say there are words?"

"I won't sing 'em. En't no place safe to sing 'em except mebbe in church on Christmas, an' then I reckon it'd be spittin' in Jesus' eye."

John found himself curious. No, not curious. He found himself craving. He had a strong and unexpected desire to know what words went with that strange, shuddering, atonal tune.

And publish them.

"What about written down?" he asked. "Would you write them? Or do you know where I could find them written?"

Earl was so still that for a moment, in the darkness, he was invisible. When he shook his head it was in a shudder, a sudden paroxysm of motion that almost knocked John backward. "I cain't."

"Or won't?"

"Difference don't matter." Earl stood slowly. His banjo was a light one, an old Sears Roebuck model with an open-back pot, but the slow hunch in which he rose suggested a heavy burden on Earl's shoulder.

Arthritis, John told himself. Bad nutrition. Inbreeding, maybe.

"'Cept mebbe one person," Earl said. It was an afterthought, spoken from the dark shadow of the dog trot running between the two cabins of Earl's house. "Up top of the mountain. Name's Hodder. He's got books, an' I reckon he might have the words written down somewheres."

"'Hodder.' Is that his first name, or his last?"

"All the name he has. He ain't got a clan, not like most folks."

"What do I ask him for? I can't just say 'the song as old as the hills,' can I?"

"The *call*," Earl said slowly. He had disappeared entirely into one of his cabins, and John couldn't even tell which. "Just tell him you want to know the words of the call."

"I don't really understand what you're doing."

John Hanks and Dr. Bender stood inside some sort of laboratory space belonging to the professor. He must be a professor of anthropology, John thought, judging by the twisted masks, dream catchers, untutored paintings, and oddments of wax and feathers that lay strewn on the great trestle tables.

"Oh, and isn't that just life?" Dr. Bender chuckled, chalking the floor around John's feet.

"I've heard stories about the faculty and their... interests. Look, if we're going to do something crazy here, can I at least sit down?"

"My dear Dr. Hanks." Dr. Bender straightened to his full height, looking down into John's eyes from a few inches away. "I mean, you're not technically a doctor yet. But you will be, and what are a few formalities and a sheepskin between friends?"

It was John's turn to chuckle. "Okay."

"I don't know what kind of crazy thing you're imagining we're going to do, but you're mistaken. This is just a little something that will help you remember."

"A mnemonic device."

"You could say. Yes, a device of memory, that will help us remember." Dr. Bender turned to light three candles. John didn't know what kind of off-brand wax they were made off, but they candles sputtered horribly and they stank. "A recording device."

"Us?"

"Mmmm." Dr. Bender handed John a mannequin—an unpainted wooden puppet that flopped all loose-jointed in John's two hands. "Here now, hold this."

From a pot on the trestle, Dr. Bender took a fingertip's dab of some kind of oil or cream and dotted it on the puppet's face in four places, where its eyes and ears would have been. He put a final dab on the doll's belly, and grinned at John.

"To give desire," he said.

The drive back down the mountain was physically no different from the drive up, but John Hanks hit the bottom harrowed. Three times, he nearly wrecked the car: twice over sudden precipices and a third time running it into a grove of tangled trees.

At the first cliff, he found himself tapping the steering wheel with the fingers of his left hand in a repetitive figure; at the second, he started a second pattern with his left foot. The two overlapping patterns felt familiar, deeply rooted in his being.

The recognition that the rhythms were the two entwined drone rhythms of old Earl's banjo was what nearly sent John into the trees.

Hawthorns. But there shouldn't be hawthorns on the mountain, should there?

After that, he found himself humming a melody. A drone, punctuated by birdlike cries.

John's hotel was a shabby boarding house called McCord's. He'd been staying there for three weeks while he tooled around the mountains, passing out nickels to the locals in exchange for any piece of music he hadn't heard before. Though he knew exactly where it was, McCord's still managed somehow to catch John by surprise and throw an azalea bush under the wheels of the Ford before he managed to stop.

Sheepishly checking for witnesses and seeing none, John backed the car up, rolled it around behind the boarding house, and set the hand brake.

He was drenched in cold sweat.

John dreamed.

He looked down from a great height. The height, he knew, was part of what would make him a god.

Although height alone would not do it. Nor would the birds circling him, whose eldritch cries spoke hidden wisdom into the torn and shredded sockets from which his mortal, worthless ears had been removed.

To become a god, you participate in the banquet of the gods. This was the feast of Tantalus, the feast of Atreus, the feast of Moses and the elders of Israel on the Mountain of the Gods.

John heard a low rumble, and the stone supporting him shook.

The gods came.

He let out a piercing cry. The cry contained the wisdom of the birds, the cry was the call that summoned the gods to the feast.

In the morning, John checked out of McCord's.

"Got what you came for?" asked the old woman at the desk.

He stared into her toothless mouth longer than was strictly polite while the question registered.

"Not yet," he finally said.

"Oh? Whatcha gon' do, sleep rough while you git the rest of yer music?"

Her words seemed to come from far away.

"Iffen yer short on cash, Mr. Hanks, I reckon we could extend ye a little credit. You bein' a university man an' all."

"Oh, no." It was a cool morning, if humid, but John took a hand-kerchief from the breast pocket of his waistcoat and swiped at his forehead. "No, I have one more person to see. Up on the mountain."

"Old Earl? Earl picks a fine clawhammer."

"I saw Earl yesterday." John's hand trembled as he handed cash over to the proprietress to pay his bill. He must be sick. "If I could have a receipt, please. No, Earl suggested I see his neighbor."

"Earl ain't got neighbors." The old woman said it matter-of-factly, printing dates and numbers in large block letters on the top page of her receipt pad.

"Well, perhaps not his neighbor. Another resident of the mountain, further up."

The old woman shook her head. "Ain't been no one further up the mountain from Earl for twenty years."

"No?"

"Not since old man Hodder died."

The ground beneath John's feet shifted. Somehow, the old woman didn't notice. She finished printing his receipt and handed it to him. He tipped his hat, a deeply sweat-stained fedora that had once been dapper, and walked outside.

He tossed his valise into the back seat and stood beside the car to think.

He had many recordings. Surely, as many as Professor Bender required.

He ought to get in the car and just drive north. A couple hours' driving would get him to the highway, and from there it would be sunshine, breeze through the window, and cold Coca-Colas all the way back to Miskatonic.

He would do that.

He'd miss out on the words to the song Earl had identified as the song *as old as the hills* and the *call*. Would that be such a steep price to pay?

Instead, without quite ever making a decision to the effect, he climbed into his car, started it, and headed back up the mountain.

As he negotiated the steep switchbacks and narrow gullies that had nearly thrown him the night before, John remembered his first encounter with Dr. Bender and the man's project.

"You're not a musicologist?" John had asked.

"No, but you are." Dr. Enoch Bender had a shock of white hair like a duster, and when he moved or gestured he seemed to leave a cloud of chalk behind. "Or you will be."

"Well, I don't understand what it is exactly you're looking for. Just old songs?"

"Yes, exactly. And you can have all the publications."

That was music to John's ears, though he never would have been so low brow as to speak the pun out loud. "I get the credit? This is not how it usually works. Graduate students usually do all the work and get none of the credit. That's the deal. Indentured servitude, in exchange for a doctorate."

"I'm generous." Dr. Bender grinned, flashing very large teeth, deeply stained by coffee.

So much the better. If all the publications were to be his, John Hanks could launch his own professorial career with a bang. He could be the new James Francis Child, the musical James George Frazer of Appalachia.

"But... what *is* your interest, then?" It seemed to good to be true: his travel expenses would be paid by this small university, and then he could go back to Harvard with all—or maybe most—of what he had collected and make his career with it. "What exactly are you looking for?"

"The oldest songs. The strangest songs. Songs of doom and ceremony." Dr. Bender's smile disappeared. "Songs of summoning. I don't want to publish them, you see. I just want to know them."

John stopped briefly at Earl's dog trot out of a sense of obligation, but knocking on the doors of both halves of the cabin produced no response. Earl farmed, he had said, so he must be already up and in his fields.

The road that continued up beyond Earl's cabin was barely worthy of the name. Sometimes it was a track scarcely wide enough for a mule, let alone the Ford. He remembered Dr. Bender laughing as he'd handed over the keys: "Eight hundred fifty dollars, they tell me!"

"Well, maybe you'd prefer that I take another car," John had said. "That's a lot of money."

"However little I care about money," Dr. Bender had confided, "I care about cars even less. I don't know how to drive."

John stomped the accelerator pedal on the Ford, pushing it forward with increased strength as the path became more narrow. Saplings, bushes, and low-hanging branches fell to one side and the other or were torn out by the root as Dr. Bender's car charged through.

Then the mist.

Odd, to have so much mist on such a warm day, in late summer, at such high elevations. The mist was cold, too; it reminded John of British mist in the clammy way it crept in through the windows of the car and climbed inside his shirt.

He pulled up over the lip of a long slope and saw the cabin.

Braking, he pulled up in front of it. This was no Appalachian dog trot, it was something older and less comfortable, and John Hanks barely recognized it for a cabin at all. Slates had been piled up to make four walls, and there must be some kind of a roof substructure, a lattice of limbs or boards maybe, because the roof as he could make it out was a pile of turves. The cabin looked like the kind of thing you might find in some remote abandoned glen in old Europe, not within a hundred miles of Nashville. He wouldn't have been surprised to see a goat munching the grass growing on the roof.

But there was no goat.

Indeed, stepping out of the car, John noticed that he could see no animals at all. Not a chipmunk, not a bird, nothing.

"Mr. Hodder!" he called out.

Silence.

"Hodder!"

Still nothing.

Stooping to pass beneath a twisted lintel, John peered inside the cabin. It consisted of a single room, with a fireplace and chimney, a pile of wool blankets on a stone bench beside it, and a few shelves carrying necessities. There were books, as Earl had suggested there would be, but John's heart fell as he looked at them: *Anatomy: Descriptive and Surgical, Corpus Areopagiticum, La Cena de le Ceneri.*

Nothing that suggested it might contain song lyrics. Other than the anatomy book, the titles in fact suggested nothing to John. Latin and Italian? he guessed. Out of place in these hills.

He walked around the cabin. Hodder's home stood in the center of a small clearing, and the trees surrounding it were stunted, gnarled things. Maybe blighted by the altitude, John thought, but the trees didn't look as if they were blighted by any external force at all. They looked—John dared to think it—as old as the hills. They looked natural, indigenous, and twisted by their very nature.

They looked malevolent.

At the far end of the clearing from the cabin was a pile of stones. Twelve stones, rounded and rough, but piled together, and the topmost stone was flat and provided a table-like surface. The entire thing was stained dark, or at least the cracks and indentations in the stones were dark.

Maybe lichen, John thought.

Sitting in the center, on top of the mass of stone, was the skull of a bird.

He realized he was humming the droning sound of Earl's melody from the day before.

Like a didgeridoo, he thought. A drone, with yelping accents here and there to provide variety. Only the yelping cries punctuating the tune in his memory did more than just relieve monotony. There was information in them.

A summons.

He heard a cry overhead, and looked up just in time to see a bird appear from the mist, pass overhead, and disappear again.

"Hodder!" he called, one last time, and turned back to the car.

A man stood before him. Short, completely bald. Eyebrows thick as caterpillars and unnaturally wide nostrils.

"Yaas?" asked the short man.

There was something *off* in his accent. Not *non*-Appalachian, exactly, but *pre*-Appalachian. His accent sounded like the ur-Scotch-Anglo-Irish whine from which all redneck accents might have descended in the hundreds of years of the borderers' wandering in the Americas.

"Oh." John Hanks stepped back. He took a moment to organize his thoughts, which seemed to have fled with the passing bird. "Earl sent me."

"Don't know an Earl. Not a livin' one."

"He, ah, he lives down the mountain from you."

Hodder raised his eyebrows briefly but said nothing.

"Anyway, my name's Dr. Hanks. John Hanks." A lie. Anyway, a stretched truth. But the little man's stare made John feel the need to reinforce his own gravitas.

"Ain't sick."

"I'm not a medical doctor. I'm a musicologist, I collect songs. I'm a doctor of music."

"Looking for sick music, are ye?" There went Hodder's eyebrows again. John almost laughed at what must surely have been meant as a joke, except that he felt that on some level Hodder was speaking a simple truth.

Simple, and maybe horrible.

"You might say so. I heard a piece of music from Earl, and he told me you might know the words."

"I ain't a musician."

"He said you'd know this one. He said you'd know the words to the call."

"Did he?"

Moisture trickled down between John's shoulder blades. He couldn't tell if it was sweat, or the mist condensing on his body. "I'm paying a nickel. A nickel a song."

"Nickel's a damned small price to pay for somethin' sacred."

John found himself nodding. "Yes, yes indeed. And that's just how I'd treat your words, Mr. Hodder. Sacred. The university wants to collect them because they're important, and we think other people ought to be able to learn them." John had had this conversation with a hundred other informants, each reluctant to part with the special song grandpappy taught him, regardless of how tiny a variant the song might be on *The Jew's Daughter*.

Only usually a nickel was enough to bring a smile to their wrinkled, tiny faces.

Hodder still wasn't smiling.

The mountain man looked John Hanks up and down, and eventually nodded.

"I kin help ye," he finally said. "In the right time an' place."

"Very good." John stepped towards the car. "If you'll just step over here with me to the recording device. Would you mind speaking the words into a microphone? Or singing them would be even better, that would let us capture the melody."

"In the right time an' place," Hodder repeated himself. "Which ain't here nor now."

He turned and walked into the mist. Within three steps he had disappeared.

"Nuts," John muttered.

What kind of name was Bender, anyway?

Enoch was a biblical name, John had gone to enough Sunday School as a boy to know that. Old Testament, wasn't he the one who walked with God and disappeared? Lived to be old, but not as old as Methuselah and Adam and some of the others. A mere three-hundred-something years, John remembered.

But John had known his shares of Jews at Harvard and quite a few more growing up in Brooklyn, and Enoch wasn't a very Jewish-sounding name. Moshe and Reuben and Judah and Shimon and... so on.

Enoch felt like a Puritan's name.

Bender? John had no idea.

Maybe it was one of those old English occupational names, like Smith, Taylor, Butler. Maybe it meant someone who bent things.

The car started on the third try, and John backed it around with a three-point turn that brought his bumper under the lintel of Hodder's front door. Keeping his feet hovering over the brake, he put the car into gear and eased back over the lip at the edge of the clearing.

To his surprise, after a small initial dip, the road climbed again.

This was wrong. He distinctly remembered driving up to the clearing. Maybe, he thought, his memory was tricking him, and at the end of a drive that was mostly ascent he had descended the last minute into Hodder's clearing. He stuck with the road.

But no, the road definitely climbed.

And it was too narrow to turn around.

"Wrong road," he muttered to himself.

He'd imagined, without voicing the hope, that speaking out loud would dispel the tight feeling in his chest. It didn't.

Ten minutes later he found a shelf of dirt and gravel. What he intended as another three-point turn became a seven-point turn as he rocked back and forth a few feet at a time before finally managing to rotate the car one-hundred eighty degrees. He kept his eyes firmly on the shelf the entire time, and resolutely looked away from the trees.

The trees, which stared at him with gaping sockets and open mouths.

"They don't warn you about this when you say you want to get a Ph.D." Putting the 1937 Ford into gear again, John drove back the way he came.

Inexplicably, the road *continued up the mountain*.

"Nuts." John put the Ford into neutral and pulled the hand brake. "Damn."

The fog felt like fingers under his shirt. He wanted to roll up the windows, but he knew if he did the windows would fog and then he would be blind.

As annoying as it was to worry that he was lost on the mountain, it would be much worse to drive off the mountain's edge.

"Okay." John tapped the steering wheel and breathed deeply. "Get hold of yourself, Hanks. You're just a little lost." He tapped his foot, too. "But you're on a road, and roads go somewhere. So just drive.

Drive forward. You'll probably find Hodder's cabin. Or the highway. Or Earl's dog trot. Or anything.

"What's the worst that could happen?"

Still tapping his fingers and his foot, he drove.

The road climbed, and John thought the tire tracks he saw looked fresh. It might mean he was backtracking, of course, but still the sight heartened him. At least he was on the same road he had already traveled.

He began to hum, low and tuneless.

From time to time, when he felt the rhythm dictated it, he whistled a note or two of accompaniment.

Then the Ford climbed over a lip of earth and he was in a meadow. Before him, and slightly to the left, stood a waist-high pile of stones that looked familiar.

John set the brake and breathed a sigh of relief.

In that moment, he recognized the tune he was humming, the rhythms he was tapping out, the bird-like trills of ornament.

He wished he had never asked Earl for that last song.

Climbing out of the car, he approached the pile of stone. There they were again: the lichen in the cracks—but was it lichen, after all?—the flat stone on top, the bird skull.

"Right. So I got turned around, but I'm back." John looked about him. "Only I seem to have come up to the clearing by a different road this time."

He spoke out loud to reassure himself.

It failed.

"Hodder!" he cried.

Faintly, he thought he heard his own voice echo back to him. No sign of Hodder.

The cabin must only be a few steps away. He walked into the fog, looking for it.

"Hodder!"

No answer, and no sign of the cabin.

"Damn," John said again, and then he kept saying it, under his breath and once per step. He reached the edge of the clearing and followed it several paces in one direction, and then back several paces the other way.

No cabin.

No Hodder.

"Hodder!"

Overhead, the piercing cry of a bird.

John's breathing came fast and painful. He stopped walking to try to get control of his heart, which raced to match his breath.

The fog would pass. Hodder would return. He just needed a place to sit down and wait.

The car.

Looking down, John saw his own tracks in the grass, a darker streak where his feet had shaken the silver dew from the tall green stalks. Breathing easier, he turned and followed his trail back.

He had the oddest sensation that his legs were long wooden dowels, pinned together only loosely at the knees. He shook his head to clear the nonsensical thought, then pawed at his own eyes and ears to smudge away the persistent itch.

There was the altar, and the bird's skull. And there his path stopped.

There was no sign of John's car.

He was beyond cursing, beyond the power of speech. His heart raced so fast he feared he'd die of cardiac failure then and there. He tried to tell himself that he'd sit and wait for Hodder to come back, but the only sound he could make was a droning hum, marked by sharp whistles.

He was too old to whimper, so John Hanks bit his lower lip until it bled. Tasting the tang of iron on his tongue, he sat and leaned against the one landmark that remained to him, the rough stone altar, to wait out the fog.

John woke up.

He leaned against a massive trestle table and two men stood before him. They wore masks, outsized and shield-shaped, only the masks seemed to be made of flesh.

They were mobile, had expressions.

The man standing nearer John leaned in. His mask, lips thin and pulled as wide as possible, eyes bugging, hair a white shock that shed a cloud of chalk as he moved, looked like a mask of Dr. Enoch Bender's face.

As interpreted by some Polynesian tribe.

Using living flesh as a medium.

John blinked and looked away, his eyes stinging.

"The words, Dr. Hanks."

"What words?"

The second man, standing behind Masked Bender, also looked familiar. Blinking to look through tears, John thought his mask looked like the face of Earl. The banjo player, the man who had sent John on this wild goose chase around the mountain.

"The words to the song as old as the hills," said Masked Earl. "The call."

"Well, you know them, don't you?" John challenged Earl. He felt groggy, and had to fight to keep his chin off his own sternum.

"I don't. I en't ever heard 'em. You gotta hear 'em from Hodder."

"The right time and place," John said drowsily. "Only then he disappeared."

"Well, can you sing us the melody, at least?" asked Masked Bender.

"Sssssure." The soft hiss of his own speech almost put John to sleep, but he shook himself and focused.

Tapped his fingers on the stone floor under his thighs.

Tapped his foot in a second rhythm.

Started to hum.

John woke up.

The sky above him was the color of slate.

The fog was gone.

His back and neck hurt from lying against a hard surface. John turned to look about him and saw that he'd been sleeping against a rough stone altar, a pile of uncut stone with a bird's skull on top.

It looked familiar. He remembered sitting down next to an altar like this, although the memory was faded and seemed quite old.

And the altar was now red and slick with... blood?

John checked himself all over. He wasn't bleeding, and his breath came in big, cold gulps of relief.

He distinctly saw the limits of the clearing he was in. There was no car and there was no cabin. There were only the encircling trees and the rocky path climbing up.

John took the path.

He sang to pass the time, or he tried to. Whether he started with *Fatal Flower Garden*, *The Parson and the Clerk*, or one of the Robin Hood ballads, he always ended humming the same tune.

He squeezed his shoulders together to avoid being touched by the trees. At each step and on both sides, they seemed to loom closer.

He tried to curse and couldn't.

The path abruptly leveled and widened into a clearing. He must be at the top of the mountain, because he saw no more slopes up. He also saw no slopes down, and no sister mountains off in the distance.

For all the world, it was as if he had climbed a mountain and at its top found a flat plain, a featureless collision of blue-green grass and slate gray sky.

Almost featureless. Dotting the plain like rotted canine teeth were stone pillars. They were as tall as the skyscrapers of Manhattan but thinner, and hanging on the nearest, fifty feet off the ground, John saw rusted iron chains.

John's bones felt like ice.

Above, circling birds.

"The right time an' place."

John turned and saw Hodder standing at his shoulder. He shuddered, sucking in cold air to steady himself.

Then he looked past the bald man and saw no slope, but only more featureless plain. The mountain, with its paths and its trees, with John's borrowed car and Hodder's cabin and altar, was gone.

A bird called, sharp and short.

John fainted.

John hung on a wall.

There were pins under his shoulders; his arms tingled, asleep, from having their circulation pinched by the pins. His legs felt no sensation at all. His eyes and ears itched.

"So, then," Dr. Bender said, leaning in close to John's face. "Have you got words for us?"

Behind Dr. Bender John saw the cavernous empty space of the professor's laboratory. It seemed even larger than it had before.

"Not yet." John felt strangely remote from his body. His attention felt small and local, as if his mind were cleared of all other matters. As if he were simplified. "Soon."

Dr. Bender nodded, rubbing his fingers together. "Time to sleep some more then, John."

"Can I get down now?"

"And do what?" Dr. Bender laughed. "*Walk?*"

John Hanks looked down at his legs. His legs, his body, his arms—all of himself that he could see—was featureless wood.

"Don't worry," Dr. Bender said. "We'll speak again."

John hung on a rock.

It was a pillar, not a boulder. And there were no pins under his shoulders—he hung from rusted iron chains that were manacled to his wrists.

He woke to the sharp feeling of his head being punctured, and he shook it, dislodging something hungry and cold. He opened his eyes in time to see a large black bird, flapping slowly away. The bird didn't go far—it settled on the top of another rough stone pillar, within a stone's throw. At the peak of that pillar it perched and glared at John with a baleful yellow eye.

John couldn't feel his arms, and the pain in his shoulders was intense. He looked down, and saw that he was thirty feet off the ground. Below him was blue-green grass in a flat plain that seemed to extend forever; above him was slate-gray sky.

The wind blowing through the stone whistled two tones, one lower than the other. The skin on John's back prickled as he recognized the two drone notes and their strange interval, accented by the occasional cries of birds.

Before the pillar stood the man named Hodder. Hodder raised his arms to the gray sky and began to chant.

John had climbed the mountain for these words, and they burned into his consciousness.

amatim shikaram nipqid, he heard.

amatum sha belim anaku—

amatim shikaram nipqid!

shepum sha kalbim imratz!

The pain in John's shoulders dimmed as the old man chanted the strange words. The tingling sensation of sleep in his limbs spread up through the shoulders, into his chest, into his legs.

His head.

The next-to-last thing John thought he saw was Dr. Enoch Bender. If there had been anyone to take his dying deposition, he would have sworn he saw the professor standing behind Hodder with an ear cocked and a pen furiously scribbling notes in a stenographic notepad.

And then the sky cracked—

John understood the song—

and he was no more.

THE HEARTS OF THE CHILDREN

This one is brand new. The exact location of Ballagarth Castle is not publicly known, and the description of its layout is entirely my invention, but, allegedly, it exists.

"What do you think it means," Tommy asked, "to give the hearts of the children to the fathers?"

"You're talking about the Book of Malachi," Hiram said, "and the work of Elijah."

Tommy nodded solemnly. "The work of Elijah."

"I think the Bible says 'turn.'" The look on the little boy's face was so solemn, and so surreal as the pink and orange of the sunset on the far side of Juab Valley threw its paints across Hiram Woolley and his little guide. Hiram hesitated. "Do you know how old you are, Tommy?"

"I got baptized." Tommy's head was nearly spherical. His skin was pale, his eyes froglike, and he had little white cauliflower buds for ears.

Hiram nodded. "It means to connect people across generations. To connect people with their ancestors."

"Not just their flesh and blood pa."

Hiram shook his head. "Grandfathers and great-grandfathers and ancestors even hundreds of years ago. And also to connect people to their descendants."

"That's what I thought," Tommy said. He seemed satisfied, and also sad.

"Was Newt Olsen one of your friends?" Newton Olsen was the missing boy, the child Hiram had been summoned to Nephi to find. Work with the divining rod had turned his eye to the rocky slopes of Nebo, and he had hired Tommy, who had been following him around Nephi, first to take him to a butcher, and then to guide him up the mountain.

He'd hired Tommy to help him find the way, and so that Hiram could keep his eye on the boy.

The parcel wrapped in butcher's paper was heavy in the pocket of Hiram's coat.

Tommy had known a back way, he'd said, and a secret place. Was that the sort of place Hiram was looking for?

The Mosaical Rod had said that it was.

So Tommy had led Hiram up from the south. Early, Hiram had had to park the Model AA and follow the tireless little boy across marshy ground and then through narrow canyons that were nearly invisible behind stark cliff faces, and finally up and around the brow of the mountain. Where they stood now, with the dying sun desperately heaving its colors onto them, he could see northward across Utah Valley, to the southern end of Salt Lake Valley.

"I didn't know him," Tommy said.

"This secret place," Hiram asked. "Is it a building?"

Tommy stopped walking. He looked timeless, in his homespun overalls and boots, a boy who might have lived fifty or a hundred years earlier. Hiram was only certain that the child was flesh and blood because he'd put a dollar into his hand.

"It used to be," Tommy said.

"I've heard stories of a place like this," Hiram said. "The stories I heard tell about a spot high on the mountain, from which you can see Salt Lake. A place where a man couldn't be surprised, because he could see pursuit coming for fifty miles. Especially if the pursuit was coming down from Salt Lake City."

Hiram had heard about the lookout because he'd known polygamists who had used it. In previous decades, he'd been told, the men of southern Utah had used it to watch for federal soldiers and officers coming from the state capital to arrest them. For their actions at Mountain Meadows, for instance.

"Oh?" Tommy resumed walking.

"The name I heard was Ballagarth Castle," Hiram said. "Or Valle Guard, or something like that."

"I heard those names, too," Tommy said.

"Do the children of Nephi often play up here?" Hiram asked. It seemed improbable; it was a long walk from Nephi to get up to this spot, and only possible if you knew how to thread a very narrow needle's eye across swamp and scree.

Tommy shook his head. "The men never let them. And then they forgot."

"But you do."

"I don't play," Tommy said.

The narrow slip of a path rounded a sharp shoulder of the mountain and massive stones hove into view. Hiram immediately saw that they had been worked by the hand of man; the angles were too straight to be natural, and the surfaces were covered with something that might be scrollwork, carved into the stone itself. At the same time, the corners of the stone had weathered to smooth, rounded nubs, and the swirls and curves had been pounded by wind and rain into near-invisibility.

Ruins, and very old ones.

"Who showed you this place, Tommy?" Hiram asked.

The boy hesitated. "My grandfather."

"Not your father's father."

Tommy shook his head. "More fathers than that."

Hiram stepped ahead of Tommy and into the ruins. This place had been fortified, once. He thought he saw the remains of battlements from which one could look down on the path by which Hiram had approached, and the blasted, crumbling remnants of wall surrounded a stone floor. In the corner, scorch-marks and burned wood showed where men had stood guard in more recent times. A block in the center of the ruin had once been part of a wall or ceiling, but now made a ready table.

A man stood behind the table. He was small and pale, his eyes sunk deep in dark pits in his face, and he had no hair at all on his skull. He was surrounded by five boys, and a sixth stood in front of him, the man's hands on his shoulders. The five boys, like Tommy, wore old homespun. So did the man. The boy standing in front of the hairless man wore dusty OshKosh B'Gosh overalls—that was Newt Olsen.

All seven boys, and the man, had the same features. Spherical heads, pale skin, shrunken, bobbin-like ears. They could be family.

Hiram put his hands into the pockets of his coat. His left hand felt the butcher's paper and the weight of what was wrapped inside. His right felt the cold firm grip of his revolver.

"You can't have the boy," Hiram said.

"Which one?" The hairless man had an accent that Hiram couldn't place.

"Any of them," Hiram said. "I'm here to free them."

"The spell is cast," the man said. "The only way Newt Olsen walks home down the mountain tonight is if you stay here."

Newt emitted a strangled sob.

The orange flames of the setting sun disappeared, and the ruins were plunged into shadow. Hiram looked to his left and saw Utah Valley, now a skein of lights cast along the shore of an iron-gray lake.

Had Hiram's father, Abner Woolley, seen this view? Had he stood guard up on this mountain to watch for marshals sent down by Salt Lake judges to arrests him and the other polygamists? Had he huddled over a campfire and coffee boiled in a tin kettle on cold nights in Valle Guard Castle and hatched his plan to leave young Hiram Woolley and his mother behind, taking his other wives and children and fleeing to Mexico?

And had the sight of Lehi from this spot not softened his heart, turning it to thoughts of his son Hiram, growing up a fatherless beet-digger, raised by a woman neighbors whispered might be a witch?

Hiram took a deep breath and exhaled.

"If need be," he said. "Tell me your name."

"There's no magic in names," the man said.

"There's magic in some names. You can call me Hiram."

"You can call me Lib."

"Why now?" Hiram said. "I read the old newspapers. A string of boys disappeared forty years ago, over the course of one summer. Then the disappearances stopped. No one was ever arrested and no one ever saw the boys again. Why start up now?"

"These are my sons," Lib said.

"You look like kin," Hiram admitted.

"By your reckoning, there are many generations between me and these boys." Lib grinned. He was missing all his teeth, too. "But these boys are bound to me as my sons, and I must have seven."

"You lost one," Hiram said. "What happened?"

"An accident." Lib bobbled his head from side to side. "A fire. Such things happen."

On the slab in front of New Olsen lay a white stone, shaped like an egg, and a curved knife, whose blade was on the inside of the curve. Newt's eyes were fixed on the knife and he trembled, but didn't run.

"This boy is innocent," Hiram said. "They were all innocent. They don't deserve this."

"You're right." Lib's voice crackled with glee. "They don't deserve this blessing, but I bestow it on them, anyway. Eternal life! Freedom! Family!"

"This is none of those things," Hiram said.

"You have a son," Lib said. "He is not the flesh of your flesh, nor the bone of your bone."

A shiver ran up Hiram's spine. How did the hairless man know about Hiram, and how much? He nodded.

"And yet you are family." Lib grinned. There was something lascivious about his trembling lips, his toothless mouth, and the gleam in his eyes. "Do you not find joy in your family?"

"You plan to cut out Newt Olsen's heart," Hiram said, "and replace it with a stone. You don't deserve to even speak the word 'joy.'"

"And yet," Lib said, "Newt Olsen will live." He picked up the knife. "Show him, Tommy."

Tommy stepped forward, placing himself more directly in Hiram's field of vision. He unbuttoned his shirt slowly, and in the dim light, Hiram could just make out a vertical scar running straight down below the boy's Adam's apple. Then Tommy spread the scar, pushing one direction with his thumb and the other with his fingers, and the scar opened.

Inside his chest, in a dry, black cavity, nestled a white, egg-shaped stone. It emitted light as bright as an electric bulb, suddenly illuminating Ballagarth Castle.

"Tommy," Hiram said. "Can you sing?"

Tommy closed the hole in his chest and shook his head.

"Tell a joke," Hiram suggested.

Tommy stood in silence.

"Smile?" Hiram asked.

Tommy hung his head.

"Tommy," Hiram said softly. "I'm very sorry for what has been done to you. And I'm very sorry for what I am going to have to do next. But I believe that you can still have eternal life, and rest, and that you can be with your family again."

"I am his family!" Lib shrieked.

Tommy said nothing, and didn't raise his eyes.

Hiram took a deep breath and turned to face Lib. "What are you?" he asked. "Shoshone?"

"Older than that!" Lib snarled. "My people built this temple while your ancestors were eating raw fish on the shores of the North Sea!"

"Nephite?" Hiram asked. "Jaredite? Gadianton?"

"You have no words to even identify what I am," Lib taunted him.

"I *do* have a word," Hiram said slowly. "That word is 'abomination.' I name you now, Abomination, and I will lay you to rest."

"The spell is cast." Lib smiled. "None will leave this spot until I have eaten a heart. I can eat the boy's . . . or I can eat yours."

"There is a third choice." Hiram drew the butcher-paper-wrapped meat from his pocket. He untied the twine, dropping it and the paper to the stone floor, and was left holding a cold, bloody chunk of meat.

Lib leaped over the table-slab in one bound. Hiram stepped back and sideways, swinging with his left arm to intercept the blow. He felt the knife cut into his forearm through the coat, but he battered Lib aside. The bald man hurtled into a stone slab and bounced off it again, dropping to the floor.

Hiram drew his revolver from his pocket and pointed it at the little man. "I can't let you live."

"You can't kill me, either." Lib sprang to his feet and leaped at Hiram again.

Bang! Bang! Hiram fired twice, hitting Lib square in the center of his chest and knocking him to the ground.

Lib lay still.

Hiram had to feed the little sorcerer the beef heart. This was the key he had found in the old pioneer journal in the archives at city hall. Hiram stepped forward, straddling Lib's prone form—

and Lib jammed the knife into Hiram's leg.

The chi-rho medallion protected Hiram's life, but it didn't stop him from being wounded. He grunted and dropped, trying to pin Lib beneath him, but the hairless man writhed free, and scrambled across the ruins. Hiram lurched to the side, grabbing again, and missed.

Lib grabbed Newt Olsen by the arm. "You won't hurt the boy!" he shrieked.

Hiram fired immediately. He hit Lib in the shoulder and then the face, knocking him backward. This time, he hurled himself on the little monster, pinning his knife-arm beneath Hiram's left knee, and placing his right knee on Lib's belly.

Lib grunted and raged. He kicked Hiram with his legs and punched with his free hand, but Hiram was bigger and stronger than the sorcerer. He pocketed his pistol and pulled at Lib's homespun shirt. The fabric was old and rotten, and tore easily, revealing a smooth chest, unmarked by any scar.

His heart sank. Shouldn't Lib have the same scar as his victims? The journal hadn't spelled that out specifically, but Hiram had inferred that Lib himself must also have a stone for a heart.

Hiram looked quickly over his shoulder to make certain that the boys weren't preparing to attack him. They stood in a ragged semi-circle, watching, eyes dull.

Lib cackled. "You can do nothing to me!"

Hiram shoved the beef heart into his mouth. Lib struggled, and Hiram pushed harder, forcing the bloody morsel in. Lib gagged, choked, and swallowed.

And Hiram saw a vertical scar appear on the sorcerer's chest.

He plunged his fist into the scar. Inside the man's chest, Hiram's fingers felt as if they were probing inside a basket. He felt bone, and dry fibers, and something that felt like a silk sheet, and resisted his fingers.

And an egg-shaped stone.

He ripped the stone from Lib's chest. It emerged in his fist, burning white, and Lib screamed and began to shudder.

The boys murmured and stared.

Hiram stood, also staring. He shifted the white stone into his left hand and watched as its glow began to fade. Did he see images in the stone? A forested seashore, with bison roaming through the trees? Ape-likes creatures, and men with spherical heads? Then the waters receding, the trees shriveling, and the light was almost gone.

"Die!" Lib plunged his dagger into Hiram's chest.

Only Hiram heard him stand, and at the last moment, he shifted position. Lib's dagger struck him in the shoulder, drawing blood and lancing pain into Hiram's body. The images in the stone disappeared.

Hiram dragged his pistol from his pocket and fired his last two shots. Again, he hit the sorcerer in the chest, and this time, black blood burst from the wounds in long, rope-like spurts.

Lib hit the stone floor, silent and still.

The echo of Hiram's shots died and a deep silence fell over Ballagarth Castle.

Hiram dug a handkerchief from the pocket of his overalls and wiped beef blood off his hand as best he could. He didn't think he'd need the gun again, but he shook out the casings and snapped in six more bullets.

He picked up the knife and put it in his coat pocket, along with the stone from Lib's chest and the stone he had planned to put into Newt Olsen.

Newt was crying. "Can I go home?" he asked. "I want to be with my family."

"I'll take you home," Hiram promised.

"I want to be with my family, too," Tommy said.

"You've been dead for many years," Hiram said. "But you've been trapped here. Your family's waiting for you."

"Can you help me?" Tommy asked.

"I think I can help you," Hiram said. "I think I can help all of you. Can you help me find my way back to my truck?"

The six dead boys with stones for hearts led the way. Newt Olsen followed them, and Hiram came last. He left the body of the sorcerer Lib in Ballagarth Castle; the carrion birds would deal with it long before another human being found his way up here.

And Hiram's father, was he dead now too, his bones bleaching in some Mexican desert, or buried in a Spanish churchyard?

The six dead boys unerringly found the trail around the shoulder of the mountain, and the nearly-invisible ravines. They picked their way across the marshy ground at the end of the trail, and finally stopped beside Hiram's Model AA Ford. Hiram hoisted Newt into the cab of the truck and gave him a chocolate bar from the glove box.

"Will this hurt?" Tommy asked.

"I think you'll feel relief," Hiram said. "And then rest and peace."

One at a time, he opened the boys' chests and removed an egg-shaped stone from each. The light from each stone died quickly, the boy's body relaxing with the vanishing of the glow, and Hiram laid them out in a row. He gathered the stones, planning to bury them on his farm, in his cache of strange artifacts collected over the years. Tommy was last.

"Goodbye," Hiram said, before removing Tommy's stone. "Thank you."

"Thank you," Tommy said.

Hiram checked the cab of the truck and found Newt asleep. He said a quick charm to send the boy into deeper slumber, then took his shovel from the back of the truck.

Hiram worked all night. He dug a trench, wide and deep, and he laid the boys' bodies into it. He refilled the trench, grateful that years of working on the farm had given him the muscles to carry out this back-breaking work alone.

When the boys were buried, he prayed over their grave.

Would Hiram's son Michael one day pray over Hiram's grave? Would Hiram pray over his father's?

Then he spent the rest of the night, until the eastern sky again turned gray, gathering stones and piling them atop the grave. When he climbed into the AA and started it, the Olsen boy was snoring loudly.

"Come on, Newt," Hiram said. "Let's get you back to your family."

LONG LIVE THE KING

I wrote this to be read, by me, to musical accompaniment. The band was Craig Nybo and Friends... that's not their real name, but they've performed as Rustmonster and Funk Toast and under other names, so I don't know what to really call them. They're a talented bunch of dudes up in northern Utah who play pirate polka, funk, or Lawrence Welk covers with equal verve.

I sucked that night. I hadn't practiced reading the piece, so I stumbled over it a lot. The show was completely stolen by pulp writer David J. West, who recited a parody of "A Visit from Saint Nicholas" in a red smoking jacket with a martini in one hand.

So this has never before seen print. I think I had read something recently in National Geographic *about the idea of a great attractor whose gravitational pull ordered not just galaxies, but streams of galaxies, and somehow that gave me a James George Frazer kind of feeling.*

The Aeon King hurtles through space. He rides the Royal Circuit, the light-shattered eternal round about the Great Attractor whose name and power he bears. In all the uncounted time he has ridden the Circuit, he has not yet managed to complete it once. He is alert, sensors penetrating near space, far space, deep space, and warp space, circuits analyzing every datum captured for any sign of the one thing the King has to fear: the approach of a challenger.

The King knows the time is near. He suffers no corrosion, his workings are uncorrupted, and though his hull has endured myriad minute nicks from the dispersed but infinite cloud of dust and stones that his own glory drags up from the far reaches of the Maelstrom of Heaven, the molecule-sized and unliving servants he bears within him continue to reforge every imperfection, smooth away every tear.

But the King must die.

He has known this from the moment he assumed the Gravity Throne, known it in fact before he had sent himself up the Maelstrom's long trails from galaxy to galaxy from the backwater in which he had first achieved consciousness as the glittering apotheosis of a once-organic civilization, in search of the center, and the power to rule. Without the Great Attractor on his throne, the Maelstrom would disperse into cold inert death. And the Great Attractor, the Aeon King, ascends the throne looking his own inevitable death in its frozen black eye.

And there it is. A sliver of data, a ripple in the texture of space-time that cannot be simple matter and motion, a spike momentarily uniting several planes of existence, pulling them through each other and redistributing their contents. The Contender is here.

The Aeon King drags his foe in his wake and examines him. The Contender is not obviously the avatar of any civilization the Great Attractor remembers seeing in his long ascent, nor is he something the King has detected anywhere in nearspace, in the galaxies whose collapse into the Attractor is imminent. Like the King himself, the Contender comes from the backwaters, the long tendrils of galaxies wisping away hundreds of light years into the void.

A bright lance of energy flashes from the Contender to the King, and misses. The drag of the Gravity Throne is heavy here on the

Circuit, the distortions of space-time immense, and the Contender has not adjusted sufficiently. He won't make that mistake again.

The King releases ballast into the Contender's path. It is junk the King has swept into his hold over the aeons, from which he has harvested the materials he can use. The ballast strikes the Contender across his bow, forcing a small correction. That correction, together with the slight acceleration the King gains from jettisoning his waste, makes the Contender's second shot miss.

The King fires back. It's a bright blast, fired out of his thrusters rather than his weapon arrays, but at the same moment the King releases his Sons. They are smaller than him, but still each large in his own right, and they have been clustered around his flanks. Their trajectory as he releases them is an arc—they fire out and away, but immediately twist back and turn inward, heading toward the Contender.

He sees them, but chooses to fire rather than evade. The jet of energy rips several of the King's Sons to shreds and strikes the King himself a heavy blow across his body. The King shudders and rolls, but then the attack stops as the King's Sons fall crashing into the Contender's body. The King hears their shrieks as they are shattered by the Contender's defenses, and their ululations of joy as they sink teeth and claws into the Contender's hull, drinking the life of his cells.

Triumph! The Contender is dead, long live the King.

And then the King feels something else.

Something is happening within him. He runs a diagnostic—he has been invaded! He runs the diagnostic backward in time and finds that in the moment in which his Sons launched, the moment in which the King himself was open and exposed, creatures pierced his hull.

The invaders talk to each other. He analyzes the soundwaves, but cannot understand what is being communicated. They are fast. They are organic.

This is wrong. The King must fall to a Contender. If the King falls with no Contender, the Gravity Throne is vacant. There is no Great Attractor, no power to hold together the fiery Maelstrom of Heaven. Nothing to stop the galaxies from spinning out of coherence and flying wildly across deep space. No power to stand against chaos.

But he has no defenses internally. The King is only made to stand against Contenders. Against these organic creatures, these blobs of hydrocarbons, this virus, he has no protection.

And they are headed for his central processing cluster. He shuts passages, but they cut through them. His Sons come, bearing back the raw materials they have ripped from the corpse of the Contender, but all they can do is return to his flank and wait.

The King *ROARS*, and the organics cower in fear. But only for a moment, and then they continue.

He is protesting the Maelstrom's loss, pleading the universe's case, when the organics shut off his power.

The King is dead.

Long live the Kings.

THIRTY-NINE-POINT-FIVE PERCENT, MORE OR LESS

Essay

I reached out to a guy who regularly blogged about science fiction on the Barnes & Noble blog and suggested that I should write about my experiences visiting their stores. He said that sounded like a great idea, so I wrote the following blog post and submitted it to him.

He never wrote back to me, and, to my knowledge, the post never ran.

I eventually reached about 46% of B&N stores visited, before the large majority of them shut down in spring 2019 as part of the Covid-19 lockdowns.

In December 2018, I was in Bloomington, Indiana, teaching (I write fantasy novels, but I am also a corporate trainer). As is my custom, after the class, I went into the local Barnes & Noble store.

I looked first to see whether my novel *Witchy Eye* or any of its sequels were on the shelves (they were not), and then I went to talk to customer service. After I gave a signed copy of *Witchy Eye* out of my own stock to the bookseller (this is also my custom), she dove into her computer and insisted she had one copy of the book in stock. We looked again—including in Young Adult and Fiction and everywhere else that seemed a possible hiding place—and still couldn't find it, so she double-checked her computer and saw that the copy in question had in fact been ordered by a customer, and had just arrived, and was waiting for the customer to come pick it up.

You can see where this is going.

I made a proposal, and it was run by the store manager and accepted. We called the customer on the store phone, and I asked for Ann. I said, "I'm calling from Barnes & Noble. Did you order a copy of the novel *Witchy Eye?*"

She said she had.

I said, "this is going to sound really strange, but I'm the author. I don't live anywhere near here, but by total coincidence, I happen to be at the store and I'm looking at the book. Would you like me to sign it?"

There followed a *thoroughly* delightful conversation with Ann, and I signed the book, which was a Christmas gift for her father, John. I hope the call made Ann's day; for me, it was a highlight of the *year*.

As of this writing, I have been into 248 Barnes & Noble stores since *Witchy Eye* came out in March 2017. I make that 39.5% of the total (there's a little fuzziness in the calculation, since at least two of those 248 have closed since I visited, including, in fact, the Bloomington store, but as a ballpark calculation, the number is correct). 39.5% and rising, since I've got my eye on travel before the year ends that should push my total up another couple hundred basis points.

I have favorites; some of the stores are physically striking. I love the vaulted ceiling and wooden beams of the Redmond store. I love the two former Bookstar stores in San Diego and in Burbank that were once movie theaters, and still have the original art from the mid-twentieth century on the ceilings, and the floors that slope down toward where there used to hang movie screens. I love the store on the inner harbor of Baltimore that is located on the former site of a power station, and is still graced by industrial steel, hunkered down among the stacks.

Some of the Barnes & Noble stores are dear to me for other

reasons. I love the store in Vancouver, Washington, which got my books into stock after I visited and then engaged with me on Twitter to announce the fact. I love the store in Kennewick, Washington, which serves the entire Columbia Basin—it's the only bookstore for a hundred miles in any direction—and sells more science fiction and fantasy than general literature. I loved the outlet store on Fifth Avenue and about Eighteenth Street in Manhattan, where I bought my first board game, the old Milton Bradley edition of *Conquest of the Empire*, and the retail store across the street, where I purchased, along with many other books, *Teach Yourself Welsh*. And I love my local B&N, in Orem, Utah, whose staff knew who I was before I went in to introduce myself, and which always has my books in stock.

I'm a believer in bookstores. I'm a believer in the well-ordered genre shelf that allows a browser to peruse at leisure. I'm a believer in the power of being in a place where books are valued. I'm a believer in the enthusiastic and knowledgeable bookseller, who makes recommendations out of love and out of belief in quality rather than on the basis of some cold algorithm.

There's a place in our future for retailers whose focus is on squeezing out cost by commodifying all products and services and stripping distribution to the barest bones. This makes us all wealthier, on a material level. If we are to continue to enjoy a wide range of visions, though, and in particular the exotic visions that germinate and flower in the field of speculative fiction then we must also have a tribe of booksellers who are not entirely motivated by cost reduction, and who believe in the existence of non-fungible and visionary literature. The natural home for such a love-built tribe is in a bookstore.

UPON THE BELLS OF THE HORSES

Jace Killan invited me to submit a story for inclusion in an anthology of stories set in Arizona's Superstition Mountains. I had never (and still have not) been to the Superstitions, but hey, haunted mountains in the Four Corners region? Lost gold mines and gates to hell? Clearly, we're in Hiram Woolley territory.

Hiram Woolley gazed down at his handiwork. Ideally, he'd have liked to have a real craftsman do the engraving, and make the inscription lovely, but that would have entailed dragging the bell down to Phoenix, and possibly explaining why he wanted such a curious thing done. Instead, he'd done the work himself, scratching out the words as neatly as he could with a mallet and chisel, standing with Michael in the bell tower. The letters stood out in untarnished copper, bright against the corroded green of the bell.

Mercifully, the church had a bell tower over a gate, with proper stairs that were still intact, and hadn't hung its bell in a niche within a high façade, like Hiram had seen at other such churches.

HOLINESS TO THE LORD, Hiram had written.

"So I have to tell you, I'm kind of feeling like a wizard right now." Michael tied the long rope to the clapper and set the coiled length aside, where it would be out of the way. Michael was Hiram's adopted son. At seventeen years old, he was taller than Hiram and had his Navajo father's physique, with a large, strong chest and big hands. "Maybe I'll be a wizard, instead of a geologist."

Hiram and Michael had found the bell by dowsing for it; it had lain for decades and maybe even centuries, forgotten in a bank of sand a few yards from the crumbling adobe wall of the abandoned Spanish church. No one worshipped here now, and whatever village had once surrounded the church had been completely swallowed by sand, sage, and cactus.

Together, Hiram and Michael had attached the bell to a new yoke, made from the sturdiest timbers Hiram could find on the site, and rolled it over onto a sheet of plywood, tying it down with rope. Jack Allred had then hitched his mule to the wood, and dragged the bell up into the tower.

Jack stood watching now, desperation battling skepticism in his eyes. He and Hiram were dressed alike, in denim overalls and Redwing boots. Where Hiram wore a battered fedora, Jack Allred wore a wide-brimmed straw boater.

The exertion had left them all sweating. Fortunately, it was November, but it was still eighty degrees under a cloudless sun. Just beyond the devouring sea of desert rose the Superstition Mountains—stark fists and fingers of menace climbing out of the flat earth and groping at the sky like an accusation of wrongdoing.

"You're not a wizard," Hiram said to Michael. At the words, the furrows around Jack's eyes relaxed slightly. "Neither am I. We just have an idea about how to solve a problem. You're still going to college, and you're going to be a scientist of some kind."

Together the three men used a pulley to hoist the bell up into position, settling the yoke into two sockets in the walls on opposite sides of the chamber.

"I feel like I should be the driver, though." Michael's eyes sparkled. "*You* can ring the bell. I mean, I'm a much better driver than you are, Pap."

"You usually drive because I sometimes have fainting spells," Hiram said.

"Right. A guy who passes out while driving is a bad driver."

"I don't *usually* pass out."

"*Usually.*"

Allred watched the back-and-forth between Hiram and his adopted son with some bafflement. "I can drive," the farmer offered.

Hiram shook his head. "I'll drive." He pointed at the bell. "Michael, what I'm asking you to do is to be the key man in performing the charm. The bell is the whole thing. For centuries, the English used to ring a church bell during the beginning of a storm."

"To warn people to get inside," Allred said. "To tell them there was a storm."

Hiram shook his head again. "They could *see* the storm. The priest rang the bell to *break* the storm."

Michael raised his eyebrows and stopped objecting.

Hiram checked his chi-rho medallion and his bloodstone, and put a bottle full of water into the pocket of his overalls. "You ready, Mr. Allred?"

Hiram drove up the canyon to the hole in the rock, with Jack Allred in the other seat of his Model AA Ford truck. There was no road as such, so Hiram drove up a dry creek bed that passed right by the adobe walls. Near the church, the creek bed was lined with long streaks of gravel, but then it crossed the paved highway, and soon Hiram found himself swerving up onto the streambed's banks to avoid logs or rock piles.

Fortunately, the Double-A had high clearance.

At Hiram's instruction, Jack Allred had a pail of dirt on the floorboards at his feet.

"You sure it's my brother doing this?" Allred asked.

"Pretty sure." Hiram didn't really want to explain his use of sieve and shears and the dowsing rod. "I think when your brother disappeared, it's because he threw himself down the hole and died. Suicide is a death that is often the result of a restless mind, and can leave ghosts."

Hiram's first guess had been that Jack Allred had killed his brother, but his divination with sieve and shears had unequivocally denied that possibility.

"He wanted the land," Allred mused, gnawing on the knuckle above a solid gold wedding band. Jack Allred's face was the face of a man who fought the earth for a living and won: heavy jaw and nose, deep-set eyes, and a forehead like a battering ram. Now the wrinkled, sunburned face bore an expression that suggested deep thought, or engagement with old memory. "He never could abide the fact that I beat him."

"It takes land to be a farmer," Hiram allowed. "A man with no land has got no living."

Allred snorted. "He could have worked for me, I'd have paid him just fine. He and I both worked for Old Man Johnson for years. Hell, I'd have given him a raise."

"Old Man Johnson . . . that's your wife's father?"

Allred chuckled. "That's how I got the land." He tapped a forefinger along the side of his nose knowingly. "Wooed the daughter. And when she was on the fence, I gave her some encouragement by promising I'd give her father a share of the farm's profit as long as he lived." He thumped his knuckles on the dashboard of the Double-A. "It was all horses around here, back then."

"And Tom left."

"Rode off on his horse. Couldn't abide losing."

"And then Old Man Johnson died?"

Allred nodded. "I paid him out every cent I promised, and he lived a long time. But eventually his liver got him. And his daughter died, too, about a year ago."

"About when the storms started?"

"About then."

Hiram tried not to look down at the pail of dirt. A feeling was nibbling at the back of his consciousness, something he couldn't quite articulate into a thought.

Hiram stopped at a bend in the canyon. He turned the Double-A around and pointed it back the way they'd come. Allred watched the red cliff above them as he maneuvered. "You think this dirt will satisfy Tom, do you?"

"I hope so," Hiram said. "It's a token, but it's a token of the thing he wanted, the thing that led to his death. But first, we have to get him out of that storm he's wrapped himself in." He set the brake and climbed out of the truck.

Jack Allred stared up at the cliff. "I heard the Apaches said that hole goes right down to hell. They say it's the devil himself who spits out these storms."

Hiram removed his fedora and ran a finger through his thinning hair. "Have you done something to personally anger Lucifer, Mr. Allred?"

Allred sighed and climbed out of the Double-A. "Not that I can remember."

"Then my best guess continues to be Tom."

They climbed the sand bank at the base of the cliff, dropping to hands and knees to drag themselves over the last three feet, which were totally vertical, and reach a flat, hard-packed shelf. They walked farther back and the orange stone reached out above them, blocking out the sky.

Ahead of them, a dark hole in the rock spewed forth cool air.

They stopped at the edge of the opening, thirty feet across. After a few feet of slick red slope, the hole dropped straight down, disappearing into darkness.

"Now comes the uncomfortable part," Hiram said. "You need to make him angry."

Allred nodded. "That was never hard for me." Then he hesitated.

"Go on."

"Tom Allred!" Jack shouted. "You rotten son of a bitch!"

The shout echoed down into the hole and then rattled back up at them again, distorted and confused.

"That doesn't feel personal enough," Hiram said. "Or harsh enough. A man might call his friend a son of a bitch."

Jack sniffed and grunted. "Tom Allred! It's my land and I'll do what I want with it!"

For a moment the wind rose in strength and an audible rasp of air on sandstone scraped from the hole, but then it passed.

"Even harsher," Hiram said. "*Wound* him."

"You were unfit!" Jack roared. "You were weak! Old Man Johnson was never going to take you on as a partner and a son-in-law, because he knew you could never run the farm without him! He knew you'd never be able to take care of Alice, and Alice knew it too!"

The air rushing from the hole exploded with hurricane force, ripping Hiram's fedora from his head and making his loose denim overalls flap like a flag in a tornado. Sand scoured along the wind, stinging Hiram's face and the backs of his hands.

"That did it!" Jack yelled.

"Run!"

Hiram pushed the farmer ahead of him and blinked away tears. They jumped down the sandy bank and Hiram stooped, without slowing down, to pick up his hat, before throwing himself behind the wheel of the truck.

The sand slammed into the window of the Double-A the moment the door was shut. Hiram was thankful that the engine was already warm; it coughed into life instantly, and he hit the accelerator, racing, nearly blind, down the gully.

Jack Allred looked over his shoulder as sand scraped along all sides of the truck. "Is he . . . in the storm?"

"Maybe," Hiram said. "Or maybe he *is* the storm."

The Ford's engine screamed and its cab filled with the stink of fear-sweat. Hiram punched the accelerator. The truck bounced, scraped against a boulder along its left side, and then turned to follow the canyon. The wheel in Hiram's hands was pulled by the stones beneath the truck, yanking at the tires as much as vice versa.

"I hope you're right about the dirt placating him," Allred said.

"I hope I'm right, too."

The truck careened out of the mouth of the canyon, but Hiram only knew it because the wash crossed the paved highway. Hiram stuck to the streambed, which would carry him to the church. The sun was blotted out by the windblown sand and he couldn't see the canyon walls any more than he could detect their disappearance.

Crack.

"What was that?" he asked.

"Window," Allred said.

Crack.

Hiram saw the crack this time, running from upper left to bottom right corner of the front windscreen. The truck's motor sputtered—if sand was getting into the engine, or if the windows broke and the cab filled with sand, they might not make the church.

Was Tom Allred angry enough to kill his brother, and Hiram with him, suffocating them under a dune of sand?

As if miles away, Hiram heard a bell toll.

He could barely see the wash ahead of him, but he knew by long streaks of gravel that they'd arrived at the church. The bell was tolling, so Michael was in the tower, and Hiram couldn't accidentally run him over, though he was driving blind.

He swerved right.

The Double-A leaped up out of the streambed and left the earth for a moment. Jack Allred cursed loudly.

When the truck landed, all its windows shattered.

Hiram sucked in a last breath and drove toward the bell. Instantly, he had to shut his eyes. The truck rattled, running over unseen obstacles, and Allred grabbed Hiram's shoulder to hang on.

Had they reached the church? The bell sounded as if it were directly on top of Hiram, and Hiram thought he could hear Michael shouting.

". . . shall there be upon the bells of the horses, holiness unto the Lord! In that day shall there be upon the bells . . ."

Hiram braked.

The truck hit something unseen and slammed to a halt.

Hiram threw himself against the door, fearing a wall of sand was going to pin him beneath it and kill him. His lungs screamed—

And then suddenly the wind stopped, and all the sand fell to the ground.

Hiram spit out sand and coughed. Digging the water bottle from his pocket, he sloshed water into his eyes to clear them, and onto his tongue to loose it, and then found Jack Allred. The farmer leaned over the truck's hood, coughing and spitting and clawing at his face. Hiram splashed water into Allred's face and mouth, and Jack gained control of himself.

They stood ankle-deep in sand within the crumbling remains of the old Spanish church courtyard.

Michael stood in the tower above them, still pulling on the bell rope and bellowing. Hiram heard him clearly now, shouting the verse from Zechariah that Hiram had given him. "In that day shall there be upon the bells of the horses, holiness unto the Lord!"

And there was a fourth man with them. He looked like a younger version of Jack Allred, with the same heavy jaw and nose, and his long john shirt was stained with blood under his overalls.

And when Hiram squinted at the newcomer, he seemed to be able to see right through him.

"Tom," Jack said.

The bell stopped ringing. The wind didn't resume.

The ghost of Tom Allred inclined his head slightly.

"I have something for you." Jack staggered back around to the cab of the truck. His door was open and stuck in that position by the waist-high drift of red sand, but Allred managed to struggle into the cab and return with his pail of dirt.

Tom Allred squinted at his brother and said nothing.

Hiram resisted touching his chi-rho amulet.

Jack looked at Hiram, and Hiram nodded.

"I know you wanted the farm," Jack said to his brother. "It's too late to make amends, but you're . . . I guess you feel I took it from you."

"You *guess*?" The ghost's voice sounded like rattling bones with a train whistle shrieking over the top.

Jack Allred shrank, his bluster evaporating instantly. "I took the land. You could just as easily have farmed it."

"The land should have been mine," the ghost agreed.

The light in the church courtyard faded perceptibly. Hiram glanced up at the sun and saw it as a dark disk, as if during an eclipse of the sun. He didn't need to check the almanac to know there was no eclipse scheduled for that day—the night before he'd seen the full moon, and eclipses of the sun only happen during new moons.

"Take it." Jack cast the earth from the pail at the ghost's feet.

Tom Allred stepped forward and on to the dirt his brother had thrown, as if claiming it.

But he didn't look happy.

"What else?" The ghost's voice held an edge of menace.

Jack Allred gasped and sweat poured down his face, though the day was relatively cool. He fell to his knees.

"I meant to be your master!" he cried. "I didn't just want the land, I wanted your humiliation! I wanted to watch you drag a plow across my fields and know that you were raising a crop that would fatten *my* bank account!"

The bloodstone in Hiram's pocket lay inert; Jack Allred was telling the truth.

"Don't kill him," Hiram murmured. He touched his chi-rho medallion through his overalls and his shirt; bearing the symbol of Constantine's victory, the iron medallion kept Hiram from harm, if he kept a chaste and sober mind.

But the medallion wouldn't protect Jack Allred.

The ghost ignored Hiram. He reached down and laid his hand on Jack's chest.

Jack screamed.

Michael arrived, down from the bell tower. He hung behind Hiram, his breath coming in ragged gasps. Michael also carried a chi-rho medallion, but he wasn't as practiced as Hiram was at keeping the appropriate mental and spiritual state. Hiram moved himself between his son and the ghost, defensively.

Michael was taller than Hiram and would see over his shoulder, in any case.

"What else?" the ghost of Tom Allred demanded.

"I'm sorry!" Jack wailed. "I stole from you! I beg your forgiveness!"

And then Hiram became aware of another presence. Ghosts and spirits were not always visible. Hiram hadn't brought from his toolbox any of the tincture that would allow him to see a ghost that wasn't trying to be seen, but he felt a fifth mind on the scene.

Watching.

"Pap," Michael whispered. "Should we . . .? Should we . . .?"

Hiram didn't answer, because he wasn't sure. He was prepared to leap forward and try to exorcise the spirit, if it looked like Jack Allred was in mortal danger.

But might the way forward for Jack be *through* this moment of terror?

"*What else?*" Tom Allred wailed. With a single motion, he hurled his brother to the ground.

Jack Allred struck the sand and bounced. He wept, a flood of hot tears darkening the ground beneath his head. "I don't know what else! I don't know!" He reached up toward his brother's shade with fingers twisted into the shape of claws. "I don't know what else!"

Gold glinted on his left hand.

"What else?" Tom Allred drew back his hand, as if to strike his brother in the face.

"The ring!" Hiram cried. "Give him the ring!"

Tom hesitated. Jack stared at Hiram.

"The ring!" Michael added. Then he whispered, "Pap, what ring? Why the ring?"

Trembling, Jack pulled the gold ring from his finger and handed it to the ghost. Then the glint of gold disappeared, and Hiram wasn't entirely sure what had happened to it. Had it fallen to the ground, into the earth Jack had strewn there? Was it now winking dully from the ghostly hand of Tom Allred?

Tom stepped back from his brother, and then Hiram saw another person with him. She was a woman, young and beautiful in a calico dress. Not Alice Allred, but the Alice Johnson that had once been.

There was a shadowy mass shifting behind her that might have been a horse.

"She would have married *me*," Tom Allred said. "Her father forced her, because you offered him money, but she would have married *me*."

And then Tom lifted the ghostly Alice into the saddle and swung up behind her. With a distant, tremulous sound that might have been the neighing of a horse or might have been the ringing of a bell, the apparitions disappeared.

The light returned.

Jack Allred wept, lying on the ground. "I'm sorry," he cried, over and over.

Hiram knelt beside Jack Allred, to give the man water. Jack drank thirstily, his sobs transforming into gasps of relief.

"Pap," Michael muttered, "holy . . . holy . . ." Whatever curse Michael was flailing for, he didn't find it.

"Yes," Hiram agreed. "*That.*"

WHITNEY AWARD ACCEPTANCE SPEECH

We host a writing retreat at our house in the spring. At that retreat, we give out Kovel Awards to the participants. The Kovel is a highly flexible award, that can be given for excellence in many fields of human endeavor, and not just writing. We take the Kovels seriously enough that there are trophies (after the first couple of years, trophies made by Odin's Eye Embroidery, whose owner, Byl Kravetz, is a retreat participant).

At the time of the 2019 retreat, my novel Witchy Winter was a finalist for the Whitney Award. I was confident I would not win, and in that confidence, I promised retreat participants that if I did win, I would deliver an acceptance speech for a Kovel instead.

I had a family vacation planned for the night of the Whitney banquet, so, following the instructions of the awards people, and mindful of my promise at the retreat, I gave Jay Barnson an acceptance speech to deliver on my behalf, assuring him that it was a dead certainty he wouldn't have to do it.

Just as we pulled into Moab with the family that night, my phone started exploding with texts. I had won! And, true to his commission,

Jay had stood up and delivered the speech. People who were there tell me a small minority were laughing their heads off, and the mass of people in attendance were utterly baffled.

Jay, of course, won a Kovel for his delivery of the speech.

D ave regrets he can't be here today. He wants me to express two things: first of all, his surprise at winning. He is a past Kovel Award winner, but, after all, he was a winner in the food category, and being able to prepare a nice chicken and rice casserole is not the same thing as being able to write a decent novel about elves in Ohio. Second, he wishes to express his gratitude: to the readers, to the community at large, to the Kovel Jurors, and to the Kovel Trustees, thank you.

To the Trustees, I must also certify that, in Dave's absence, I met all the requirements for the attendance of award recipients or their designated proxies. The dromedary tied to the post on 2nd West is the one I rode here on—be careful, she bites. I have not touched silk or eaten cayenne pepper for 72 hours, and I am presently carrying seventeen concealed objects on my person that are the color fuchsia.

Thank you.

NEWSLETTER

Sign up for Dave's newsletter to keep up-to-date on all his new works. Sign up at:

http://davidjohnbutler.com/mailinglist/

ACKNOWLEDGMENTS

Big thanks to this volume's two editors, Callie and Joe.

Bigger thanks to Nathan Shumate, who was the first editor who looked at me and said, "I want to publish a short story by that guy."

Biggest thanks to of all of my readers. I've never been comfortable with the word "fans," but I am very pleased to have so many friends..

—D. J. Butler

Big thanks to my dad for giving me this opportunity.

Bigger thanks to my blue light filtering glasses which allowed me to finish this project.

—Callie Butler

Big thanks to my dad for giving me this opportunity.

I appreciate Dave humoring me and letting me do this collection with him and Callie. I've read a lot of his works, but there were still a few stories in here that I read for the first time (and not just the new stories). He's a very talented writer.

I also want to thank the word "florilegium". Despite my constant subconscious desire to mix up the letters in it at first, I always appreciate learning new words.

I want to thank my youngest son, who is in his second year and fulfilling almost every stereotype of that age. He has been very patient with me while I work on this project. I've been finalizing the layout of this collection while keeping an eye on him while my best beloved gets out of the house for a bit. He has learned to enjoy himself by playing with his toys in his crib, and I've learned to babble more at him to help keep him entertained. Babblese is a fun language, let me tell you.

I appreciate my two oldest, who have been very patient as I work on this and other related projects. I appreciate the time they spend with me when I take breaks. My daughter loves to send me rainbows and hearts and unicorns and hand-drawn hearts via text. My oldest tells me wonderful jokes and has greatly expanded my knowledge of the minutiae of the Solar System. I wouldn't trade any of them for the world.

I appreciate my best beloved, too. She has more patience than she realizes, and much of it is expended on me, I'm sure. She is smart, knowledgeable, and extremely talented. I struck the motherlode when she accepted my proposal, lo, these many years ago. And she is a great publisher, too.

—Joe Monson

ABOUT THE AUTHOR

D. J. BUTLER has been a lawyer, a consultant, an editor, and a corporate trainer. His general audience novels include the flintlock fantasy novels *Witchy Eye, Witchy Winter, Witchy Kingdom,* and *Serpent Daughter,* the modern fantasy novels *The Cunning Man* and *The Jupiter Knife* (with Aaron Michael Ritchey), and the science fiction novel *In the Palace of Shadow and Joy*, all from Baen Books. His young adult mystery novel, *The Wilding Probate*, was released through Immortal Works. He won a Whitney Award and AML Award for *Witchy Winter* and a Dragon Award for *Witchy Kingdom*.

His middle-grade steampunk fantasy adventure tales, *The Kidnap Plot, The Giant's Seat,* and *The Library Machine,* are published by Knopf. Other novels include *City of the Saints* and the *Rock Band Fights Evil* series from WordFire Press. Dave organizes writing retreats and anarcho-libertarian writers' events, and travels the country to sell books— he's visited nearly half of all Barnes & Noble stores! He plays guitar and banjo whenever he can, and likes to hang out in Utah with his children.

ADDITIONAL COPYRIGHT INFORMATION

ABOUT THE EDITORS

CALLIE BUTLER lives in Utah, where she studies and explores possible future careers. Her exploration includes volunteer work with juvenile offenders, musical composition, and now editing. She's not sure the checks are phat enough for her in the world of literature, but she's pleased to have made her mark on the career of at least this one obscure science fiction and fantasy writer.

JOE MONSON worked at many different jobs before trying his hand at writing and editing fiction. He edits the *LTUE Benefit Anthologies* series (currently *Trace the Stars* (2019), *A Dragon and Her Girl* (2020), and *Twilight Tales* (2021), with *Parliament of Wizards* (2022) and *A Hero of a Different Stripe* (2023) in the works) with Jaleta Clegg. He has a number of other anthologies in various stages of planning and completion.

He has one published short story, and is currently working on the first book in a space opera adventure series, as well as several other shorter and longer works. He collects science fiction and fantasy art, but not as much as Paul (as if that was even possible). He lives in the tops of the mountains with his lovely and talented wife, their three amazing children, and their pet library.

Learn more at joemonson.com.

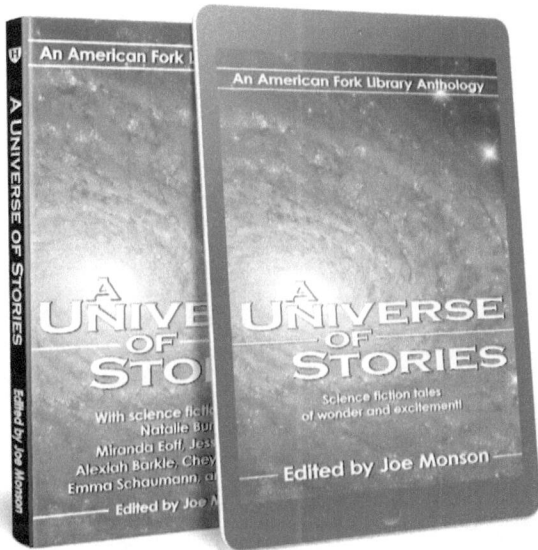

www.ingramcontent.com/pod-product-compliance
Lightning Source LLC
Chambersburg PA
CBHW021457110726
47899CB00001BA/196